RECKLESS REBELLION

The Possession Chronicles #8

By

Carrie Dalby

For Jennifer Lamont, a terrific beta reader,

and the music of Bill Leverty,

for fueling my writing time with songs like "You're a Natural,"

"The Bloom is Off the Rose," "Strong,"

and the Southern Exposure *album.*

Prologue

Monday, January 6, 1919

Dearest Claudio,

I hope this letter finds you settled and well in Italy, though I regret not having sent a letter since early December. Hopefully, you will forgive me since a new letter would not have reached you before you left New York. It is still a bitter thought to know you moved away just as I was planning to join Alex in Mobile. It would have been lovely to share more time with you—and have you near to help keep my husband in line. I say that in jest because he's been wonderful, though we all know Alexander is capable of much mischief.

As I said in my last letter, you were missed at our wedding ceremony. And again at Christmas. The party we hosted for the Davenport and Adams families turned out beautifully—in spite of your absence. Tabitha stole the limelight with her piano skills, and Alex led the carols. Henry missed the celebration, but Darla was able to enjoy herself because he is safely on his way home.

Though I complain about missing you, I understand why you left. That being said, the next news is about the Davenports. If it is too difficult for you, please skip to the next paragraph. Frederick still uses a cane most of the time, but he and Melissa were able to waltz at our Christmas party. Alex is her new Turkey Trot partner until Darla and Henry teach us the newest dances. Melissa is well, almost back to her old self in appearance and mood. Whenever we get a moment alone, she asks if I have heard from you and tells me to send her regards.

The last message also included, "tell him his light keeps me aflame." (I am only passing that on because she promises it isn't as scandalous as it sounds. Is it?)

As for the current news, I will start by saying the family is happy and healthy. Kade and Simon will join Asher at UMS when the schools reopen after the governor closed them last October because of the influenza epidemic. It will take adjusting to a more rigorous academic experience, but they will do well. Tabitha will attend the little school with the Davenport girls. The plan is for Frederick to collect her in the morning as Alex sees the boys off to school. Half the time, all the children gather here, the other half at the Davenports'. On Wednesday afternoons, Alex and I see them all to the stables.

We've bought a second automobile to help transport everyone. I attend women's auxiliary meetings and volunteer at Sacred Heart Residence twice a week, along with Melissa. Little Sisters of the Poor are open to both of us helping despite the fact we don't attend Mass. Thank you for suggesting them as a service opportunity. (And forgive me for mentioning Melissa again! Our lives are all intertwined these days. It is refreshing to know all seven children are welcome at either home.)

Speaking of children, there is news. I feared telling Alex, afraid he would be upset at the quickness of it since he and Lucy waited so long for Asher, but he was joyful when I told him last night. I am beginning to understand Alex hides his vulnerability behind his flamboyant actions. He is even more tender and gracious than I imagined. I know Douglas must have gnashed his teeth in Heaven when I married Alex, but surely he sees all that is good in Alex by the way he treats me, our children, the Davenport girls, and Asher. We are all blessed by his love and generosity. As happy as I am to welcome another child into the world, it is strange to think I will be the means of further extending the Melling family. I always ask to be addressed as "Mrs. Alexander Melling" or "Magdalene Melling", never <u>Mrs. Melling</u>. That name still harbors ill feelings within me.

Your special day is next week, but I am sure this will be late in arriving. All the same, I hope it's a blessed birthday, Claudio. I wish you the best with your exorcist training. Let me know if your experiences are a help or hindrance to your studies. If they are troublesome, I apologize for my part.

Much love and prayers,

Your modern Mary Magdalene

Sunday, August 24, 1919
Dearest Claudio,

She's here at last! Amelia Rose Melling was born a week ago today, a Sabbath angel with brown hair and her father's blue eyes. I allowed Alex the choice of names, and he chose to honor his first wife and sister, both gone from the world too soon. He says if Amelia had been a boy, he would have chosen a name to honor Douglas. I know he splurged on sending you a telegram, so I did not rush to send word—a blessing because it was a taxing week. Darla informed me I lost more blood than normal, and it took me until today to feel decent. During my labor, Darla kicked Alex out of the room twice: once for his innuendos and another for nearly fainting. (But please do not mention that to him.) Alex spent the week at home with us, and has been a great help with the children out of school for the summer.

Phoebe claims Amelia ruined her birthday. She had to have her birthday supper at her father's house last Wednesday because Alex refused to allow a boisterous party to disturb our rest. Phoebe also missed three days of riding with Alex and begged Henry to take her and Kade yesterday. Horatio and Simon went along with them, and Tabitha and Asher spent the morning at the Davenports, allowing Alex and me a few hours of peace with our new arrival. Though he's different than Douglas (and I ache with pain for him from time to time), Alex is every bit a devoted and proud father as my Scottish love. I am sure it is naughty, but I cannot help but imagine what it would be like to have them both with me. Lest I turn into Lucy, I keep those thoughts in check and relish the time I have with Alex rather than pine for the one no longer with me—though I still feel his love and support like a guardian angel.

I shall have to wait until the weather cools and I finish recuperating before resuming my volunteer work and riding. It will be wonderful to return to the trails. Alex promises to go back to taking a morning off each week for us to go riding without the children, as our private time is rare. He is already planning what masquerades and parties he wants to attend as the previous Carnival Season was closed due to the influenza. He tells me I am opening the doors to society for him, but I assure him he had the power all along. I love him more each day, especially after seeing him with our daughter. He loves her so much already— another thing Phoebe is sore about.

Since you asked in your last letter, I am pleased to report that Melissa is doing well. She kept volunteering at Sacred Heart when I could not attend, bringing along the girls during the summer. Bethany is sewing lap blankets for the residents to give at Christmas. She recruited Naomi and Sharon to her project, as well as several students at school, and I pledged to make half a dozen as soon as I am able. Melissa and Frederick appear to be restored to their relationship as it was before their terrible loss. No, not restored because we can never go back completely after heartache, but at least their devotion and passion have returned (little touches and looks in passing, fervent kissing when they think no one is looking.) I know you will be pleased she is cared for properly. Her eyes shine with joy more often than not these days.

Tabitha sends her love and wishes to tell you she practices accompanying the violin to Valentino's recordings. She hopes you will send your cousin here when she is a better pianist so they can do a duet. (But let it be known her mother does not want Valentino De Fiore in the same city as her precious girl, no matter their age difference.) The boys send their hellos and Asher a hug for Uncle Claudio.

Please be sure to tell that priest to stop teaching all possessed people willingly sinned. My oppression was a result of location, not grievous mistakes. Those came after. Don't you agree? I try to be moral, but I do not count my pleasurable moments with Alex as mistakes. Compared to what we now share, they were hollow examples of all he could offer, but the experience taught me much.

Love and Prayers,

Magdalene, Posseduta *no more*

Tuesday, February 15, 1921
Dear Claudio,

How long must they keep you for training? It has been over two years! I hope you will request to return to Mobile when you become an expert at exorcism. Surely there is no shortage of need here, though fortunately, the need does not reside with the Melling family at present. I would not put it past the Davenports, though.

Phoebe is becoming more like her mother every day, but I am fearful of ever saying that to Alex. Pray for her—and us! It could be her growing pains of reaching that tumultuous age of thirteen or the upset over Doff dying last month, but she is completely disrespectful to me. I have gone so far as to ask Alex not to invite the girls over without discussing it with me first, but Tabitha and Bethany are so close, it does not seem fair to keep them apart. And Louisa, Simon, and Asher are tight as peas in a pod themselves—Horatio too. The girl is surrounded by boys at playtime, but at least she has all girls during school hours.

As much as Phoebe has it out for me, I worry more over her relationship with Kade. I had hoped he would grow out of her as he formed bonds with classmates, but he's as smitten with her as ever. At the stables, they take off together on their horses. The worst argument Alex and I ever had was the one about buying them horses for Christmas. Alexander is too generous— extravagant! You would hardly recognize him these days. He has mellowed into a respectful businessman, father, and husband. (Did you think I would put up with anything less?) He's as passionate as ever, but can last a full supper party without removing his shirt or swiveling his hips. (I insist he saves that for our private time, but do not tell him I told you.) We have enjoyed three Mardi Gras balls so far this season, with invitations to two more before the end of the month. He keeps me well attired in dresses from Mademoiselle Bisset and the focal point of each gathering as much as possible.

Did he tell you he joined a committee for a Cathedral lawn party to raise money for a family who lost their home in a fire last month, and that for Easter, he is planning on going to Sacred Heart to sing while Tabitha accompanies him on the piano? He's trying to talk me into making it a duet, but I am refusing for three more days because I enjoy his means of persuasion too much to give in quickly. (Do not tell him I told you that, either!)

Darla and Henry are expecting their third child this summer. Their Ginny and our Amelia will have a new playmate. I am glad the pictures arrived and that you think Amelia favors me over Alex, but her eyes and smile are all Melling. Kade and Simon are their father's sons, but I have my Tabitha to claim. They are all growing too quickly—the Davenport and Adams children too. You need to hurry back and see them. Surely you have cast out enough demons by now to be able to handle anything.

Hugs and Best Wishes,

Magdalene

Tuesday, July 17, 1923
Dear <u>Deacon</u> De Fiore,

Yes, I have demoted you because you have not returned. Taking a position in Naples should not have been an option! Melissa informs me it is not near your family, and nothing but family would keep me from being upset for you failing to return to us. (Despite her and Frederick being as solid as ever, Melissa looked disappointed when I gave her the news.)

Thank you for sending the lovely mantilla for my birthday, even though it is black. We spent the last week at Seacliff Manor with the Davenports to escape the heat of the city. I do not feel forty, but I assume my body knows of the change. I am sorry to inform you, but I was pregnant for a few months. I lost the babe in June. I found Alex crying in his den one night after the loss. He curled into me and told me of his other heartaches—things I never knew! Lucy was pregnant when they broke their engagement, and she lost the little girl. He felt it was punishment for his part in the death of Twila (a story I had never heard!) when he was at college with that loathsome man he used to call a friend. He believes his penance continued when he had to wait so long for Asher to come to him and Lucy once they were married. My dear husband has suffered much.

"I thought I was beyond punishment when we had Amelia so easily," he told me as I held him. "But maybe the Lord thinks I've been too blessed lately."

I had to console him, reminding him that unfortunate things happen to good people all the time—that he is a wonderful man and I am pleased to have him in my life, no matter how many children we have together. When he finally came out of his depression, he emerged fully and took me on Lucy's chaise for the first time. It was glorious! (Do not tell him all that I share!)

The loss has brought us closer than ever, and my birthday week on the bay was splendid. The children are all tan and healthy. Claire and Joe Walker stopped by for a few days with Abraham while we were there. Kade is now sixteen, and he enjoyed time with his best friend. He and Abe get into as much trouble as they did when they were running wild on the island together, but I am sorry to say Kade is still devoted to Phoebe, and he snubbed Abe to please her several times during their visit because she is jealous of their friendship. Phoebe is blossoming into a woman and is every bit as lovely as Lucy. Frederick nearly lost his temper when he found her kissing Kade in the parlor one evening at Seacliff. He went so far as to sit in the hallway the rest of the night (much to Melissa's distraction). Bethany spent several days making new dresses for all the girls—the simple, drop-waist style that's all the rage. Beth and Tabby wear it well, but Phoebe is too curvaceous for it to work prettily on her. She had Beth alter things so it better showcased her figure (much to her father's displeasure).

As you can see, there is never a dull moment with us. I am beginning to think I need to ask you to burn these notes after you respond. Please pray for our family. Amelia will be four next month, and still, you have not met her. Know that I love you and wish you well in Naples—though I'd much prefer you to be in Mobile.

Love and forgiveness,

Magdalene

One

Late morning on Christmas Eve day 1925, Bethany Davenport snipped the last thread from the dress she made and placed the final present from her long list of hand-sewn items into a box. She set the gift on the pile in the corner of the bedroom she shared with her half-sister, Louisa. After smoothing her bobbed hair, she descended the stairs.

In the study, her father lectured Louisa about mathematical equations. Her older sister, Phoebe, was draped across an armchair in the parlor, a *Vogue* magazine in her lap as she kicked her bare legs to the rhythm of the jazz record playing on the gramophone. Hoping to find her stepmother, Bethany continued to the kitchen.

Melissa wiped a tear from her cheek with the corner of her apron as she stared at the lump of dough on the counter.

"Sissa, you shouldn't be alone right now." Bethany wrapped her arms about her stepmother. She was almost as tall as Melissa and used her size to bring her to the table. "I miss him too."

"He would have been ten today," she managed to say before the tears began in earnest.

Every Christmas Eve it was the same, though Louisa was too young to remember and Phoebe too wrapped in herself to care. Junior's birthday happening at the holidays was torturous to his mother, but she suffered silently. Kissing her stepmother's hand,

Bethany lowered her brunette head over their joined limbs and prayed she wouldn't have to hurt alone.

"Sissa," she whispered, "I'm going to get Daddy."

"No, Beth." She wiped her nose with the apron. "He mourns in his own way. Your father doesn't need—"

The door swung open and the imposing figure of Frederick Davenport stepped into the kitchen.

"I don't need what?" Assessing his wife's condition, he pulled her into his mighty arms and nestled against her neck beneath her short copper curls touched with gray. "Beloved, we should be celebrating a birthday, but we're missing him another year."

Melissa cried harder, but Bethany couldn't help smiling because it was the first time she'd seen her father hold his wife during her time of anguish. Taking a fresh apron from the pantry hook, the fifteen-year-old tied it on and prepped the forgotten dough for the baking pan. A minute later, her father steered Melissa out of the room. She listened to them climb the stairs as she rolled the dough, thinking of her mother and the way her stepfather used to sweep her off to their bedroom. Blushing—because now she understood what the Mellings did so often in their room—a pang of guilt over thinking of her deceased mother involved in sensual encounters caused her face to heat with embarrassment.

Louisa came in and grabbed an orange from the basket on the table. "Did you finish Phoebe's dress?"

Bethany nodded.

"Wasn't Mom was doing the rolls?" Louisa dropped the peels into the rubbish can.

"She needed a break. I think I'll stay home from Mass tonight so she and Daddy won't be alone."

"Tabby will be sore if you miss."

"I'll see her tomorrow."

Bethany thought of Kade, her best friend's older brother, and grew melancholic over skipping a chance to see him. But they would both be at her stepfather's house for Christmas dinner. While Tabitha Campbell and her brothers weren't relatives in an official sense, they spent so much time together, they were practically cousins—which made Bethany think her feelings for Kade were awkward, though he seemed to have no qualms about showing affection for beautiful Phoebe. He'd been sweet on her since they were kids, back when he lived on Dauphin Island with his parents and only came to Mobile for monthly visits.

Louisa took her orange out the backdoor. Bethany watched her from the window until she settled on the double swing, wishing she could be twelve again when things were less complicated. But even at twelve, Bethany had been without her mother four years.

After the rolls were in the oven, her father returned. "Thank you for taking over. How are you doing, Little Princess?"

Bethany smiled and hugged his broad form. He still went to the gym three times a week—something she never knew him to skip except during his months in the army.

"I'm sad," she said honestly, "but I'm happy you finally saw Sissa's despair."

He kissed her head. "Is she always this upset?"

"Yes, but she said you grieve differently and didn't want me to tell you. She's like this on Junior's birthday and every July seventh."

"Please don't keep secrets like this, Beth. Melissa is stubborn and independent, but I need to be able to comfort her."

"That applies to both of you, Daddy."

He chuckled and hugged her to him. "So it does."

"I'm going to stay home with you tonight."

"And miss Christmas Eve Mass with the Mellings? I know you've always enjoyed that."

"I feel like I need to be home this time, but I'll give you privacy if you need it."

He nodded, the gray in his dark hair shining in the sunlight coming through the window. "I appreciate your thoughtfulness, Beth."

***

Long past supper, Bethany sat in the parlor in her new flannel nightgown and robe. Her father and Melissa were cozy on the couch with cups of coffee when Louisa bound down the stairs. She twirled into the room in her lacy, drop-waist dress.

"Phoebe gave me ringlets!" She fluffed her auburn hair that hung just below her shoulders in a more orderly fashion than typical for the dense mass. "Am I old enough for a bob like her and Beth?"

"No," their father said. "You're beautiful the way you are, Littlest Princess."

Melissa smiled. "Run up and get my fur cape. It's chilly tonight."

"I can use the fur?" she squealed. "Phoebe will be jealous!"

Louisa dashed out of the room. Before she returned, eighteen-year-old Phoebe entered dressed boldly in a short green art deco design, without a stitch of shapewear beneath.

"You're not to attend the cathedral like that, Phoebe Camellia."

Phoebe laughed and started in on the Charleston. "Momma would have approved. Besides, I'll have a wrap on the whole time. It's not nearly as scandalous as you think, Daddy."

"I don't appreciate my daughter running around town looking like she belongs in a speakeasy."

"I'm not running anywhere. I'll be in Poppy's car and then the cathedral. You're the biggest bluenose out of any father I know." She sashayed out of the room returning with a mint green cloak that didn't cover her exposed knees, but at least she had stockings on under her T-strap shoes.

Automobiles rumbled into the yard, followed by doors slamming and laughter. Alexander let himself and the stream of Mellings and Campbells in the front door.

"Merry Christmas, Davenports!" Arms wide, he went first to Phoebe who stood in the middle of the parlor. "How are my darlings?"

"Wonderful! Merry Christmas, Poppy." Phoebe kissed his scarred cheek.

Frederick and Melissa stood to welcome the others but Bethany stayed huddled in the corner armchair, wishing she hadn't already dressed for bed with the room full of holiday finery. Tabitha looked beautiful in an emerald sheath and black cape. Her sleek bob and bangs made her look twenty instead of sixteen.

"Are you sick, Beth?"

"I feel like staying with Daddy and Sissa tonight."

Phoenix Asher, her thirteen-year-old half-brother, joined them, followed closely by Tabitha's brother, Simon—the same age as his stepbrother. "You aren't coming, Beth?"

"Not this time, but I'll see you all tomorrow."

Louisa bound straight to the boys, holding out the fur. "Look what I've got!"

Simon shrugged with indifference, but Asher paused to feel the texture of the black wrap around her shoulders.

"That's swell, Louisa."

"She gets to use the fur?" Phoebe's voice shrieked above the din of the conversations.

Kade was at her elbow, his blue eyes ringed with dark lashes looking intense.

"You already have a matching cloak, Phoebe," Melissa said matter-of-factly.

"But Daddy doesn't think this outfit is appropriate. I would have changed to have—"

"What's done is done, Princess," Frederick said.

"Maybe next time, Phoebe Camellia." Alexander kissed her cheek. "Let's head out. Oldest with Kade, youngest with me and Maggie."

He took Amelia's hand as the crowd filtered out. The six-year-old pointed to the corner and Alexander came for Bethany.

"Are you ill, Bethany Iris?"

"I felt I should stay home with Daddy and Sissa tonight."

He gave a bittersweet smile. "You have a tender heart, Knight Bethany."

Amelia climbed into her lap and hugged her. Amelia Rose already shone as the prettiest of the girls with her mother's coloring and her father's blue eyes. While Phoebe was flashy, Tabitha stylish, Louisa classic, and Bethany plain—according to her own standards— little Amelia was a beauty like the pictures of Eliza Melling.

"I'll see you tomorrow, Amelia." Bethany promised as she saw the Mellings to the hall.

Planning to make hot chocolate, she then went to the kitchen. When she pulled a cup out of the cabinet, the door swung open behind her.

"Tabby said you were staying home, but if you want to change your mind, I'll wait for you to get dressed."

She turned to Kade, who looked more attractive than ever in his gray suit with his piercing eyes and rich brown hair.

Clutching her robe closed, she shook her head. "Thanks, but I feel like I need to stay home tonight."

"What is it, Tiger?" He touched her floral-print sleeve.

Looking past his broad shoulders up to his furrowed brow, she imagined he cared for her as she did for him.

"Today is Junior's tenth birthday," she whispered as a tear threatened to spill out.

"Tiger," he whispered as he gave her a quick hug. "I wish Phoebe were as thoughtful as you."

With his parting words, Bethany hoped the hot chocolate would replace the chill he left.

Two

Halfway through Mass, Phoebe Davenport followed Oscar Easton's lead in slipping outside. She went with her cousin to the square across the road where Robert Woodslow and Jane Spangler sat on a bench, smoking. From his jacket, Oscar pulled a flask and drank from it before passing it to Phoebe. She nipped from it twice before handing it to Jane and accepting the cigarette her cousin lit.

"You look good enough to eat, Phoebe," Robert said with a leering smile. He was only seventeen but already outshone many of their peers with looks and class, including Oscar's university friends.

Phoebe wasn't one to let appreciation for her go unrewarded. She shrugged the cloak from her shoulders, shimmying to let him see what pleasures her unbound curves offered. "You want a taste, Robby?"

He stomped out his cigarette and kissed the hollow of her throat as he wrapped his arms around her. "Don't look now, but your boyfriend's coming."

She shook her unruly platinum hair as Kade hurried down the portico steps. "He's not my boyfriend."

"Your brother then." Oscar laughed. "Man, what I'd do to you if we weren't cousins!"

"Don't be crass. I claim Kade neither brother nor cousin."

"That's good because the poor sop can't keep his eyes off you." Robert pressed against her. "Shall I make your poor relations jealous?"

The smolder in Robert's gaze called upon her base desires. She ran a hand through his blond hair, tousling it so a wave fell over his forehead. He locked his arms about her waist and rubbed against her.

"Hey there, Kade Campbell," Jane called. "These two are making me feel lonely. How 'bout you sit with me a minute and warm me up?"

Before he could reply, Phoebe broke from Robert and took Kade's arm with a venomous glare at Jane. "He's not here for you, are you Kade?"

His smile showcased his perfect teeth and dimples. "Sorry Jane, but I need to keep track of Phoebe. I'm her ride tonight."

"Don't you wish, Campbell." Oscar sniggered. "The closest you'll get to being her ride is Phoebe straddling your horse at the club."

Kade clenched his fists and stepped toward the smaller man. "Talk like that to me if you wish, but not in front of the ladies."

"If you think these two are ladies, you've got a lot to learn. I believe Jane here would be more than happy to teach you."

Jane's wicked giggle stopped when Kade threw a punch at Oscar.

"Kade," Phoebe shrieked, "that's my cousin!"

"But unlike his father, he's not worth a lick in a fight." Kade glared at Oscar. "Learn some manners, Easton."

Kade started back toward the cathedral.

"I hear you're shoveling stables, Campbell," Oscar called. "How's that working out to win the ladies?"

"Unlike you eggs, some of us work for their money rather than rely on family for everything."

"You mean your stepfather is withholding funds because you're trying to bed his first wife's daughter?"

Kade ran at him, punching Oscar in the stomach.

Robert took Phoebe by the arm before she could interrupt. "Stay back, doll. Oscar has it coming to him."

Phoebe pushed Robert away and lunged at the men. "Leave him alone, Kade Campbell! You don't need to prove a point."

His body relaxed under her touch. "Sorry, Phoebe."

Phoebe ran her hands down his arms. "We can all see how strong you are without an exhibition of your strength."

"I want a hands-on demonstration." Jane giggled.

Phoebe huffed and linked her arm through Kade's. "Let's go wait on the portico."

Once they were across the street, she increased her attentions in hopes Jane would get the hint to leave Kade alone. Pressing him into one of the columns, Phoebe gazed into his blue eyes.

"I appreciate you trying to defend my honor, but don't waste your time."

"I wish you'd agree to be my girl. Then guys like Oscar wouldn't say things about you—especially in front of me." The brightness of his luminous eyes almost made her drop her guard, and when he took her by the waist she wanted more. "You can't tell me you don't like me after all the fun we've had together through the years."

"You know I like you, Kade." She kissed the corner of his mouth and brushed a knee across his thigh. "Meet me in the camellia garden after Christmas dinner and I'll let you know."

When the cathedral doors opened, they stepped apart as the parishioners filed out. Their siblings joined them and they headed across town.

Frederick waited in the parlor, but Melissa and Bethany were upstairs for the night. "Did you enjoy yourselves?" he asked Phoebe and Louisa.

"Yes, Daddy. Simon and Asher are fun, even at church. Merry Christmas." Louisa kissed him and went for the stairs.

He turned to Phoebe. "And did you keep yourself covered, young lady?"

"Yes, Daddy," she lied. "I'll see you in the morning."

***

"It's gorgeous!" Phoebe held the red, sleeveless evening dress to her chest before tossing it over her shoulder and throwing herself at Bethany. "It's as pretty as something from Mademoiselle Bisset's shop!"

She ran for her bedroom where she pulled off the flannel nightgown and slipped the silk chiffon over her head. Her unbound breasts tingled at the cool softness and Phoebe smiled at her womanly peaks in the mirror. The pleated gathering of the drop-waist hit just above the widest part of her hips, the asymmetrical slit from the knee-length gown showcased the shapeliness of her leg, and the scarf-like detail on the opposite shoulder drew attention to her arms—toned from her hours with Prince, her horse.

Knowing her father would have a fit if she attempted to attend the family dinner without anything under the dress, she removed it to pull on a silk camisole, panties, garters, and stockings. Reassessing her image, she grabbed the silver scissors Grandma Easton used to keep in her crocheting basket. The weight of the metal shears always calmed her. She focused her newly found serenity to snip a few locks of hair to better frame her face.

"You look gorgeous!" Louisa exclaimed when she returned to the parlor. "Here, take the present from me and Mommy!"

Inside the harlequin box was a red and gold beaded circlet for her head. "You all coordinated and now I'll be the Christmas queen!"

"Not yet, Princess." Her father crossed the room with his typical stiffness of the morning hours, compliments of his war wounds.

Phoebe allowed him to kiss her cheek and embrace her so she could have the box that looked to be the perfect size for jewelry. She wasn't disappointed with the extra-long strand of pearls that afforded itself to be knotted so it hung enticingly below her chest.

"Thank you, Daddy!" She gave herself a moment to feel the security she used to enjoy in his arms—before he abandoned her to play soldier in France. "Now I need to pick out my shoes."

She disappeared into her room, not joining the family until it was time to leave for the Mellings' house.

Louisa insisted on sitting in the middle of the backseat. She wore a new dress from their sister too—a sweet blue collared one that made her auburn curls brighter. The seamstress wore a sophisticated black sheath that showcased her locket splendidly. Phoebe didn't compliment Bethany on her looks though the ensemble made her look at least two years older.

At the mansion, Phoebe allowed the rest of the family to walk ahead of her with the presents so she could make a grand entrance.

Phoenix Asher held the front door open and whistled. "Wow, sister, that's some get-up!"

"Thanks, Ash." Phoebe kissed his cheek. She'd always had a soft-spot for her half-brother—partly because he looked so much like his father.

After handing Asher her capelet like he was a servant, she sashayed into the front room. Tabitha continued to play carols while Bethany joined her on the piano bench. Louisa had Simon captivated with her new book of magic tricks while the adults were engaged in an animated conversation with spoiled Amelia in the center of them. Worse than the lack of attention was Kade missing from the room.

Alexander raised his head. Phoebe caught the way his ice-blue eyes widened and the wistfulness in his expression that betrayed his true feelings for a fleeting moment. An empowering surge of energy pulsed through her veins. So what if it was because she looked like her mother standing boldly in red—the distinguished Alexander Randolph Melling yearned for her, even if only a second.

As though sensing her husband's attentions elsewhere, Magdalene looked to Phoebe and crossed the room.

"You're a vision, just like your mother." She graciously linked their elbows. "I bet Lucy would have loved the fashions these days. You wear it wonderfully, Phoebe. Is this what Bethany made?"

"Yes." She smiled though she hated to hear her mother's name from the lips of her replacement.

"Beth," Magdalene said loud enough to be heard over the piano, "all the dresses you made are gorgeous. Phoebe sparkles and Louisa is a ray of joy, but you outshine them all with your classic style. Come turn around so I can see it properly."

Phoebe sat on the loveseat.

Kade came in as Bethany took her turn in the middle of the room. Phoebe noted the way he smiled at her sister's above-average looks. Bethany must have noticed too, because a blush crept onto her cheeks.

"You look terrific, Tiger. Merry Christmas," Kade said as he distractedly kissed her cheek before continuing to Phoebe.

Phoebe smirked at seeing the disappointment in Bethany's eyes when he didn't stop, and patted the spot beside her. Her kiss left a lip stain on Kade's cheek. "What did you get me for Christmas?"

"Nothing at the moment."

"You've always been cruel, Kade Campbell." She crossed her arms, squeezing her bosom into more of a showcase.

Tabitha left her spot at the piano and wiped the lipstick off her brother's cheek. "And you've always been spoiled, Phoebe Davenport."

Magdalene was quick to try to smooth things before they escalated. "Why don't we exchange presents before dinner?"

Simon dove for the tinseled tree in the corner, followed closely by Asher and Amelia. The next several minutes were spent with the baby of the family dispensing the boxes to the appropriate receiver. Phoebe was bored with the whole event until the porcelain child brought her a large box she struggled to hold.

"For you, from Poppy and Mama and all of us."

"Thank you, Amelia." Phoebe turned quickly to Kade. "Does this mean I don't get anything special from you?"

"That depends on what you tell me in the garden later," he whispered.

Phoebe smiled devilishly as she tore open the box and ripped the tissue paper to unveil a gray chinchilla stole. "It's gorgeous!" She caressed her cheek with it before tossing the fur around her shoulders. "I love it!"

She kissed Kade first, then went for the younger brothers. Tabitha received an air-kiss and Amelia a real hug.

"Thank you, Miss Maggie." She quickly hugged Magdalene.

"You're welcome, Phoebe. I'm glad you like it. It was all Alexander's idea."

The glimmer was in his eye when she caught his gaze.

"Thank you, Poppy!" And with his name, the spark was gone. But Phoebe pressed against him as they embraced, kissing his cheek a little too close to his mouth.

"You're a lady now, Knight Phoebe, and deserve a gift befitting your debut season. I hope you'll wear it to the New Year's ball."

"It would be an honor to wear your gift." She fingered her pearl necklace as she caught his eye. "Maybe even Daddy's too."

Phoebe resettled beside Kade as Amelia brought him a present. Looking at the tag, Kade smiled across the room at Bethany. From the box he pulled two monogramed handkerchiefs. Beneath those, a silk bowtie and cummerbund set in the exact shade of blue of his eyes—and the same color as the thread used for his initials on the fine handkerchiefs.

"Thank you, Tiger." He lovingly folded them back into the box and went across the room. Pulling her up from the sofa, he hugged her. "I'll proudly wear it to the ball next week. I wish you were coming so I could get a dance with you."

"You could always take her for a spin before going." Tabitha adjusted the fringed shawl Bethany gifted her.

"I just might have to."

Bethany's perfect gifts ruled the conversation the next quarter-hour rather. Asher and Simon each got a necktie and handkerchief, Alexander a stylish riding vest, Magdalene a silk robe—much too like their mother's old kimono for Phoebe's liking—and Amelia a turquoise hooded cape.

Miss Charlotte came to the doorway. "Dinner is on the table."

"Why are you so snippy with Amelia?" Kade asked Phoebe as everyone headed for the hall.

"She's unmanageable and greedy for attention."

Kade took her elbow. "You know that's not true. Don't tell me you're jealous of a six-year-old."

"But she has the finest half-brothers in the world." Phoebe eyed the sprig of mistletoe hanging at the cross-section of the halls and nudged Kade until he was beneath it. "I can't wait until our rendezvous after dinner."

The others were in the dining room so she allowed her fingers to trail across his broad shoulders. Bringing her mouth to his, she hooked a leg around him as she parted her lips with Kade for the first time. Hands skimming her waist, his fingers splayed her lower back, tenderly nudging them closer as his tongue tangled with hers.

Why does he have to feel so good? He's trying to trick me into thinking what we have is real when he just wants to use me like the other guys. She clung to him until he stepped back with a glorious smile.

"Are you my girl, Phoebe?" A hand trailed up her bare arm to her chin, lifting it like a master gazing at his creation.

The quiver in her stomach answered *Yes!* but her head shouted *I belong to no one!* She teased her hand along his belt. "You'll just have to wait until the garden to find out."

The dinner table wasn't as full as typical for a holiday since the Adams family was in Chatom. The dozen Davenports, Mellings, and Campbells settled around the space comfortably. Phoebe sat between Kade and Asher, though she didn't make much conversation. Often Tabitha glared at her, but she also caught Alexander looking, as well as a grim-faced Melissa. Her stepmother was keen and knew Alexander well. *I bet she knows he's looking upon me with want, imagining I'm his Lucy in red this Christmas.*

After dinner, Tabitha and Bethany disappeared upstairs and the youngest four went to the morning room for games. Without speaking, Kade and Phoebe walked the hall to the open den and out the French doors onto the patio. A few steps into the camellia maze, he took her hand. The bushes had grown taller over the years, the pathways slightly narrower as Magdalene preferred them to keep a natural rounded appearance rather than the squared sides of a traditional labyrinth.

Phoebe pinched a pink blossom from a bush and tucked it behind her ear. She was heady with the thought that she was almost to the spot where her mother and Alexander met romantically twenty-one years ago—that she was there with a man as equally smitten with her as her stepfather had been with her mother. After the taste of Kade under the mistletoe, Phoebe felt ready to commit to him, at least temporarily.

When they were a turn away from the center, a laugh sounded from the area of the bench. Kade stopped, squeezing Phoebe's hand and nodding back the way they came.

"Oh Alex, you're sweeter every year."

That imposter is in my mother's place!

"Phoebe," Kade whispered, "let's go somewhere else."

She shook her head, platinum curls striking her face.

"I'm not going to spy on my mother." He stepped back and paused, but when she didn't move, he left.

Let him leave! It shows what coward he is. I can't believe I was ready to throw myself at him when he isn't man enough to claim our rightful place in the garden!

Phoebe crept toward the corner, leaning her head around an inch at a time until she had a view of the bench. Magdalene sat beside Alex, her legs over his lap and his arms about her as they kissed. Behind her right ear, a white camellia shone in the sunlight. Phoebe saw red as her nails dug into her palms.

He defiles Momma's flower with the likes of that woman—the daughter of a country blacksmith who snared him only six months after Momma died!

She peeked back once more. Alexander's hands roamed Magdalene's chest, their mouths locked together, and her dark hair waving in the breeze. Phoebe yanked the pink camellia from behind her ear and threw it on the oyster shell path before huffing back to the house.

I'll make them pay! Every last one of these Campbells and my traitorous Poppy too!

Three

Alexander Melling paced the patio outside his den. He was on his second cigarette, and the chill evening air began to be too much for him as apprehension over the New Year's Eve ball climbed. A hired car would soon arrive for him and Magdalene. Bethany and Louisa were expected any minute—the Davenports were dropping them off on their way to accompany Phoebe to her first masquerade.

Phoebe Camellia Davenport.

His unease about the evening was because of her. She looked more like her mother every day. Several times on Christmas, he had felt a prickle of remembrance. The red dress beneath her blonde hair, the lift of her Easton chin, and her blue-green eyes all crashed together in a symphony of longing for his first love. The pink camellia he'd seen on the garden path Christmas afternoon stuck him as a sign. Someone saw him in the garden with his wife. Phoebe was the likeliest person as she'd always had a penchant for the maze. Then in parting, she'd caught him under the mistletoe and kissed him on the lips with a naughty gleam in her haunted eyes.

Alexander took a final drag and snuffed the cigarette into the ashtray before entering his den. Magdalene came in from the hall as he closed the drapes.

"I'm ready, Alex."

Turning to her, his fears melted into joy. Magdalene's dress showcased her gorgeous body from scooped neckline to the knee-length slit. The creamy, silk gown was trimmed in royal blue velvet which ruffled the bottom foot of it, and then tapered to the left shoulder on the sleeveless gown that draped like a faux cape. His smile grew as he approached and then doubled when he trailed his hands over the exciting textures, including the embroidered florals spanning the area where the two fabrics met with a sprinkling of rhinestones and ivy.

"And I'm ready for you, Magdalene." He swayed with her.

She clung to him, fulfilling his needs as she always did. Her lips on his shaved jaw were electric as she kissed her way to his mouth. It started soft, but he escalated it to tantalizing within seconds. Trailing his touch up her arms to the column of her unadorned neck, he took advantage of her up-do to nibble beneath the dangling earrings that sparkled becomingly.

"I wish we had a room at the hotel tonight, sweetness." He inhaled the floral scent that clung to her neck. "Why don't we escape to Seacliff for a few nights before school starts, just the two of us?"

Magdalene angled away. "The older children are self-sufficient, but what about Amelia?"

"She adores Tabitha. I'm sure they'd all get along fine. Maybe bring Charlotte in earlier in the day to make sure they get two decent meals."

Her smile made him want to feel her lips and teeth on him.

"Which days?"

"I don't have any court dates until the thirteenth and everything else can be rearranged. Please say yes." He tasted her neck and lower. "I need unrestrained time with you. I've been good, but I need to let go."

"I love you and your fiery appetites." Magdalene laughed and flicked her tongue on his earlobe. "I could use a few wild days myself. I'll make plans tomorrow."

"Bless you!" He planted a firm kiss on her lips, and went for his black tuxedo jacket on his desk chair.

Thinking of the vision of Magdalene in their bedroom at Seacliff Manor caused him to collide with Frederick in the foyer.

"Get your head out of the clouds, Melling."

Alexander clapped Frederick's broad back. "It was in my bed, not the clouds. Where's Maggie?"

He nodded to the front room. Tabitha was at the piano and Magdalene, Asher, Simon, Louisa, and Amelia sat about the room watching Kade waltz with Bethany.

At the end of the tune, Kade kissed Bethany's rosy cheek. "Thank you, Tiger."

She smiled and straightened his bowtie. "I'm pleased it looks as well as I imagined. Have fun tonight."

Frederick's face was full of pride for his daughter as he turned to his friend. "Thank you for having them over. I'll see you there, Alex."

Alexander set down the rules with the children staying home, and said goodbye to Kade, who was picking up friends on his way to the party. Then Alexander snuggled with Magdalene in the back of the hired automobile—one hand on her thigh beneath her dress.

"Kade and Beth would make a handsome couple in a few more years," she remarked. "I much prefer to see him with her if he's going to be attached to any of the Davenport girls."

"Bethany Iris is the sweetest and her vest fits me perfectly."

"Yes it does. And it was a joy to remove it from you after riding yesterday."

They touched and teased. By the time they reached the hotel, Magdalene's lips were red from use. She looked years younger than she was and Alexander gloried in her beauty—inside and out. The jeweled embellishments on her blue mask coordinated with the details on her dress, glimmering under the chandeliers.

Rather than the back slaps, elbows to the gut, and other jostling he received in his younger years, Alexander and Magdalene were received with warmth from the people in the crowd. Where his relationship and marriage to Lucy brought him notoriety and gossip, his current one blessed him with respect from his peers. No matter her humble beginnings, Magdalene proved her worth and staying power within the society circle. Appreciated by the women for her philanthropy and kindness, and by the men for her graceful ways and shining beauty, she held Alexander's heart with more power than he thought possible when he first looked upon her nearly twenty years ago.

"Mellings!" Maxwell Easton greeted them with hugs. "I've claimed your name for my table, is that all right?"

"We'd be happy to join you, Maxwell," Magdalene said, "so long as there's room for Freddy and Melissa."

He nodded his gray head. "I claimed the Davenports too."

Alexander inwardly groaned, but as he led his wife across the room, he realized Phoebe would rather be forced into last season's clothes than spend her first masquerade at her father's table. Relaxing his guard, he kissed Lottie's cheek, saw Magdalene to her seat, and went to greet one of his associates. Before he could return to the table, a towering brunette caught his arm.

"Alexander," Kate Walters simpered, "does F.L.D. have any idea what beast he's unleashing on the city tonight?"

Though remarried after her divorce from the now deceased Rupert Lyons, Kate was still stabbing with her gossip. Her hair was too dark—as though she'd recently used a coloring on it to disguise her graying tresses—and her brown eyes were as cold as ever. Fortunately, the worst Kate could say about Magdalene was she was raised in the country and shockingly married a chauffeur for her first marriage.

He removed his arm from her talons. "What do you mean, Kate?"

"His oldest daughter out in society looking exactly like her mother. Does it bother you to see those Easton threads on the next generation?"

Following her gaze, he fought to control his shock at seeing Lucy's lily print gown repurposed into a modern creation.

"Isn't that the dress Lucy wore to the New Year's ball the first time you were seen together?"

And to the opera the night I proposed. Damn her for having Beth alter it! And damn Freddy for allowing her out of the house in it!

"You're as keen as ever, Kate. Enjoy your evening."

He turned away from the vision of Phoebe in the fabric he'd ran his hands over while marking Lucy for the first time. Halfway across the ballroom, a bare arm linked around his sleeve, her bosom straining within the broad neckline as her chest pressed against him.

"I'm excited to finally be at a masquerade with you, Alexander."

He was certain the surprise at Phoebe using his given name showed on his face. He stared at her red lips beneath her gold Columbina mask.

"Since I'm an adult now, I think it's time to retire my childish names. Don't you agree?"

He looked into her eyes—*the wrong thing to do!* The shadow from her mask made them appear green and the smoldering intrigue there was the perfect blend of Lucy's mischievousness and Opal's venom.

"If that is what you wish."

"It is, Alexander." She rolled his name from her tongue like her mother had often done in her moments of want.

Trying to ignore her, he looked down. The long slit on the left side of the skirt flashed her shapely leg with a peek of her garter strap as she walked. Jaw clenched, Alexander refocused his gaze to the table they approached. Magdalene conversed with Melissa and Frederick with Maxwell and Lottie.

"Phoebe," Maxwell said with his charming smile that was still youthful, "like all the Easton women before you, you're the prettiest debutante this year. Of course, the year Cora and Emma were out, it was a tie."

She accepted his hug and kiss. "Thank you, Uncle Max. Will you save a dance for me?"

"Don't waste your time on this old man. You'll have no shortage of dance partners."

"Family isn't a waste." She linked her arm through her father's. "Will you dance with me if Sissa can spare you?"

"Of course, Princess."

"And Alexander won't deny me." She flashed a grin that would have set fire to his soul in his youth. "But dance with me now, Daddy, before your leg tires."

After Maxwell and Lottie went to the dance floor, Melissa pulled Alexander into the seat between her and Magdalene. "What's going on between you and Phoebe?"

"Nothing," he said as he rubbed the burn marks on his jaw, "but I think she's planning something."

"I've noticed a change in her since Christmas." Melissa looked to Magdalene. "Have you?"

"She hasn't been over since then." Magdalene's voice was soft but Alexander knew she was holding back something.

Alexander took his wife's hand and kissed her palm before linking their fingers. "I think she might have seen us in the camellia garden."

Melissa gasped. "Alex, with everyone—"

"No, nothing like what I would have done with Lucy." He caressed Magdalene's wrist.

Melissa's short, copper waves swooshed as she shook her head. "Everyone knows your story. That was your special place with Lucy. Phoebe will be resentful."

"I can't avoid every place Alex and Lucy had intimate encounters. If I did, there'd be no place left for me." Magdalene's straight face broke into a pleasing smile as she looked to Alexander.

"Everywhere is fresh when I'm with you, sweetness." He caressed her cheek as he drew closer for a kiss. The classic waltz ended and a modern tune, perfect for fox trotting, began. "How about a dance, Magdalene?"

"Take Melissa this time."

Knowing Frederick only waltzed in public, Alexander stood and offered a hand. "How about it, darling Sissa?"

"It would be an honor, dashing Poppy."

Melissa was a better dancer than Magdalene, and Alexander enjoyed his time with her, though a hint of sadness over her losing that outlet with Frederick always tainted their dancing. Halfway through the song, Henry cut in and switched partners. The Adamses were the best dancers of all. Alexander tried to match Darla's expert Charleston with his own cunning moves, but it turned sultry. Darla shot him a warning look while she continued with her quick kicks. He laughed because once his hips found the rhythm, there was no stopping him. It was carnival season, after all. Magdalene would forgive him, and his friends would only joke that the old Alex was back.

But Darla didn't stand for it. Frowning, she crossed her arms in front of her shapely golden gown and turned away. Smiling—and still dancing—he turned toward the table to collect Magdalene. He found himself facing a shimmying Phoebe. The slit of her long gown afforded the outlandish moves, and her unbound breasts moved beneath the scooped décolletage, threatening to erupt. She smiled as she closed the distance between them.

Alexander immediately stopped and stepped to the side. "Don't make a spectacle of yourself."

"But isn't that what you and my mother did?" Her cold voice snapped with electricity as she followed him off the dance floor.

"Don't ruin your chance for a match with a decent man, Phoebe."

"I didn't come to you for fatherly advice, Alexander."

He grabbed her wrist, nostrils flaring. "Then why are you coming to me?"

"If you don't know what I want, you're less of a man than I thought you were." She yanked herself free and stalked away.

Four

At twelve-thirty in the morning, Bethany stirred a pan of milk on the stove in the Mellings' kitchen. The back door slammed and she turned, wooden spoon raised against possible danger.

Kade's angry face faltered into a laugh. "Easy there, Tiger, though it's good to see you have enough pluck to defend the castle."

She smiled and turned back to the stove. "Hot chocolate will be ready in a few minutes, if you'd like some."

Stopping directly behind her, he placed a hand on her shoulder. "I would, thank you."

Her racing heart filled her ears as Kade held his position, his body heat warming her back as much as the stove's flame kept her hand warm as she stirred. She turned off the burner and mixed in the cocoa and sugar.

"You make the best hot chocolate," he said. "Remember that winter at Seacliff when it sleeted? Our parents were all in their rooms for the night but you, Tabby, and I went downstairs to watch the storm from the back porch."

"Yes." She sighed, remembering her thirteen-year-old self in awe of Kade's strong figure building a fire in the porch hearth while she made hot chocolate in the kitchen. "That's one of my favorite memories at Seacliff."

Kade stepped back while she ladled the drinks into mugs.

"What about the others?" He stood by the corner table and undid his bowtie.

"The boys and Louisa are playing Parcheesi and Tabby brought Amelia upstairs last hour. She never came back, so I checked on her fifteen minutes ago. She's sleeping too."

"You were alone when the clock struck midnight?"

She nodded and handed him his cup. "I don't mind."

"I was in the middle of a crowded ballroom, but I held no one's hand and didn't kiss any girls." He took her cup as well, setting them both on the table. "May I kiss you now as a belated New Year's well wishing?"

The tenderness in his blue eyes drew her in, showcasing his hurt and disappointment in the evening's festivities. She nodded and turned her cheek to him, but he took her chin and brought his lips to hers. A soft, quick one. Then he returned with a longer kiss, nestling into her hair when he was done.

"Tiger," he whispered in her ear as he tugged her waist closer.

Melting against him in the moment she'd been waiting for, Bethany savored the smell of him—smoke and aftershave—as she tentatively trailed her hand up his chest to the hanging bowtie. "I'm always here for you, Kade."

He kissed her cheek and exhaled his frustrations. "Why can't Phoebe be more like you?"

The words were a knife to her heart after his gentle attention. She knew he didn't mean to slight her—that he spoke from his own disappointment in whatever happened or didn't happen between him and Phoebe at the masquerade. Kade took the nearest seat without further comment. Slowly lowering to the seat diagonally from him, Bethany held her cup without drinking, not wanting to wash the taste of him from her lips.

Halfway through his cup, he smiled at her. "Still the best chocolate, Tiger."

She grinned and finally took a sip knowing that from then on, hot chocolate would taste like broken fantasies.

Catching his eye, she offered a friendly smile. "Do you want to talk about the ball?"

He shook his head, his brown locks falling over his forehead in clumps from the hair oil. "But your handiwork was admired. Both my set and your sister's dress."

Bethany blushed. "I hope one didn't detract from the other."

"As if there was a chance of that." Kade leaned back, his shoe brushing against her foot as he stretched his legs. "She hardly spoke to me the whole evening, but that twit Jane wouldn't leave me alone."

Bethany nodded, knowing Jane was an octopus.

"I think Phoebe asked her to keep me occupied because she was too busy flaunting herself in front of Poppy."

Bethany choked on her chocolate. "Poppy?"

"Yes." He struck the table with his fist. "It was disgusting. Poppy wasn't playing into it, but your fath—"

"Beth! Louisa!" Frederick Davenport's strained voice called from the front of the house.

Kade grabbed her hand. "He's mad, but don't let him take it out on you."

"He never does."

"I didn't think he would." He caressed her hand. "And Tiger, I shouldn't…I'm sorry I kissed you."

"And I'm sorry you feel that way." She stood and bit her lip to keep it from trembling as she brought her cup to the sink.

Kade stood to follow her. "Ti—"

"Beth?" Her father pushed through the door. "We need to get home."

"I have to wash—"

"I'll see to the dishes." Kade stepped around her to reach the sink first. "Thank you for the hot chocolate and your sympathetic ear."

"Goodnight, Kade," she said without meeting his gaze.

"Louisa's already in the automobile," Frederick said. "Get your wrap."

Bethany matched his stilted pace to the front door where Asher stood to see them out. "Happy New Year, Beth. Mr. Freddy."

"Thank you for the fun evening, Asher." She hugged her half-brother goodbye.

On the veranda, Frederick's steps slowed.

"Did you dance too much, Daddy?"

"Not nearly as much as I wanted. Fortunately Alex, Henry, and your Uncle Max helped keep Sissa satisfied on the dance floor. And a few others that I would have liked to shake my cane at if I'd had it with me."

"Daddy!" She giggled as they neared the automobile.

"She's beautiful, and I'm not the only one who appreciates her company."

"Sissa loves you," she whispered.

"At times I pity her devotion to this broken man."

Bethany squeezed his arm and kissed his cheek. "You're still a strong, kind, handsome man any woman would be proud to be with."

When they reached the car, he led her around to the driver's side. "Sit up front with me."

Phoebe was in the backseat with Melissa—her blonde head in their stepmother's lap as she lay curled on her side. Bethany met Melissa's gaze. Her stepmother shook her head to prevent Bethany from asking questions. Sliding onto the bench seat, Bethany sat between Louisa and their father for the mile drive home.

"Get the house unlocked and Louisa inside, Freddy," Melissa said once they parked in the porte-cochere. "Beth can help me with Phoebe."

He motioned to Louisa as he opened the car door. "You heard your mother. Go on and get in your nightgown, Littlest Princess."

Melissa sighed and shoved Phoebe off her lap. "Come on," she grumbled. "I'm done coddling you."

Phoebe moaned and reached for the open door. "Beth, help me!"

Bethany put out a hand to steady her sister. "Are you drunk?"

She laughed, head lolling. "Oscar spiked all the punch and then shared his extra flask to help us debutantes enjoy carnival season properly."

"You behaved shamefully." Melissa grabbed her arm and started for the house.

"Leave me be." Phoebe tried to push Melissa away.

"I'm seeing you to bed like the child you are. Next time you want to act wanton by throwing yourself at your stepfather and getting drunk at a respectable ball, make sure your father isn't there to witness your nauseating display."

"So I have permission to behave as such without Daddy around? Is that why Uncle Eddie says you behaved scandalously during the war, because Daddy wasn't here to see it?"

"Your uncle knows nothing about what happened that year. I slapped him once and will do the same to you if you spread those vicious rumors."

Bethany looked to her stepmother with shock as they stumbled up the front steps with her sister.

Phoebe laughed and clutched Bethany as they entered the house. "Uncle Eddie says Miss New York and Uncle Claudio had an affair when Daddy was gone to war, same as she did with men all over the world in her travels."

Melissa took Phoebe by the arms and yanked her upright before slapping her. "I never gave my body to *any* man except your father, and that was after our wedding! If you and your disgusting uncle wish to spread gossip, I demand you keep it out of my house!"

She let her go, and Phoebe crumpled to the floor.

"I'm sorry, Sissa! I didn't know. Uncle Ed—"

"Why don't you ask your *precious* uncle about his life's choices rather than discussing mine?" Melissa stomped up the stairs.

"Beth," her father called down, "shall I help you?"

"No, I've got her." She heaved Phoebe up off the floor and nudged her toward the stairs. "Come on, and keep your mouth shut. Your breath stinks and you can't hold your tongue."

Phoebe sniffled and leaned on Bethany to help navigate the stairs. "I didn't mean it about Sissa. Now she hates me too. Daddy is furious, and Poppy and Miss Maggie know I'm wicked, but I couldn't help it."

"Shh, be quiet."

Louisa looked out from her shared room. Bethany waved her back as she led Phoebe into her private space.

Phoebe collapsed onto her double bed. "He didn't appreciate what I did."

"Who?" Bethany removed her sister's heeled shoes.

"Alexander Randolph Melling." Shoes off, Phoebe lifted her legs, kicking them until the lily print skirt was about her thighs. Her hands met the garters and released her stockings. "That's why I wanted you to makeover this set—to remind him of Momma—but he said I made a spectacle of myself by trying to dance with him."

"Phoebe, he's our poppy!"

"Exactly!" She flung her stockings at Bethany. "He was Momma's and ours before he was Maggie's! She's taking over everything, erasing Momma from his memory!"

"He loves Momma and would never forget—"

"You didn't see him in the camellia garden on Christmas! He was all over Maggie like she was his everything!"

"She is, now," Bethany whispered. "But he still loves Momma. I've seen him crying at the mausoleum when we're at Seacliff. He brings her roses every time he goes."

"That's nothing when he's making love to that woman in the sacred spaces from his time with *my* mother!" Phoebe unfastened the skirt and sat up to undo the top.

Fearing she'd rip the seams, Bethany helped. When she finally freed herself, Phoebe lay back on the bed and Bethany hung the clothing neatly in the closet.

"You know they made love everywhere," Bethany whispered. "I never told anyone, but I walked in on them once when I was five. I didn't understand what they were doing at the time, but now—"

Phoebe was up in a flash. "Where?"

Bethany blushed. "The chaise in his den. I never could sit on it after what I saw."

She laughed bawdily and licked her lips. "I always expected as much. Was he thrusting on top of her?"

"Phoebe!"

"I need to know! Mother isn't here to teach us."

"Sissa can explain things before you get married."

"Women today are free to explore what men have to offer without ties of commitment." With a noxious exhale, Phoebe clutched her breasts, running her hands over her silk camisole. "Do you know how many have touched these already? Ten, and I only know five by name. And I've kissed twice that many guys."

Not wanting to hear more, Bethany turned for the door. "You need to sleep this off."

"I may be drunk, but I know what I've done. You have to tell me, Beth. How did you finally know what Momma and Poppy were doing?"

She sighed and sank to the bed beside her sister. "A couple years back, Miss Darla left one of her birthing books in the study when she was visiting with Sissa. The other kids were in the yard so I looked through it. I read passages about what medical professionals call 'conception.' It had drawings of naked bodies, both male and female, and all the parts inside and out."

Phoebe giggled. "I think I'll have to pay a call on Miss Darla and ask to spend time in her library. Oscar and his friends have shown me pictures of real people. One of his college friends even asked if I'd model for one to add to his collection."

"He didn't!"

"He did, but I told him no—for now." She pinched Bethany's cheek a little too hard. "Now how were Momma and Poppy?"

"They were naked, with one of those velvet blankets she loved beneath them." Bethany looked away, trying not to picture the scene because she knew she'd never look as bold as her mother. That no man would ever look upon her and touch her with such fervor.

"And he was moving on top of her?"

She shook her head, afraid she was tattling. "He was lying down and she was straddling him. Her hair was so long it was like a cape about her shoulders and it shifted across her back as she rocked on top of him."

Phoebe giggled. "Momma knew how to work it! What was he doing?"

Bethany's face heated further. "It's not for me to say. That was their private moment and I shouldn't have gone in there."

"Beth!" she whined. "You have to tell me!"

"He was touching her," she whispered. "He was rubbing her breasts to the rhythm she was moving to. I'd never seen him with such a peaceful expression on his face. Eyes half closed, a little smile, and the love. I could feel it in the air and knew it was a special moment for them."

"Don't you see? He should have respected that love rather than transfer it to Maggie! It isn't fair to Momma!"

"Momma told him to remarry. I heard her tell him that during those final weeks and it sounded like it was something he'd heard from her many times because it annoyed him. He was too worried to want to discuss a future without her."

"She didn't want him to be alone, but surely she didn't want him throwing himself at Maggie because she was the closest woman available. He could have waited for the right—"

"He loves Miss Maggie. They were good friends for years and I'd seen them kiss before. Surely it's a great thing to marry a friend, someone you already respect. He has scars for her, the same as for Momma."

Phoebe shook her head and moaned, fisting her hair. "You don't understand!"

Bethany stood. "You need sleep."

Her sister clutched her forehead. "Could you bring me some headache powder and a glass of water?"

In the bathroom, Bethany stripped to her underclothes and pulled on her robe before returning with the medicine.

"Thank you, Beth." Phoebe said after swallowing it all. She took her hand when Bethany went to retrieve the glass. "Would you stay with me?"

The desolate look in her eyes and the humble tone of her voice made Bethany pause.

"I feel so alone, like everyone hates me. If you stay, I'll know that my only full-sibling still loves me. I'll be able to rise for a new day."

Bethany turned off the light and crawled under the covers.

Phoebe embraced her. "Don't ever hate me, Beth, I couldn't stand for it. I try to be good, but no one's as good as you."

She stayed quite, afraid to admit that Phoebe's choices had already caused friction between them. Several minutes went by and Bethany thought her sister had fallen asleep.

"I was cruel to Kade," Phoebe whispered." I think that hurts me more than what I did to Poppy and how angry Daddy and Sissa are. I don't know what to do about Kade, Beth. I love him, but I don't think it's the same way he loves me."

"Don't worry about it tonight. If he truly loves you, he'll forgive you." *And he'd feel guilty for kissing your sister.*

Five

Monday, January 11, 1926

Dearest Claudio,

We managed to have a horrific New Year's, but this past weekend made up for it. The bad news first: Phoebe Camellia Davenport is following in the footsteps of her mother and aunt. I haven't been so bold as to discuss it with Alex, but Melissa and I agree. At the New Year's ball, Phoebe threw herself at Alex each time he was on the dance floor. It didn't matter who his partner was, she wiggled herself between them. Frederick was livid. After he scolded her, she got drunk and made it worse. Melissa told me she had to slap Phoebe when they got home because she started rehashing what Edmund said about you two during the war. Phoebe has been around the Eastons too much!

After that night, Frederick turned to Darla for help securing items to have on hand should Phoebe have an episode like the ones that plagued Lucy. There's small comfort knowing he has the means to subdue her should it be needed, but I fear the damage is already done. Poor Kade still fancies himself in love with her despite her actions. He's been moping around since then, but he's back to his studies this week. Hopefully, he will forget her and concentrate on this semester's work. His professors are impressed with his aptitude and are encouraging him to choose a field of study so he can apply himself to what will serve him best for his career. Part of me thinks he's waiting for Phoebe to say what type of man she'll marry before he declares his major, but the other part of me thinks he's confused from being raised among the laboring men on the island

and being thrust into society with lawyers and accountants. He knows there is good in both worlds, but needs to choose which one works best for him. Thanks to Alex, he has a solid education for anything.

Besides dealing with the she-devil, we've been well. Amelia, Asher, and Simon enjoyed Christmas, Tabitha too. She'll most likely be out in society next year, but stayed home New Year's Eve with the youngest this time. Louisa and Beth spent the evening with them. Dear Bethany made everyone's Christmas presents. She said she mailed you a wool scarf—did it arrive? Her skills are as good as anything professionally made. I wish Kade fancied Beth instead of her sister.

As for the good news, Alex and I escaped to Seacliff Manor the end of last week. We left Tabby and Kade in charge of the children and Charlotte came to cook a second meal each day. I asked Melissa and Darla to drop in unannounced to check on things. The children did fine, of course, and Alex and I needed the space. It was even more necessary after the awful masquerade. (Part of me is still in shock, but the other knows it's been coming all these years because Phoebe is too much like Lucy.) I commanded Alex to forget society and decorum. We asked Rosemary to stock the kitchen and we were blessedly alone for two whole days and nights, eating and making love where and when we felt like it. By the second night he—well, I'll keep that private. I tell you too much as it is! Needless to say, we ended our stay smiling, sated, and a tiny bit sore. (Another letter to burn!)

Alex is looking forward to Lucy's Azalea Blossom *being reprinted for the twentieth anniversary this March. I can't help but think of seeing him with that pink book my first weekend at Seacliff Cottage. It was one of the mysteries that drew me to him. Well, maybe not completely mysterious as there were the pull of the demons and the raw magnetism he possessed (or rather, still possesses!), besides the bright romance novel within those dark walls.*

I am pleased to know your work in Naples has been helpful to those you serve. Even with all your success, please remember I am the first you delivered from demons. Though you passionate Italians seem plagued by evil spirits, please be mindful what we are facing here. Alex might need you if things continue to decline with Phoebe. Maybe a sabbatical trip to your dear friend is in order. We have a lovely guest room and you would be most welcome. In case travel is in your future, it would be best to stop feeding those stray cats near your home so they will not be too spoiled by the time you leave.

Love and Prayers,

*****

It took the better part of January for Phoebe to arrange the perfect plan. The morning of Tuesday, January twenty-six was the chosen day. All the siblings would be in school, Magdalene would be at Sacred Heart for her charity work with Melissa, and Charlotte didn't arrive at the Mellings' until mid-afternoon. Two weeks before, Oscar telephoned Melling and Associates to set-up a fake appointment with Alexander for ten that morning. At nine, Phoebe called the office and pretended to be the frantic secretary of "Mr. Brinker" apologizing for the late cancelation. Ten minutes later, she telephoned again, acting as Magdalene. She told the secretary to send word to Alexander about a pressing document she left at home to be brought to her at Sacred Heart.

"It's about donations, and I simply must have it this morning. I left it on his desk," Phoebe said into the telephone in Alexander's den.

"Of course, Mrs. Melling. His appointment next hour just cancelled. I'm sure he'll be happy to assist as you do so much for the community."

Phoebe rolled her eyes and gave her thanks before hanging up. Leaning back behind the massive desk of the Melling men, she savored her cunningness. Then, she stood and adjusted her mother's kimono that she'd changed into when she arrived.

After spreading a velvet blanket she'd found in one of the upstairs closets over the chaise, she pulled the drapes shut and lit the candles she'd arranged on the desk beside a partial brandy bottle she'd filched from her father's stash. It was the last of his brandy, and she knew she'd get in trouble, but it would be worth it.

She poured two glasses and took a swig from the bottle so the taste was on her tongue. Bringing the lapel of the silk robe to her nose, Phoebe inhaled the familiar scent of her mother, kept fresh because she stored Lucy's clothing with lavender sachets.

Alexander's whistling announced him in the hallway. She moved into the corner so she would be behind the door when it opened. It swung inward, and his whistle turned to a pleased hum. He moved into the middle of the room, stepping out of his shoes and pulling off his jacket.

"Where are you, sweetness?" he called as he dropped the jacket onto the nearest chair and loosened his tie. "And brandy, you naughty woman. Have you called me home to seduce me?"

Phoebe shut the door. "At last, we're on the same page."

She wasted no time crossing the room, lifting a shoulder so the expertly hung kimono slipped open several inches with the movement. Before he could resist, her arms were about his neck and her lips on his, tongue spreading the taste of the brandy to his mouth. With a groan, he pushed her away, causing her to stumble back several feet.

Alexander wiped his mouth on his shirtsleeve. "You need to leave, Phoebe."

"I'm here to give you another chance with your queen." She returned to him. "The sights, scents, sounds, tastes, and touches from when you were fulfilled by your true love."

He shuddered.

Phoebe took the opportunity to trace his sensual lips. "Cleave to me, and be with your queen once more."

She kissed his jaw, gently pressing their bodies together.

"You see her when you look at me." She nudged him toward the desk as his hand went to her hip. "I saw the longing in your eyes on Christmas, the desire on New Year's Eve to feel my curves beneath that gown. I'll be your queen, Angel."

They'd reached the desk. Phoebe set a tumbler in his hand. "Old cravings don't need to be denied. I'll fulfill everything."

He inhaled sharply. "Lavender and brandy."

His whisper strummed her tight body. "She misses you as much as you've missed her. Remember her words?

'I've waited

And will continue to wait

Until we make

our escape

Free to explore everything

With sight, touch, and taste

Only then will we belong to each other.'

Drink and remember, Alexander."

He opened his eyes, and brought the glass to his kissable lips—much too fine to be wasted on an aging woman like Magdalene. Alexander took a few tentative sips before slinging it back. Phoebe followed his lead with hers.

"You need to leave." He sounded stronger, but his eyes betrayed him.

Phoebe moved fluidly toward the chaise, not breaking eye contact.

"'White and pure

Until you touched me with your soul

Now I'm pink with desire

Cravings for you flooding

As I wait for the red your touch will bring.'

Show me everything. I'm your second chance to rediscover your first and last love affair."

His icy eyes lit with fire as she lay back on the velvet blanket, hands trailing the kimono to showcase her curves, opening the fabric a little more to expose the valley of her breasts. He looked away long enough to pour himself another glass, and then sauntered forward with a look between amusement and disdain.

"'Your hands over my skin

Mine on yours

Your scent all around me

In me.'"

She rose from her position and circled him. "I want you in me. Take me and make me scream in passion."

Meeting no defiance, she pulled his tie free and opened several buttons on his shirt until she could kiss the scars showing on his chest.

"Those marks were to protect Magdalene. Don't touch them." His harsh voice loosened fear inside her.

"Your queen enjoyed kissing your scars." Phoebe settled her arms on his shoulders. "You'll find me just as willing."

His gaze softened and a slight smile found his lips. "Lucy was extraordinary."

"And you tossed her memory aside for the commonness of another woman." She removed his cufflinks and opened a few more buttons, causing his breath to hitch. "Allow the exceptional back into your life."

"Sweets." He abruptly turned. "My queen always needed sweets."

"Alex, don't go!"

He paused at the door. "I have just the thing in the kitchen. It will only take a minute."

Phoebe poured more brandy and settled on the chaise, legs displayed from feet to thigh. She adjusted the folds of the top of the kimono to cover a few inches that had previously been open.

If he's going to run out, he'll have to work for more.

Alexander returned with a plate of cookies, holding the offering before her.

"There's only one sweet I want right now. Would you like this heavenly body above you? My form is magnificent on a stallion. You taught me everything I know about riding, but it's time to learn more."

He smiled like an angel, slaying Phoebe with what she took as consent. When he came back from placing the plate on the desk, she pulled him to the chaise.

"I knew you felt the same way, Alexander." She nuzzled into his neck, kissing him. Her kimono opened more in the process. The deliciousness of their skin touching sent sparks through her. She moved to straddle him. "I can be your everything. We'll need no other."

"Phoebe, slow down."

"You don't—"

He touched her lips with a finger. "Do you want things to be exactly like your mother?"

"Yes!" She sat halfway up, her breasts nearly spilling out of the robe.

"I didn't take Lucy the first time she offered herself to me."

Muscles taunt with expectations, her body felt like it would snap. "You didn't touch?"

He laughed and freed his legs from beneath Phoebe, kissing her cheek as he shifted to sit beside her. His laughter didn't hurt her feelings—it only endeared him more, for she saw the love on his face shining through.

Love for Momma, love for me.

"Darling, we couldn't get enough of touching and kissing! She was passionate and I was blessed to be the one she chose to give herself to, but I made her wait." He smoothed Phoebe's hair behind her ear. "I loved her too much to take advantage of what she offered. I waited until we were engaged before I allowed myself the honor of making love to her."

"So you only want to touch and kiss me today?"

He nodded, the light in his eyes changing.

"You could mark me yours," she whispered, pulling the kimono aside to expose the area of her heart.

He closed the robe, fingertips trailing her chest. "I can't allow that, Knight Phoebe. I love my wife too much, and your father would kill me."

Panic flooded her as he embraced her like a child, hugging her to his torso as he trapped her arms.

"My father?" She jerked, trying to free herself.

"I called his office when I went to the kitchen. He's on his way."

"No! It isn't supposed to be like this! You love me!"

His lips on her forehead calmed her a moment. "I've loved you as a daughter for fifteen years. You need help, Knight Phoebe. Your father and I will see that you get the assistance you need."

"The only help I need is you!" Her voice warbled. "Take me and make me a woman! Fill me as you did my mother so I can feel the love you shared!"

"Phoebe Camellia Davenport!" Frederick stormed in with the assistance of his cane, but stopped as he took in the details of the room. His countenance switched from anger to pain to rage to fear within seconds.

"Help me, Daddy!" She struggled more. "Poppy tried to seduce me! Kill him!"

His faltering steps brought him closer as he pulled a cloth from his coat pocket. "Lies don't become you, Princess. Be brave."

She screamed as her father covered her nose and mouth with the wet cloth. Then everything went cold and dark except the feeling of Alexander's warm arms around her.

Six

Alexander sat on the chaise, the dead weight of his stepdaughter in his arms as Frederick used the telephone. Unable to look upon Lucy's robe, he closed his eyes. But he couldn't block the cloying scent of lavender, the silk against his skin, the taste of the brandy, or the fragments of Lucy's poems echoing in his mind.

"Mother Mary, save me!" The anguish in his voice startled his soul, but it wasn't enough to stop the tears.

"Alex, get a hold of yourself," Frederick commanded.

Alexander couldn't respond. He could only feel the body trembling in his arms as he shook from his torment. Hands tried to pry her from him, but he clung tighter in hopes of hanging on to his Lucy.

"Let her go, Alex."

Another figure arrived, blue eyes blazing with resentment. "She needs to be stretched out until they come for her, Frederick. Take her, and I'll pull him away."

The two worked in tandem until Darla had Alexander by the arm. He was a sniveling wretch, and she looked like she wanted to slap him.

"You need to get out of here, Alex."

Frederick looked up after covering Phoebe with the velvet blanket. "This isn't his fault, Darla. He called for help when he found her here."

"You can't tell me he didn't drink with her. I smell it on his breath. And Phoebe dressed in Lucy's—"

"You've always been cruel to him!" Magdalene snapped as she rushed into the room.

Alexander immediately fell against her, breathing in her rosewater scent in an attempt to rid the memories. "It's like losing her all over again. I ache for my queen like never before. Don't let me go."

"I'm here, Alex."

Then Melissa was on his other side. The two women helped him to the morning room in his grief-blinded state. Magdalene lowered to the sofa with him. He straightened enough to pull the pins from her hair and then curled into her side, nestling beneath the veil of brunette locks and clutching her middle as though a frightened child. Magdalene's touch spoke of her love as she stroked his arm, her steady breath an anchor to his present life.

Father would shun me if he saw me behaving as such, but I need my wife. She's my courage when besieged by demons.

"You were brave," Magdalene whispered to him.

"I'm riding to the hospital with Freddy," Melissa interrupted. "Darla is going to collect Charlene from Henry because she dropped her off at the office before coming over. She'll pick up the girls from school when she gets Ginny, and is happy to keep them all for the evening if needed. I've asked her to send Louisa and Beth home by five so Miss Sharon can give them supper at their regular time. Shall I send word to the boys' school for you, asking Asher and Simon to go to Darla's with Horatio?"

"No, but thank you," Magdalene replied. "I'll have them study before supper. Ask Darla to send Tabby and Amelia home by five as well, please."

"And Kade?" Melissa whispered.

Magdalene's sigh shuddered beneath Alexander's cheek. "He'll be at the dormitory until Friday. I won't bother him until we have a better understanding."

"I'll keep you posted."

"Thank you, Melissa."

The Mellings listened to the ambulance arrive and waited expectantly in the stillness after everyone left.

"May I get anything for you?" Magdalene asked.

"Stay with me. All the pain resurfaced from losing my Lucy."

"You treated them both with utmost care. It's not your fault they unwound like they did. It's their Easton blood, nothing you had control over."

"She tricked me into coming home. She called my secretary pretending to be you, asking me to fetch a paper from the den."

Magdalene sharply inhaled, and Alexander sat upright to look her in the eye.

"Phoebe had the room closed, candles burning and a bottle of brandy out. I thought you'd planned a romantic interlude for us and began undressing."

"Please know I'd never give you brandy." She kissed him, gently brushing his nose with hers.

"I called out that you were naughty when I saw it, but then Phoebe showed herself. She attacked my senses with her play of seduction, making me think of my queen. Even when I lost the battle to drink, I fought to stay in control."

"I'd expect nothing less from you, my lion." Taking his discolored hand, she smiled.

"I told her I love you and wouldn't allow her to touch your scars." He brought the hand she clasped to his chest within his opened shirt and she splayed her fingers over the lines. "My body is yours, Magdalene. Please know I only love Phoebe as a daughter, that her looks and actions haunt me with memories of Lucy, not longing for her. Is it a crime to still love the one we lost after all this time? To spill tears, though my life is filled with your amazing passion?"

She took his cheeks and pressed her forehead to his. "You promised we'd cherish our memories, that we wouldn't replace our first spouses, but add to the present and future. And we have. I love you and your tender ways. I love that you feel so deeply. That's the bravest thing about you, Alexander—your true heart."

He tasted the words on her tongue, lowering her to the sofa as his hands followed her figure from shoulders to hips.

"Magdalene, my head's swimming from the brandy, but I need you."

Her lips stretched into a smile. "Build me a fire and I'll get the drapes."

Hands trembling over the kindling, he managed to start a low blaze in the hearth. *Alex of the marble palace ... I'll mount her like a good gent.* His old limericks jumbled in his mind as he removed his shirt. Magdalene stood by the front window, the blue draperies a pretty backdrop to her functional beige ensemble. Dressed for charity work, the outfit had no pleasing textures but it wouldn't take long to dispense of it.

As though reading his thoughts, she met his gleam with a bold stare as she released her dress to the floor. Wearing her silk slip, she haphazardly tossed a few pillows from the sofa at him. He dropped them to the floor in front of the fireplace and stepped out of his pants, grabbing the back of the nearest chair to steady himself.

Magdalene was at his side in an instant, a hand on his elbow.

"I think I'm drunk, sweetness."

The feel of her bare arms about him as her tongue plundered his mouth was excitable. They were on the carpet, their yearnings heating them more than the flames as they surged together.

"You taste like Seacliff Cottage—those times in the parlor with brandy and the fire when you tried to sway me."

"Magdalene, I don't want to hurt you, but I can't promise I won't." His mouth was at her throat, hands on her soft curves. "I haven't drunk for a long time, but before … I've gone too far."

Her brown eyes sparked with intrigue. "Show me what you wanted to do to me in Seacliff Cottage. I promise I won't stop your advances this time."

With a primal groan, he released two decades of passion, allowing his body to lead unrestrained. The pillows used for comfort and positioning were shoved aside as Alexander's enthusiasm swelled. When he turned too intense, Magdalene took over—just as hot in her fervor. Afterward, he fell asleep with her cheek against his heart, the soft weight of her body covering his.

***

"Alex." Toes nudged him in the ribs.

He groaned and rolled to his side, noticing the blanket he was under though still on the carpet before the fire.

"It's lunch time. I've got coffee and a sandwich for you. Would you like it here or in the kitchen?"

He took hold of her ankle, trailing his fingers higher as he looked up at his wife through cracked lids. "You want it in the kitchen, spicy Magdalene?"

She laughed as he reached the back of her knee. "I'd be surprised if you could walk there right now. I'll bring a tray."

"Thank you."

After she left, he crawled to the hearth and added another log to help remove the chill from his bare skin. He settled with his back to a nearby armchair and pulled the red blanket around his lap. His clothing was folded over the arm of the sofa, the rest of the room pristine beyond the nest of pillows in front of him.

Magdalene returned with the promised nourishment and a smile. She settled on a pillow, placing the tray between them.

"Where's yours?"

She blushed and retrieved a teacup. "You made me ravenous. I had to eat while I prepared things."

"You know how to exude more energy than I ever thought possible." His teasing smile and wink made her laugh again. He chewed his first bite of food. "I doubt either of us would still be here if things had progressed between us back then."

"How's that?" The quirk of her lips made his loins ache.

"Our young passion would have set our souls on fire." He leaned forward to kiss her but grew dizzy, falling against her shoulder instead. "I'm still a wreck, but I need to telephone—"

"I already contacted the office and informed them there was a family emergency, and that you would be out the rest of the day. I plan on feeding you, seeing you to the shower, and then a nap or—"

"Or make love to you again." His lips didn't miss the mark that time.

"I think one of us should be able to answer the telephone at any given time the rest of the day." In response to his pout, she kissed him. "But bedtime is another story."

She drank her tea and watched him eat. When he set his empty cup on the tray, Magdalene took his hand. "What are we going to tell the children?"

Her voice held heartache, and he pulled her to his chest. Kissing her face and neck, he relished in her warmth before replying.

"I'll explain it like I did to Ash when Lucy worsened. It's the easiest way. They don't need to know what happened here, what showed how far she's fallen."

"But Kade?"

"He's too much like his father and Frederick for his own good. Lucy nearly ruined Freddy. I'd hate to see Kade's heart trampled, especially this young. At least when Frederick lost Lucy he'd already gone through the heartache of losing his first wife. He had more worldly knowledge and a few years on Kade at present. But Kade doesn't need to know the details, nor can we make Phoebe appear as forbidden fruit. He needs to make that decision on his own, which will hopefully be easier after her behavior at the New Year's ball."

By the time Asher and Simon returned from school, Alexander poured over old notes in his den from the time he investigated asylums for Opal. The files were horribly out of date, but it was a starting point should Frederick require assistance in that regard.

Magdalene came to the doorway. "Where would you like to speak with the boys after they're done eating?"

He closed the file, clasped his hands behind his head, and leaned back. "The parlor."

"You don't think it too formal?"

His sock-clad feet were silent as he crossed the room to embrace her. "What would the boys think if I rushed out of the morning room with you in the middle of a serious talk because I caught the scent of what we enjoyed earlier and wanted more?"

"You're as naughty as ever, Alex." Her hand went to his backside and pinched.

"And you wouldn't have me any other way."

"I'll have you any way I can get you."

He tugged up her skirt to get at her thigh. With an old reflex, she punched his stomach. Laughing, he caught her around the waist and brought her out of his room. "You feisty tease."

The smell of fresh oatmeal cookies filled the hall. Asher and Simon exited the kitchen.

"Come with us to the front room, boys," Alexander said. "There's family news."

"Don't tell me Mama's going to have another baby." Simon smirked around his final mouthful of cookie.

Asher pushed him and rumpled his brown hair. "That isn't a way to speak about your mother. Amelia is a fine sister. I'd take another if the baby is like her."

They elbowed their gangly bodies back and forth until their shoving match ended with Asher on the sofa and Simon sprawled on the floor at his feet. Smiling at their rambunctiousness, Alexander sent a silent prayer of gratitude for his son having such a close stepsibling. They'd become almost twins in their years together. Simon's sensible upbringing on the island and his six months head start gave him a tad more maturity than Asher, but he was prone to hijinks while Asher was more level-headed. The two balanced each other and kept themselves out of trouble more often than not.

Settled on the sofa between them, Alexander put an arm around each of their shoulders while Magdalene took a chair across from them. "Phoenix Asher, do you remember what I told you about your momma when she became sick?"

Asher's easy-going smile fell from his face and he ran a hand through his blond hair. "That she had scars in her head that made her angry and upset, but it was from nothing any of us did."

Magdalene covered her mouth to muffle a sharp inhalation.

"That's right. Do you understand that, Simon? That sometimes people have scars inside instead of on their skin? Scars that make them different, sometimes unable to function like they used to?"

"Yes, Poppy." Simon grew solemn as well.

"It appears that Phoebe has scars inside her. She had to be brought to the hospital this morning for help."

"But that killed Momma!" Asher was on his feet looking down on his father as though he'd given his sister a death sentence.

"It might not be exactly the same, Ash. It's too early to know. Phoebe is being tested and getting help, but one thing will be different no matter what the results are from her hospitalization." Alexander took his son's hand and guided him to his seat. "Phoebe won't be sleeping over here ever again."

"And what of Beth? Do I no longer get to see my sisters?"

"Bethany will continue to come, but it's too soon to say what Phoebe's schedule will be. Depending on how she's doing, we'll decide about the best way for you and the rest of the family to visit with her. We'll have to wait and see, but we wanted you to know so you can pray for her."

Asher folded his arms, eyes downcast. "Are Momma's scars inside me and Bethany too?"

Alexander hugged his son. "I don't think so, Phoenix Asher, and I'll do all I can to keep everyone safe."

Seven

Bethany ran from the streetcar, not stopping to make sure Louisa was behind her.

"Daddy! Sissa!" She called as soon as she was in the front door.

A moment later, Louisa stumbled in behind her.

Miss Sharon came out of the kitchen. "Miss Melissa said she'd be home or telephone by five-thirty, so you two best wash up and be ready for supper at six."

"Have you heard—"

"I haven't heard anything other than what I told you, Miss Bethany." She wiped her hands on her apron. "Now why don't you settle in and sew on something to calm yourself."

"Yes, ma'am. And I'll answer the telephone if it rings." Turning to her sister, she took charge in an attempt to gain control over her emotions. "Put away your school supplies and wash up, Louisa."

Bethany washed her face and hands in the guest bathroom to be near the telephone. Her current sewing project was a dress for herself, but it didn't feel right to work on it when Phoebe was in the hospital suffering in an unknown condition. She sat with her history book at Melissa's desk in the study, staring at the telephone as a finger trailed the gold lettering across the unopened book.

At five-fifteen she answered the telephone on the first ring.

"Hello, Beth."

"Sissa! What's going on? The only thing Miss Darla said was that Phoebe had to be hospitalized."

Louisa hovered in the doorway, dark brows drawn together.

"Phoebe had an episode similar to what your mother used to have. She was out of control, and your father had to bring her to the hospital for help."

Bethany's blood went cold. She knew Phoebe was acting different lately. Guilt crept in over not telling someone.

Melissa kept talking. "She's sleeping right now, but she woke when her first medicine wore off. She was still agitated, so they had to give her something else to calm her. Your father wants to stay until eight to see if she wakes again before coming home for the night."

"You'll be home to see us to bed?"

"Yes, Beth, I promise. Ask Miss Sharon to stay with you until then if you want. I can drive her home so she isn't on the streetcar too late."

"That's okay. You'll be tired, Sissa."

"Please ask her to put our food in the refrigerator ,and we'll eat when we get home. Is Louisa nearby?"

"She's looking right at me."

"Let me say hello to her and we'll see you in a few more hours."

"I love you, Sissa. Hug Daddy for me."

Later, after saying goodnight to Sharon, Bethany sent Louisa up to shower. She slipped into the study to telephone the other house.

"Hello."

"Ash, how are things over there?" Bethany asked.

"Fine. Is Phoebe home yet?"

"Our dad isn't even home from the hospital. Have you heard anything?"

"No," he whispered, "but Sissa called and talked to Miss Maggie for a long time."

"Could I speak with Tabby?"

"Simon, get your sister. It's Beth."

Bethany took a deep breath. "How's Poppy?"

"He's been sad. Everyone is except Tabby."

"Give it to me, Phoenix Asher!" Tabitha demanded. "Beth, are you okay?"

She smiled at the concern in her friend's voice. "Just worried is all. My dad and Sissa are staying at the hospital until eight in case Phoebe wakes up. I won't know anything until later. Have they told you anything over there?"

"Only to keep our mouths shut about it to Kade. Mama doesn't want to worry him when he's at school, especially since there isn't anything to say yet."

"He'll be sick over it."

"Let him be! After that stunt she pulled at the masquerade, he doesn't need to give Phoebe any thought other than being friendly at family suppers. Mama did say Phoebe wouldn't be staying over any more, so that's one good thing on this end. I wouldn't put it past her to try to climb in bed with Poppy."

"Tabby, that's my sister!"

"And be glad you're nothing like her. The things people are saying around town about her because of New Year's Eve aren't fit for your ears, dear one. Kade needs to scrub his soul of her, the quicker the better."

Gooseflesh tingled Bethany's limbs. "I think I hear Louisa coming. I better go."

***

After school on Friday, Bethany and Louisa rode to the Mellings' house with Tabitha, Amelia, and Magdalene because it was Bethany's weekend to stay over with her stepfather. Rather than stop for something to eat in the kitchen with the others, she continued to her bedroom. When Alexander had married Magdalene, they moved the girls to the wing where the guest rooms were. Phoebe and Bethany shared and Tabitha—who now shared with Amelia—got the one next to them. The Davenports' old room adjacent to Asher's became the Campbell boys' space, though Simon had since moved into Asher's room.

Tabitha had warned Bethany her mother wanted Phoebe's things packed that weekend. Bethany stood in the middle of the room, gazing at the shelf of horse statues and trophies, then at Phoebe's crowded dressing table. Slipping into the corner chair, she continued soaking in her sister's collections.

"What are we going to do, Tiger?"

Turning to Kade in the nondescript suit and tie he wore to classes at the university, Bethany caught her breath at the pain reflected in his blue eyes. He looked as Phoebe had New Year's Eve—hopeless. She went to Kade and hugged him, not knowing what to say. She couldn't speak of her sister's despair over hurting him, so she held him and reminded herself that his arms about her were nothing more than a hurting friend needing comfort. That he had apologized for the New Year's kiss. She'd never be anything more to him than Tabitha's best friend and Phoebe's little sister.

"Why didn't you tell me, Tiger?"

"Your mother didn't want you distracted when there was no information to—"

"I should have known about Phoebe these past four days!"

"It wouldn't have changed—"

Kade stepped away. "I thought you understood how I feel about her. You should have realized I'd want to know, even if I couldn't do anything about it."

"I didn't know what to do." She dipped her head to hide the tears welling in her eyes. "Daddy and Sissa are near breaking and Louisa's scared. She idolizes Phoebe and doesn't know what to do without being able to follow her around every evening. I'm not one to break the rules, Kade, and things at my house are too tense to make a telephone call."

He lifted her chin and searched her face before hugging her. "You're stalwart in all you do, Tiger. I forget how young you are."

She sniffed and wiped a hand against the worst of the tears. "I'm not a baby, even if I snivel like one."

Kade laughed and patted her cheek. "You're the steadiest female I know."

"Thanks a lot, Kade." Tabitha walked into the room, wearing a fresh drop-waist dress that would take her through supper and evening plans. "I guess you won't be up to taking us *unsteady* females to the Crown Theater after supper. Mama said it would be good for the three of us to get out for the night."

Kade frowned and stepped away from Bethany.

"I know we're not as sophisticated as your co-eds, but Beth and I won't detract from your plans if you don't want to be seen with us."

His face relaxed. "Being seen with two classy brunettes at the cinema won't hurt my standing. You look like a college girl and if Beth wears that little cloche hat of hers, she'd pass for a sweet sixteen at least."

Tabitha laughed and smoothed her fringe of hair. "And people think you don't care, but here you are with it all planned out."

Louisa ran in. "Mom and Daddy are coming for supper. I get to stay until we go home afterward!"

Before Bethany could respond, her half-sister ran down the hall shouting for Asher and Simon. Kade excused himself, and Tabitha opened the closet to help Bethany pick out a dress—a blue one she said brightened her complexion and would look great with the black hat. After changing, Bethany was the last one to gather in the living room before supper.

Alexander was nearest the door, standing watch over his family. Not having seen him that week, Bethany noticed he looked older, like her own father did. There even seemed to be a bit of silver in the stubble of his unshaven face.

"Knight Bethany Iris." He embraced her, kissing her cheek. She was as tall as him now and rested her head on his shoulder rather than tucking it under his chin. "Are you doing all right?"

She kissed above his shadow of a beard in return. "Yes, Poppy."

His blue eyes looked pale against the dark smudges beneath them. "You three have fun tonight. In the morning, you're welcome to join us at the stables. It's been awhile since you and Tabby have done that. I'm sure Amelia would like to show off and you'd be welcome to ride Prince."

Phoebe's horse. "I'll see how I feel."

Charlotte announced supper. Bethany hugged her father and Melissa before following the group down the hall. Taking her typical seat between Tabitha and Kade, Bethany smiled at Asher across from her, who sat with Simon and Louisa. Louisa was a full year younger than Simon, but only six months separated her and Asher. The three of them were at that age when Phoebe and Kade's relationship began to change. Bethany wondered if something would kindle between her half-sister and either boy to mar their camaraderie. She was glad there was no worry of Louisa going into hysterics, but she and Asher had the same mother. Could they be touched in the head like Phoebe?

It was a brooding subject to dwell on, and it kept her silent most of the meal. Bethany wasn't the only one quieter than usual. The whole table held an air of unrest beneath the forced smiles and pleasantries. After her parents and Louisa said their goodbyes, Bethany took a few minutes to look at a catalog with Amelia while Tabitha finished putting on her makeup.

"Poppy says I can pick out any dress. What color would be best for spring, Beth?"

"Something to blend in with the flowers," she replied. "Would you like to match an azalea or lily?"

Amelia snuggled against her as she turned the page. "Azaleas."

"A fuchsia would look lovely with your complexion."

Kade came to the doorway. "Time to go, Tiger."

"Thank you," Amelia said as Bethany stood. "The boys are no help and Tabby is too busy on the piano to bother."

She kissed her forehead. "Anytime, Amelia."

"Will you go to the stables with us in the morning?"

Bethany nodded. "But I might have to sit out if my riding clothes no longer fit. I haven't ridden since last summer."

Kade took Bethany by the elbow to hurry her along. "I'll have her wear my clothes if needed," he promised Amelia.

He walked Bethany to Alexander's automobile where Tabitha already sat in the front passenger seat.

"It's about time, children," she chided. "Are we going for sodas before or after the show?"

"After, like good college kids." Kade said as they headed for Dauphin Street.

After the double feature, they gathered at the drug store counter for colas. Several of Kade's friends stopped by and gave attention to Tabitha, but Bethany slunk to the corner, shadowing her face with her hat to prevent making eye contact with the flirting guys.

All that changed when Oscar Easton arrived with a boisterous group.

"Come greet your cousin, Davenport!" he hollered above the noise of the shop.

The well-known name brought the attention of customers and workers alike. Not wanting to prolong the scene, she hurried to Oscar. He looked sharp in a suit and fedora, his Easton chin shaved smooth. Taking her hand, he spun her around and whistled.

"You're turning into a choice bit of calico, Davenport. Be glad you aren't of age as one of my friends here would snatch you away." He nudged his closest friend in the ribs. "She's only fourteen, Jimmy, so forget it."

Bethany pulled away. "I'm fifteen now, Oscar. Last November."

His hazel eyes sparked with mischievousness. "So you are. What's the latest on our doll, Phoebe? Is she still in the hospital?"

She nodded.

"Let me know when she can have visitors. I'm sure she'll be more than ready for a smoke and a nip of something."

Bethany agreed, though she knew anything Oscar heard would be from his father, secondhand information passed on from Uncle Maxwell. "I need to get back to my—"

"Poor relations." He patted her shoulder. "I understand."

Red faced, Bethany returned to Kade and Tabitha. "Could we please go now?"

"I'm at your service, Tiger." Kade slung back the remainder of his cola and stood, putting an arm around her shoulders as Tabitha took the lead.

Oscar whistled when they passed. "How come you didn't come out this year, Tabby Cat? I'd take those legs of yours dancing any time."

Tabitha sneered and made clawing motions with her fingers. "In your wet dreams, Easton."

Eight

After school on Monday, Bethany and Louisa found Naomi at their house with Melissa.

"Miss Naomi!" Bethany ran into the parlor for a hug.

"Oh, sugar, you've got to stop growing. You're as tall as your father, aren't you?"

She shook her head. "Just Poppy and Sissa. Are you staying for supper?"

"No, Paul finished a project early and took Sam fishing after school, so I decided to pay a short visit." Naomi looked to Melissa. "If you want to go to the hospital, I'll stay with the girls an hour."

"Thank you." Melissa looked relieved. "I'd like to be there when Freddy and Alex arrive."

Bethany knew her parents were making preparations for Phoebe's move from the local hospital, though she hadn't heard the details.

Once Melissa departed and Louisa settled in the study with a geography book, Bethany sat beside Naomi on the sofa and sighed.

"Now, tell me how things really are, Bethany."

Tears welled in her eyes before one escaped down her cheek. "I saw Phoebe acting differently since Christmas, but didn't tell anyone. I'm afraid she'll end up hurt because of it. She's been in the hospital a week and Sissa said they only took off the restraints Saturday."

"It isn't your fault. Phoebe's always been a bit wild."

Bethany clutched her hands. "Is she like Momma?"

Naomi's rich countenance remained cheerful. "Possibly."

"Am I going to be like her? And Asher? Will we all fall into madness as we mature?"

Naomi hugged Bethany. "Sugar, you only got the best of your momma. And Asher is his father all over. Phoebe seems to have gotten every bit of the Eastons—the good and the bad. There's nothing you could have done to stop that from showing. I knew your momma since girlhood, and known all you children since birth. There's nothing that concerns me in any of your generation besides your big sister."

"I don't think Phoebe will be coming back."

"They aren't going to send her away like they did to your aunt Opal. She hasn't done anything bad enough to merit that." Naomi patted her arm. "Now, I keep hearing about these dresses you've been making. Would you show them to me?"

Upstairs, Louisa modeled the dresses Bethany had made for her and the seamstress showed the clothing she'd made for herself and Phoebe.

"It tickles me to know I helped start you on your sewing journey and now you're beyond anything I could ever do," Naomi said. "I'm sorry to have to leave, but it's time for me to see to supper for my boys."

They said their goodbyes, and then Bethany settled at her sewing machine to complete a red and black silk ensemble her father commissioned for Melissa's Valentine's Day gift. By the time her father and stepmother returned, supper was laid on the table by Miss Sharon.

"Phoebe looked much better today, girls." Frederick said as he helped Melissa to her seat. "Her cheeks had color and she'd made an effort with her hair for the first time since being there."

"How did she wear it?" Louisa sat forward.

"Brushed to one side," Melissa replied.

Louisa smiled and patted her own side part.

"If she's steady the next few days, we'll see about you two going for a visit."

After supper, Frederick sent Louisa and her mother upstairs to ready for bed, and took Bethany to the parlor.

"Are you holding up, Little Princess?"

"Yes, and I would like to see Phoebe when she's up to it, but not with Louisa."

"It would be best to have no more than two people at a time."

"And visitors more often might be nicer for her."

"You're forever the thoughtful one. If you need anything, no matter how stressed you think I am, please ask. I'll do everything I can for you." He cupped her cheek and kissed her forehead. "I know you're being strong for everyone, but don't forget to take care of yourself. You're too much like me in many ways. I know you'd rather sink yourself than burden anyone, but I don't want that as an option for my Bethany Iris."

Part of her wanted to complain about the staring eyes at school, the mocking of people like Oscar, or not feeling adequate around Kade, but she buried herself on his shoulder instead. "Thank you. I love you, Daddy."

Bolstered by her father's attention, she peacefully slipped into bed a few hours later, though dreams of Phoebe and Kade disturbed her sleep.

***

Saturday morning, Bethany rode to the hospital with her father. Phoebe had held steady that week, accepting her first visitors besides her father and medical personnel: Melissa and Louisa the day before. While both Melissa and Alexander had been to the hospital many times, neither had gone into the room with Phoebe—a fact that disturbed Bethany.

"Whenever you want to leave, tug your ear and I'll make an excuse for an exit."

Bethany tightened her grip on Frederick's arm and steadied her breathing. She was nervous, and it wasn't good that her father could tell. That meant Phoebe would too.

Outside the locked door, they waited for a nurse to open it. Bethany took the moment to smooth the wool pleats on her blue dress though they weren't rumpled. Her leather t-strap shoes matched the black cloche hat Kade admired.

"Beth!" Phoebe flung herself on her sister as soon as the door was opened, kissing her cheeks and crying. "I've missed you!"

Bethany patted the back of her sister's cotton nightgown and Frederick gently nudged them further into the room so the nurse could lock the door behind them. Bethany noted his look of love as he watched over them—Lucy's girls.

"Are you here to take me home, Beth?" Phoebe spun to her father, blonde waves disheveled, childlike voice pleading. "May I come home today, Daddy?"

"We've talked about where you'll be going when you leave the hospital, and it isn't home."

Frowning, she flopped onto the bed in the sparse, clay-colored room. The small window in the wall was frosted glass. Nothing of the outside world could be seen. All she had for a view was the tiny observation window in the door to the hallway.

Hoping to bring a bit of cheer to her sister who had been locked in such drabness for two weeks, Bethany turned to her father and held out her hand. With a smile, he retrieved her gift from his coat pocket.

"Here, Phoebe. I embroidered this for you." Bethany passed the white handkerchief on which she'd stitched the silhouette of Phoebe's horse surrounded by flowers and vines.

"Prince! And it smells like home. Thank you, Beth." Phoebe kissed the image of the horse as silent tears fell. After a minute, she wiped her face and looked to her father. "Did Sissa tell you I apologized for what I told her after the ball?"

"Yes, Princess, but don't worry about that any more. Focus on getting better."

"I think Oscar's been poisoning me with Uncle Eddie's stories. I know Sissa loves you and I've gotten over you abandoning me that year."

His smile was bittersweet, gaze lost in the past. "It was a difficult time for everyone."

"But we all survived, except Momma and Douglas Campbell." Phoebe pursed her lips and sniffed. "At least Poppy and Miss Maggie are no worse for the heartache these days."

Frederick cleared his throat. "That's enough on that subject, Phoebe. It's been almost nine years since I joined the army."

"And eight years this May since Momma left us." Her voice cracked with the words. "I think I better sleep now. The medicine they give me makes me tired."

Phoebe theatrically arranged herself on the narrow bed and her father pulled up the blanket.

"I love you, Princess." He knocked on the door for their release as Bethany stepped to the bed.

"Take care of yourself, Phoebe. Everyone's worried about you," she whispered.

"Even Kade?"

Bethany nodded.

"Good." She closed her eyes, a mirthful smile on her lips.

Once they were outside the hospital, Bethany breathed in the fresh air and tried to rid her mind of the smug look on Phoebe's face.

"Where shall we go, Beth?" Frederick asked. "Do you want to shop for something?"

"I always enjoy window shopping, but if it's too much walking—"

"Don't worry about me, Little Princess. Walking is good for me, even if I have to slow down at times."

He parked the automobile near the gym and stopped in to say hello to the regulars.

Thomas Charles made a fuss over Bethany. "I remember when Davenport won the title and walked the ring with you on his shoulders. You're growing into a fine young lady, Bethany. There's a woman's boxing club starting down the street if you want to take after your old man," he added.

"No, thank you. I'll stick to swimming."

"Melissa often takes her to the pool while the others are at the stables," Frederick explained as he leaned nonchalantly against an exercise bench to take the weight off his bad leg. "All three girls learned to ride, but Phoebe is the only one who fell completely in love with it."

"She won some competitions last year, didn't she?"

Frederick nodded, his smile fading. "We better move along. I'm sure Beth doesn't want to spend all our time here."

"Good to see you and your daughter, Davenport." They slapped each other's backs. "Tell the rest of your ladies hello."

They walked several blocks, looking at the clothing displays in the windows and greeting people they passed. Usually Melissa, Phoebe, or Louisa stayed by Frederick's side, allowing Bethany to accompany the family without being remarked upon. But with her arm around her father's, she accepted more compliments than ever.

They took their luncheon in a corner booth at their favorite diner, Bethany relaxing in the semi-privacy.

"The dress you made Melissa for Valentine's Day is exquisite," he said as they waited for their food. "Do you wish to make sewing into a career?"

"It's what I enjoy best. Tabitha and I worked extra at school this past year and will have enough credits to graduate this summer. I meant to talk to you about that, but with everything going on…"

Her father's warm hand surrounded hers. "Don't be afraid to talk to me, Little Princess. Though I don't think I'll be able to call you that much longer."

"I don't mind, Daddy." She returned his smile. "Tabby wants to finish school to focus on the piano, and I'd like to try selling some of my designs."

"Locally?"

She nodded. "For now. I'm not in a hurry to leave home, especially as I won't be of age."

"Alex and I have talked about debuting you two next season. I had Phoebe wait until she was eighteen because her maturity level is different than yours, but we both think you and Tabitha could handle it, if you're interested."

"I'd like to if Tabby does."

"That firecracker? I'm sure she will."

After eating, Frederick paid the bill and tucked Bethany's hand under his arm. His steps were quicker from after the rest. Before she realized where they were heading, he reached for the door of Mademoiselle Bisset's store.

"Daddy, I couldn't." She clutched her locket with the portraits of her parents inside it.

He laughed. "It's high time you get acquainted with the fashion leader in our fine city."

Bethany blushed at the thought of speaking with the Parisian shopkeeper who'd dressed her mother from foundation to flowing gowns. Phoebe had gotten a few dresses at the shop in the last two years, but Bethany hadn't been old enough.

The tinkling bell on the door announced their entrance. Mademoiselle Bisset herself stepped out of the back, her buxom form clad in a tasteful black dress as Bethany always remembered from her visits to the store as a child.

"Mr. Davenport, it's always a pleasure to see your handsome face." She approached with outstretched hands and they kissed each other's cheeks. "You're as fit as ever and I can say the graying in your hair is much handsomer than on mine. What shall we do as we grow older but see that the next generation is appropriately attired?"

Without allowing time for him to respond, Mademoiselle Bisset turned to Bethany and took her chin in a soft hand. "And you, my dear, I have waited for this day! While those dark, arching brows are devastatingly handsome on your father, they are utterly enchanting on you. Coupled with the chin of your mother's family, and that smile you guard like the best kept secret, you shall win the hearts of all you meet!"

Frederick laughed fully. "Mademoiselle Bisset, may I present mine and Lucy's youngest, Bethany Iris."

The woman kissed Bethany's cheeks. "It's the happiest of days for me, Bethany. Your older sister is all flash and leaves nothing to the imagination. But you, my dear, are the pinnacle of true beauty—dark and bewitching."

Bethany clasped her arms behind her back to hide the tremble the heady words created. Knowing where Kade's affections lie, she dismissed the compliments. "I'm nothing like that, Mademoiselle Bisset, but you're most kind."

The woman took Frederick's hand. "Tell her, Mr. Davenport. She doesn't believe me."

"Bethany, the most important thing to remember about Mademoiselle Bisset is that she *never* flatters. Customers trust her not to lie to make a sale because she wants everyone walking out with her clothes to look their best. And you are remarkable, Little Princess." Looking to the shopkeeper, he smiled "We came today to make introductions. Bethany is a fine seamstress and has a career in fashion on her mind. She's made this dress and many others for her family and friends."

Mademoiselle Bisset whispered in French as she circled Bethany, fingering the cuffs buttoned at her wrists and the shoulder seams. Bethany stood still, face warm from the scrutiny. "My dear, I must see more. Bring me your creations."

"She does alterations as well," Frederick added.

Mademoiselle Bisset gasped. "The lily gown on Phoebe New Year's Eve was you?"

"Yes, ma'am. I've updated several of our mother's dresses for her."

"Mr. Davenport, why have you kept her hidden? You must loan her to me. I shall introduce her to my friends in Paris and shape her career!"

Laughing, he took his daughter's hand. "She graduates this summer."

"I cannot wait months to see the dresses. Bring them to me so I may inspect them, Bethany."

Smiling, she nodded. "I will, Mademoiselle Bisset. Thank you."

Nine

Phoebe stayed in the hospital a total of three weeks before being moved to a private residence. Dr. Stephen Moore and his spinster sister, Verbena, agreed to take her in for room and board, with the help of round-the-clock nurses. From their visit to meet Phoebe at the hospital, and the doctor's frequent stops thereafter to track her progress, she knew he was at least two decades older than her father and sour in countenance, but kind.

When her father and the first shift nurse brought her to the Moores' home on February fifteenth, she didn't notice the details in her drug-induced state. As her vision sharpened after her nap, she noted the bars on her window and a grim-faced nurse with a chest span as large as her father's sitting in a chair facing her bed.

"Are you thirsty, Miss?" the nurse asked.

Phoebe sat up, swinging her feet to the hardwood floor. "Where's Daddy?"

"He went to his office, but said he would stop in on his way home. Do you need a drink?"

"Whiskey would be wonderful."

The nurse frowned, and went to the door. Using a key she had tied to her belt, she opened it. "Miss Moore," she called. "Could you send in some iced tea when you get a chance?"

"Yes, Nurse Gloria," the answer came. "And I'll bring a dinner tray since she slept through that."

Phoebe looked around the bedroom. While more decorative than the hospital, it lacked charm. Single bed, dresser, writing desk, and two armchairs—one of which the nurse used. A crucifix hung above the door and a single painting of a dreary forest over the dresser. Besides the door to the hall, there were two others. Standing, she stumbled to the nearest door.

One of her red everyday dresses similar to the blue one she wore hung inside the bare closet. Rustling through the dresser drawers, she found underclothes and several nightgowns. On her way to the opposite door, Phoebe felt like she was walking on a ship. She reached a hand for the bed's mahogany footboard.

Nurse Gloria took her elbow. "It'll wear off soon, but we had to dose you up to keep you docile for the move."

I'll show you docile! Phoebe wanted to claw the woman's eyes out, but instead pulled from deep within to give voice to her sweetest tone. "Would you be so kind as to help me to the bathroom?"

Once she used the facilities and washed her face, she took her brush and tried to smooth her wayward locks. *If I'm going to get out of this prison, I need to be on my best behavior—and that includes keeping up appearances.*

Meek as a mouse, she ate and drank though everything was tasteless. She spent the rest of the afternoon sitting placidly by the window, enjoying the sky for the first time in weeks—even though bars obscured the view. At four o'clock, Nurse Gloria left and another arrived.

"Do you remember me, child?"

Phoebe gazed at the graying hair and kind eyes of the nurse. "You sat with Momma!"

"That I did."

She was the nurse on duty when Momma attacked Uncle Eddie. She knows what we're capable of.

"It's good of you to agree to stay with me, Nurse Bertha. I've already taken a nap and would like to continue sitting until supper."

The next time the door unlocked, her father entered.

"Daddy!" She hugged him, sniffing the odor of adding machine ink that was woven into his suit as much as the threads.

He kissed her forehead. "How do you like it here, Princess?"

"It's much nicer than the hospital, but still a bit plain. If I'm really to stay here long, could I send for some of my things?"

"Of course."

"Could Beth come and we could make a list together?"

His smile turned down at the corners. "No visitors for a few days, but you could make a list or telephone the house."

"But you're here, Daddy."

"Only me until you settle in. Then you can take dinner with Miss Moore and supper with her and the doctor if you're up to it. We'll see about visitors after that."

"I'll need more clothes if I'm expected at the supper table and when visitors call. I only have two dresses, Daddy. It isn't fair! I need to speak with Beth. She'll know what to pack."

"I'll call the house and see if she's available."

With a nod to Bertha, he was out the door and it securely locked behind him. Phoebe began pacing the room. When she saw the nurse watching her, she forced herself to perch on the chair. Minutes passed before her father returned.

"I've got Beth on the telephone."

Phoebe's first clear look at the Moore's house showed it to be clean but cluttered. Bookshelves lined the hallway, and the bedrooms she passed on the way to the front of the house were stuffed with furniture and doilies from decades past. Her father pointed to a narrow chaise beside a tabletop telephone in the corner of the front room. Miss Moore's hawk-like eyes watched her from her corner chair as she crocheted lace-work.

"Beth," she said into the telephone. "Do you have something to write this down with?"

"Yes." Her reply sounded thin through the connection. Phoebe wasn't alert enough on the drive over to know what part of town she was in, but her sister sounded miles away.

"I want my trophies, copies of Momma's books, stationery, my photographs, and all the items from my dressing tables from home and Poppy's house. Perfumes, lipsticks, everything!"

"All right, Phoebe. And what of clothing?"

"I only have two horrid everyday dresses. Sissa must have picked them out for their functionality. I'll need at least two dozen outfits and a few gowns. I trust you to choose the best, and shoes to coordinate. And I want a riding set included." She looked at her father's frown and narrowed her eyes. "It doesn't matter if I can't go to the stables at the moment, I want to be prepared. And I want my pearls, the silk Chinese pajamas I got on my last birthday, and Momma's kimono. I had it with me that day and I'm not sure where it went, but it's not with my items from the hospital. I demand it be returned."

Frederick's arms crossed his muscular chest as he stared at his daughter.

"Anything else, Phoebe?" Bethany asked.

She pursed her lips in thought. "I'll leave that to you. You know what I like. I hope to see you soon, Beth."

Her father walked her back to her room.

When she settled on the chair, she smiled up at him. "Did you and Sissa have a good Valentine's Day?"

"It was fine, Princess. Is there anything I can do before I leave?"

She clutched his hand. "You'll be back tomorrow?"

"Yes. Would you like me to bring you lunch and eat with you or stop in after work?"

"A sandwich from the deli please, Daddy. And fudge from George's."

He pulled her to her feet and crushed her in a hug. "You are your mother's daughter, Princess. I'll see you tomorrow."

***

On St. Patrick's Day afternoon, Phoebe received word that Bethany and Kade had arrived at the Moores' house to visit her. She brushed through her hair and adjusted her assets beneath her dress before she was brought to the parlor.

"Kade Campbell!" She threw herself at her visitor, not caring if Nurse Gloria or Ms. Moore thought her scandalous. She wrapped a leg about his and kissed him on the mouth.

"It's great to see you, Phoebe."

He wasn't in a hurry to let her go and she clung to him— happy to feel a man's arms around her. *It's been almost two months since Alexander held me!* She breathed in the aftershave at Kade's neck, nipping a kiss below his ear in the process. Kade tightened his hold.

"I've missed you, Kade. It's been too long. Promise me you won't stay away."

He cleared his throat and pried himself free, taking her hand to lead her to the sofa. "I had to wait until I was cleared for visiting privileges."

"But Beth's been coming to me for weeks." She looked to her sister sitting primly in the nearby armchair. "She brought me the new edition of our mother's first book last Thursday."

"Daddy wanted you to be reintroduced to people one at a time so we don't overwhelm you," Bethany said.

Phoebe sniffed and raised her chin. "I'd much rather have seen Kade before Sissa and Louisa."

"And me?" her sister asked defiantly.

"Tiger," Kade whispered with a warning tone.

Phoebe laughed and rolled her eyes. "Still using her pet name from that silly stuffed animal she carried around the whole time Daddy was gone. You really are a child, Beth. Too sweet and naïve for your own good—most of the time."

Bethany looked from her sister and Kade to her hands, choosing to keep her gaze down.

She's too easy to cow. "Tell me, Kade," Phoebe urged, "what have you been up to?"

"School, work, and riding."

"Poppy said you two take turns riding Prince, and that Bethany has even taken him out twice."

"He's well cared for and I see to his stall myself four days a week."

"But it isn't all work and school. I talked to Oscar on the telephone last week and he said you've taken Beth to the petting pantry a few Friday nights since I've been indisposed."

Bethany turned pink and Miss Moore scarlet. As though fearing the woman might choke, Nurse Gloria escorted the lady of the house to the kitchen, leaving Phoebe and her guests alone.

"I see how it is, Kade Campbell." The electricity snapped in her voice. "You can't have me so you go for my little sister. Just remember how young she is and the fact that she isn't built like me."

"It isn't like that. Tabby goes to the cinema with us and—"

Phoebe was on his lap in an instant, tongue searching his mouth as she brought his hands to her chest. Kade resisted at first, but with a groan of submission he kissed Phoebe back. His hands trailed to her hips with a pleasing grasp.

"Miss Phoebe!" Gloria pulled her away. "Your father will hear of this! Go to your room!"

"Don't stay away from me, Kade!"

He looked from Phoebe to Bethany and placed a gentle arm about the younger girl's willowy frame in a show of comfort to still her tears.

"Let him love me! I need purpose to these dreary days!" Phoebe continued her shouts as she was locked in her room with the nurse.

"If you'd like me to put you under, keep up that racket. Otherwise hush," Gloria said.

"There's no point to being awake for this existence!" She fell face-first onto her bed and cried until she fell asleep.

Phoebe woke in her dim room to the sensation of someone holding her hand.

"Why must you behave like this?" Her father whispered. "It pains me to have to shut you away from your family and friends."

She sat up and hugged his neck. His hair was slightly damp, like he'd just come from showering at the gym. "Daddy, I'm sorry! I didn't mean to behave shamelessly. Don't keep Kade from me, please!"

"I understand things get beyond your control, and I trust Kade more than other men, but I'm afraid Miss Moore will be difficult to convince."

"You haven't trusted Kade since that summer you found us kissing at Seacliff and sat in the hall all night!" Her cheeks burned.

"It caught me off guard, but he's a fine man. I understand he has feelings for you, but you can't allow these moments of mania to overpower your good sense."

"What is sense when love is involved?" she countered. "He loves me, Daddy!"

"But your mind is too muddled to know if *you* love him."

"But I could give him what he wants for the time being."

He kissed her hair. "If you love Kade, Princess, spare him the heartache and let him go. It's the kindest thing you can do though it might hurt the most."

She buried her face on his powerful shoulder and sobbed.

Ten

Monday, May 3, 1926

Dearest Claudio,

I'll begin with the news I must forward you: Melissa offered a pretty smile and her thanks for your birthday wishes. Though her birthday is today, we celebrated with the families during Sunday dinner. We find it easier to have family parties on Sundays now because the oldest like to go out Friday nights. When we had a few minutes alone, Melissa confessed the birthday you spent with her during the war was one of her best.

When Alex and Frederick walked in on our conversation, Alex exclaimed "It seems Melissa caught the 'Seacliff Gaze', as Douglas called it." Upon realizing what he insinuated, he looked to Frederick and said "don't worry, it passes quickly." Melissa stood to excuse herself—probably to regain her composure. Frederick caught her arm and pulled her to him with a kiss so powerful that I thought Alex was going to swoon. "My life began again when you accepted me fourteen years ago," Frederick told her. "I love you more each year we share together." It was beautiful to witness—how he turned her pain into passion.

I tell you all this to reassure you it would be safe to come back. Melissa cherishes your memories, but the Davenports are strong—all except Phoebe. She's been steady since she pulled that stunt with Kade in March, but he's only visited her once since then, with Frederick chaperoning. It was the only way Miss Moore would allow it. Phoebe behaved that time, but what could she have done with her father watching?

I finally went to visit Phoebe last month, but I wish I hadn't. Her pale eyes are dead, her smile shallow. She kept looking at Alex like he was a lost dream and she didn't offer me a kind word beyond saying I was as lovely as ever—which sounded more like an accusation than a compliment. The rest was endless chatter about Prince. Alex is going to speak with Frederick about Phoebe possibly having riding privileges. He believes it would be therapeutic to her, but I think it's more of a selfish desire to hold her horse's care over Alex and Kade because it gives her some control. In reality she's nothing but a lost child and I feel sorry for her, though more so for the Davenports. They've endured so much already.

I refuse to bring Amelia to see Phoebe, though our youngest asks about her after family dinners. Thankfully, Simon has no interest in going and Tabitha declines to visit. Those two never got along—not that I blame Tabby. Asher has been several times with Alex or Bethany, but he was closer to her—closer than she ever was to Louisa.

If late summer is the earliest you could visit, it would be better than nothing, but truly, we could use your physical blessings more than your prayers offered on our behalf. The short of it is that we'd be happy to see you whenever you arrive, so surprise us if you must. Surely you've driven out enough devils from Naples for the people to be safe if you leave for a month or two. I've been wearing the crucifix bracelet you gave me since Easter. I always wear it for that holiday, but I've kept it on this time and often find myself touching it and thinking "what would Claudio advise me?" when I'm confused or sad.

I hope your copy of Azalea Blossom *Alexander mailed a month ago arrived. I'm glad you are having a lovely spring and that book is perfect for reading in this weather. Think of me and our days on Mobile Bay when the summer heat begins.* Posseduta *is in need of your help once more—and Alex and our children. I hope you enjoy the Easter family portrait I'm including. I still find it humorous Alexander ended up with the most children—his two, my three, and Lucy's girls. I'll try for a photograph of the Davenports next time, but I doubt it will include their oldest. Come soon, Claudio. We need you!*

Love and prayers,

Magdalene

P.S. Be on the lookout for Tabitha's and Bethany's graduation invitations arriving separately.

***

On the third Wednesday in May, Alexander sprung from his automobile parked beside Magdalene's at the riding club. He had dressed for the stables at his office and rushed across town for his ten o'clock date with his wife. In another few weeks—when the summer heat settled over the area—they'd switch to early morning rides. For now, they worked around his appointments.

Magdalene was in Daphne's stall, her back to the entrance as she brushed her horse's mane. In the stall beside them, Apollo nickered as his owner passed. Alexander took hold of Magdalene's hips and ran his hands over her rear, which was expertly displayed in her riding breeches. She arched like a cat as his hands continued to roam.

"What you do to me should be considered criminal." He kissed her neck.

She turned to him with a cheeky smile. "Would you press charges?"

"I'd press more than charges against you, Magdalene." He raised his eyebrows and thrust his hips to hers, relishing the feel of their bodies colliding, even with the riding wear between them.

Magdalene licked her lips. Alexander knew she'd never allow things to progress in their present location, but he couldn't help going for more. Grasping her braided hair in one hand, he took a hip with the other and tangled his lips with hers.

To his joy, she nudged him toward the wall as she deepened the kiss and pulled his shirt free to get to his skin. With a voice dripping want, she panted his name.

"You'll allow this?" he hissed as her fingers reached his chest scars.

A shout outside from one worker to another broke the mood.

Smiling, Alexander pulled away a few inches. "Shall we make a quick ride and reconvene at home for a longer one?"

The gleam in her eyes as she nodded matched his own, causing a throb below his belt.

Alexander fixed his shirt and readied Apollo. Magdalene waited for him outside the stable—a striking sight atop Daphne's glossy brown coat. With a slight flick of the reins, Magdalene headed toward a wooded trail. Alexander followed at a brisk pace, but not quick enough to catch her. He enjoyed the view of her back—the movement of her braided hair between her shoulder blades and the splay of her hips in the saddle. The few times he'd ridden Apollo with Lucy, she'd been between his legs and afforded him no view, though the touching was exquisite. But what his first love lacked in equestrian skills, she more than made up for with her uninhibited ways. Not counting the inaugural ride on his birthday, when she carried Phoenix Asher in her womb, Lucy on Apollo always ended with her and Alexander on the forest floor or against a tree.

After a quarter of an hour, he brought Apollo to Daphne's side along a wider portion of the trail. Tightening his knees to keep his seat, he leaned over to kiss his wife.

"I enjoy time like this with you as much as when we share our bodies." He took her hand in his and they traveled side-by-side until the path narrowed.

He motioned her ahead, and she winked at him as though she understood his preference. They rode another mile before taking a side trail to bring them back to the stables. After passing a tip to one of the grooms, Alexander helped Magdalene down, relishing an excuse to put his hands on her. He fingered a tendril of her hair that had come undone from her braid.

"Follow me home?"

"Gladly, Alex."

After a chaste kiss, he offered his arm and they strolled to the parking area. The crosstown drive had him more eager than ever to feel every inch of Magdalene against his skin. He haphazardly parked in front of the garage and forced himself to wait for her to turn off the motor before opening her automobile door.

"In the bedroom," she said in a soft, teasing voice, "let's see who can get undressed first."

"I'd rather undress you one piece at a time."

She linked her fingers through his as Alexander held the gate open for her. "I've perspired too much for that. I need to get in the shower."

He stuck the key in the backdoor and licked below her ear. "But you taste divine."

She attached herself to him as soon as they were inside. A trail of clothing marked their path to the bedroom.

"As much as I've loved seeing you in pants since the hurricane at Seacliff, I much prefer getting you out of them." Alexander nibbled her neck as he knelt over her. "You were tangy then too from the heat of the storm."

She caressed his scars. "And you're every bit as fiery as you were back then. How could it be twenty years already? I'm barely that old."

He laughed and admired the lines crinkling at the corners of her brown eyes as she smiled. "Being spicy keeps you young."

"And I thought it was all the lovemaking that did that." She gripped him and raised her eyebrows in challenge.

"That's when you're the spiciest, just as your mighty Scot always told you." He brushed the hair back from her face and studied her. The sting of loss melted into longing for the present. "I hope I cherish you as you deserve, Magdalene."

***

On June eleventh, Tabitha and Bethany graduated from their private school in a ceremony hosted at the Mellings' home. Three graduates, the other dozen students, and the two teachers were in attendance as well as the families of the girls. A white canopy was erected over the chairs for the audience while the gazebo held the graduates, teachers, and Father Quinn.

Bethany and Tabitha looked stunning in their white gowns, though the younger girl clutched her bouquet nervously. After the ceremony, Alexander put his arm around Bethany and kissed her cheek.

"Don't worry so much, Bethany Iris. You'll do well with Mademoiselle Bisset, and the ladies in Mobile will be all the prettier for your efforts."

"Thank you, Poppy." She hugged him, straightening the collar of his seersucker suit as she did so. "And thank you for the party. Everything's lovely."

"Not as lovely as Magdalene." His gaze followed his wife's progression through the crowd with a tray of crystal cups. Her sky blue dress—the same color as his summer suit—was charming against her creamy skin and dark hair. "Are you happy the Campbells are in our lives?"

She nodded. "Miss Maggie is wonderful. Tabby is my best friend and Simon is Asher's. And Kade is... special to me."

"Tiger!"

After hearing her words, Alexander watched with interest as his stepson approached.

He took Bethany's elbow and kissed her cheek. His grin was bright, eyes playful. "Congratulations, Tiger. You're practically a woman now. After your debut this winter, there will be no stopping the line of suitors for you."

Her smile glowed at him in return, but faded when Kade left to find his sister. Bethany watched him several seconds before sighing.

"Don't lay your heart out for a man until he's ready to appreciate it, Bethany Iris."

Her brown eyes widened in fear as she looked at him.

"Your secret is safe with me." Alexander smiled. "He'd be worthy, but he isn't ready."

Before she could respond, Frederick and Melissa were there. Bethany hugged each one and then put an arm around both Frederick and Alexander.

"Sissa, a picture with my fathers, please."

Alexander swallowed the lump in his throat and flashed a grin at Melissa's raised camera. Bethany left him with a kiss, and the Davenports moved on to speak with Darla. Scanning the party for Magdalene or Tabitha, his gaze fell to Naomi Rollins standing on the side of the patio. He hurried over, raising her bronze hand to his lips.

"My day is complete, Miss Naomi, and you look marvelous in green. If there's dancing, you must save one for me."

"Mr. Alex, you old flirt." She laughed. "I won't be staying long. I had to see my sugar before she steps out into the working world. I can't help but praise the Lord she's still with us. That was a brave thing you did for her when she was a little girl."

He clutched the old bullet wound on his arm. "There was no other choice."

"Say that all you want, but I know the truth." With a smile she nodded her farewell.

The chill of what he'd seen in the belly of the cathedral returned. Wondering if Phoebe was capable of what her aunt was, he shivered despite the heat.

"Poppy!" Arms went about his legs.

"Amelia Rose, my precious." He lifted his daughter into his arms, kissing her angelic face. "Are you enjoying the party?"

"Yes! The lemonade is delicious. You put extra love into it, didn't you?"

He squished her to his chest. "I did."

"Will you make lemonade and give me a party when I graduate?"

"I most certainly will. It will be the biggest party yet!"

Amelia giggled and hugged him tighter.

Magdalene kissed each of them. Alexander looked from mother to daughter who shared the same complexion and rich brunette hair. He loved his stepdaughters, but there was something special about his own—the perfect blend of him and Magdalene like a jewel of their love for the world to see.

Amelia squirmed to be set down and ran for Virginia Adams across the lawn.

"I love you. Both of you." He nestled into Magdalene's neck, slightly damp from the heat. "You know we made the prettiest girl ever."

"I'm glad you think so." She decorously slipped out from his too familiar embrace given their surroundings. "Would you serve me a glass of your lemonade I keep hearing about?"

Taking her elbow, he leaned to her ear. "I'm saving the last cup for later, so I can lap it from your naval."

With a sensual lick below her ear, he stepped back to enjoy the look of surprise transform into a spark of yearning. A naughty smile graced her countenance, and he swaggered to the refreshment table.

"I'm surprised Maggie hasn't punched you yet, dashing Poppy." Melissa held out her hand for him to serve her a glass.

"I believe she has come close several times, darling Sissa, but she's behaving herself as hostess. Though pray for me once I'm alone with her."

"Pray for you and evacuate the premises because it's sure to be a rowdy time."

Laughing, he spilt the cup he'd prepared for Magdalene and went to refill it. "She's not as loud as Lucy was," he whispered.

Melissa choked on a snort. "Loud enough! I have vacationed at Seacliff with you two."

"I can't help it if I drive my women wild."

"They're in good hands, I know." She touched his shoulder and kissed his cheek. "Try to behave. Father Quinn is watching."

"I know no remorse unless it's Claudio."

"Lies! You've got a guilty soul and know it. That's what makes you so tenderhearted."

He puckered his lips and accepted a quick kiss from her. "It's good to know you care, darling Sissa."

He passed Frederick on his way back to Magdalene. "Be sure you keep an eye on your wife, Freddy. Her topics of conversation might be too much for the main populous of the party."

Eleven

As the graduation party came to a close, Bethany and Tabitha each ate an extra piece of cake in the kitchen while Miss Charlotte washed dishes. Bethany had already said goodbye to the remaining guests and was happy to leave Alexander and Magdalene to their roles of host and hostess. She mulled over what Alexander told her about saving her heart, wondering if that was his polite way of telling her to move on from what he thought was an infatuation because Kade would never want her compared to Phoebe.

"What has you so broody?" Tabitha lifted another forkful of cake to her painted lips. "It was a terrific party and you're staying the weekend. I'm sure Kade would be happy to bring us to the cinema tonight. Think of all the lovely clothes on the screen and how you would improve them."

Bethany's face warmed at the memory of Phoebe calling out her and Kade at what she referred to as the "petting pantry" when she'd visited her sister with him. *Just because she let guys touch her in a dark theater didn't mean all girls did.*

"I'm missing Phoebe and feeling sorry for her not being able to come."

Tabitha rolled her dark eyes. "She would have been jealous our party was bigger than hers, but that's what happens when Poppy and Mama host the whole graduation. Still, she'd have tried to make us miserable."

"I suppose."

"Did you see Louisa after we cut the cake? She took off into the camellia maze with Asher, Simon, *and* Horatio."

"They're all friends."

Her brown hair swung across her cheeks as she shook her head. "You need to have a talk with her. She's thirteen now. People will start to talk, especially with Phoebe as a sister."

"So people speak badly of me?" Bethany countered.

"No, but you don't spend all your free time with boys. Kade hardly counts because everyone knows he's had it bad for Phoebe. She was always out with him, plus Abe when he's in town, and that obnoxious cousin of yours and all his cronies. Not to mention Robert Woodslow, who's already got a reputation and he's not even in society yet. He's handsome enough to look at, but I'm not sure what Phoebe's up to by letting him kiss and touch her. And her friend, Jane, is talked about as much as your sister. It's said she's been with more men than she has fingers, but I'm not sure she can count that high."

"I can't help what people say, and I'd rather not put ideas into Louisa's head."

"Then I'll speak to Simon about it. He's the oldest out of the lot."

"But Asher is more discreet. He'd be sensitive about something like that."

"Because of your mother?"

Bethany nodded.

"Perhaps you're right. We can corner him this evening." Tabitha leaned back and stretched her fingers. "It's time for the piano."

Tabitha left her at the table with their dirty dishes. Bethany carried them to the counter. "Thank you for everything, Miss Charlotte. Would you like help washing?"

"I couldn't accept help on your special day, but thank you kindly. You go on and relax or do whatever it is graduated young ladies are up to these days."

She knew better than to argue with Charlotte. When she passed the kitchen telephone, it rang.

"Mellings' residence."

"Beth, I need Alex!" Melissa's voice sounded frantic.

Not knowing what could have happened in the twenty minutes her family had been gone, she thought the worst. "Is it Daddy?"

"No, but be quick."

"Poppy!" she shouted from the back door. "Telephone. It's an emergency!"

The few remaining guests watched him hurdle the bench on the patio. A second later, Magdalene ushered the others out the gate.

"It's Sissa."

He grabbed the receiver from the box on the kitchen wall rather than go to his den. "Melissa?"

His face grew worry lines. "How long has she been gone? Has she had any telephone calls lately? Visitors?"

Alexander continued to listen. "I'll go to the Moores' as well."

In the moment he hung up the telephone, Alexander appeared to burn with anger. He yanked off his tie and opened his top buttons.

"Did she run away?" Bethany whispered.

"Did she hint to you at all?" his voice was hard.

"No, I only guessed from what you said."

Alexander nodded and raced to Magdalene on the patio to explain the situation before running out the back gate. She sank to a chair and covered her face with her hands.

Bethany put her arms around her. "I'm sorry, Miss Maggie."

"It's not your fault, Beth. And I'm glad word didn't get to us until the end of the party. I would have hated her if she'd spoiled yours and Tabitha's celebration."

Bethany fingered her locket. "Phoebe doesn't always mean to be spiteful."

"But when she does," Magdalene's voice was cold, "she does it fully."

***

Supper was subdued without Alexander. Bethany had never felt like an outsider in that house, but at the table without her stepfather in attendance, she felt decidedly Davenport. Magdalene and Amelia were solemn. Neither Kade nor Tabitha spoke of going out, and the younger boys kept their hijinks to a minimum.

After dessert, Amelia slipped her hand into Bethany's. "Would you read with me, Beth?"

Moody piano chords already drifted from the front of the house, so Bethany went to the morning room with her. Magdalene and Kade followed, but settled on the sofa while Bethany and Amelia stretched before the unlit fireplace.

Halfway through a Beatrix Potter book, Alexander appeared in the doorway. "Bethany, I'd like a word with you in my den."

Once she started for the door, Kade stood to follow.

"This doesn't concern you." Alexander's voice was firm.

To keep Kade from following, Alexander walked behind Bethany and shut the door as soon as they were inside his room. He motioned to the chaise, but she took the seat that faced his desk. He patted her shoulder on his way to his chair.

"Is she back with the Moores?"

He sank to his seat. "We can't find her. We checked with her friends and all the Eastons. The police have been notified, but there aren't any clues to go on other than the kitchen door was broken into at your house and half her remaining clothes and a suitcase are missing. From her room at the Moores' she took clothing, Lucy's books, and her dressing table items."

"Do you think she's run away for good?"

"I don't know." Raking his hands through his dark blond hair, he grimaced. "We're done for the day, but the police will keep an eye out tonight. Freddy and I will start looking again tomorrow."

"You've both done your best with her," Bethany whispered. "Don't blame yourself."

"I can't help but to." He dropped his head to his arms on the desk.

Seeing his shoulders shake as though he were shedding tears, Bethany went for Magdalene.

"He needs you."

Magdalene hurried out with an anxious countenance she didn't usually allow. Bethany stood frozen in the middle of the mourning room.

Kade gripped her arms. "What's happened to Phoebe?"

"She's disappeared." Without further comment, she went upstairs.

For several minutes, she stared at the empty bed across from her own, trying to decide what to do. Where would Phoebe have gone?

Tabitha and Kade came in, shutting the door behind them.

Tabitha hugged Bethany. "Don't allow her to control you."

"I think I know where she went," Bethany whispered.

Kade took her by the shoulders, spinning her from Tabitha's grasp. "Where?"

"Seacliff. The last time we were there, she talked about how Momma's money is running everything and it should belong to us, not Poppy. She might have gone to stake what she believes is her rightful claim."

"We can go on the morning ferry."

"Shouldn't we tell Poppy and my father?" Bethany looked to Kade with trepidation.

"We don't want them to waste their time crossing the bay on a whim. We'll check it out first, you and me, Tiger."

"And me," Tabitha added.

"You and Phoebe hate each other," Kade said. "If she's there, it might be more difficult to persuade her to return if you two start fighting."

"Or it might cause her to show her true colors and give reason for her to be locked up properly!" Tabitha glared at her brother. "You know what her mother did to that priest and nun. Phoebe is just as capable of attacking people. I'd gladly allow myself to be victim if it will get her where she needs to be."

Kade scowled. "You're awful."

"I'm a realist!" Tabitha held her head high. "We all have clothes at Seacliff and can travel light. We should be able to slip away in the morning without much trouble, and take the streetcar to the docks."

"I'll wake you both at seven-thirty if you aren't up." Kade hugged Bethany. "You made a beautiful graduate today. Try to rest, Tiger."

The Campbell siblings said their goodnights and Bethany took a long bath. Wrapped in her nightgown and robe, she descended the stairs a final time to see if Alexander or Magdalene needed anything. His den was closed, the other spaces empty. She returned to her room and lay in bed for hours as images of Phoebe reigning at Seacliff Manor danced through her mind.

Twelve

Phoebe woke when the morning sun caught the room in a bright glow. Sitting up in the four-poster bed of the Mellings' master suite at Seacliff Manor, she found one of Oscar's friends face down beside her on the blue bedspread. Poking him until he rolled over, she was glad to see him fully clothed. She ran her hands over her own body, but didn't feel anything out of the ordinary.

Good! He looks ridiculous and I don't want my first time to be with someone who sleeps with his mouth gaped open.

After washing her face and slipping on a silk mint evening gown, she paused in the doorway to the hall.

"Oscar Easton!"

It took five shouts before he stumbled out of the room two doors down, pulling on his pants.

"Get this guy out of here! Not just from my bedroom, out of my house!"

"Who'd you end up with?" He stumbled to a stop in the room. "Jimmy, ha! I would have steered you clear of him. Word is he's only good once, if he hasn't drank too much."

A deep snore shook the bed.

Oscar laughed. "He's a goner. Get yourself a real man today, Bearcat."

She lit a cigarette. "I plan to."

Oscar had Jimmy by the arm. "Come on, you've lost your chance. The queen of Seacliff Manor wants you out!"

Phoebe settled herself at the dressing table to apply fresh makeup and take a morning cigarette. She used Magdalene's powder jar as an ashtray. Once she felt presentable, she sauntered down the hall, throwing open all the bedroom doors, surprising various couples and groups. At her father's room at the opposite end of the hall, she held her breath before trying the knob.

Locked.

Good. This weekend is about the Mellings, not taking revenge on Daddy.

The first thing she did before unpacking her things yesterday was secure her father's suite from houseguests. Partying was welcome anywhere but there, and she was pleased the group Oscar invited last night respected that rule. But Saturday, with a whole day to gather revelers, might be a different story.

"Everyone up!" she yelled. "If you want to stay, you better be on your feet in five minutes or you're getting thrown out! I'll not stand for people who don't hold their drinks or think they can laze about my house!"

Thirty minutes later, Phoebe was down to eight houseguests including Oscar, Jane, and Robert. The others were college friends of Oscar's he'd rounded up and thrown on the ferry yesterday afternoon. Phoebe took a new cigarette to the front porch. She settled on the swing, hiking her skirt so she could tuck her legs underneath.

"Phoebe!"

Thinking she must be dreaming, she looked to the figure of Kade Campbell running up the driveway, their sisters following him.

Perfection! She tossed her cigarette butt into the ashtray on the table.

"Phoebe, I'm glad we found you!" He embraced her when he reached the porch. "You look good."

"So do you." She moved her hands across his broad chest and down his thick arms. Nudging him onto the swing, she straddled his lap and attached her lips to his.

The screen door opened.

"I see today's flavor has been found," Oscar announced. "And you sent for more girls—excellent! I'm sure these fresh faces will be all the rage."

Fear over what her little sister would be subjected to caused Phoebe to pause. Arching back from Kade, she turned to her cousin. "Don't you dare pawn Beth on anyone!"

"Or me." Tabitha pushed past Oscar and stalked into the house. A moment later, her shout reached the porch. "Who put drinks on my piano?"

Phoebe laughed.

The pounding music began as Tabitha took her frustration out on the keyboard.

"Oscar, be a dear and see that Beth gets coffee. She looks positively exhausted."

"Come on, Davenport. Big sister wants alone time with your poor relation."

After Oscar ushered Bethany inside, Phoebe returned her attention to Kade. "How did you find me?"

"Beth figured it out." His hands caressed her bare shoulders. "I've missed you, Phoebe, but I wish you hadn't run away. When you get back, it'll be more difficult for me to visit than it has been."

"I'm not going back. This is my rightful home."

Robert and a couple of the college guys piled onto the porch. "We're going to the Pink Elephant to round up some moonshine."

"Hurry back, fellas."

"Get her primed for us, Campbell," one of them shouted.

Kade's fists clenched but Phoebe immediately shoved her tongue into his mouth, doing a grinding motion in his lap to help him forget what the others said.

"Do you still love me?"

Nestling into her neck, he kissed her. "You know I do, Phoebe. I've been worried sick these past five months."

She allowed herself a moment to melt against his warmth, feeling him as a man who loved her rather than a conquest on her path to revenge. Then she stood, holding her hand to him.

"Let's get a drink and settle somewhere private."

Phoebe marched down the hall, ignoring Tabitha at the piano in the front room and Bethany looking uncomfortable in the library with a steaming cup of coffee as one of the college boys talked her up. Grabbing a bottle of bourbon and two glasses from the kitchen counter, she ignored Oscar's smirks and ran upstairs with Kade. She went for the master suite, but he paused.

"It's the quietest room in the house. It's been so long since we've been together, I want to talk." She clicked the lock behind them and poured them each a drink.

Patting the bed beside her, she smiled welcomingly. "It's okay to sit, Kade Campbell. We're safe here. Tell me about Prince."

As he spoke of her horse and riding, he relaxed, sipping the bourbon he wasn't used to. She needed him drunk for what she was going to do because he would never go along with it in that space otherwise. When he finished his first glass, she removed his tie and then refilled it. Halfway through the second, she had his shirt unbuttoned.

Hard body, blue eyes, dark lashes—he was gorgeous.

It's your body craving him. You want this man to be your first full experience, but it doesn't matter to your heart. Stay in control. You can claim him and get your vengeance at the same time.

As though he heard the battle within her mind, he stroked her cheek. "Are you my girl, Phoebe?"

She kissed him and gasped as his hands found her breasts on their own for the first time. She had wanted Alexander, but this was the next best option—precious Magdalene's son. *How far the perfect Campbells will fall! Alexander and Magdalene will be devastated when they learn we marked their bed with a forbidden love affair.*

Frantic, her hands felt across his skin as he kissed her collarbone and lower. She went for his belt as they fell back on the soft bedding.

"Phoebe..." His mouth made its way back to hers with a probing kiss as his hands tugged her dress higher. "I'll love you forever."

"Make me yours, Kade. Make me yours again and again!"

***

Phoebe expected Kade to sleep because that's what Jane told her happened after she was with men. But Kade had held her for half an hour after their first time, strong arms about her waist. Then he kissed her all over and his attentions turned them both frenzied. Sharing passion with him the second time, the inhibitions of inexperience were gone. Their third coupling proved exquisite. Phoebe didn't want to let go.

Two virgins taken in passion within these walls. Seacliff is ours once more.

"If I had known it would be like this, I would have been yours a long time ago, Kade Campbell."

His fingers trailed her spine and he kissed her ear. "Do you want me to find a justice of the peace so we can get married this weekend?"

"What? No!" She scrambled to sit, looking down at him. "I'm not marrying you!"

He pulled her into his arms. "But you're my girl, Phoebe. I've waited years for you. We shared this." He planted a kiss over her heart. "Let's make it official."

"Marriages are nothing but broken promises!" She freed herself and pulled on her mother's kimono. "You need to leave."

"Phoebe, we don't have to rush. I only thought since we—"

"I don't need to be married to share my body, Kade Campbell. I'll go to bed with any man I want!"

Pleasure your body with everyone you wish. Devotion is a lost cause.

Kade's gentle hand caught her arm. "But I know I was your first. You were mine too."

Before she could stop him, he kissed her with enough passion to make her forget her anger. Pressing his forehead to hers, his sweet exhalation showered her face as he caught his breath enough to speak. "I'll care for you always, Phoebe Camellia Davenport. I love you."

She shoved him away and kicked his trousers at him. "Get out of my room!"

"Do you need time to think it over?" He pulled on his pants, never breaking eye contact with his intense gaze.

"Stop looking at me, stop loving me! It was all a mistake. I don't want you!"

Kade reached out to comfort her but she let out a piercing scream and he shrunk back.

"Phoebe! Phoebe, are you okay?" Bethany's voice called through the locked door.

"Get him out of my room!"

"You aren't in your room," she called back.

With a low groan, Kade seemed to take in their surroundings.

She went for the door, but Kade blocked her. "Don't do it, Phoebe. I'll slip out quietly when there isn't an audience."

"Don't you want your precious *Tiger* to know what we've done in here?" Seeing the shame in his eyes spurred her on. "My sister will be the first to know how sinful the mighty Kade Gabriel Campbell is. I'm sure it will tarnish her glowing opinion of you. Not to mention the pain your father would feel knowing that you aren't as in control of your natural man as he was with his lovely Maggie before they wed. What will it do to your dear mother and Poppy when they find out we tumbled their bed? The bed that was *my* mother's!"

"Phoe—"

"Get out!" She flung the door open.

Bethany stood pale in the hall, brown eyes wide. Looking from Kade half-dressed to the state of the bed behind them, she flushed.

Phoebe stepped boldly into the hall. "Robbie! Robbie!"

"He ain't here right now!" Oscar hollered back. "Whatcha need, Bearcat? There are plenty to satisfy you."

She sauntered to the top of the stairs. Tabitha's piano playing filled the air, but Oscar's whistle shrilled over the chords.

"I need a man." She glanced back at Kade clutching his clothes to his chest in the doorway of the bedroom.

"Have you met Hans? He's an artist living in Fairhope. I bet he'd love to sketch you, among other things."

"Send him up."

"Sure thing."

Phoebe dropped to the top step, leaning seductively against the wall and angling her legs so nearly every inch was on display beneath the silk to those who climbed the stairs.

Kade pulled on his shirt. "Why did you share that with me if you're only going to throw yourself at a stranger?"

"I'm not a good girl ready to cast away her youth because the stable boy thinks I'm pretty."

"Don't do this, Phoebe."

It hurt to see the pain in his eyes, so she narrowed her gaze to distort her vision.

Finish him and move on to the next.

"I don't love you, Kade. I never have."

He flew down the stairs in an angry rush, shoving people out of his way until he slammed out the front door.

Phoebe's frown turned to a smile as a tall man in a half-buttoned white shirt ascended the staircase.

"Miss Phoebe?" he asked with a New England accent.

"Hans the Artist?"

"Your lovely form would be a treasure to capture." He reached the step below hers and held out his hand.

"You wish to draw me?"

"Perhaps a sketch at a later time. I'm a sculptor and need to explore my subject with my hands."

"Come to my room and explore away."

Thirteen

Pinned to her spot in the hall by the pain of Kade's and Phoebe's rampant immorality, Bethany watched her sister accept Hans's offer. The man had approached her downstairs the previous hour, seeking a private audience, which she refused. He had to be thirty—twice her age—and it sickened Bethany more than flattered her.

"I found my new muse," he told her as they passed.

Phoebe stopped, anger flashing in her blue-green eyes. "Don't tell me I'm a stand-in for my baby sister!"

Hans tilted his head, shaggy brown hair brushing across his forehead as his hand touched her wrist. "She was the most interesting figure downstairs, but I didn't know what beauty hid up here."

She smiled at his smooth excuse before flashing a snide grin at her sister. "Don't wait around for me."

The door shut and Bethany's tears fell. Running downstairs to escape the vileness of her sister, she tried to go for Tabitha, but half a dozen guys surrounded her as she played the piano, and as many couples jitterbugged around the front rooms and hall. Seeing the library empty, Bethany locked herself inside.

Knowing she was beyond handling things, she telephoned home.

"Davenports'."

"Sissa, I need Daddy!"

"He's not here, Beth. Is some—"

She hung the receiver a second before dialing the Mellings.

"Mell—"

"Poppy!" she broke into sobs.

"Bethany Iris, where are you? We've been worried sick! When I came home for lunch, Maggie had me call—"

"We found Phoebe."

"Thank God! Where are you?"

Bethany began to tremble as cold tentacles of something unseen slithered up her legs. Stories she'd overheard the adults speak of when she wasn't supposed to be listening flooded her mind as the horror of understanding what she was up against engulfed her. She managed a short scream before her chest constricted.

"Bethany! Where are you?"

Lips trembling, she forced her mouth to move.

"Seacliff."

It was more whisper than word, but she knew he'd heard when he sucked in his breath.

"Help me, Poppy."

"Beth, dear God, get out of there!"

"I can't move." Hot tears streaked her face. "Can … barely … breathe."

The telephone receiver slipped from her grip, clattering against the wood floor as Alexander's shouts sought her reply in vain.

Bethany closed her eyes so she wouldn't see the curtains fluttering without the use of a breeze. The tightening around her continued. She prayed, moving only her lips because she didn't have breath to speak. As she prayed, the unseen bands began to slacken and she raised her voice. Once free, she gasped for a full breath of air and slipped to the floor as she fainted.

***

In the darkness, voices shouted.

"Tabby, where's Beth?"

Kade! She thought he was long gone from the house of pain.

"I haven't seen her for a couple hours, but she often hides in the library."

"Has anyone seen Beth Davenport?"

She heard the doorknob rattle, then knocking. "Beth, are you in there?"

More pounding.

"I swear if anyone touched that girl, I'll kill them!"

"Calm down and let me check the kitchen drawer for a key," Tabitha hollered.

Bethany tried to answer, but no sound escaped her lips. Movement was impossible. She laid on the floor and listened as the door flung open. Kade fell to his knees beside her, taking her face in his hands.

"My God, Tiger! What's happened?" He felt down her arms and put a gentle hand on her chest to feel for movement.

Opening her eyes, she looked first to Kade and then to Tabitha, who reset the telephone.

"Tiger? Are you okay? Did someone bother you? I shouldn't have left like I did, but I had to get out of here and think things over. If one of these Eggs put a finger on you I'll—"

She shook her head.

Kade's blue eyes glistened. "You scared me."

"Let's get her up on the chaise," Tabitha said. "You didn't hit your head, did you?

"No." Bethany's voice cracked.

Kade breathed a sigh of relief and hauled her up under her arms. Nestling her beside him on the leather chaise, he pecked her cheek with a kiss. "And no one's bothered you?"

She cleared her rasping throat.

"Get her something to drink, Tabby." Kade hugged her closer once his sister was gone. "Are you upset because what happened upstairs?"

When she didn't respond, he continued.

"I thought she loved me. I didn't realize how bent on revenge she is. I don't think I can forgive myself for playing into her trap."

Tabitha returned with a glass of iced tea and Kade helped Bethany straighten, a hand on her back to keep her steady. When she swallowed several times, she looked to Kade once more.

"The demons are back."

His eyes widened. "How can you—"

"They tightened around me until I couldn't breathe. I managed to telephone Poppy first, but then I couldn't move or speak."

Kade paled. "He knows where we are? He's coming?"

She nodded.

"When did you call?"

"After Phoebe took that man into the bedroom."

"Which one?" Tabitha asked. "After Hans came down, Robert went up."

Kade's face went red. "She's really come undone, hasn't she? I guess I should be grateful I was first."

"Kade Campbell, don't tell me you laid with that tart!"

They glared at each other.

"The demons," Bethany said to hopefully break some of the tensions. "You've heard what the demons had your parents, Poppy, and Uncle Claudio doing."

A look of hope brightened Kade's countenance. "Then that means Ph—"

"Don't even go there!" Tabitha crossed her arms. "Everyone knows she's crazy, you've just been too blind to see it."

The sound of shattering glasses followed by Phoebe's squeal of delight made the three turn toward the open door. Tabitha went first, going for the front room where shouts and whistles replaced the momentary silence after the break.

"Not on my piano, you whore!" Tabitha screeched.

Kade dashed from the room, his voice carrying the loudest. "This has gone too far! All of you, out!"

"My mother's money pays for this house!" Phoebe yelled. "I'll not leave until I'm ready and my guests have every right to stay!"

"Then take yourself, your lovers, and your disgusting audience to your room," Tabitha shouted. "You don't need to defile other people's things like a bitch marking territory!"

Bethany began quaking as a damp chill settled over her skin. Fearing another fall, she laid sideways on the chaise to save herself from possible injury. Kade brought his sister back to the library, arms around her to keep her from returning to the confrontation.

He released Tabitha and came to Bethany's side. "Tiger, stay awake. Don't give in to the darkness!"

Her eyes closed. The chill turned to fire and her spasms increased.

"It's like that day of the boxing tournament." Tabitha sounded scared. "She was only two, but she was overcome with an evil spell from that emerald brooch."

"I remember!" Kade took Bethany into his arms. "Sissa brought her inside because she was burning with fever. Her father put her in a cold bath to keep her body temperature down."

"But Uncle Claudio had to pray over her and—"

"We have no priest, but start a bath! Tiger, stay with us." He murmured as he carried her up the stairs.

The rushing water filled the space with humidity. Tabitha removed Bethany's shoes while Kade continued to hold her.

"I think we should remove her dress, Kade. She does have underclothes on, unlike her shameless sister. Hold her upright and I'll pull it off."

When she was lowered into the water, Bethany revived enough to scream. Clutching Kade, she sobbed a moment before trembling once more.

"Push her down," Tabitha instructed as she moved to the head of the claw foot tub. "She needs the cool water over more of her whether she likes it or not. I'll hold her head and make sure she doesn't slip under all the way."

"I'm sorry, Tiger. I wish it wasn't like this."

He pried her fingers off and pushed her knees down with one hand and her belly with the other. Bethany shuddered once more before returning to the darkness.

Fourteen

Alexander knew he was blessed to have caught one of Joe Walker's boats at the dock on a Saturday afternoon. Captain of the ship was the Walkers' oldest son, Emmett. He agreed to help without question and ferried Alexander and Frederick across the bay with young Abraham as first mate.

The Eastern Shore automobile Lucy had bought Alexander for his thirty-fifth birthday sat cockeyed in the yard. A man passed out on the porch with a moonshine jug in his lap should have tipped Alexander off to what awaited him inside, but he hurried to the front door.

Not waiting for Frederick and the Walker boys who took a slower pace up the cliff path with the war hero, he threw open the screen door. The evil within Seacliff Manor roiled as soon as Alexander stepped inside. He hitched in a breath and crossed himself, saying "Hail, Mary" three times before advancing further. The noise of furniture scraping the floor grated from the front room.

"You've got the best bubs in town, Phoebe. Thanks for giving me another go since Stan chickened out after Kade's tirade."

"Stop talking and go faster!"

Alexander staggered, swallowing bile as the front door opened behind him. "Freddy, give it a minute before you—"

Frederick pushed around him. "Phoebe Camellia Davenport!"

To keep his friend from killing someone, Alexander followed him into the room. Frederick yanked Robert Woodslow off his daughter on the sofa and repeatedly punched Robert's face.

Alexander caught his arm on the fourth swing. "Freddy, that's enough."

"No it isn't!" He pulled his arm free and struck again.

"Uncle Fred—"

He dropped Robert and lunged at Oscar Easton, pounding him just as hard. "How dare you sit by while your cousin—"

"She asked for it!" Oscar squealed between strikes as he blocked his face with his arms. "She invited us here for a party."

"If you touched her, I'll kill you *and* your father!"

"I'd never touch her, Uncle Freddy!"

"That's right." Phoebe stood defiantly, pulling down her dress. "I only invited Oscar and the others to watch the last two times."

Frederick's anger turned on his child. He did what Alexander could never do—backhanded Phoebe across the mouth. "I'm glad your mother's dead because this would have killed her!"

The tears started as she fingered her bleeding lip. "Daddy—"

"Not another word." He turned back to Oscar. "You know how sick she's been, that she hasn't been safe for proper society! Not that there's a decent man amid this lot of junior Dardennes. I hope you all rot in Hell when I'm done beating you!"

Frederick managed to strike three men before the Walker brothers had him restrained at Alexander's command. Between the fighting and yelling, the house cleared of everyone on the main floor. Before Oscar could slip out, Alexander took him by the wrist.

"Give me the names of every man she was with."

He shook his head. "You won't like it, Uncle Alex."

He tightened his grip. "Tell me!"

"Robbie Woodslow, Hans—"

"My new artist friend who aims to sculpt me for his next project. But you forgot to mention Kade. He took me first." Phoebe lifted her chin, strutted to the hall, and hollered for the whole house to hear. "Kade Gabriel Campbell, you need to tell Poppy how you ravished me three times in the bed your mother stole from mine after she'd been dead less than six months! Tell him how you kissed every inch of me because he didn't accept me when I offered myself to him in January!"

Frederick took Phoebe from behind, pinning her arms with one of his as he brought a chloroform-soaked cloth to her face and laid her on the sofa.

"Poppy, are you really here?" Tabitha called from upstairs.

"Tabitha!" Alexander mounted the stairs three at a time. "Where's Bethany?"

"The demon has her!"

The convulsing form in the tub made him pale.

Kade held Bethany's head steady against a folded towel on the edge of the porcelain. "She was burning and—"

"She's turning blue. Get her out and dry her!"

Alexander went to his room for a talisman. The sight of the rumpled bed, Phoebe's items tossed about the dressing table, and assorted men's clothing discarded on the floor caused his anger to flare. Trying to ignore the surroundings, he went to his dresser and pulled the small box from the top drawer. Inside the wooden case was his mother's gold and garnet cross that was given to Lucy upon his return from Louisiana, tucked safely away to subdue the painful memories associated with it. He had told Lucy on her last morning he would pass it to Phoebe. He had saved it for her marriage day, but knew that would never happen.

It wasn't in that blasted will and I'll be damned if I give it to Phoebe after this. Bethany is more in need of it right now, though I'll pass it to Amelia Rose one day—daughter of my flesh and blood.

Frederick heaved himself to the top of the stairs as Alexander went for the Davenports' wing. Gripping the top of the banister, the war hero looked exhausted. "Abraham is watching over Phoebe, and Emmett is making sure everyone else is gone. Where's Beth?"

"They brought her to her room. They tried to help her the way you did when she was overcome by the brooch all those years ago." He held up the cross. "I'll do what I can for her, Freddy."

The bed was stripped of sheets and blankets. Tabitha leaned over her friend, rubbing her arms with a towel as Kade tried to keep her legs wrapped in another as she twitched.

"Get away from my daughter!" Frederick growled the words.

The pain and fear in Kade's eyes made Alexander think of Douglas's expression when he came out of his possession during the hurricane.

"I never meant to hurt your family, Mr. Davenport. I love and respect you all. I shouldn't have gone into the bedroom with Phoebe. I'll forever hate myself for not respecting her enough to protect our innocence."

Alexander went to Bethany as the two men stared at each other.

"It wasn't in your control, Kade." Alexander tied the black ribbon around Bethany's slender neck. "The house is infested. No one is safe."

"But I—"

"The demons used your love for her to lure you into temptation," Alexander continued as he smoothed Bethany's hair from her forehead and drew a cross with his fingertip, "just as the demons used her illness to spur her to such heights of revenge that she wasn't satisfied with bedding you when it's clear that was her main purpose. It was the thing she knew would hurt me and Magdalene the most."

"She'll never be well enough for a normal relationship." Frederick's countenance was broken with anguish but his tone softened. "Do yourself a favor and move on."

Kade stood to his full height, staring at her father. "I've loved her since I was a boy, Mr. Davenport."

"I'll tell you what a friend once told me, Kade. A childhood infatuation is good when you're young, but you need to find a woman to love as an adult. A woman who loves you completely in return."

Heart breaking moisture clung to his dark lashes. "How can I after what we shared?"

"It didn't mean anything to her!" Frederick's voice turned hard. "She doesn't have the faculties to care and love. She's sick. The sooner you accept that, the better off you'll be."

"Please," Alexander whispered, "I need to pray and then someone might need to go for a priest in Fairhope."

The room settled with an uneasy hush. Alexander prayed in Italian and then English, words he had often heard Claudio speak, closing with "Please, God, relieve my daughter from suffering and send help."

Bethany's body quieted, chest no longer heaving.

Frederick went to his knees beside her, kissing her hand. "Thank you, Alex."

"It's only temporary." Alexander stood and ran a hand through his hair. "I'm going to check with Emmett and Abraham."

"Abe's here?" Kade asked.

Alexander nodded.

"I'd like to go speak with him, if you don't need me."

Frederick's scowl was his reply so Kade went downstairs with Alexander.

Emmett met them in the hall. "All the rooms are clear except the Davenport's suite. It's locked."

"Phoebe told me she locked it yesterday," Kade offered, "to keep people out of it."

"At least she had a shred of respect for someone." Alexander sighed and went into the front room. "Kade would like a word with you, Abraham."

As the three young men took their conversation down the hall, Alexander sat across from Phoebe. *She looks so innocent lying there, like Lucy the night after the Mystics of Dardenne masquerade, when she collapsed on the settee and Frederick watched over her from the porch.*

The ring of the telephone startled him from his thoughts. He answered the extension on the side table. "Melling."

"Alex, you made it!"

"Darla?"

"You'll never guess who arrived on the train after you left." Darla continued without allowing him a word. "Claudio! Melissa brought all the children to me while Maggie secured a boat for the trip over. They should be there soon."

"Claudio?"

"And Maggie and Melissa! Maggie's been begging Claudio to come for months. The last thing she told him was to come whenever he could, so he surprised her."

Melissa traveling with Claudio—what will that do to Frederick in his current state?

"Thank you for watching the children. I'm not sure when we'll be able to get back."

"Don't worry about any of that. Henry is seeing to the horses, and I the children. Call when you can, Alex."

After hanging up, he exhaled with relief. Phoebe didn't stir during the telephone call, and Kade and the Walker boys were still conversing in the game room. Alexander dashed upstairs. Tabitha sat at the foot of Bethany's bed. Frederick was in a chair, holding his daughter's hand.

"We have more company coming. I'm going to watch for the boat."

Frederick nodded absently.

Back downstairs, he went for the boys—men, as they were all of age, and by his actions, Kade had made himself a man that day.

"I want at least two of you in the room with her at all times. There's another ship coming. I'm going to watch for it."

"Who?" Emmett asked.

"I'm not sure who the captain will be, but my wife, Melissa, and Claudio are passengers. If Phoebe wakes, call Frederick down and have Kade sit with Bethany." Seeing his stepson's concern, he ventured to explain. "I don't want you around Phoebe when she's awake. She's liable to make the situation worse than it already is. Do you understand I wish to protect you?"

He met his gaze. "Yes, Poppy."

"And if Bethany wakes, she'll need comfort. Can you be supportive for her?"

Kade nodded.

"If you don't think you have it in you send Abe, but you're to leave Phoebe, no matter what."

"I'd be more than happy to help Tiger," Kade assured him. "She's dear to me."

Alexander nodded and left the house. Traveling the well-worn path to the sepulcher, he felt an empty yearning in his chest. Realizing he held no offering in his hands, he shoved them into his pockets until he reached his destination.

Falling to his knees on the marble steps, he crossed himself and prayed before entering. With a finger tracing the name marking her place he stared at the bold script.

Lucille Amelia Easton Davenport Melling

Loving wife, mother, and queen.

June 24, 1884- May 25, 1918

"Lucy, my queen, Forgive me. I've failed to bring you flowers for the first time. I'm doing my best, but it's not always enough, just as I warned you. I don't know how to handle your oldest, and it seems Freddy's best efforts aren't enough either. Maybe Claudio will be able to help."

He pressed his lips to the cold marker before turning to lay a hand on his sister's name.

"He's been gone eight years, but will stop to see you, Eliza Rose."

Closing the door behind him, Alexander went for the cliffs, staying a safe two dozen feet from the edge. When a small steamer approached, he descended the cliff path to the dock.

As soon as the boat was secure, Magdalene dashed into his arms. Squeezing her in the tightest hug he'd ever given, Alexander kissed her neck and breathed in her essence. Her arms were just as strong around him.

"I had to come, in part because I didn't think it wise to tempt fate by sending Melissa and Claudio alone, but also so I could be here for you." She leaned away, a hand going to his cheek. "Is everything—"

"It's worse than I imagined. I'd rather you not go inside. You can wait in the stable."

She jerked back, hands on her hips. "With the ghost of Douglas while my husband confronts evil within Seacliff Manor?"

"It was hell, Magdalene. Bethany is overcome and—"

"Beth!" Melissa was at their side. "How's Freddy?"

Claudio's hand went to her shoulder and Alexander raised his eyes to his friend standing behind her. His Romanesque features were the same, though more lines were etched into his olive skin and hints of gray marred his black hair. Stepping around the women, Alexander embraced the priest, kissing each cheek as Claudio did likewise.

"You're just in time, Claudio. So much evil happened within the walls, I fear to allow the ladies to enter."

He raised his black bag. "I have come prepared for Seacliff, *amico*, but I know better than to tell these women what to do. If they wish to enter with us, I only ask to bless them before and after."

Alexander nodded in resignation.

"That's Emmett's boat, isn't it?" Magdalene asked. "Should I send our hire along?"

"Yes, he and Abe agreed to stay until we're finished."

After Alexander and Magdalene thanked the captain and arranged for payment, they led the way up the path. Hands clasped and bodies close, a sense of calm began to fill his chest despite the peril. When they reached the old stable, Alexander stopped and gazed at his wife.

"It does me a world of good to have you here, but if you don't wish to—"

"I'll not leave your side, Alexander Melling. Demons can't stop our love." She threw her arms about his shoulders and kissed him.

Sucking the healing balm from her lips, he trailed his hands over her until one pressed the small of her back and the other felt the pulse in her neck.

"I see things are not much different for Alexander." Claudio smiled when his friend turned to him.

"Forgive me for seeking to fill my reservoir with goodness before returning to the evil." He held Magdalene to his side. "Horrific things happened before Freddy and I arrived, some continuing for us to witness when we walked in."

"Tell me, and spare no details. I must know what we face."

Alexander tightened his arm around Magdalene. "I'll hold you should you weaken. Claudio, you might want to stay close to Melissa."

After a deep breath, he explained Phoebe's escape with Oscar's assistance, their gathering of friends, and the upheaval in the house from sexual encounters.

"And sweet Beth walking into a situation like that." Melissa covered her mouth as though to swallow tears before they could erupt.

Claudio put an arm around her. "She is susceptible to the demons because of what she went through as a child."

"And that was my fault." Melissa buckled under her remorse and let the tears come.

Claudio tucked her to his chest. "*Eroina*, do not think that way."

As Claudio comforted her, Alexander continued the story with Phoebe's unscrupulous liaisons and reassuring them all that Tabitha was fine—the one bit of good news. Then it was Magdalene's turn to cry as she heard what Kade did with Phoebe, followed by what Alexander and Frederick walked in on and finding Bethany overcome.

Melissa stepped out of Claudio's embrace. "I need to help Freddy."

"*Eroina*, I must bless you first." After his blessing, he kissed her on the forehead. "He needs you. Cling to him."

After she disappeared through the backdoor, the men's eyes met.

"How does it feel to see her again?" Alexander whispered.

Claudio crossed himself. "It feels glorious and heartbreaking, but now Magdalene needs my care."

Alexander released his wife to Claudio and the priest held her a moment, resting his head on hers.

"I refuse to allow you to become *Posseduta* again. You shall carry St. Benedict's Cross and stay away from Phoebe. If you feel weak, allow me to bless you again. You may kiss your husband, but only him."

She punched his arm as she straightened, a smile breaking through her sadness.

"There." Claudio pinched her chin. "Keep your spirit up, Magdalene. It will serve you well. You must be strong for your children and husband."

"Seeing your face is enough to strengthen me."

Fifteen

Phoebe heard the murmur of voices and willed her body to hold still until she understood her situation. She remembered Robert filling her, her father beating him, and Alexander looking disgusted.

Was he disgusted over Daddy for fighting or for what I did?

"Hospital."

"Control."

The words came to her in uneasy fragments.

"She's beyond your help, Freddy."

Sissa wants Daddy to lock me up! I need to escape before that happens.

She peeked an eye open but only saw the ceiling of the front room.

"Phoebe," a familiar voice whispered. "Are you awake?"

Slowly, she turned her head. Wide hazel eyes with wisps of unruly red hair falling over his freckled forehead met her gaze.

She clutched Abraham Walker's hand. "I need to get away. Will you help me, Abe?"

Abraham glanced toward the hall and whispered. "Mr. Alex says you're sick."

She raised a finger to his lips. "I've only been sleeping because my father drugged me. They think my lifestyle is unsavory because they don't understand the passion our generation has. You have passion, don't you?"

He gave her his broad grin. "Every day."

She returned his smile. "Show me how experienced you are. I'm not wearing any underclothes."

Abraham's eyes seemed to glaze in ecstasy as a hand trailed up her bare foot. He reached her knee and she spread her legs. His work-calloused hand was a new sensation as his fingers brushed along her sensitive skin.

Phoebe moaned in pleasure when he reached her thigh.

"Abe, you fool!" Emmett jerked him away.

She sat, head spinning, but managed to keep a seductive smile on her lips. "No need to fight, Walkers. I'd welcome both of you."

"*Principessa,* it does not bode well for you to behave as such."

"Uncle Claudio!" Phoebe felt the coldness in her heart increase as he stepped closer with a crucifix outstretched. She was a girl the last time she saw him, but he was larger than life in her memory: the priest who arrived in town when Alexander came for her mother, the one who married her father and Melissa, his visits to St. Mary's School, and his joyful countenance at Friday suppers.

"Cease to do wickedness, Phoebe Camellia Davenport. You will not find peace with these actions."

His dark eyes were kind, but she sensed his displeasure. Guilt hardened in her chest. "I can't help it! I want to stop, but I can't!"

"Come to the light." He switched to speaking in Latin. Words that stung and clawed at the vileness inside her.

She screamed in anguish. Her body convulsed.

"Phoebe!"

Kade!

"Stay back!" *Alexander.* "Abraham, keep him away!"

Then her father lowered her to the sofa with bandaged hands as Claudio continued the Rites. She shouted curses at him as her father's strong arms held her down. In a final, desperate attempt at freedom, she cried out.

"Please, Daddy! He's hurting us! He's trying to take them away, but I want to be here with them. I safeguarded your bedroom. I know I'm not perfect like Beth, but I tried. I tried so hard, Daddy. Allow me to live here with what emotions I still feel—lust and pleasure!"

"You deserve more, Princess."

In a moment of clarity she saw Frederick Davenport as he was—stretched thin from the stress of family and loss. Deep-set lines rimmed his mouth, gray hair framed his forehead, and pain filled his brown eyes. When his arms slackened, she moved in for the final blow.

"I'm more like Momma than you realize. Just as she needed Alexander to feel satisfied, I need to be filled. Alexander could have done that for me, but he refused. Kade alone wasn't enough. I'll never get enough to satisfy this hole in my soul, but I have to keep trying. Don't hate me, Daddy. Hate Alexander for what he did to this family by taking your Goosy before you could claim her. Think of it—life with Lucy at the Eastons' old home, your pretty daughters and a houseful of others like you always dreamed. Maybe even a son that lived beyond infancy to carry your name so the Davenport line doesn't die out. Momma gave Alexander a healthy son instead when we all know the Melling name is the one that deserves to be extinguished."

Frederick flinched as though struck. Claudio shifted to fill the space but Melissa cut in, taking Phoebe by the shoulders.

Laughing maniacally, Phoebe tried to wriggle free, but her stepmother held fast. "We didn't say a word against *you* this time."

Melissa's eyes blazed as fiery as her hair.

"They whispered to me. They told me how to coax Kade to lie with me, how to position myself so Hans—"

Claudio reached around Melissa to press the crucifix to Phoebe's hand. Screaming in pain, she flung her stepmother away. Claudio fell across her to still her thrashing body.

"Did you come to finally make Melissa yours, Priest? What will it do to noble Davenport if she leaves him while both his daughters from Lucy are overcome? Will you allow her to take the youngest when you leave so Frederick has nothing left of her when she's gone?"

Chanting in Latin, he pressed the crucifix to Phoebe's lips. She screamed until she lost her breath and everything went dark.

***

"Daddy! I'm sorry, Daddy!" Phoebe grew dizzy in the dim room, immediately falling back from where she'd sat up on the sofa.

Frederick was beside her, smoothing her hair and kissing her cheek. "Shh, Princess. Catch your breath and calm down."

"I love you. I didn't mean to hurt you or Sissa." More tears fell. "I couldn't stop myself. The voices kept telling me what to do, what to say."

"I know, Princess. Don't worry." He sat on the sofa and pulled her onto his lap.

She felt his unconditional love, but goose pimples marred her limbs. "I'm cold. So cold."

One of the throw blankets from an armchair was handed to them. As her father tucked it around her, she turned to the giver. His mouth was tight, pale eyes sad.

"Thank you, Poppy. I'm sorry for what I did in your bedroom." And when the admission was out, the pain became raw. "Would Sissa be willing to speak with me?"

"I'll check if she's available."

Once Alexander was gone, Phoebe snuggled against her father's broad chest. "Will I ever be well, Daddy?"

He sighed and kissed her head. "I don't know, Princess. Your mother had periods of good days and weeks, but once she'd had an episode, there was no going back."

Melissa walked in.

"How is she?" Frederick asked.

"Still unresponsive. Maggie and I got her changed into a flannel nightgown and her bed made with fresh linens."

"Beth?" Phoebe's voice cracked.

Her father nodded.

Why couldn't it have been Tabby? "Sissa, could I speak privately with you?"

She crossed her arms and glared.

"Daddy could wait in the hall. I'll stay here and you can sit over there. I don't think I could stand on my own. You'd be safe."

"Your words would reach me."

"You're too stoic for words to wound—the only woman I've ever met strong enough for my father."

"Don't overdo it, Princess," he whispered.

"It's true."

He hugged Phoebe tighter. "I know it is."

Frederick left, and Melissa settled on a nearby armchair. Gathering her courage, Phoebe readied for the conversation she never thought she'd have with her stepmother.

"I need help, Sissa." Phoebe shifted, causing the soreness to be more pronounced. She placed a hand between her legs. "I hurt. Down here. Now that the demons are gone, I can feel the damage they drove me to."

Concern flashed across Melissa's face and she leaned closer. "Phoebe, how many times did you—"

"At least eight. Kade was gentle with me, but the others weren't. I feel sore and dirty."

Melissa paled and gripped the armrests. "And how many men?"

"Four." Tears fell. "Kade will never forgive me."

Melissa stood. "I'm going to call Darla and ask her a few questions. Stay with your father."

Melissa didn't stop to explain anything, but Phoebe felt her father's all-knowing gaze upon her and fidgeted under the scrutiny.

When Melissa returned, she spoke matter-of-factly. "I need help getting Phoebe upstairs to wash. Who would you like me to ask? And don't say you'll do it, Freddy. You've done too much to your body already." She motioned to his bandaged knuckles.

He frowned. "Emmett would be fine."

Melissa and the young captain took either side of Phoebe and helped her stand. After they were alone in the bathroom, Melissa kindly explained Darla's advice of a vinegar wash. She'd brought the supplies upstairs before collecting Phoebe, and set about preparing the mixture and soaking the sponge in the bowl.

"It could sting if you have abrasions, but it needs to be done. After, you may shower and finally soak in the bath if you'd like."

From the look on her face Phoebe knew Melissa took no joy in the task. The cleansing of her intimate area caused Phoebe to cry.

With Melissa's steadying arm, she was able to shower and wash her hair, but she was too exhausted to bathe.

Wrapped in towels, she leaned against Melissa. "Can I just go to sleep?"

Her stepmother set her in the wicker chair in the corner. "Let me ask where you can rest and collect your clothes."

Ten minutes later, Phoebe wore one of the functional cotton nightgowns she kept at the house and was tucked into the freshly made bed Louisa usually slept in. Melissa guarded the door, but Phoebe was too weary to mind that they didn't trust her.

Sixteen

Bethany came into consciousness with the strange sound of foreign words being chanted, a cold touch on her forehead, and something warm around her hand. Her eyes fluttered open, but the room didn't offer much light.

"Beth!" Tabitha appeared behind Bethany's father—the one holding her hand.

"Thank God!" Frederick kissed his daughter's cheek. "I was beginning to lose hope."

"I believe that even after all my training, Frederick Davenport has no faith in me."

She looked to the voice and realized it was his words that had awoken her. "Uncle Claudio!"

Her father moved out of the way so the priest could come to her. Removing the crucifix from her forehead, Claudio kissed her there and then on each cheek.

"You look just as I remember you, Uncle Claudio."

"And you, Bethany, are most extraordinarily a young woman now. But I still see the little girl you were in your eyes, nose,"—he touched the tip of it with his finger—"and that pert chin. You have done well with your schooling and sewing. I wore your scarf during the winter and was asked each day by at least one person where I bought such a fine piece. I am sorry to have missed the graduation ceremony for you and Tabitha. I was to arrive Thursday, but my ship across the Atlantic was delayed."

"I'm glad you're here." She sat up and hugged him, looking over his shoulder at Kade, Tabitha, Alexander, and Magdalene. "What's going on, and why is everyone here? What time is it?"

Frederick sat on the edge of the bed, taking her hand in his bandaged one once more.

"What's the last thing you remember, Little Princess?"

Thinking past the darkness, the fever and chills, Bethany remembered the telephone call she made to Alexander. The shock of seeing Phoebe take a strange man into the bedroom. The pain of seeing Kade emerge half-dressed from it before that.

"Phoebe," she whispered as she felt the blood drain from her face.

"Claudio has freed her as well," her father said. "It's after two in the morning. She's been resting for several hours. Sissa is with her. I want you to eat and drink, if you're feeling up to it."

Bethany nodded.

Alexander and Magdalene came to her for hugs.

"May I fix a tray for you, Knight Bethany?"

"Please, Poppy. I am hungry."

"I'll take over for Melissa so she can see you," Magdalene told her.

"Bring me, please." Frederick reached for Magdalene with stiff motions and bandaged hands.

"Daddy, what happened?"

"I took a few rounds with the revelers when I arrived. I'm afraid my body isn't used to that type of exertion and my old wounds are yelling at me because of it."

Kade held his position near the door when his mother left with Frederick, but Tabitha perched on the foot of the bed, smiling with relief. Melissa rushed in and Bethany's concerns lightened more as she was enfolded in her stepmother's arms beneath Claudio's watchful eyes.

"Beth, Sweetie. We were so scared."

"I won't be left alone, will I?"

"I'll make up the other bed for Tabby. She's refused to sleep while you were in danger. Kade's been here too." She smiled at the Campbell siblings before her gaze paused on Claudio. "And Claudio. Thank you." Melissa kissed him on her way out.

When Alexander returned with the promised refreshments, Melissa and Kade made the other bed. By the time Bethany finished the sandwich and tea, Tabitha was in her nightgown. Melissa called for Claudio, and he blessed each young woman and then the room.

"Kade," Melissa spoke softly, "the Walkers are camped in the game room if you want to join them."

"I won't be able to sleep. Would it be all right if I sit in the doorway and watch over the girls?"

Bethany's heart warmed at his concern, but Melissa glanced uneasily at Claudio.

"Kade will need a special blessing of protection and diligence." The priest smiled and handed him a crucifix. "Hold to it always this night."

Melissa kissed Bethany goodnight and slipped out. Tabitha's eyes closed, but Bethany studied Claudio as he prayed over Kade.

Afterward, he hugged the young man and in a low voice spoke more. "….your father succumbed as well…morally strong…forgive…."

Throughout it all, Kade nodded and then embraced Claudio in return. After the priest left, Bethany waved Kade over.

"Thank you for staying. I'm scared, but didn't want to burden my parents. I'll be able to sleep comfortably knowing you're here."

"How can you after what I did?"

She squeezed his hand. "Don't shoulder the blame."

Kade took the desk chair to the doorway where Bethany studied his profile until she fell asleep.

***

Bethany found Kade standing over her when she woke.

"Morning, Tiger. Tabby got permission for us to go down to the beach for a swim if you want to join us. Abe's coming too."

Curling onto her side, she tried to ignore his stare by closing her eyes.

"Are you feeling okay?" His fingers feathered across her cheek.

His touch was passionate as he made love to Phoebe. He reveres her as a woman, but you'll always be a child—a sniveling girl who needs a nightlight and someone to protect her.

A tear slipped out, followed by the constricting of her limbs.

"Tiger?" He took her hand. "Should I get your—"

"Uncle Claudio!" She managed to call before the seizures began.

The bedroom filled with concerned family, but Claudio pushed to the bedside, crucifix and prayers at the ready.

Minutes later, Bethany breathed normally.

"She needs out of these walls," Claudio said as he stepped away to allow her father to come to her.

"The others are going swimming," Magdalene said. "Alex and I will go with them and bring Beth."

Everything was arranged while Bethany sat quietly. Tabitha and Melissa helped her dress and then Kade carried her piggyback. Trying not to think about his hands under her bare knees and her pounding heart against his back, she tucked her head alongside his.

The June morning was already hot. Bethany asked to be left in the shade of the cypress trees. Dressed in her black swimsuit, Magdalene arranged their breakfast basket nearby while Kade, Tabitha, and Abraham ran to the shoreline.

Alexander settled beside Bethany. "He has matured into a man in more ways than one during the last twenty-four hours."

Bethany nodded as she continuously followed Kade's antics while wrestling with energetic Abraham. They threw each other into the bay, splashing and shouting. The islander's broad grin was easily seen, even at that distance. The sun glinted off Abraham's red hair as he emerged from a dunking. Bethany smiled.

"Kade's decided to go away for the summer."

Her attention snapped to her stepfather.

"He spoke with Emmett and Abraham yesterday, and Maggie and I this morning. He's going to work on the boats and stay on the island with the Walkers until the autumn term begins."

"But what about his work at the stables?"

"His place will be easily filled. There's always willing kids looking to make money when out of school. I might even offer Simon and Asher for the position a few days a week. It'd be good for them." Alexander patted her hand before releasing it. "You're young, Bethany Iris. Don't worry too much over things you can't control. Focus on your own job. What day do you report to Mademoiselle Bisset?"

"Tuesday." She tucked her hair under her swim cap as Magdalene settled on the other side of Alexander.

He nipped a kiss at his wife's neck and winked at Bethany. "I promise not to buy lingerie for Maggie while you're working."

Magdalene punched him in the stomach but he caught her arm and pulled her to him, falling so she was on top. Alexander's hands roamed the back of her swimsuit.

"Alex!" Magdalene pushed him away.

"Excuse us, Bethany," he said as he straightened them upright. "The fresh air does wonders for me."

"Any type of air, Alexander." His wife jabbed him in the ribs.

Kade and Abraham ran up, dripping cool water onto Bethany. "Are you ready to join us, Tiger?"

Happy to leave Alexander and Magdalene some privacy, she nodded.

"Good!" Abraham snatched her ankles as Kade grabbed her wrists.

Together they carried her into the water, swinging her between them until they released her into the bay with an undignified splash.

As soon as she righted herself, Bethany torpedoed under the water. Kade and Abraham yelped as she pinched the backs of their thighs before she swam toward Tabitha with strong strokes to out distance the guys. The four of them spent half an hour swimming and playing while the Mellings necked at the picnic spot.

After eating, Alexander went to the house, and Abraham joined his brother inspecting the boat. Bethany and Tabitha went back into the water, but Magdalene asked Kade to stay with her. Bethany kept watch while she floated. After hugging his mother, Kade retreated to the cliff and Magdalene waved the girls ashore.

By the time they toweled off, Alexander returned.

"You didn't even get wet, sweetness." He kissed Magdalene's cheek.

"We have a whole summer ahead of us to enjoy the water."

"We can come whenever you like, for as long as you prefer. And getting to see you in your bathing suit is never a wasted effort."

Tabitha rolled her eyes before stalking up the path.

Alexander nodded Magdalene toward her daughter and offered Bethany his arm. "Will you walk with me?"

"Gladly, Poppy." She kissed his cheek, knowing he liked a fuss made over himself. "It looks like the Walkers are getting the boat ready. Are we leaving soon?"

He nodded. "I called the Watts to help us because of the state of the house. Melissa had Phoebe clean up the worst of things and gather dirty linens for laundering, but Leroy is to oversee new locks on all the doors tomorrow. I've promised to send them a bonus this week for the trouble, especially for having them come on a Sunday."

When Bethany and Alexander came within sight of the house, Rosemary Watts rushed out the kitchen door.

"Bethany Iris, you gave your daddy and everyone such a fright!" Rosemary hugged her. "It's a good thing Father De Fiore was in town. I shudder to think what would have happened otherwise. This land has seen too much sadness for its own good, but congratulations on your graduation. I didn't expect to tell you so soon after your special day."

Bethany thanked Rosemary and assured her she was fine. Then Melissa was there, ushering her inside.

"We want to be off within the hour, Beth," she told her. "Take a quick shower. I'll have something ready for you to eat when you're dressed."

"Sissa—" The word choked in her throat when she saw Hans at the front door with her father.

"Go on," Melissa whispered as she nudged Bethany up the stairs.

"What's he doing here?" she asked once they reached the bathroom.

"He's come because Phoebe agreed to go with him today."

"He was with her—with her after Kade." Bethany's arms sprouted goose pimples.

"We know, Beth. Your father's handling it, and Alexander will be sure he doesn't physically over-handle things like he did yesterday."

Seventeen

Since Frederick blocked the front door inside, Alexander went around the house to the porch. Lighting a cigarette, he sprang up the steps and casually parked himself on the swing as he exhaled a smoke ring.

Hans Caldwell turned to him while forcing what had been a frown into a pleasant smile. "Mr. Melling?"

"Yes."

"I'm H—"

"I know who you are, Mr. Caldwell. You have a glowing reputation in the local art community, as well as with the nudists in Fairhope."

Frederick's fists looked like they would burst his bandages.

Hans straightened the sleeve of his lightweight suit. "I'm not quite sure what to say to that, other than the human body is the most beautiful form on Earth, not something to be shy about."

"The Esherick and Anderson families are well known. When you're brought into their fold, word gets out."

Hans cleared his throat and lost a bit of his bravado. "I understand you're Phoebe's stepfather. Perhaps you would be willing to discuss the arrangement I made with her yesterday since her father refuses to hear me out."

Alexander took another drag and settled back. "I'm happy to listen, but it's not my consent you need."

The sound of bare feet running the hall clamored to a stop behind Frederick.

Phoebe tried to push around her father but he held firm. "I'm of age and need no one's consent!"

"Phoebe, go back upstairs." Frederick's voice was hard.

"I won't unless it's to get my suitcases to leave with Hans. I promised to model for him. He has a cottage with a guest room I can stay in while he works on the sculpture. I can stay for free as well as receive a small allowance for my modeling time. My first job!"

"*Principessa*," Claudio said from behind her, "come sit in the front room with me."

"No! This is my life they're discussing and I should be a part of it!" She reached a hand around her father's solid form in desperation. "Don't leave without me, Hans!"

The man straightened his tie and smiled as though he enjoyed being begged for, souring Alexander's stomach. *He's up to the same thing Hazel Kline accused me of doing with Consuela—installing her in my home to use as I wish. My intentions were good then, but this man is over-sexed and seeking the adoration of an unstable girl to become her conqueror.*

"I'll do my best, Miss Phoebe," he replied, "for I won't be able to work until I capture your lovely figure in wood."

Wood being the keyword.

"Mr. Caldwell," Frederick spoke through gritted teeth, "my daughter hasn't been well this year and is much too young—"

"Daddy, I'm eighteen! You're letting Beth start work this week and she's only fifteen!"

"You're asking to live with a man you just met. A much older man."

"I am but thirty, Mr. Davenport, and much younger at heart. I see no reason for you to imprison your fully-grown daughter against her wishes."

"She needs to stay where she has someone looking after her."

"As my muse, her well-being will be the center of my concern. If she turns sickly—which I don't foresee happening as she's a blossom of health—the medical clinics in Fairhope are top of the line. I'll see to her care personally."

"She's unstable and cannot—"

"Then lock me up, Daddy! If I'm that bad, why am I not in an asylum like Aunt Opal? If I'm only as bad off as Momma, then allow me what she had—home life with someone who adored her, though in her case he was *her* muse." On her tiptoes, she peered over her father's shoulder at Alexander. "And I remember the frequent indulgences with her muse are what helped her most."

Frederick's face reddened while Alexander felt his own pale.

"There's no shame in differing emotional states," Hans said calmly. "They run rampant in creative types. I bet I can find Miss Phoebe's creative streak, and utilizing that outlet will improve her wellbeing."

Find her giftedness as you bend her body to your will. She'd be a talented lover, just as her mother was. Lucy, my queen! He'll ruin her more than I ever did you. We loved each other! This man has no love other than for himself.

"Daddy, I'll not be caged in the Moores' house again. Lock me in an asylum or let me go with Hans. I'm either dangerous or not. What would Momma want for me, prison or passion?"

Frederick hung his head as he slumped against the doorframe.

"Frederick!" Alexander snapped. *The devil within her! She knows how to manipulate as well as Opal!*

Raising his gaze to meet Alexander's, Frederick's countenance was one of defeat. He turned to Hans. "You'll care for my daughter?"

"As long as she's with me, Mr. Davenport."

Alexander ground his cigarette into the ashtray and stomped off the porch. He hid himself in the stable-turned garage, plopping onto the swing Douglas had built for Magdalene.

Anger burned his vision until the shadowed world was a blur. He closed his eyes against the pain.

"Alex?"

The love in his wife's voice brought him back from the edge of agony. Her beautiful face was pinched with concern as she cupped his stubbly cheek.

"She's gone, isn't she?" he asked.

A tear fell from Magdalene's eye when she nodded.

"Freddy's damned her to misery," he lamented.

"She'll find misery wherever she is, you know that."

"Freddy should have—"

"He's tired, Alex, tired of fighting for everyone. You know what sending Phoebe to an asylum would do to him—the same thing it would have done to you had you sent Lucy. He has a wife and two other daughters that need him. You saw what Phoebe did this weekend, what she's capable of. Isn't it possible that she might be better off taking responsibility for herself, especially since she's recently exorcized?"

"That won't last five minutes once she's gone from here! That man doesn't love or cherish her like I did Lucy! She's his conquest and she'll be worse off than ever when he's used her up!" Alexander shoved Magdalene and stomped three paces away before realizing what he'd done. He tenderly took her in his arms and kissed her neck. "Maggie, forgive me."

She clung to him, kissing his lips twice before pressing her forehead to his. "I know you're hurt and angry. You have every right to be, but it's beyond your control. Let it go."

"I don't know if I can."

"Allow me to help, Alexander." Her hands trailed his back then around his chest in an erotic caress.

"Magdalene." He swept his tongue into her mouth and splurged on her sweetness rather than the pain. In that moment, he knew what he had done for Lucy, Magdalene did for him. Hands gasping her backside until she was lifted to his hips, he walked them to the automobile. He leaned against it to support her while they indulged.

Nipping her neck, he paused to speak. "Did you ever go at it with Douglas in the stable?"

Her smile said it all.

"It would be a first for me, Maggie."

"Virgin territory with Alexander Randolph Melling?" Magdalene gave a whoop and slugged his arm. "I've waited two decades for this! Come on!" She tugged him to the foot of the ladder.

His smile faltered. "Is it safe up there?"

"Leroy keeps everything repaired on the property." She was halfway up before she turned, looking down and motioning with a hand for him to follow.

Alexander stared at her, eyes wide. "Hold on, Magdalene!"

"I've been climbing ladders since I could walk. I slept in a loft at my parents' and then in the carriage house my first few weeks with Douglas." She impulsively switched her single-grip to the opposite hand so she could kiss the ring her first husband had given her.

"Maggie!"

She laughed and easily turned so she faced out from her precarious height. "I do believe you're scared, Alexander Melling."

He crossed his arms, looking up the knee-length dress. He mustered an impish smile. "Maybe I prefer the view from down here."

She tugged her hem higher to show more. "Come on, they're bound to look for us soon."

He grabbed the ladder with both hands. "I can't, Maggie."

Standing before him on the ground seconds later, she kissed him. "Don't tell me you're afraid of heights."

He nodded and she cocked her head to the side as she stared at him.

"You never go to the cliffs."

"Not if I can help it, but I did look out from the forest to see your boat coming yesterday."

Her pretty smile coupled with a spark in her brown eyes created a yearning below his belt. "And you wouldn't climb up there, even if it meant you'd be more than satisfied?"

"Magdalene, I would if I could, but I can't! I never look out a window that's higher than the second floor and that loft has no railings or—"

She kissed him hard as her hand teased his belt. "It's safe and we won't stand on the edge. We'll set up a blanket near the back. You'll be so impressed with what I'm doing that you wouldn't care if we were on the roof."

He stroked her curves and went for her lips.

"Not until we get up there. You go first. I'll be right behind you. I won't let you fall. Just keep moving, slow and steady, one foot above the other."

He took the first two rungs without issue. "Why can't we play in the backseat of the car instead?"

"I want a location that I share with no one else in your memory." She pinched his backside playfully.

"Maggie!" He stopped on the fourth rung, white knuckles straining around the ladder. "You'll be the death of me if you touch me again."

"I'll try to contain myself, but now that I know what type of view you enjoyed, I can't help appreciating your tight derriere from this angle."

He laughed and gained two more rungs. "I just ask the fondling be delayed. The hayloft might be new for me, but what about you?"

"Douglas proposed to me up here. We might have been necking in the hay pile when I felt a bulge in his pants, but it turned out to be the ring box."

Alexander stopped to laugh. Noticing how high he was, he froze. "Mag—"

"You're almost there. Think about what awaits you when you conquer this ladder. And you better pull out something other than a ring."

He groaned and took another step. "I can see into the loft but there's no hay."

Magdalene laughed. "No horses, no hay."

"I think I'd like to see you with some hay stuck in your hair after a tumble together. Maybe I could bribe a worker at the stables to clear us a window of privacy so we could take an extra ride one day."

When his waist was level with the loft floor, he crawled until he was more than six feet away from the edge before standing.

"I did it! God knows I've wanted to do that since I was a boy. Thank you, Magdalene. This is exactly what I needed after the heartaches of the past two days."

"I love you, Alex." Her embrace was pure joy to his triumph. "You overcame this, my lion. We'll make it over any other obstacle that appears before us."

"Together." He kissed her.

"Always together."

Eighteen

Miss Charlotte managed to prepare Sunday supper at the Mellings' house for nineteen people with only a few hours' notice. Bethany kept thinking there should have been twenty souls around the table with the Mellings, Davenports, Adamses, two Walkers, and Claudio. Phoebe's escape after five months made her absence more pronounced because instead of being safe at Dr. Moore's house a few blocks away, she was with Hans Caldwell in Fairhope.

Bethany expected Kade to be melancholy, but he joked with Abraham and Emmett like life was great. Asher, Simon, and Horatio hung on the young men's words like opossums from a branch. On her other side, Tabitha answered all the questions Louisa threw at her. Across from Bethany, Claudio sat between Amelia and Charlene—the two who joined the group since he moved to Italy—but he often watched Louisa as though he remembered all the time he spent with her while her father was overseas.

"Even though it's the Sabbath," Alexander announced as the platter of cookies passed around, "I believe we should enjoy a bit of dancing after dessert. That is, if Father De Fiore will indulge our wicked ways."

Claudio laughed. "If only dancing was the worst of the offenses."

Darla tapped on Henry's shoulder and motioned to Virginia slumped with her head on her mother's lap.

"I'm afraid my family needs to leave after the children are done eating," Henry looked to their host. "Ginny isn't feeling well and I know the others must be tired after having company over last night."

"But Dad—" Horatio stopped his complaint after a stern look from his father, though Bethany could tell he didn't want to be parted from his friends.

When the group dispersed, Bethany stacked dishes to help clear the massive table. After she took the first load to the kitchen, Asher joined the work.

"Was it real bad at Seacliff?" His blue eyes were luminous as he gathered stemware.

Bethany nodded.

"Poppy said Uncle Claudio had to exorcise you. Did it hurt?"

"That didn't hurt, the demons and sin did." She set the pile of plates she'd collected on the table and dropped into the nearest chair. "My heart aches, Ash."

His thin arms were about her in an instant. "You're safe now. Kade won't be here this summer, but I'll protect you. Simon, too."

She cried, knowing those boys were no substitute for the friendship and love she'd wrapped her life around in regard to the oldest Campbell. "It's too late. My heart's spoiled, my fairytale gone."

"Then write a new one. Momma always told me it's up to us to write our own happy endings. Your story isn't over, it's just beginning."

Unable to stop the tears, she sobbed unashamed in her half-brother's embrace until Miss Charlotte came to collect the remainder of the dishes.

Bethany sent Asher ahead of her and stepped into the morning room to gather her emotions. Leaving the lights off, she went to the window overlooking the backyard. There were two figures on the patio. Melissa, white summer dress bright in the dark, turned to Claudio as he lit a cigarette for her. He briefly cupped her cheek as he kissed her forehead with deliberate tenderness. Once they were both smoking, his arm went about her waist and she leaned into him.

Phoebe's biting words rang in Bethany's troubled heart. *"Uncle Eddie says Miss New York and Uncle Claudio had an affair when Daddy was gone to war." And he did leave soon after Daddy came home.*

Pain began to spread in her chest. She remembered Melissa's passionate rebuttal to the accusation, but after knowing what true-hearted Kade was capable of, Bethany wasn't sure what was real and what was nightmare. Least the tears begin anew; she turned for the hall and ran straight into her father.

"Little Princess." His sturdy arm went around her.

Without thinking of anything other than understanding the upheaval in her world, she led him to the window and motioned to Melissa nestled beside Claudio.

"I may have graduated, but I still don't understand life. I don't mean to cause trouble, but I don't know what to think when I see Sissa so comfortable with another man."

He gazed out the window several seconds before walking Bethany to the sofa and clicking on the side table lamp with his bandaged hand. "You're old enough to know the truth, Beth."

Heart pounding, she gripped his bandaged hand. "You and Sissa are—"

"Melissa and I are stronger than ever. Do you remember when Junior died and the year after?"

"You only came home to tuck us into bed, Pancake Time was miserable without you, and everyone was sad."

"I made choices that magnified the pain for the whole family. Instead of being there for my wife and daughters, I wallowed in my grief alone. I'm ashamed to say I left Melissa when her pain was just as acute. Not only did she lose her son, she lost me as well, though she bravely cared for you girls without physical or emotional support.”

“Daddy, who could blame you? Your only son—”

“Junior was her son too.” His voice was hard, but he brushed a tear off her cheek with a gentle stroke of his thumb. “I was selfish and did one of the worst things a husband can do—emotionally abandon his wife. Then I compounded the injury. The day we began healing, I joined the army without discussing it with her. Another betrayal.”

“Sissa didn’t know? But she never—”

“Melissa is a brave woman. She handled her pain and kept going, refusing to slander me or my choices before you girls or the city, as she had her newspaper readers. But my leaving was the last straw. She couldn’t go on without love and support after almost a year of neglect.”

“Claudio.” Bethany breathed the name as understanding filled her. “Uncle Claudio was there. He had meals with Sissa and Louisa, danced with—”

“Yes, and I don’t blame either of them for what intimacies they shared because it was my fault they were needed.”

“What is sin when it comes to a man and woman?”

“You know the commandments, Beth. Melissa may not share our faith but she’s a good woman—the best. She didn’t go too far with Claudio, and he was a gentleman with her. I, on the other hand, erred once again. After my injuries, when I’d failed Chuck and the others, my despair was worse than ever. A nurse offered relief. I indulged in more than I should have in an attempt to numb my pain.”

Bethany pulled away, shaking her head to stop the words she didn’t wish to hear.

“Details aren’t important, but it was Melissa who saved me from taking a physical connection too far. Her letters and articles, her wondrous words, finally caught up with all my transfers. I received a mountain of mail after the silence in time to stop me from making the biggest mistake in my life. But it was I who had forgotten home in the absence of the mail—not her. But still, I hadn't learned my lesson. I struck an equally jarring blow to her—to all of you—my first morning home."

"Momma," Bethany whispered as more tears filled her eyes.

Frederick nodded. "In my pain over losing your mother, I thought only of my need to see Lucy. All the infractions Melissa had forgiven me for surged back when I left. I thought she'd leave me after having to walk you girls here to say goodbye. And then you cried out for me, do you remember?"

"Yes, Daddy."

"You cried in your anguish, and I wasn't man enough to face her wrath to see to you. I hid, Beth. I hid from myself and my family in my shame. Alex, despite all his suffering, was the bigger man and father figure to you. I'm sorry I failed you all."

Bethany collapsed in his arms, wetting his shirt with her tears. "But don't you see? It takes Poppy and Uncle Claudio to fill your place, not to mention Mr. Henry and everyone else who helped us. And Sissa was hiding from you as well, but you finally comforted her in her pain on Junior's birthday this past Christmas. No matter what, you're my champion father."

"I love you more than you know, Bethany Iris." He kissed her forehead, hugging her close. "I told you all this to help you understand not everyone is perfect. I fear that while it looks like you're holding together on the outside, on the inside you're lost and scared, just like me."

"I am, Daddy." She curled against him, resting her head on his shoulder. "Everything's changed. I don't know what to do but hide myself away as protection from more heartache."

"I won't allow that, Little Princess."

"Tiger?" Kade's voice shouted down the hall as footsteps approached. "There you are! We've been waiting. All the guys want a spin with you."

He held out his hand, smile and bright eyes dazzling amid the heavy atmosphere.

"I'll be there in a minute." Bethany stood by herself and then put her arm out for her father. She walked past Kade and led Frederick through the den and out the French doors. Melissa and Claudio turned at their approach. There was no guilt on their faces, but Claudio hastily took the cigarette from her and snuffed both in the ashtray.

Bethany flung herself into her stepmother's arms. "Thank you! Thank you for loving us and protecting Daddy's reputation. I understand now, but back then it would have been too much."

She turned to the priest before Melisa could respond and took him in a hug as well. "I've always loved you, Uncle Claudio. Now I love you even more, understanding all you did for Sissa when she needed support. You've always been there for everyone."

Bethany took Melissa and Claudio both into an embrace before stepping back to see the astonishment on their faces and enjoy the laughter from her father. Seeing the obvious warmth and love between Melissa and Claudio gave her hope that her friendship with Kade didn't need to suffer in spite of Phoebe's actions.

She kissed her father's cheek. "I'm going dancing."

The gramophone played a Charleston tune while Alexander out danced Tabitha. Magdalene partnered with Emmett, Simon with Louisa, and Asher spun little Amelia. Feeling the loss of the weight from her shoulders, Bethany sashayed to where Kade and Abraham lounged on the couch. The islander was quickest, jumping to snatch her hand. He led her across the floor and staked the spot by the piano.

Unselfconscious and free from guilt, she enjoyed the dance with gangly Abraham more so than any other partner in her life. He didn't dance well, but that didn't stop him from having fun. His charming smile and mass of freckles created the illusion of mischievousness more suited to boys Asher and Simon's age.

"You're really something else, Beth," he told her while Alexander changed recordings. "I was always wrapped up with Kade on my visits that I never paid you mind, but now I know why he thinks so highly of you. Could I call on you when I'm in town?"

"No you don't." Kade went between them as the next tune began, a sultry Latin beat filling the air. Bethany blushed as Kade's right hand settled low on her back in mimic of the style of tango Alexander indulged in with Magdalene. When she looked over, Alexander had his wife in an amorous hold, their hips pressed together as he dipped her back.

"Don't worry about them, Tiger. I know you aren't ready for anything like that."

She giggled, which turned into a grin as Melissa entered the dance floor on Claudio's arm while Frederick settled beside Louisa on the sofa. Across the room, Abraham followed Tabitha's lead because he had no sense of rhythm.

Seeing her interest in the other couple, Kade shook his head. "I heard what he said to you. Don't think of him as a possibility, Tiger."

"Aren't you supposed to support your best friend in his endeavors?"

"Not if a sweet girl like you is involved." He pressed closer and swayed her into a shallow dip.

"I've known Abe as long as I remember, same as you, though I haven't been around him as much."

"He's a good guy, but a bit of a cad when it comes to girls. It'd be safer to stay clear."

And what of you and your infractions? Would Abe warn me away from you as well after your hours with Phoebe?

As though he read her mind, he reddened and changed the subject. "You seem happier since you started dancing. Did you have a good conversation with your father?"

Not trusting her voice at the moment, she nodded and looked to Melissa and Claudio. While not as scandalous as Alexander and Magdalene, they were just as passionate with their precise motions and their cheeks touching. Seeing where her attentions were, Kade leaned closer.

"I don't know if I can match their style, but I'd be a heap better at attempting than Abe."

"Don't start comparing yourself to set yourself up as the better man."

He laughed, dimples on full display. "You're special to me, Tiger. You always have been but in the last few days—"

The song came to a close and the room quieted.

Frederick stood. "I think it's time for me to get my girls home."

"Is Beth staying?" Tabitha asked.

"Not this time. You have a house full with the Walkers and Claudio." Frederick went to Alexander and Magdalene to tell them goodbye. He made his way around the room, nudging Louisa away from her friends. When he got to Kade, he shook his hand. "All the best this summer, Kade. Remember what I told you and think about it."

"Yes, sir. Thank you." Kade left a kiss on Bethany's cheek. "Take care of yourself, Tiger, and enjoy your job."

"Thanks. You too." She turned to Abraham for a hug. "Take care of Kade for us."

He slapped Kade on the back. "I'll teach him everything a good sailor needs to know, both on and off the boats."

Claudio followed the Davenports to the vestibule, a hand at Bethany's elbow. "I'll see you tomorrow for another blessing, *Principessa*."

"Thank you, Uncle Claudio."

"Could I get one, too?" Louisa asked.

"Of course!" He grinned. "Blessings for all."

"Come for lunch or supper and we could have a picnic like we used to. We could, couldn't we Mom?"

"Claudio is always welcome, and I'd be happy to host him for a meal," Melissa said.

"I'll telephone in the morning," he assured Louisa.

On the veranda, Frederick paused to kiss Melissa. Bethany tugged Louisa ahead to give them privacy but she heard Melissa's words.

"You don't need to worry, Freddy."

"I know, Beloved. But I want to remind you how grateful I am to have your devotion."

Nineteen

Alexander stepped out of the bathroom, towel riding low about his hips. Magdalene sat at Lucy's old dressing table, fixing her hair for the supper auction they were attending that night—some fundraiser for one of the charities she volunteered with. Her lips were pulled down at the corners. Their bedroom door was open, but for once they were alone in the house. The hour previous, Claudio left with the children to spend Saturday evening with the Davenports.

Alexander boldly crossed the room to kiss her bare shoulder. "What is it, Maggie?"

"I'm worried about Kade."

He kissed her other shoulder beside the sparkling red strap of her evening gown. "You saw him this afternoon when he stopped in. In a week's time, he's still alive and well. Tan and lively, even."

"He did look happy, but I'm worried how everything with Phoebe affected him."

"Kade's a man now and will figure it out. He's the spawn of your mighty Scot, after all."

Magdalene laughed. Upon catching sight of her reflection, she leaned toward the mirror, fingering the smile creases at the corners of her eyes. "We were supposed to grow old together. Douglas wanted to hold hands in rocking chairs on the porch as our grandchildren ran about."

"I'm honored to fill the vacancy, though I'd much rather rock a bed than sit in a chair." Alexander tasted her neck, breathing in her rose infused scent. "You grow lovelier each year, Magdalene."

She stood for an embrace, soft hands skimming his scars across his humid skin. "And I love you more each day we're together."

"Show me." He thrust his tongue into her mouth and allowed his hands to drift down the dress as he shifted backward. He broke the kiss as his legs met the bed. "There's only a towel between you and the man of your dreams."

Her shove placed him on his back, and she smiled down at him on the bed. "We have a supper party to attend."

"But we have the house to ourselves. How often does that happen?"

Magdalene's earrings sparkled with the lowering of her chin for her to better observe him.

"I know you like what you see, Magdalene. The group already has our money for the dinner tickets. Do we need to go bid on something that will sit on a shelf and gather dust? Wouldn't you rather be here, in these arms with this tongue doing all sorts of tantalizing things to your body?" He brought his legs around her waist, locking his ankles behind her.

Her squeal of surprise turned into a laugh. "You know I would, but our food would go to waste and—"

"I'll grovel and beg. I'm shameless in my pursuit when it comes to your touch."

"We'll go to eat, but leave before the auction."

He sat up, hands replacing his legs for purchase of her waist. "Supper only. I want my dessert here. And here. And here." He touched her womanly parts with the words, ending on his feet with his mouth pressed to hers.

"It's a deal. Now, please get your tuxedo on."

After dressing in his white tails, Alexander drove them to the country club and escorted his wife into the banquet room. The prideful gaze he'd inherited from his father shrouded him with an air of distinction, Magdalene on his arm a glowing award.

While she chatted with the coordinator, he watched from their table. The red fringed short gown and sleeveless cut made her warm tones burn with delectableness. Lucy in red always excited him because it was at odds with her pale coloring, but Magdalene in red appeared to be her natural state—feisty and bold.

An unknown man reading place cards slowed. Leaning over the empty seats on the opposite side of the round table, he paused at the back of the chair on the other side of Magdalene's at the eight-person setting.

"Here I am, at last." The man grinned at Alexander and offered a hand. "Bradford Petty."

Alexander stood and took his hand. "Alexander Melling."

Bradford Petty appeared to be a bachelor in his late twenties—polished but lacking that finishing touch a woman would have seen to, like his crooked bowtie and one lock of hair disheveled on his side-parted, dark hair.

"I moved here at the beginning of May from Montgomery as part of the engineering firm that plans the highways for the state. The local boss told me I need to get out to events like this to mingle with the right people if I'm to have a proper time."

Alexander nodded, resettling in his chair, attention already back on Magdalene's figure across the way. "Fundraisers are big in Mobile. Almost as big as Mardi Gras."

The younger man followed his gaze. "And the women appear to be exceptional for the most part. Can you image what type of lady wears red to a charity function? I'd like to see if the view of her front is as fine as the backside."

Magdalene turned to speak to another lady who joined her group, causing Mr. Petty's eyes to widen with interest. "I wish it were carnival season. From what I hear, some of the masquerades are quite loose. I'd like nothing better than to approach that one with a private invitation. Either that or touch first and ask permission later. What do you think, Mr. Melling? Would that be allowed during Mardi Gras?"

Alexander stared opened mouth at the man, dumbfounded that anyone would dare speak to him in such a way about his wife.

"Come on, I saw you gawking at her. Would I have a chance to handle a woman like—"

"*You*, absolutely not." Alexander's tone clipped the vulgar speech.

Mr. Petty smirked. "But you think someone else would have a chance?"

"Just one person. *Me.*" Alexander stood for Magdalene's return. "And if you ever speak about *my wife* like that again, I'll strike you."

Mr. Petty blanched. "I beg your pardon, Mr. Melling, I had no idea. I've never seen a man look upon his wife like you were."

"That's because no man has a wife as fine as mine."

Alexander went for Magdalene as soon as she turned fully to the table. Kissing her lips, he lingered a moment before tucking his arm around her. At the table, Bradford stood in greeting, cheeks ruddy from his indiscretion.

"Our tablemate, Magdalene, Mr—"

"Bradford Petty, at your humble service, Mrs. Melling."

"It's a pleasure to meet you, but please call me Magdalene." Her brilliant smile brought a gleam to the man's green eyes.

"I'm new in town. Could I impose on you to help me meet the best possible Mobilians that an unattached gentleman of twenty-eight would find agreeable?"

"If you mean charming young ladies—"

"None could be as charming as you, Miss Magdalene, but any way you could assist me would be wonderful."

Alexander did his best not to grumble while Magdalene conversed with him before their other table mates arrived. Grateful for the attention Sean and Hattie Spunner paid the newcomer when they joined, as well as Mr. and Mrs. Marley and their unattached daughter, Alexander took the opportunity to place his hand on Magdalene's knee.

"Remember we're taking dessert elsewhere," he whispered in her ear. She nodded and moved to lean back, but he gripped her knee. He softened his touch and trailed a fingertip over her silk stocking. "If we aren't out of here in one hour, I'll not be responsible for my behavior."

Magdalene placed her hand on his thigh, squeezing in a pulsing rhythm, and winked.

He groaned—all eyes at the table turning to him as Magdalene calmly removed her hand.

"I'm sorry," he told the group, "but I'm not feeling well. Maggie, I'm afraid I won't be able to make it much longer. I know you were looking forward to the auction."

Sean Spunner, now a respected judge and father of four, choked on a laugh as he looked to Alexander with a knowing smirk.

The others settled back into their conversations as they finished their crab cakes and salads. When Alexander tried to make his exit twenty minutes later, the judge intervened.

"Come on, Alex," Sean said as he stood and placed a hand on Magdalene's bare arm. "You're capable of getting yourself home. Allow Magdalene to stay with us. Hattie will look after her."

Alexander grimaced as though in pain, but it was over his annoyance at Sean thwarting his getaway.

Magdalene smiled at Sean. "I really should administer to my husband."

"He's always been a tad delicate." Sean leaned close, but spoke loud enough for the whole table to hear. "Melling was the puniest scamp on the block. Pale, putrid. Yes, you better get him home before he faints. Shall I escort you out, in case I need to carry him?"

She took a moment to control a laugh. "I'm sure we'll be fine, Judge Spunner. Thank you. Good night, everyone. It was lovely to meet you, Mr. Petty."

Alexander slowly walked Magdalene across the room and through the lobby. At his automobile, he removed his tuxedo jacket and slid behind the wheel. With a provocative smile, she settled under his right arm as he pulled out of the parking lot. He thought of driving to the stables because it was closer than home, but he didn't think Magdalene would appreciate the sentiment in her evening gown. By the time they were in town, his arousal was so intense that his knuckles strained over the steering wheel.

A cool breeze helped chase the lingering heat of the day from the air. He pulled into the garage knowing what he wanted and where. They held hands to the backdoor. As soon as they were inside, he scooped her into his arms and deposited her at a swing bed on the upstairs sleeping porch. The area was lit only from the patio lights below and the moon above.

"I'll be right back!" He dashed inside and brought back two crisp sheets and several pillows.

Alexander settled the sheet over the mattress, each of them tucking a side under. Smiling across the bed as they worked, Magdalene's appreciative gaze caused an ache in his groin. They wasted no time shedding clothes, and were soon in each other's arms between the smooth sheets.

"Don't feel you need to rush things. I'm in heaven holding you like this." He kissed her slow and deep until her roaming hands cause him to hiss with awareness of his needs.

It was all about sensations from then on—the chirping buzz of the cicadas in the trees, the cool sheets warming from their friction, and the salty-sweet tang of her skin. Whether above or below, Alexander relished in the moment and the connection he shared with Magdalene. *Sweet, sensual Magdalene Jones of Seven Hills. My wife, my lover, my friend, my all.*

***

Several hours later, Alexander lay in the hammock on the patio with a cigarette. Claudio stretched in the nearby lounge chair with his own smoke. Strains of Tabitha's piano chords floated into the night—soft and dreamlike as Asher, Simon, and Amelia were in bed.

Alexander exhaled. "How was your evening at the Davenports'?"

"Wonderful, but I am worried about Bethany."

"So am I. She's as stubborn as her father and has already been tested too much in her innocent years."

"Yet she worries deeply, like Lucy." Claudio folded his legs and leaned forward. "She is changed from her ordeal in Seacliff Manor."

"But it's not all from the demons." Alexander looked to his friend. "She was in love with Kade. It broke her to see how far he was swayed. She lost her trust that day in her sister and her first love. In many ways, it's like what happened between Freddy, Lucy, and I."

Nodding, the priest took another drag. "But it worked out for you all with time."

"She's young—five years younger than Lucy was that year, seven from me and Freddy."

"At least her work keeps her occupied. She is happy when discussing what alterations she does and the ideas she has for designs of her own. Melissa is watching her closely."

"And how is it between Melissa and Freddy and you?"

Laughing, Claudio opened his collar. "I return with no strangle marks or black eyes, but Frederick watches. Not untrustingly, but with an air of a man in awe."

"As if he feels honored Melissa chose to stay with him when a smooth-talking Italian lover presented himself?"

Magdalene exited the French doors. "You're not far off, Alex. Freddy knows what a treasure he has with Melissa, how he broke her heart those years, and the fact that she loved her time in Italy—which included a liaison with a certain winemaker."

"That was nothing compared to what we share." Claudio took a satisfied drag and leaned back.

Magdalene frowned. "And how can you possess the infamous Seacliff gaze when you and Melissa never—"

"But they did!" Alexander sat up so fast he almost spilled from the hammock. "That Christmas we spent there while Freddy was at war. She was depressed and I sent for Claudio to come for the day. I even brought him to her bed one time."

"Alexander!" Magdalene's hands were on her hips, defining their luscious curves beneath the loose house dress she'd changed into after their intimacies.

"She needed to be cuddled and I wasn't about to crawl into bed with her myself, at least not with Lucy there."

"So you would have otherwise?"

Unable to resist a tease, Alexander raised his brows and produced a mischievous smile—made more realistic from the flash of memory of the kissing session he'd shared with Melissa. "You know I'd do *anything* for Melissa."

"In that case…." She dropped onto the lounge chair, snuggling to Claudio until her head rested on his chest and her leg tightened around his like a hook. "I know Claudio would do anything for me, and I for him."

Alexander found himself on his knees in an attempt of springing out of the hammock. Their laughter brought him to his feet, and then he launched himself atop them both.

"Then share the love, you sinful creatures!" He kissed Claudio's cheek and then Magdalene's lips. "You know there's enough of me to go around."

Laughing, Claudio wriggled out from beneath him. "I think this is my hint to say goodnight, Mellings. Are we attending early Mass?"

"Yes." Alexander settled beside his wife, nuzzling into her neck.

"You may leave me at the cathedral for the day as I am to meet with Bishop Allen in the afternoon. I would like to spend the morning in contemplation and prayer on the grounds."

"He's checking in with his wayward deacon, is he?" Alexander teased.

"It is I who sought the appointment. I wish to offer my services as an exorcist to the diocese."

Magdalene reached for Claudio's hand with a huge smile. "It's about time, Claudio."

Twenty

Phoebe groaned when Hans yanked opened the curtain in her room.

"I hear your curves crying from the wood to be set loose."

"It's not even six yet!"

"Free room and board, love. You're at my disposal any time."

"But my father will be here with—"

"All the more reason for me to work early since I've promised you time off. You might want to do some cleaning when I don't need you posing. It would help give your father a more favorable impression of your living situation. Ten minutes." He left, showcasing his bare backside beneath his smock.

Phoebe rolled her eyes and cursed under her breath, stumbling to her washbasin to splash water on her face. It was empty.

She never thought to ask Hans if he had indoor plumbing before agreeing to move in, or a cook or housekeeper. All her fine clothes were worthless because Hans preferred her nude as she moved about. She didn't mind the arrangement until last week when he'd asked her to scrub the primitive wood floor. Afterward, he'd lugged in bucket after bucket of water for her to bathe in the tin washtub situated in the dumpy kitchen. It was a luxury she relished—until he invited three of his artist friends over to sketch her so he could compare their visons to his own images of her before beginning the sculpture. She'd sat in the cold water almost an hour until she pulled the strength from her anger to stand before the unwanted attention and marched herself dripping wet across the clean floor.

In her sleep deprived situation that morning, she slipped on her mother's kimono and stalked to the pump off the back porch with her pitcher. She washed her face and set the coffee pot on the stove to heat water before hanging the kimono on the back of her door. With a disgruntled sigh, she flopped onto the table before his work station.

"I don't need your theatrics, love. Do I need to kiss the impertinence out of you?"

Her heart rate increased. "It wouldn't hurt to try."

"That coy smile tells me it's all in your control, so drop it." He turned back to his tools.

The familiar anger she felt toward him while he worked returned, as well as the flush across her cheeks which she saw in the mirror on the wall across from her. Sitting for an artist wasn't the romantic scene she had in mind—at least not with Hans. His regular self was passionate, but the working artist was objective and vilifying in his drive. Expecting the first of the two—a handsome sculptor gazing upon her with lust so each session ended with him making love to her—she was disappointed to not only be ignored by his natural man, but to be chastised if she tried to urge him toward desire while he worked.

Fixing them both a cup of coffee, Phoebe set his in the designated place so it wouldn't disturb his work if jarred. She drank hers quickly and returned to the perch to be looked over for her figure rather than what she could bring to a relationship. Hans spoke not a word when ready, only inclined his head in approval of her positioning. Three hours she sat, her short breaks used to tidy the cottage. When she was dismissed at nine, Phoebe dressed in the sensible blue pleated drop-waist that Bethany made her and hung her father's pearls around her neck—both the strand from her birthday when he was gone to war and the longer one from the previous Christmas.

Phoebe brushed her hair, then snipped a few wayward curls with Grandma Easton's scissors. After setting her makeup, she returned to the main living area. Hans carefully draped the massive chunk of oak that was his present canvas, but the nude sketches of her were tacked all over the wall in the work corner. There would be no hiding those from her father or the priest. With the last of his supplies set in order, Hans looked at Phoebe as though seeing her for the first time.

"I'm reminded why I chose you—the way that blue affects your complexion is marvelous. You look good enough to paint, Phoebe." He took her in his arms and brought his mouth to hers. A lock of his wavy hair tickled her forehead with the motion.

She kissed him back with full awareness of the growing desire he had for her. It didn't take much for him to coax her into his bedroom. Hans was skilled enough not to leave her wanting, though his main concern was his own release. Half an hour later, she was no worse from the romp and presentable when a knock sounded.

Phoebe didn't think a few weeks would make a difference, but a lump formed in her throat when she opened the door. She flung herself at his broad form and pushed back the threat of an emotional reunion. "Daddy!"

"Princess."

Frederick's hug was tight, comforting, and she was pleased he wasn't in a hurry to release her. *He's not mad. He still loves me!* She found no bitterness in her own heart.

"Did you have Pancake Time this morning?"

Her father laughed. "We did, and still miss you each week."

She turned to the priest. "Uncle Claudio, it means so much that you wished to see me before going home."

"I could not leave you without another blessing, *Principessa*." His hug felt almost as secure as her father's. "You are loved and prayed for."

Phoebe stepped out of his arms and looked to her father. "Would you care to walk to the pier or—"

"I would like to see your living arrangements first."

"I'm not sure if Hans is—"

"Of course I'm up, love. Bring your guests in." Hans stood behind her, strong hand on her shoulder. "I was hard at work early this morning. When I do that, I typically nap afterward but I didn't want to miss seeing you, Mr. Davenport."

Dressed in a day suit—the same one he'd worn when collecting Phoebe at Seacliff—Hans made an imposing figure. Phoebe smiled at him admirably.

"I'm afraid my workspace occupies most of the room, but you're welcome to sit." Hans motioned to a weathered settee and collected two chairs from the rickety dining table further on.

But her father didn't seem to be in a hurry. He walked toward the work area, hands clasped behind him and Claudio at his side. The men didn't gawk at the drawings, but they took them in with a sweeping glance and then looked over the recently finished carvings of native birds on the shelf below the sketches.

Frederick nodded at Hans. "Your talent is great."

"Thank you, Mr. Davenport. I manage to make a living with it, though humble at present. I believe Phoebe will help me reach my next level of success." Hans lifted her hand to his lips and kissed the back of it. "Show your father your room, love. It's her sanctuary and she sleeps alone there each night. I only enter it to wake her if she's needed to model in the mornings."

It was true. Hans never took her in rapture in her tiny room—he entered only when he needed her artistically. All their sex was had in his larger bed or the common area without remorse because he'd presented her with a diaphragm her first day there. The only bad part was he kicked her out as soon as he was done with her.

He's never held me in his arms like Kade did that day.

Claudio took a seat on one of the dining chairs while Phoebe led her father to her room. Walking in, she realized the sparseness of the pine board space was in line with the barrenness of her room at the Moores'—which she complained about relentlessly.

The only decoration beside the small mirror over the dresser was her mother's novels on the window ledge because there was no functional furniture besides the narrow bed and dresser—which was piled with makeup and the wash basin. Freddy crossed the room and fingered the pastel book spines.

"It's different than what you're used to. Are you truly happy, Phoebe?"

She bit her lip and nodded. "As much as I can be with my muddled thoughts."

"Do you wish to come home?" he asked, brown eyes expectant.

"I can never go home, Daddy. You told me that at the hospital."

"I might have been wrong, Princess." His hands were on her shoulders. "That does happen from time to time. I've pushed those I love away before."

She hooked a tear from the corner of her eye before it could streak her face. "It's not fair to the others for me to be there, staining their lives with my mistakes. I'll be fine here. Hans does care for me in his way. He doesn't show his project to others, but I've seen glimpses of his carving. It's going to be a knockout. He'll make money from it, Daddy."

"I have no doubt it will be lovely because it's of you." He kissed her forehead and then pulled her to his chest. "You're beautiful, just like your mother."

***

Two hours later, Phoebe entered a Fairhope café on her father's arm, Claudio behind them. She'd forgotten what it was like to walk the streets with Frederick Davenport and was surprised by the amount of people who knew him on that side of the bay. Many were weekenders from the city, but even the locals knew of his war heroics and boxing championships from the previous decade.

They settled at a corner table after their productive morning of shopping and seeing the sights. The three had gone to a secondhand store and picked out a small bookcase for her bedroom, as well as an armchair for the main room so she'd have a pleasant spot to read in. Buying her several new books was also part of their excursion, along with setting up a charge account at the nearby grocer beginning with a five dollar credit to start her off.

"We have to move on after we eat, Princess, but we'll see you back to Hans. We promised Alex we'd stop at Seacliff, and Claudio wants to visit his old parish. We'll take the ferry from Daphne. If you change your mind, get on the ferry here and we'll meet you aboard this evening."

She shook her head before reaching for her coffee.

"The offer is there any time you need it, Phoebe." His voice was soft, loving. "But they do a fine Fourth of July celebration over here. You should enjoy that next weekend."

"Will anyone be at Seacliff for the holiday?"

A shadow crossed his eyes. "It isn't for me to say, but I think it's best no one comes to visit you in your present circumstances, especially unmarried family members."

"You'll give Beth a hug from me and tell her I miss her, won't you? And tell Sissa and Louisa I love them."

"Of course." Her father took her hand.

"And Poppy and Asher?"

He nodded with a bittersweet smile.

"Kade," she whispered the name.

Her father looked away.

"He is gone for the summer, *Principessa*."

"What?"

They were quiet while the waitress brought their food, and Claudio thanked her before answering Phoebe. "He went back to the island with the Walkers. He is working on the boats until his next semester at the university begins."

"But he had a job at the stables! Who is seeing to Prince?"

"Asher and Simon now work there four days a week. Your horse is well cared for."

Phoebe stayed silent, mulling over the idea of sending Kade a note of apology. Her father picked up on her mood and as they finished their sandwiches.

"Let him go, Princess. It's for the best." Turning to Claudio, he spoke louder. "I'd like to secure the hired car. Would you meet me at the corner in a few minutes."

"Certainly, Frederick."

He left the money for their meal on the table on his way out.

"*Principessa*, where would you have your blessing?"

"There's a lovely oak with good shade near the cottage."

"Then you must stop us when we reach it."

She nodded, gazing into his dark eyes. "Uncle Claudio, do you love Sissa?"

"*Sì*, very much," he said without delay.

"Uncle Eddie told me you and Sissa had an affair, though she denies it."

"Melissa is an honest woman, no?" His accent was more pronounced than Phoebe remembered, probably from his years spent back in his homeland.

"Yes."

"Then do not allow questions in regard to her character to cause trouble. She has been a wonderful mother-figure to you and deserves your respect." He stood and offered his arm. "Let us find your father."

Frederick waited for them outside, a hand behind his back. When they stopped beside him, he brought forth a box of chocolates.

"I hope you'll allow me to look in on you when I'm in the area, Princess."

"Yes, Daddy." She flung her arms about his neck. "I'm sorry for all the trouble I've caused."

At the oak, the little group paused for Claudio to bless Phoebe. Afterward, he took her chin in his hand. "I hope to return, *Principessa*. Do not fear asking for help if I am not here. Your father and Alexander know who to turn to."

"Thank you, Uncle Claudio." She hugged him and then took her father's arm to go the rest of the way to the cottage. She paused on the pathway beside the automobile that would take them north. "Thank you, Daddy. I had a great time and I appreciate everything."

"Shall I see you inside?"

"No, but I appreciate it." She kissed his cheek and hugged him. "Be sure to tell everyone hello and give them a hug from me, especially Beth."

"I will, Princess." He kissed her forehead. "Telephone or come whenever you'd like. I love you."

Phoebe managed to smile and wave, clutching her chocolate box in the other hand. When the automobile pulled away, she opened the screen door and found Hans sprawled in her new armchair with the newspaper, naked as the day he was born.

"There you are, love. Be on the table in five minutes."

Twenty-One

Monday, October 25, 1926

Dearest Claudio,

Thank you for the telegram seeking to find out our safety the other week. I hope Alex's reply got to you in a timely fashion to relieve your fears. If you haven't heard yet, the hurricane on September twentieth made landfall near the Florida state line. We were on the better side of the storm, as is said, but suffered damages just the same. Not our sound home, but the area in general. As you can imagine, we were all frantic about our island friends and Phoebe across the bay— much closer to the major destruction—but all are accounted for.

It took me so long to reply because I was busy with volunteer work and seeing to the children. While the schools were closed, I kept us all at work on relief efforts: gathering donations and supplies to those near the waterfront as well as my regular hours at Sacred Heart and other auxiliaries. All is back to normal in our household, but prayer and work are still needed elsewhere.

Have you heard about Bishop Allen? He passed away last Thursday. It may be selfish of me, but I wonder how this will hold up the possibility of you transferring here. Alexander said it could be next year before a new bishop is called, but I don't think that's soon enough. I can't speak of my concerns to him because he was deeply affected by the bishop's passing. As many times as he had been admonished by the man, Alex did love and respect him. I don't wish to sound like I am complaining about not having you here when all the parishioners in the area are mourning, but I miss you, dear friend. Please be persistent in your request to return to Mobile. I had my heart set on you being here for Christmas, but I suppose that won't happen.

Now for some good news. Tabitha is seventeen. We had a birthday supper for her with the extended family. As it was a Friday, Kade took her out dancing with his friends afterward. Bethany was invited, but she declined. She's kept herself isolated much of the time since the drama at Seacliff, working extra hours at home on her sewing projects, besides the days in the shop. Tabby only gets her to attend the cinema once a month when they used to enjoy that weekly. We had hoped that when Kade returned she would join in with him and Tabby like she used to, but she hasn't. Hopefully things will change when she and Tabby debut this winter.

Amelia is shining at school and an amazing rider. I'm still upset over Alex buying her a pony for her seventh birthday since she's the youngest and there will be no one to pass it to, except maybe the Adams family, when she's outgrown the dear thing. Henry and his children are often at the stables. Horatio works there with the boys twice a week. Simon and Asher loved working there so much over the summer they've kept it up two afternoons a week as well as Saturdays. Kade and the boys were a great help with clearing the trails after the hurricane.

Yes, Kade is back at the stables when he isn't at school, but he finally declared his major last month—mathematics. It appears Freddy, being the dear he is (and most likely in an attempt to prove he held nothing against him for what happened with Phoebe), offered him an internship at Davenport and Adams Allied Accountants if he was interested. He should have enough credits to begin at the office next year while he finishes his degree with the specialized courses. Though he doesn't say it, I know Alex is a bit disappointed Kade didn't choose law, but there is still Simon, Asher, and Amelia to go. One of them is bound to want to follow in his footsteps, and if I had to place a wager, it would be on Amelia. She thinks her father hangs the moon each night—and I'm certain it was Alex that gave her that idea, the scoundrel.

Melissa's told me she began writing you last month with Freddy's blessing. I think it's lovely, though my first reaction was jealousy that I'm not the only woman you're writing. And now my letters will be that much shorter without having to give news of the Davenports, as you will have the news straight from Melissa. If that isn't a reason to return to us, I don't know what is!

Love and prayers, both for you and the Pope or whoever installs new bishops and exorcists in our city,

---

***

Bethany woke early on Thanksgiving. Checking the mirror on her dressing table to see if she looked a day older than sixteen, she shrugged at her familiar reflection. The Davenports had a quiet supper party with just the four of them the night before, but today would be more festive with a Thanksgiving meal and party combined at the Mellings' house. She dressed in a new design of her own—a Madonna blue knee-length sheath—that she coupled with her first set of Parisian lingerie, her gift from Mademoiselle Bisset.

As always, she clasped her locket around her neck, kissing the engraved iris before lowering it to her chest as she whispered "I love you, Momma."

Across the hall in Phoebe's old room, Louisa still slept. Her half-sister took over the space earlier in the year, allowing Bethany more freedom. She often sewed late into the night or woke early to complete a project before going to work. Passing her parents' room, the rustle of someone dressing sounded through the closed door.

After eating a muffin and drinking tea alone, Bethany joined Melissa in the study. Her stepmother worked her way through a stack of nonfiction books from the library in hopes of finding her next great adventure. Bethany spent the morning browsing *Cultural Fashions from Around the World,* the book Melissa gave her for her birthday, and dreaming up ideas she could tackle on the electric sewing machine her father gifted her.

When they left at eleven, Frederick took his daughter's arm. "As the young woman of honor today, I want you to ride with me upfront, Little Princess."

"You must, Beth," Melissa told her. "Father's orders."

Once they were parked at the Mellings' house, Louisa ran through the back gate in search of the boys.

Her father once again linked arms with Bethany as they walked to the front veranda. "I'm worried about you, Beth. Don't hide away. Enjoy the day and your family and friends."

"I'll try, Daddy."

Asher held the door open. After the Davenports were inside, he hugged his half-sister. "Did you have a good birthday, Beth?"

"Yes, thank you. And I'm sure I'll have a great second birthday today."

Asher turned to take Frederick's coat and Melissa's wrap. The adults went into the front room, but Asher took Bethany's hand and went for the hall.

"Not yet, Ash!" Alexander called. "Bring her in so Maggie and I can tell her Happy Birthday."

Bethany went first to Magdalene. Then Alexander took her in a hug that lifted her off the floor.

"Hello, stranger. I'm beginning to think I need to speak with Mademoiselle Bisset about giving you Saturdays off so you can stay with us like you used to. Seeing you once a month isn't good enough for me, Knight Bethany." He set her back down and smiled up at her. "See, it's a shock that you're taller than me now! When did that happen?"

"Poppy, I love and miss you too." She hugged him, smelling his familiar sandalwood scent that was just as comforting as her father's aftershave.

"Then come stay with us or I'll think you've disowned me."

"I'd like to return to my weekends here, but I'd never disown you, Poppy." She opened her locket to her mother's and his side and smiled. "I kiss this every morning when I put it on. You're family, always."

Alexander gazed at the miniatures with a wistful smile before taking Bethany's cheek in his hand and kissing her forehead. "I love you and will always love your mother. Never forget either information. Now go on and see the others."

Asher put a protective hand on her shoulder as they went down the hall. "We all love you here."

"I know you do, Ash. I've missed everyone, but it's been good to work these past months."

"So you don't think too much?"

She nodded. "It's comforting to know you understand me."

When they walked into the morning room, a great shout of "Surprise!" erupted.

Louisa, Amelia, the three Campbell siblings, the whole Adams family, Maxwell Easton, and Abraham Walker were there in silly party hats. Her fathers and their wives came up behind her, Alexander nudging her forward until she was besieged with hugs and kisses—including a quick one on the mouth from Abraham that resulted in a scowl from Kade.

Then, Bethany was seated in a prominent armchair with a tiara on her head.

Amelia brought the first gift. "For you, Beth, from Poppy and all of us."

"But we couldn't have done it without Max." Alexander motioned to his brother-in-law, sitting with Frederick.

"Oh!" was all Bethany could say when she lifted the lid on the exquisite silks from the Orient. Bolts of jewel toned solids as well as several floral prints embellished with golden threads filled the deep box. She ran her fingers over the rich fabrics, relishing the cool silkiness of them. "They're gorgeous! I never would have asked for anything so perfect. Thank you!"

"You deserve the luxury, Knight Bethany. And you're to make things for yourself with *at least* half of the yardage. Don't give it all away." Alexander kissed her cheek before returning to his seat beside Magdalene.

"Amelia, bring mine now." Maxwell gave a smaller box to the girl who ran it over.

Inside were specialty threads, ribbons, buttons, and other notions that would coordinate perfectly with the fabrics.

"Thank you, Uncle Max." She set the gifts aside to cross the room and embrace him—the patriarch of the Easton family. Knowing they'd planned months ago to place the orders and have it shipped touched her all the more. "Everything is wonderful."

Tabitha gave her a recording of a new dance song as well as a special edition magazine about the latest Hollywood styles. Virginia Adams delivered the gift from her family. Inside the handsomely carved box was a new pair of fabric scissors.

"Give them to me or Kade to sharpen at least once a month," Henry told her.

She nodded and looked to Kade for the first time since he'd hugged her after the surprise. The corner of his mouth turned up in a smile.

"I'd be happy to assist you, Tiger."

Then Abraham launched himself from his seat and pulled a small box out of his jacket pocket, offering it to Bethany.

"Happy Sixteenth."

"Thank you, Abe."

He squatted beside her chair as she opened the box, displaying a strand of tiny seashells. "I've been collecting them since I was a boy. These are the daintiest of the lot. I always wanted to make them into jewelry for a pretty girl. It took me a while to figure out the best way to secure them, but I think it turned out well."

Bethany took the strand and marveled over the workmanship. "You did it yourself?"

"All except the clasp. I wanted something secure, so I brought it to a jeweler for that." His freckled face—so like the speckled shells—looked pleased. "May I put it on you?"

"Yes, thank you." Bethany held out her wrist.

"It's not a bracelet. I didn't want to give you something that could snag on the fabrics when you work. It's an anklet."

She felt her cheeks warm as he gently lifted her foot, setting it atop his bent knee to fasten it over her stocking. Amelia, Virginia, and Charlene were immediately at her feet as Abraham walked away with a cocky smile.

"Look, Ginny!" Amelia exclaimed. "There's pink and a rainbow of colors. Do you ever see shells like this when you go to the island?"

Skin tingling from Abraham's touch, Bethany looked to Tabitha on her right.

Her friend grinned and leaned closer. "Kade's redder than you."

Maxwell said farewell so he could return to his family for the holiday. The adults went for the front room and the youngest to the backyard. Tabitha stayed with Bethany, going through the silks.

"I know what Poppy said, but if you can bare to part with some of the—"

"Tabby," Kade said as he crossed his arms, "you know if you say what you like Beth would give it to you, even if it's what she had her heart set on. She knows what colors look best on you and will take that into consideration when choosing for herself."

Tabitha lowered her head a moment. "I'm sorry. They're all beautiful, Beth. What did you get from your parents?"

"Daddy got me a new sewing machine and—"

"More of an excuse to ignore your friends." Tabitha frowned.

"I'm doing what I like." She defended herself with too much force. "But I'm sorry if I've been neglectful. It's nothing against you, Tabby."

"I'm here all weekend," Abraham announced as he plopped onto the floor before Bethany, huge smile charming its way into her heart. "I'll make sure you don't ignore Tabby by taking you both out tomorrow night. Saturday too, if you'll have me."

"I'm off tomorrow, but work until four Saturday."

"Then I promise not to keep you out too late."

***

Friday afternoon, Bethany worked a simple pullover dress for Louisa on the electric sewing machine to get the feel of it. Her little sister was at the Mellings' to spend time with Asher and Simon since they had the day off from work and school, and her father and Melissa were on an automobile ride through the north county, enjoying his extra day off from the office. When the doorbell rang, she huffed at the interruption but hurried downstairs.

Abraham stood on the porch, half a dozen pink roses in his hand, rusty hair shining in the sunlight. "Hello, Beth."

"Abe!" She looked beyond for the familiar form of Kade, but Abraham was alone.

"I hope it's okay I came by. I wanted to spend some time with you before we all go out tonight. Brought you some flowers even."

"That's sweet. Thank you." She accepted the flowers as she opened the screen. "I'd invite you in but I'm alone. Daddy always told Phoebe she couldn't have callers inside if he and Sissa were gone. I assume it's the same rule for me, though the situation hasn't arrived."

"I can't be the first guy to call on you, Beth."

She smiled and looked at her bare feet—staring at his anklet. "You are."

"It's an honor to be your first. I'd be happy to sit out here or take you for a walk."

"We could sit out back. I'll put the flowers in water and meet you by the kitchen door. Would you like anything to drink?"

"No, thanks."

Heart racing, Bethany stopped at the mirror in the foyer, fingering her wavy bobbed hair. She looked down at the trousers which she liked to wear when sewing and the rumpled shirt with wayward threads stuck to the sleeves. It was too late to change into something more respectable, but she brushed the threads off her clothes. After placing the roses in a vase, she continued to the breakfast porch and slipped on her yard shoes.

Abraham looked her over with a broad grin as she jumped off the back steps. Feeling childish, she raised her chin and made an effort to walk respectfully to him.

"Don't get proper on me, Beth. I like to see your exuberance. You're too serious much of the time." He took her hand and led her to the double glider.

Sitting beside her, he immediately put his arm around her shoulders. Remembering Kade's words over the summer—that Abraham was a cad when it came to girls—gave her pause for two seconds. Bethany leaned slightly against him, letting him know she wasn't shying from his contact.

"Mind if I smoke?" he asked.

"I'd prefer you didn't if you plan on ki-ki—" She stuttered to a stop, cheeks warm.

Abraham turned to her, hazel eyes sparking mischief. "You want me to kiss you, Beth?"

"I thought *you* might want to after giving me the anklet and flowers, but it's fine if you don't. I'm sure I have some silly notions about how this is supposed to go."

His laugh echoed off the back of the house. "I'll take notions like that when they come from you, but they aren't silly. I snuck that quick kiss on you yesterday, but I'd like nothing more than to do it up right. Have you had a proper kiss yet, Beth?"

"Just once. He said he was sorry he'd done it, making me think I did something wrong."

"That boy was a damned fool. May I kiss you?"

She smiled and nodded. Abraham tilted her chin upward as his mouth lowered to hers. His lips were soft in comparison to his calloused hands. Keeping it slow and gentle, he pressed and nibbled against her lips longer than Bethany thought possible.

Leaning back, Abraham smiled. "Did you like that?"

Bethany nodded, happy to see the joy on his face.

"Would you like more?"

Nodding again, she went limp as he took her around the waist and pulled her closer. The heady sensation of his lips on hers and his hands splayed on her lower back created a tingling in her stomach and lower. She found herself wanting nothing more than to keep him there and moved her mouth provocatively to see that it happened.

Abraham clutched her tighter and kissed from her lips to her ear. "You're so sweet, Beth. May I taste more?"

Not understanding what he asked—but knowing she wanted everything—Bethany whispered in the affirmative.

Her breath hitched at the way the gold flecks in his eyes caught the sunlight. Then his mouth was back on hers, tongue slipping along the seam of her lips. And she understood. Opening to him, she tried not to think of the oddness of his tongue dancing with hers. It was hot, encompassing, and strange—but exciting. Bethany wrapped her arms around Abraham's shoulders and kissed him all the more.

What felt like hours later, he pulled away with his confident grin on display. "You're something special, Beth. Don't let anyone make you feel inferior."

Twenty-Two

Alexander dozed on the sofa in the morning room with Amelia after attending early Sunday Mass. The far-off ring of the telephone roused him. His arms tightened around his daughter and she snuggled onto his chest. With a sigh, he recalled his beautiful girl sitting with him and Asher while they sang the hymns beneath the glorious stained-glass windows of the cathedral. The moment could have only been more perfect if his wife was beside them.

As though conjured, Magdalene came to the doorway. "Telephone, Alex."

"Take a message, please."

She stepped closer. "It's Beth."

Knowing Bethany never asked for anything, he made her call his priority. Kissing Amelia, he shifted her so he could stand.

Pausing by Magdalene, he kissed her as well. "Stay with her?" he whispered.

She nodded and trailed a hand down his arm, squeezing his hand before he walked away.

Alexander closed himself in his den and found the extension waiting for him. "Good morning, Bethany Iris."

"Hello, Poppy. I need to speak with you, please."

"What can I do for you?"

"I want to talk in person. Would it be okay if I come over in half an hour? I'll come in the back and could meet you in your den if you leave the patio door open."

The remembrance of Phoebe tricking him into meeting with him in that very room ten months previous seared his mind. "Would you want Tabitha or Maggie to sit in?"

"Not Tabby, but if you think Miss Maggie would be interested in helping, that's fine."

She doesn't mind if Maggie is here so she's not coming to trap me. Of course she isn't—it's Bethany!

"Maggie's always happy to help."

"Thank you, Poppy. I'll be there in half an hour."

Alexander ran a hand through his hair and returned to the morning room. Amelia was curled on her side, her brunette hair a shiny cape around her shoulders while her pouty lips turned down at the corners in her slumber.

"I could watch her sleep all day, our perfect girl." He trailed his hands down Magdalene's back. "Bethany wants to speak to me privately but says you're welcome to join us."

"She's shy. I'll leave you to your discussion, but call for me if you think I should join."

"That's exactly what I was thinking."

Taking advantage of their quiet moment, Magdalene tightened her hold until she gripped his backside and pressed them together.

He nipped her earlobe. "Do you want me now, Magdalene?"

"I want you always, my lion, but I'll be patient."

"You know that's never been my strong suit." His kiss devoured her mouth and his hand claimed a breast through her soft blouse.

Her moan of submission unleashed his primal need. He ran for the stairs because he couldn't chance Bethany arriving early and finding him and Magdalene in raptures on the chaise. In their master suite, he escorted her to the bed and turned away long enough to lock the door. Alexander stepped out of his trousers on the way back, pulling his shirt over his head before joining his wife.

Ten minutes later, he was limp on the bed with a huge grin.

"You're everything I need. Please help me watch the clock and force me to dress in five minutes."

Magdalene laughed and fingered his scars. "I love spontaneous times with you as much as the planned for seductions."

"Speaking of seductions," he said with a teasing smile, "how about wearing that purple nightgown tonight?"

"The one cut down to here?" She trailed a finger between her breasts until it reached her navel.

"That would be the one."

He indulged in several kisses, and then pulled his clothes on.

"I'll be down soon," Magdalene promised. "Invite Bethany to stay for dinner."

Alexander didn't know if it would be best to have more company in the house while Kade was on bad terms with Abraham. When the boys had returned from taking Tabitha and Bethany to the cinema the previous night, they were arguing loud enough to wake Alexander from his sated sleep.

In his den, Alexander opened the French doors and lit a fire to take the chill out of the late November air. He was nursing a cigarette when Bethany stepped onto the patio, gold locket glinting at the chest of her black dress.

"Thank you for seeing me, Poppy." She shut the door as she entered and he snuffed his smoke in the ashtray before meeting her for a hug.

"Anytime, Knight Bethany. I'm happy to help, as is Magdalene."

Her smile shone from her Davenport eyes to her Easton chin. "I'd rather get right down to the matter."

Alexander nodded and motioned to the chaise.

"I'd prefer the desk, Poppy." She took the chair opposite his and waited for him to settle behind the mass of mahogany. "I was hoping you could see that Abe secures an invitation to the Order of Mayhem's ball and host him here for New Year's."

The eager yet dreamy look in her soft brown eyes said it all. Alexander immediately understood the disagreement between the guys. Family friend or not, he was sure Joe Walker's youngest wasn't the type Frederick would approve of for his daughter, and Kade would know it. A deckhand—wharf rat as Douglas had called them. Even if he was on his way to being a captain, Abraham was just as rough around the edges as any of the other islanders his age with scant education and prematurely weathered skin.

"Poppy? Could you?"

He reached for his cigarette case, flipping it over in his hands. "You want him here for your coming out ball?"

"Yes, but I don't think Daddy would approve of me having an official partner for my first masquerade."

"Do you have an understanding with Abe? Is he expecting an invitation?"

"No, neither. We like each other and had a pleasant time the past few days." She blushed, making her look even prettier. "I thought it would be fun to see him dressed up."

"Bethany Iris, you know I'd do anything for you. I'll extend the invitation and ask Maggie to speak with Claire to make sure Abe is welcomed at our home for the long weekend."

"Thank you, Poppy!" She jumped from her seat and hugged him.

"Would you take noon dinner with us? Magdalene wanted you to stay."

She nodded. "I'll go see if she needs help."

"I'll call your father and let him know you're staying." Alexander smiled after Bethany until the door closed once more.

He wasted no time dialing the other house.

"Davenports'."

"Darling Sissa."

"Dashing Poppy. Did Beth make it over all right?"

"Yes, and she's staying to dine with us. I hope that's okay."

"You know it is. Is everything all right? She seemed distracted when she left."

Alexander laughed. "She's more than all right. If I'm not mistaken, she's been grazed by one of Cupid's arrows."

"Oh no, and she went to you for advice?"

"I'm sure she'll confide in you before long. Our Beth needed my assistance securing an invitation to the New Year's ball for the lucky guy."

"Who?" there was an edge in Melissa's voice.

"My lips are sealed."

"Ha! Maybe if sucking on—"

His laughter cut through her words. "You vulgar woman!"

"I could have been about to say a grapefruit."

"Oh, I'm sure. Be patient, Melissa. Bethany will be back by dark."

"Take care of our girl."

"I always have." He hung up the telephone and found his youngest stretching on the sofa as she woke from her Sunday nap.

"Amelia Rose, my precious."

She ran to him, throwing her arms about his middle. "Poppy!"

He bent to kiss her. "Would you do me a favor?"

"Yes." Amelia's blue eyes lit with joy.

"Would you find Abe and ask him to see me in my den?"

"Yes, Poppy."

He watched her run the length of the long hallway before returning to his lair. By the time he'd added another log to the hearth, Abraham Walker stood in the doorway, crisp Sunday shirt and tie still in perfect condition from his trip to the cathedral with Alexander and the Melling children.

"Come in and close the door, please."

"Yes, sir." He adopted a formal tone and did as asked. Taking the seat across the desk from Alexander, Abraham's hazel eyes watched the host, an easy smile on his lips.

"Smoke?" Alexander leaned forward with his case and lighter.

Accepting the items, the young man lit up, tucked the cigarette into his mouth, and passed the things back. "Thank you."

"Do you know why I called you in?"

"I've got a pretty good guess, Mr. Alex." His smile was as much of a scoundrel's as his father's, though Joe was a decent man.

"Bethany Iris asked me to invite you to the New Year's Eve ball and to stay here for the weekend. I told her I would, and that Maggie would speak to your parents to be sure you were allowed the time off."

His grin doubled. "That's kind of you."

"You know what this ball is to Bethany, the significance?"

"It means she's a woman in the eyes of society and available for serious suitors."

Alexander shifted forward, hands clasped atop the desk. "She's still young and won't be left unguarded. Do I need to remind you what Frederick Davenport did to those men we found at Seacliff with Phoebe?"

He cleared his throat. "No, sir."

"It wouldn't hurt either to remember that I've taken bullets for that girl. Not to mention Kade is protective of her, as well as Asher. And Henry Adams, her uncles, and an Italian priest. If you need more reasons to treat her with respect, I'd go so far as to say Melissa, Magdalene, and Darla wouldn't shirk from whipping a young man should he take liberties with—"

"I'd never, Mr. Alex. I know how everyone feels about Beth and I feel the same."

Alexander smirked. "Not *quite* the same."

"I suppose not." Abraham chuckled. "But I'm fond of her."

He studied the earnest gaze amid the young man's freckled countenance. "What had you and Kade arguing last night?"

"He saw me kiss Beth goodnight when we dropped her off. He said he wasn't jealous, but why else should it matter to him if I kissed her? It's not like I was cleaning her teeth."

Alexander bit back a laugh. "If you're respectful of Bethany, you'll have nothing to fear. You'll probably find her in the kitchen helping Maggie, if you're interested in speaking with her."

"Thank you, Mr. Alex." He stood and offered his hand, man to man. "I appreciate your assistance in seeing to Beth's wishes."

Alexander nodded toward the bowl. "Take a mint on the way out. Women appreciate that."

He disposed of the cigarette in the ashtray and took two mints before leaving. Alone, Alexander let his head fall to the desk and groaned.

God, please don't let Frederick to kill me if I've done wrong!

Magdalene found him in his misery. "Lunch will be ready in five minutes. Do you need anything?"

His head snapped up. "Where's Bethany?"

"Setting the table with Abe."

He jumped to his feet.

"What is it, Alex?"

"I need you to talk to Claire and see that Abe gets to town by the afternoon of December thirty-first. He'll be staying here the weekend and attending the Order of Mayhem's ball."

"Wonderful! Did Kade ask for him to attend?"

"No, Bethany did. Please don't tell Frederick it was my doing."

Alexander rushed for the dining room, stopping short before the door. Peering around the corner, he held his breath. Abraham had a finger under Bethany's chin as he whispered to her. Her cheeks were pink with the attention.

Leaning back against the wall, Alexander crossed himself and turned to Magdalene. "Start digging my grave. Freddy is going to kill me."

Twenty-Three

Bethany stopped at her full-length mirror for the third time. The flowing A-line of the soft vertical sections of the evening gown skirt created just the right amount of movement. The circular details, growing larger as they trailed from the V of her neckline to the hips, gave her the appearance of a more womanly figure. All-in-all, the jewel-toned Chinese silks and matching sheer panels of the skirt assured her she would make a bold statement at her first masquerade. She stepped into her gold slippers and tied on her fuchsia mask—the same color as her painted lips—and made her grand entrance in the parlor.

"You outdid yourself, Beth!" Melissa exclaimed.

"I want one just like it when I debut, please!" Louisa begged.

Frederick smiled, opening his arms for a hug. "You're exquisite, Little Princess."

She reached for her locket, but her neck was unadorned to allow the dress to be the focal point. "Thank you, Daddy."

"Come on!" Louisa tapped her foot. "Let's get to the Mellings so the boys can get a look at her."

In the foyer, they paused long enough for photographs then her father lovingly placed outerwear around each of his girls. Bethany tied on the velvet-lined emerald cloak she'd made to go with the dress. On the drive to the Mellings, she warmed at the memory of Abraham stopping by the shop when he got to town. She'd only seen him briefly three times since her birthday weekend, but each meeting was like he never left. That afternoon, his hair was covered by a knit hat, his coat smelled of salt air, and his smile was infectious. Mademoiselle Bisset took an immediate liking to him and allowed Bethany to leave half an hour early. He saw her home on the streetcar, leaving her with a kiss on the front porch.

Louisa ran ahead when they parked at the mansion.

"Go on, Beth," her father told her. "Melissa and I will wait for you here."

She stepped through the front door as she flipped the cloak opened.

Asher stood by the stairs, a huge smile on his face. "Momma would have loved that dress. You look amazing."

"You always know what to say, Ash."

"Everyone else is gone already, but Amelia and Simon are in the morning room and Miss Charlotte in the kitchen. We're stuck with her since you and Tabby are grown up now."

Bethany greeted the others, enjoying the delight Amelia showed over the rainbow of colors. "I'll make you a pretty dress too," she promised before returning to the automobile.

At the hotel, Bethany placed her cloak at the coat check with an air of anticipation. Frederick took his daughter's arm and escorted her into the ballroom, Melissa directly behind them.

The first people she saw were Alexander and Magdalene. His arms opened and Bethany happily embraced her stepfather.

"Bethany Iris, you dazzle!"

"Thank you, Poppy."

"Save a dance for me if you can."

"I will."

Magdalene led the Davenports to their table where Maxwell and Lottie Easton gushed over the debutante. Then Tabitha, in a brilliant gold and white gown from Mademoiselle Bisset's shop, collected Bethany to bring her to the table where their friends gathered.

Kade was at her side in a flash. "You look beautiful. May I have the first dance, Tiger?"

She shook her head. "Sorry, I'd like that to be with my father. He'll come for me soon."

"Afterward then."

Bethany nodded, saying hello to the two other young women sitting at the table and the guys standing behind their seats before her gaze settled on Abraham. The double-breasted black tuxedo looked sharp, and his smile bright. Her heart swelled knowing he must have gone to a lot of trouble to secure the clothing.

"You're prettier than ever, Beth." Taking her hand, he kissed her cheek. "Would you do me the honor of sitting with me?"

"Yes, thank you. You look terrific yourself."

She took the seat he'd pulled out and he sat beside her.

Tabitha chatted with one of their friends who'd graduated from their school two years before. "Doesn't Beth look like the bee's knees with makeup?"

"I thought she'd be the only deb without any on," Lee Ann replied.

It was just lipstick, but hearing the girls discuss it made Bethany blush.

"It looks terrific," Abraham whispered, "but you do fine without it."

Frederick came, dealing a harsh look at Abraham's closeness to his daughter. "Ready, Little Princess?"

Bethany was grateful her father said nothing about Abraham while they waltzed, but his lack of conversation was almost as alarming. Bethany studied his face for clues, noting it looked thinner than usual, but it could have been the stiff way he held his jaw as though pained.

Alexander met them as the song ended and swept her across the room.

"Thank you for getting Abe here. Did you help with his tuxedo as well?"

"That was all him. Claire told Maggie he pulled from his savings to buy it. He cleans up well, doesn't he?"

Bethany nodded, thinking about the way he looked that June morning on the beach at Seacliff, all freckles and laughing in the borrowed bathing suit as he took her ankles to throw her into the water. The anklet now marked the spot he'd previously touched.

"Kate Walters already had a word with me." Alexander's smile was bittersweet. "She approves of your style and grace, but be mindful of her ever watchful eyes. What she observes can be just as troublesome as your father seeing. More so as he and the rest of the city would hear an embellished version of it."

"I'm not going to cause a scandal, Poppy. I only want to spend time with Abe."

When the song ended, he kissed her forehead. "I know you're level-headed, but love can do crazy things to people."

Bethany felt the blood drain from her face. She'd never said "love", not since her feelings for Kade were shattered. Fondness, enjoyment, and a little romance—that's what she and Abraham shared. She wasn't ready for *love*, not if it hurt anything like the disappointment over Kade's words dismissing the kiss a year ago or seeing him coming out of a bedroom with Phoebe.

Before she returned to the table, Oscar's familiar call of "Davenport!" boomed above the murmur of the crowd.

She turned in time to see Edmund slug his son's shoulder. "That's no way to get a young woman's attention."

Mustering a smile, she approached the two Eastons. "Hello Uncle Eddie. Oscar."

Her uncle kissed her cheek. "Your grandma would be proud. She always fussed about the perfect dress, and I think you found it."

Bethany blinked back the threat of tears. "Thank you. That means a lot to me."

"Now that you're out," Oscar said as he took her arm, "how about meeting some of my friends?"

"No thank you, Oscar." She moved to step away. "I've promised a dan—"

"She promised me the next dance." Kade took a firm hold on her other arm. "Please excuse us, Oscar and Mr. Easton."

He didn't wait for their reply and led Bethany away. "Stay away from your cousin. He's trouble."

"I know he is. They caught me unaware."

A Charleston tune started up, but Kade kept the conversation going. "You have to be on guard, especially looking like you do, Tiger. All the guys have their eyes on you and—"

"Don't try to flatter me."

"It's the truth! And what's going on with you and Abe? He refuses to answer my questions."

"We enjoy each other's company." Bethany said as a means to defending herself, but Kade stared at the doorway. She followed his gaze and stopped moving as well.

Black-masked Phoebe on the arm of Hans Caldwell walked the main aisle with a full-length mink coat about her. They stopped at a table with empty seats, exchanged a few words with the guests there, and then Hans removed her coat. Bare beneath a sheer black dress, Phoebe's body commanded the room's attention. Strategically placed stars embellished the bust enough to cover her nipples and a sparkling crescent moon accentuated her bellybutton. The waist was banded and beaded in a dipping line much like a woman would wear in a harem. Solid panels hanging from the center of the front and back of the braiding offered the only full coverage, all the way to her feet. The striking black sections accentuated the gauzy covering of her hips while the ornamental chain of trinkets that hung down the center of her lap drew attention to the core of her sexuality.

Rather than continuing to stare, Bethany—with a racing heart—pushed through the ogling crowd to her family's table. Melissa's face was the same color as her hair. Frederick stood, gripping the back of his chair like he was about to crush the wood.

"Daddy, please don't make a scene! Pretend she's not here if you must. She'll probably get thrown out and there's no reason for us to lose your company if you start something."

He looked from where Phoebe and Hans waltzed to Bethany, cupping her cheek. "It's your night, Little Princess. I'll keep my peace."

Magdalene looked furious, but Alexander took her into his arms, tucking his face near her ear so neither saw the display.

"She's ruined Tabby's and Beth's debuts," Magdalene said.

"Don't worry, Miss Maggie. We'll have a splendid time." But even as she said the words, Bethany knew Tabitha would be more upset than her mother.

She rushed to the other table. Words surrounded her flight.

"I'll have to go straight to confession after seeing *that*."

"She's as shameless as her mother."

"What's a girl to do without a mother, bless her heart."

"I need a cold drink."

"What do you expect from a girl with divorced parents?"

"If my wife sees me looking, remind her I forgot my glasses and was just trying to see what the fuss was about."

"When the parents live in sin, the children will follow suit."

Kade added to the spectacle, trying to cut in on the dance. He was ignored by both Hans and Phoebe while the whole room watched.

Bethany was near frantic when she reached her friends' table. Tabitha's straight brows were pinched together, red lips gritted in a scowl.

Bethany took her arm. "It doesn't matter what she does, Tabby. We can still enjoy ourselves."

"I'll not sit by and watch her make a fool of *my* brother!"

Phoebe looked like one of Ziegfeld's sex goddesses but Tabitha, with her fringed short gown and golden circlet over her sleek dark hair, could have walked off the cinema screen. Her lean body and good looks appeared too much for greedy Hans when she walked up behind Phoebe and tapped her shoulder though it wasn't a double rush. The artist made the transition of partners without a second glance at his lover. Kade pulled Phoebe close.

Unable to watch either couple, Bethany sunk to a chair as the room continued to buzz as the new couple tangoed.

"That's Melling's stepson."

"Never in all my life!"

"She's a stepdaughter of Alexander Melling."

"You would think this was a Mystics of Dardenne ball with all the degrading behavior."

"There has to be a law against siblings dancing like *that*."

Bethany was about to hide her face when someone took the seat adjacent to hers.

"I got you some punch. I think it's spiked. That might take the sting away for a bit, but drink slow."

She turned to his hazel eyes, as deep and warm as his voice. "Thank you, Abe."

While the rest of the room watched the dancers, Abraham kept his attention focused on Bethany. She took her first sip and smiled at him.

"It's good, but I'll go slow."

"You're beautiful, but I'm going slow too." He fingered the wave of hair that hung beside her cheek, tucking the strands behind her ear.

She felt his touch from her face to her toes. Wanting nothing more than for him to kiss her, she hid her yearnings behind the glass.

"Thank you."

"What for?" he asked.

"For sitting with me."

His hand went to her knee. "It's the most pleasant experience in the world to be near you."

Twenty-Four

From their table, Alexander watched Tabitha follow Kade onto the dance floor with trepidation. Hugging Magdalene to his chest, he prayed she would continue to hide her face. But Magdalene wasn't a woman to stay defeated. When she turned, her mouth gaped.

"She did it for Kade," he whispered. "He was being ignored when he tried to cut in, so Tabby did the cutting for him."

"Of all the—look at everyone watching! What people will say about my—"

"They're adults, Maggie. Kade is nineteen and this is Tabby's coming out. Anyone with a lick of understanding will know they're beyond your control." Seeing her anger growing, he tried another tactic. "Why don't you let Freddy take you and Melissa home and I'll keep an eye on things here?"

Frederick turned to him. "Did you not hear Beth beg me not to do something would cause me to be removed? I'm not leaving her."

Alexander frowned. "I'm looking for solutions."

"Then get your stepson away from my daughter!"

Melissa rubbed Frederick's shoulders and kissed his cheek before turning to Magdalene. "I'd be happy to take you home or over to our house, Maggie. You might wish to partake of the cellar's offerings."

Magdalene's brown eyes widened and she turned to her husband. "You'll keep an eye on them and bring Tabby home?"

"I swear to you I will."

She fingered his upper arm where he took the bullet for Bethany and nodded. *She knows how far I'll go for my darlings, stepchild or otherwise.*

"And Kade." She sighed. "Box his ears on Douglas's behalf if you must."

"I think Freddy will be more than happy to help in that regard." Alexander kissed her until she pulled away. "Try to relax and have a good evening with Melissa."

Melissa and Magdalene took their coat tickets and retreated, causing a new stir in the room as the notable women walked away— one from her own children and the other from her stepdaughter.

"We can thank Lucy for leaving this legacy of scandal," Frederick muttered.

Alexander snorted a laugh. "I'd like to think she would have worn something like that only for me, but toward the end, when she was running high and hot, I think she could have pulled something similar to this." He thought of Lucy's glorious breasts squeezed into her butterfly gown, wanting to go to supper with her cleavage spilling over the top. "God bless my luscious Lucy and the girls you created with her."

Frederick turned toward the table the younger set claimed. "Abraham's with Beth. I should bring her over with us."

"Let her have her evening as much as possible. Besides, we might have to rush at the others if they go too far, and then she'd be here alone since it looks like Max and Lottie abandoned us."

He huffed and eased into his seat, keeping his bad leg straight. "I hope the ladies don't drink the rest of my whiskey. I'm going to need something for a nightcap and my stores are running low."

Alexander laughed. "I hope Maggie gets into it. She's uninhibited when drinking, and I have a feeling I'll need a good tumble when I get home."

Their conversation was something they might typically have saved for the den, but as the masqueraders were giving them wide berth, they had plenty of room to speak privately.

That all changed when Kate Stuart Walters approached them. "Well gentlemen, I hope you're proud of your offspring, both natural and otherwise. They've managed to put on the finest display of debauchery this side of a Mystics of Dardenne party. I'm reminding people that it shouldn't be that much of a shock with Alexander Melling as stepfather to all three. But the Davenport name, F.L.D., that's the kicker. Though I suppose that one is more Easton. Shall we lock up the nuns to be sure she doesn't go on a tirade?"

Knowing Frederick would ignore the woman, Alexander stood. "We can do without your commentary."

Kate laughed. "Stay sharp, gentlemen. This brood will keep you on your toes for hours and all the other ones for years to come. How old is your youngest, Alexander?"

"Seven."

"That promises more than another decade of fun for the spectators. The little one might look demure like her mother, but I see the spark of Eliza in her. I'll chat later."

Alexander scowled as she walked away, but then Sean Spunner was there.

Still sore over how his old friend played him at the charity auction that summer—and annoyed with Kate—Alexander was curt. "What do you want, Judge?"

"I'm here for Davenport. Don't take this the wrong way, Freddy, but your girl is as lovely as her mother was."

"All of my daughters are beauties," Frederick said, "but if I catch you looking too much at my improperly clad oldest, I'll chip another one of your teeth."

Sean's broad grin showed the aforementioned flaw in his otherwise immaculate smile. "You could always best me in the ring, but I have no need for debutantes with my lovely wife always at the ready for me." He looked between the two men. "We're all blessed in the regard, are we not?"

"Yes," Alexander replied, "but ours unfortunately have left—fled from the sight of Phoebe's spectacle."

"If you get lonely, I'm sure Hattie would dance with either of you, as a favor to Melissa and Magdalene."

"Thank you, Sean. We'll keep that in mind."

Alexander turned toward the dance floor and was relieved to see Phoebe back with Hans. Kade danced with Jane, but Tabitha eluded him. It took two visual passes after Sean's farewell to locate Tabitha as she danced swiftly around the space with none other than Bradford Petty. He'd been cozying up to Magdalene at fundraisers since last summer, and now he had her daughter in his arms.

He looked to Frederick. "I'm going to cut in on Tabitha."

Frederick nodded and looked over his shoulder at his youngest. "I think I'll be doing the same thing if Abraham brings Beth out there."

"Beth isn't the concern tonight," Alexander reminded him.

"She's my daughter. I'm always concerned with her well-being."

Alexander drew upon his Melling pride to make his way across the room to Douglas's only daughter. He skirted between people in the middle of discussing his family. *What would Douglas do? What would Magdalene have me do? Argh! She likes Petty and would probably be pleased to see him dancing with Tabby. If she had heard the way he spoke when he first laid eyes on her, she'd be singing a different tune.*

Phoebe and Hans whirled by. She smiled at him as though hoping he was coming for her, but frowned when he kept walking. Reaching the couple he sought, Alexander tapped Bradford's shoulder before he could move away.

"May I cut in?"

"Mr. Melling, why of course." Bradford Petty bowed to Tabitha. "It's been a pleasure, Miss Tabitha. I'll be sure to look for you again."

She smiled at Bradford in a way Alexander had never seen from her, and looked back at her stepfather with a pinch of annoyance—much like her mother when he interrupted her charity work.

"I finally had a partner I was interested in and you broke us apart. That's not fair, Poppy."

"Neither was throwing yourself on Caldwell."

"Phoebe was making a fool of Kade. Or rather he did it to himself, but I wasn't going to stand by and let the whole room laugh at him!"

"No, instead everyone discussed the shameful display of the Melling stepchildren, all *three* of them."

"Did I hurt your glowing reputation, Poppy?"

Blast it all! Her sarcasm is heavier than Magdalene's ever was. "In case you forgot, your mother has my name. I hope you're satisfied you were part of chasing her from the ball. Sissa too, as we weren't going to send Magdalene off on her own."

Tabitha craned her neck as they continued through a flowing box step, seeking the table to see the empty seats for herself.

"If you had let well enough alone, Phoebe would have been the only one making a spectacle, and Kade would have realized he was a mooning fool before long. But no, all three of you are in the muck of it until the next scandal blows in to replace that sight."

"I'm sorry, Poppy. I didn't think about all that. Phoebe gets me so mad, I just—"

"You're a woman now, Tabby. You need to learn to let that go."

She nodded, looking forlorn.

"Focus on yourself and your friends, not your enemies. This is your special night." The song came to an end and he took her hand in both of his. "I'll watch over you, but promise to keep my distance. Look for me at twelve-thirty. We'll have to drive the Davenports home as Melissa took their car."

"Yes, Poppy."

"And be mindful of men that are too old. Petty is pushing thirty."

"Don't be a bluenose, Poppy." She kissed his cheek and turned away.

Alexander stopped at the refreshment table. A few curious people asked about Phoebe, twice as many people leaning close to hear.

"Is she engaged to that man?"

"Are they moving to Mobile?"

"You need to ask her directly," he replied.

Seeing they weren't going to get information from him, they moved on.

Bradford Petty took their place. "Don't tell me you're looking to trade your lovely wife in for a younger woman, Mr. Melling. Not that I fault your exquisite taste. I knew that one was a firecracker when I saw her interrupt the daring couple. And who could blame the other man for trading in that knockout blonde for the willowy beauty of the other? I'll have to try my hand at getting a dance with the blonde, but Tabitha was something else. Just the type I was seeking when I asked you about Mardi Gras this summer. I saw you got a kiss from her, how do you think I could arrange that—or more?"

Left staring at the man like a simpleton once again, Alexander gathered his thoughts before speaking. "I suppose you'd have to marry her mother, but that's not going to happen."

"Marry? Magda—Mrs. Melling?" Bradford's eyes went huge.

"Tabitha Campbell's father was killed in the war. I'm her stepfather and active chaperone tonight. I cut in for the express purpose of getting her away from you."

"It seems I'm always sticking my foot into my mouth around you. I'll just keep my thoughts and eyes on the blonde."

"Before you get any more harebrained ideas, I'll let you know the 'knockout blonde' is my stepdaughter from my first wife's previous marriage." A surge of glee coursed through Alexander at the sickening pallor that overtook Bradford. "And I've got another stepdaughter here tonight, so before you choose your prey for New Year's Eve, keep in mind she might be my daughter. But even if the young woman isn't, she's someone else's. Be sure you treat her with the appropriate respect and watch your tongue."

Bradford's Adam's apple bobbed. "My apologies once again, Mr. Melling."

Alexander dipped his head a fraction of an inch to show he'd heard him before walking away with a pleased smile for putting the fop in his place.

Twenty-Five

Hans lacked the flare Phoebe was used to with dancing. She had learned from the best—Davenports, Mellings, and Adamses—and most outsiders proved to be a disappointment. But Kade was bold enough to claim her even though it took Tabby cutting in for him to accomplish it. *She thinks she's all grown up with her flapper gown and sleek style, but she's a child, same as Beth. My poor sister probably hasn't danced with anyone but our fathers.*

When the song ended, she wasted no time. "I'd like a drink, please."

Hans sauntered off the floor with her on his arm—right up the path the onlookers cleared for them. Feeling the rush the attention, Phoebe put a little extra sway in her hips and kept her shoulders back, which shifted the embellishments on the top. Ignoring the women's glares, she winked at the coveting men.

I know you all want to touch me, glory in my curves. Hans taught me what power there is in the human body. I'll use it to my best advantage.

Hans deposited her at their table before collecting the refreshment. She was alone less than ten seconds when one of the Order of Mayhem's officers approached her.

"Miss Davenport." He smoothed his mustache as he tried not to stare at her breasts beneath the sheer fabric.

She purposely shifted to showcase their pert youthfulness. "Yes, sir?"

He cleared his throat. "There appears to be an overwhelming consensus in the room that people are uncomfortable with your spectacular gown. Would it be possible for you to wear your lovely coat the remainder of the ball?"

"I don't think you've done the math properly. By my calculations, I have at least fifty percent favorable reviews. The only unfavorable, or *uncomfortable* as you say, opinions seem to be from the female population. I think they might be jealous they don't have such a lovely gown, don't you?"

His grin turned into a grimace when he caught the eye of another officer. "Miss Davenport, I'm sure you understand our need to protect the fair ladies who are our guests. I don't wish to cause a scene, but—"

Phoebe pushed her chair back and stood atop it before climbing onto the table. She kicked the centerpiece aside.

"Listen up, you hypocrites!"

The live music faded and all eyes were on her above the crowd.

"Sending a spokesman from your group to ask me to put on my coat is a mockery of double standards! How many of you sneering women would have asked my father to put on a shirt when he was in the boxing ring? How many of you turned away when he climbed through the ropes for a match because too much of his body was on display? None of you! You sat by your husbands, fanning your hot little faces because what you saw excited you! Tonight, your husbands are enjoying the sight of a woman at her peak. Let them have their fill of glory while you sit back and remember your own lusting after Frederick Lionel Davenport!"

Phoebe paused on her soapbox, posing to the whole room in turn before accepting Hans's extended hand to help her step back onto the chair and then the ground.

"Well said, love." He kissed her long and deep as the whole room watched.

She drank her glass of punch, grateful for the dash of alcohol, and sent Hans back for more.

Oscar hurried over, a sleazy brunette on his arm. "Way go to, Bearcat! You told those old biddies where to stuff it. I'll be sure you and Hans receive invitations for the Dardenne masquerade."

"Thanks, cousin." She winked at him and smiled in invitation at the next man who caught her eye.

His black hair had a precise side part, but it was the fire in his emerald eyes that took her attention. Despite his delicate features—slim nose and lips with thick eyelashes—he was bold and sensual. Motioning him over, she saw the hesitation melt from him in an instant. Holding out her arm, she waited until he bowed over her hand to kiss it before speaking.

"I see the desire in your gorgeous eyes. Why the hesitation?"

"Bradford Petty at your service, Miss."

"Phoebe Davenport." Her painted lips smiled. "It's a pleasure to meet you, Mr. Petty. I noticed you dancing with Tabitha Campbell earlier. I can assure you I have much more to offer than that frigid cow."

He took a step back and cleared his throat. "She's a nice girl."

"She's seventeen, Mr. Petty. I'm two years older and much wiser in the ways of the world. Why do you keep backing away?"

Bradford ran a finger under his collar. "Your stepfather warned me not to—"

Phoebe laughed. "Dear Alexander! I'm afraid he thinks himself much bigger than he really is. Don't worry about his threats. It's my father you need to be wary of. If Frederick Davenport hasn't warned you, you'll be fine."

"That's good to know."

"Ah, here's my drink. Thank you, Hans. Hans, this is Bradford Petty. He wants to dance with me but was too shy, so I asked him instead." She downed the contents of the offered glass and stood. Taking Bradford's arm, she led him to her fathers' table. "Daddy, this is Mr. Petty and he's harmless. Poppy, I asked him to dance, so don't hold anything against him."

They let loose on the dance floor with an uninhibited display. Halfway through the tune, Phoebe saw the bold colors of Bethany's gown across the room and laughed to see her with Abraham Walker. They both looked to be enjoying themselves, not even glancing at her like the other couples in the room, but Abraham needed all his concentration on his gawky moves so as not to step on Bethany.

"Would you mind a switch, Bradford?"

"Anything for you, Miss Davenport."

"You'll get a chance with my kid sister. That's something not many men will be able to say tonight—that he danced with all of Alexander Melling's stepdaughters."

She saw the terror in his eyes but laughed. "Just keep your hands off her feminine areas and our fathers won't kill you."

When they danced closer, Phoebe threw herself at the islander. "Abe Walker! How's my favorite naughty sailor? Would you like another chance to finish what you started last summer before your big brother pulled you away?"

Bradford was quick to take Bethany's hand and started jitterbugging, but her placid face turned stormy as she looked to her sister and Abraham. Since Bethany was too far away to hear Abraham's protest, Phoebe wrapped a leg around him and put his hand on her nearly naked hip to prove her point.

"You were ready to pleasure me last time we were together. What's changed?"

He stepped out of her reach, hazel eyes turning dark. "I now recognize what a selfish bitch you are."

Her laugh was bawdy as she tried to cover the sting of rejection. She danced around him, tauntingly. "Don't tell me you've gone soft on Beth! Are you going to try turning into some upright, moral character when I've heard plenty of stories from your lips about your escapades the last few years. Even if she falls in love with a shabby deckhand, Daddy isn't going to go for that. He won't let you within a mile to court Bethany and you know it."

"Just remember it was you who ruined your sister's first masquerade. She's sweet, but I wouldn't blame her if she never forgives you for this debacle of self-gratification. You haven't shamed your family, Phoebe. You've only cemented what a conniving slut you are in the eyes of the whole city."

Phoebe slapped his freckled face but Abraham took it like a man and inclined his head to her. "I held back a lot of what I wanted to say."

She watched him leave, trying not to feel the sting of truth that she'd hurt Bethany. Abraham cut in on Bradford and guided her sister across the floor before he wrapped an arm around her.

Kade came to Phoebe's side. "Looking for a new partner?"

She took in his clear, bright eyes and handsome face before running a hand down his thick arm. His tuxedo sleeve was soft, but she knew how firm his muscles were beneath it. Closing her eyes, she remembered their hours together in Seacliff Manor—his loving attentions she'd yet seen repeated by another man.

"Dance with me, Kade." She breathed deeply until she was sure he'd memorized her heaving chest. "Then take me somewhere else if you'd like."

A song with a tango beat began. He clutched her to him. Hands hot through the sheer fabric, burning the skin of her lower back while desire pulsed to the thrumming drums.

****

The first thing Phoebe did when she and Kade returned to the ballroom was look for their family. None of them were there and the crowd was considerably smaller.

"Shall I bring you to Hans?"

"I can get to him myself." She put a hand on his shoulder. "Thank you for everything, Kade. Let's keep in touch this time."

Phoebe didn't watch him walk away because she wanted the image of him on top of her fresh in her mind rather than his retreat. She knew if she'd have gone off with any other man her gown would be in tatters. Kade had carefully placed her thin dress over the driver's seat and laid his tuxedo jacket on the bench so she wouldn't be against the cold leather as he made love to her. He was as gentle as he had been their first time as he expressed his passion in the backseat of the Mellings' automobile.

"There you are, love." Hans put both his hands on her hips and kissed her. "This party is as dead as my grandmother. How about we invite a few people to our hotel room and live it up for the stroke of midnight?"

"That sounds good."

"Anyone you want special? That blue-eyed guy that keeps following you, perhaps?"

"No, but that's sweet of you to ask. I'll be happy with whoever joins us."

"Go say goodbye to your family. I'll meet you by the door in five minutes."

Hans placed her mink coat—borrowed from a Bostonian couple who was wintering in Fairhope—over his arm. Phoebe walked the room a final time.

Oscar leaned in conspiringly as he placed an envelope into her hands. "Here are your invitations to the Mystics of Dardenne ball. Do you think Hans would be up for sketching women if we set him a special stage and easel? I'm sure the guys would like to watch real art in action."

"He doesn't typically let people to watch him work, but I'll ask."

"I know ladies don't like to wear the same gown to different balls, but there will be no complaints if you wear this number again, even if you give your cousin unholy thoughts."

"You scoundrel." She kissed his cheek. "Did you see my father leave?"

Oscar nodded. "Last hour with Uncle Alex, Tabby, Beth, and that spotted islander."

"Thanks, and Happy New Year, Oscar. I'll see you later."

"Hopefully the Dardenne ball, if not before."

Phoebe sashayed her way through the middle of the crowd to reach the exit, allowing the revelers one last look before she would be on full display for Hans and his friends.

Twenty-Six

Even if everything else went wrong, Bethany was pleased to leave the masquerade tucked in the backseat of the automobile between her best friend and Abraham. Everyone's masks were gone, as well as high hopes for their debuts. Tabitha sat with her head hanging out the window to dry her tears, and Abraham held Bethany's hand in the space between them.

Alexander parked behind Frederick's car in the Davenports' driveway. The two men made their way across the dark yard toward the glow of the porch lights.

Bethany nudged her friend. "Come on, Tabby. I'll make us some hot chocolate."

"I'll wait here. Poppy and Mama will come back in a minute."

Abraham helped Bethany out of the vehicle and tucked her arm around his. Outside the front door, she paused for him to open the screen. He leaned in and kissed the corner of her mouth. Her smile in reply brought forth his broad one as his eyes crinkled at the corners. Giggles erupted from the parlor, followed by a groan. Abraham and Bethany looked at each other in the hall, not knowing what to say or do.

"Melissa," Alexander said, "giving her a drink is one thing, but it looks as though she's drunk the whole bottle!"

"Only three cups of whiskey, my lion, but now I don't care what Kade and Tabitha did." Magdalene's words slurred.

"I left her alone for two minutes to telephone Miss Charlotte," Melissa explained. "I'd forgotten what she once did with a bottle of Scotch during the war when left unattended."

"I can only imagine! But what am I to do with her when she can't even sit up?"

"Take me to bed, Alex. You know exactly what to do with me there."

"Amelia has no need to observe her mother like this. I don't want the boys to see you on a toot either."

"Carry her up to the guest room and we'll keep her," Melissa suggested.

"Yes, take me to bed and—"

The parlor doors clanged together and Frederick limped toward them. "Beth, there's a bit of a delay with the Mellings returning home just yet. Could you offer Tabitha and Abraham some refreshment?"

"Of course, Daddy." She looked to Abraham. "Would you make sure Tabby knows she needs to come in?"

He nodded and slipped out the front door.

"I'm sorry your evening was spoiled." Frederick hugged Bethany.

She clasped her hands around his shoulders—something she'd never been able to do about his girth—and hugged him back. "It's not your fault, Daddy."

"I could have had her institutionalized, and then this never would've happened."

"I'm still with my family and friends. That's what matters most to me."

He looked at his watch. "Ten minutes to midnight. How would you like to have wine to toast in the New Year?"

"Could we?"

"It's fine with me, and I'm sure Joe wouldn't mind us sharing with Abraham, but I'll need to ask about Tabitha. Can you be discreet about it?"

"Of course. It's so grown-up rather than spiked punch or moonshine like others will be drinking."

"Go wait in the kitchen."

Bethany pulled out crackers and cheese, things she remember Melissa serving with wine when it was still legal. Abraham and Tabitha found her in the kitchen.

Tabitha turned her nose up at the plate. "Cheese with hot chocolate?"

Frederick pushed through the door. "Gather the glasses, Beth. You know where they are."

Once three goblets were on the counter, he opened the bottle and filled them halfway with burgundy wine. "For the debutantes and their guest. May you have a Happy New Year and a glorious season."

"Thank you, Daddy."

He took two glasses plus the remainder of the bottle with him as he retreated. The friends settled around the little table with their food and drinks.

Abraham stood and raised his glass. "To the prettiest debutantes of the year, who I'm lucky enough to have a private party with."

Tabitha frowned. "I'd rather be dancing at the ball. No offense, Abe. But the wine is a nice touch."

Magdalene's giggles pierced the stillness of the house followed by knocking on the stairs as though someone stumbled. "Oh, Alex! Just take me here!"

Tabitha jumped out of her seat, pushing through the swinging door. "Mama, are you drunk? Poppy, stop laughing and help her! And you're allowing me to drink when you see what it does to her? My father would throttle you!"

"I didn't give her the whiskey, and only agreed for you to have one glass of wine."

"Stupid Phoebe, idiot Kade, and now drunken Mama! The only good today was meeting Mr. Petty."

"Don't start in on that fop!" Alexander yelled in return.

Bethany stared at Abraham, not knowing what to say. But he knew what was needed. Gathering their glasses he brought them out the backdoor and across the yard to the gazebo.

The night shadows were long and deep, instantly giving them an air of security. Setting their goblets on one of the benches, he looked at his watch and then at Bethany.

"It's nearly midnight. Would you enjoy kissing to bring in the New Year?"

In response, she met his mouth with her own. He wrapped his lanky arms under her cloak, pulling her closer as firecrackers sounded around the neighborhood. Abraham was warm and sweet, but strong and unafraid. Bethany finally had to rest her head on his shoulder to counteract her lightheadedness.

Abraham's hands shifted across her back as he kissed her neck. "Happy New Year's, Bethany Iris Davenport. I'm the luckiest guy in the world to be holding you right now."

"And there's no one else you'd rather be with?"

"Phoebe behaved inappropriately. I let her know it wasn't welcomed."

"I heard what she said in the beginning. Did you have a relationship with her?"

"I was always beneath her—Kade's annoying friend dividing his attention." Abraham's gaze was tender and he brushed his thumb along her cheek.

Bethany held her position to gather the full story. "She called you 'naughty'."

"I wish I could tell you otherwise, but I'm no saint. I've always enjoyed a pretty face and have been with a few girls and kissed a lot more." His warm lips pressed gently to her forehead. "That day at Seacliff when you were overcome, I spent time watching Phoebe while she slept. My thoughts were swayed but it was working with what was already within me. When Phoebe woke, we were alone and she encouraged me to touch her. I'm ashamed to say I was more than willing to do it, but Emmett shook reason into me. She hasn't been a temptation to me except that one time. We've never even kissed. She was always Kade's girl to me, Iris," Abraham whispered. "May I call you that? Your name is beautiful, just like you."

"Momma named me." Tears pricked the corner of her eyes as emotions flooded her. "You may call me whatever you like, Abraham Jeffery Walker. Were you named after Lincoln?"

His charming smile returned. "No, but my namesake might have been. Ma named me after Private Abraham Jefferies of Massachusetts, a solider she fell in love with when she was a nurse during the Spanish-American War."

"And that doesn't bother your father?"

He shook his head, a wave of shaggy hair brushing across his forehead. "He was a victim of the race riots when he tried to save a little Negro boy."

"He was—"

"Colored, yep." He flashed his grin once more. "I'm probably the only white boy in Alabama named after a Black man."

"I think it's romantic. Miss Claire and her star-crossed lover. I'll look at her with even more respect the next time I see her."

They settled together on the iron bench, whispering and drinking for the next fifteen minutes. When they brought their glasses back to the kitchen, Tabitha pounded out disjointed chords on the upright piano in the corner of the parlor, Frederick and Melissa were drinking together in the study, and odd keening sounds came from upstairs.

Blushing, Bethany looked to Abraham. "Do you mind if we go back outside?"

"No, but are you warm enough in that?"

"I'll be fine if you stay close."

They settled on the double glider under the magnolia tree. Abraham stretched his long legs to the seat across from them. With a carefree attitude, Bethany rested her legs atop his.

Leaning forward, he fingered the anklet. "It means a lot to me that you wore it tonight. I know you could have embellished your dress with gold or pearls or anything, but you chose my humble shells."

"The shells are lovely and I like you, Abe."

"And I'm fond of you, Iris." His kiss was soft and quick. "But I'm not sure your father will approve of us getting close."

"Daddy won't mind. He's always liked your family."

"Ma maybe, but Pa turns him sour. I've seen him stomp away from him and Mr. Alex when they're cutting up."

Knowing her father loved Alexander even though they had different opinions settled any concerns over the differences of the Walker family from the Davenports. "Poppy wouldn't have invited you to stay the weekend if there was a problem with my father."

"I hope so because I'm at the point where I don't want to think about not seeing you again." He took her face in his hands, making her feel delicate and loved. "I won't ask anything of you, but I want you to know I won't be stepping out with any other girl. I'll do my best to see you at least once a week, but it might only be a quick hello between runs to and from the island."

"That's fine, Abe. I'll enjoy whatever time we have together."

They kissed until she sighed with exhaustion.

"Lay your head on my lap and rest." He slipped off his tuxedo jacket and folded it into a pillow. Bethany curled on her side and he arranged her cloak to cover her completely. Stroking her hair, Abraham hummed a little tune. She drifted to sleep knowing 1927 would be an amazing year.

***

"What's the meaning of this?" Frederick's harsh voice woke Bethany with a start.

She pushed against Abraham's knee to sit upright, vaguely remembering lying down. "Sorry, Daddy. Are the Mellings ready to go home?"

"They left last hour, and I've collected Louisa already." He crossed his arms.

Bethany stood on the glider platform and looked to Abraham who was fully awake and looking pale under his freckles. "No one told us and we were sleeping so well we didn't even hear the automobiles. Do you think it was the wine?"

"Don't blame a glass of wine on this behavior, Beth! Get yourself inside while I teach Abraham Walker how I feel about men who push the boundaries with my daughter."

"We came out here to escape the turmoil. Tabby and Poppy were arguing and Miss Maggie was making a shameful display of herself. Even you and Sissa retreated into the study. Don't blame us for coming out here."

"I'm not blaming *you* for anything." He glared at Abraham.

Bethany took Abraham's hand and lifted his wrist to her face to read his watch in the dark. *Three in the morning!* "Did it take three hours for you to realize I wasn't around? And what of Poppy leaving his houseguest? It's not our fault we were forgotten in the commotion."

"Maybe not, but that's no excuse for him to take liberties—"

"Abe was a gentleman, making sure I had a lovely evening despite the failure of my debut ball."

Her father's face softened. "I am sorry how it all turned out, but know I'm proud of you."

"Then stop berating my friend and implying more happened than two people resting."

Father and daughter stared at each other without speaking.

Abraham stood beside Bethany, the glider swaying with the movement. "It's okay, Iris."

"I'll not have my father think poorly of you because we were chased from the house and forgotten."

Frederick's scowl lessened. "All right, Beth. I'm sorry for thinking the worst."

"Thank you. I'd be happy to drive Abe to the—"

"Absolutely not! Especially after drinking your first glass of wine. You get to bed and I'll bring him."

"Thank you, Mr. Davenport, but it's no trouble for me to walk. I'm sure you'd like to get to sleep." Abraham pulled on his tuxedo jacket.

"But you don't have a coat," Bethany protested.

"I'll be fine, Iris. Don't worry about me."

She bit her lip and turned to her father. "Could Abe come for Pancake Time?"

"There's no telling when it will be with everyone up late. It's liable to be at noon for all I know."

"I could telephone when—"

"No, Bethany. Leave it at that and say good night."

She tucked her arm around Abraham's and stepped off the glider platform. "I'll walk you to the road, Abe."

Not caring if her father watched, she leaned close as they went through the porte-cochere. "He's tired and upset. I'm sure it's nothing against you. Come to me tomorrow—later today. We can go downtown or anything else you want, no matter what Daddy says."

"You're certain, Iris?"

"I've never been more sure of anything in my life, Abraham Jeffery Walker." She sealed her words with a devoted kiss.

Twenty-Seven

Tuesday, March 1, 1927

Dearest Claudio,

The most important news first: in case you have not heard, as of yesterday, Bishop Toolen is the new head of the archdiocese here. Start planning your means of swaying him to the need of an exorcist in Mobile.

After the New Year's debacle—and no, Alexander still has not quit teasing me about how much like Lucy I was when drunk, so please ask him to stop—I am happy to say Tabitha is finally getting over her disappointment. She has gone out twice with Bradford Petty (who Alexander cannot stand) and has joined a jazz ensemble as pianist. Needless to say, her days are busy with practice, performances, and primping her public image.

After Frederick took away the option of Kade interning with him (I hope I don't need to remind you of his shameless behavior on New Year's Eve, which seems to have forever soured Freddy to him), he's switched his studies to law. Alex has promised him a position at Melling and Associates if he passes his exams and is not involved in any more scandals. I'm not sure if he will be able to keep to those guidelines because he is not the same since the masquerade. He's hardly at home on the weekends, and it's not just work at the stables that keeps him out because he is gone until all hours of the night and not attending church. I'm beginning to think he needs an exorcism as much as Phoebe.

Simon and Asher continue to excel. Alex's idea of having them work has proven ingenious. They are more focused at school and in life. Simon is playing polo and Asher, while he enjoys riding for fun, is spending his spare time on artistic endeavors. It appears he inherited Eliza's talent. I coach him as best I can, but he's surpassing my skills. I hope to find him an art mentor soon.

Our dear Amelia Rose is still a joy and no heartache. Her horsemanship is superb. Alex says she's doing better than Phoebe did at her age. I ride with her as often as possible, but she prefers riding time with her father. Alex still dotes on her terribly. Amelia is staying top of her class, though Ginny Adams gives her a lot of competition.

I'm sure Melissa has told you about Beth, so I won't use space to update you on her life, but it's lovely to see her so often. Do write soon and include a plan of action we can put into play on this side of the ocean to help your cause for a transfer.

Love and fervent prayers for your return,

Magdalene

***

Alexander paced the veranda that overlooked the budding azaleas. He took a shaky drag from his cigarette and realized allowing Bethany and Abraham to meet at his home the last two months was beginning to take a toll one him. Abraham had arranged his schedule so he was off the weekends Bethany stayed with Alexander. She, in turn, worked only half days those Saturdays, giving her and Abraham the freedom to go to the cinema, Mardi Gras festivities, or whatever else they wanted in the afternoons. They took supper with the family each day, but often went out to see Tabitha's band or other such amusements Friday and Saturday nights. Home by midnight without being told, Alexander happily waited for them to be sure they separated at the top of the stairs, Bethany to the far wing and Abraham to Kade's room—who was usually still out when they returned.

What they were doing would eventually bring about Frederick's wrath, but the vibrancy in Bethany's countenance made the threat of exposure worth it. Her seriousness was replaced with joy. She shone with love and laughter, even the days Abraham wasn't in town. Alexander was glad she didn't bend to her father's will when he refused to allow Abraham to call on her at their house. The young man had proven his sincerity and good character the past few months: always respectful, helping around the house without being asked, and pampering Bethany to no end. There was no doubt the two were in love, though Alexander never heard them mention the word.

When the next streetcar stopped at the nearby corner, Bethany hopped off. Purse dangling from her wrist, she waved to the neighbor and smiled at the pedestrians she passed. Her bucket hat was charming, and her blouse and wide-legged trousers the height of fashion.

"Poppy!" She hurried up the front walk, and kissed his cheek. "I love seeing the house skirted with flowers. It reminds me of Momma's *Azalea Blossom*. I almost walked home to take in more of the buds around town, but I didn't want to miss spending time with Abe."

"He's not here yet." He snuffed his cigarette against the closest pillar and brushed the ashes off. "I've been thinking, Knight Bethany, thinking a lot."

Her arched brows narrowed.

"I think we should let Sissa in on your relationship with Abe."

"She would tell Daddy, though I wouldn't want her to keep a secret from him."

"Yes, and I think she's the one who could best explain things."

"What if she doesn't approve?"

"Do you believe that?" When she shook her head, he continued. "Your father is in a difficult spot, Beth. After what he went through with Phoebe, he's determined to protect the rest of you. I doubt there will ever be a man he thinks is good enough for either you or Louisa. He made a menace of himself over Abe on New Year's and is stubborn enough to stick to it, even if he knows he's wrong. The only person who could persuade him to change his mind is Sissa."

"You're probably right. I appreciate all you've done for us."

He took her hand and left a peck on her forehead. "You deserve it, and Abraham is a good man. I'll telephone and see if Melissa will stop by this weekend."

Abraham's whistling carried up the street. Bethany passed her purse to Alexander and dashed down the walk. The two convened at the edge of the property, Abraham swinging her around and leaving a kiss on her lips before tucking her to his side opposite his drawstring sack. Alexander was certain Abraham's smile could be seen five blocks away.

"Good evening, Poppy." He shook Alexander's hand.

He found it amusing Abraham had picked up his nickname and hoped that one day he would be the young man's stepfather-in-law. "Welcome home, Abe."

Bethany took back her purse and the two went inside to put their bags away, chatting animatedly all the way up the stairs.

Upon telephoning Melissa, she assured Alexander she would come after supper. When he stepped out of his den, Tabitha was hollering for Magdalene.

Alexander met her in the front hall. "She's gathering flowers for the dining room. Anything I can do?"

Tabitha gave him a patronizing smile. "I have a change of plans. Brad is picking me up at six-thirty and we're taking supper out before my show."

Alexander grimaced in return. "I'm sure your mother will be pleased."

"My mother has lovely taste in men, *most* of the time." Tabitha gave him a cutting look before walking away.

"I love you too, Tabitha," he called after her.

Alexander hurried through his den to the yard, relieving Magdalene of her gathering basket near the back fence. He set it on the ground, hands roaming her yellow dress. Relishing the feel of her melted his stress.

"Shall we rendezvous in the camellia maze?"

"Lock me in your den, my lion."

He scooped her into his arms.

"My tulips!"

He set her down and snatched the basket before running for the house. The flowers were on the table and the hall door locked by the time Magdalene stepped in. Once the patio entrance was closed, his hungry eyes roamed his wife as his body pulsed with need.

He went for his buttons. "We need to make it quick. Beth and Abe are upstairs and—"

She punched his stomach. "Alex! We need to set a good example."

He lowered her to the chaise without ceremony. "Have you forgotten they heard you drunk, Magdalene?"

"You insufferable—"

He silenced her with a searching kiss. "What better example can there be than a loving husband and wife? Pure desire and devotion between a couple bound in holy matrimony is the most beautiful thing in the world."

With his impassioned words, the light in her eyes changed. Alexander took full advantage of wooing her. He wished for one second Magdalene was as uninhibited as Lucy in forgoing underclothes, but it was only a slight setback before their pleasure.

After their pinnacles, Alexander hugged Magdalene.

"I still think you're insufferable," she whispered with a smile.

"And I think you're glorious. Your daughter on the other hand…." He sighed. "I think Tabby got yours *and* Douglas's sarcasm combined."

Magdalene laughed as she smoothed her yellow dress. "What did she say?"

"Petty is taking her to supper before her gig tonight and she inferred you had a misjudgment of your fine taste when it came to marrying me."

"Is that what this was, a means to rebuild your bruised ego?"

He tucked in his shirt. "You know you're more to me than that. Besides, Melissa is coming after supper. I wanted to be sure to show you how much I adore you in case our company stays late."

"The Davenports haven't come over since December."

Because Freddy hasn't wanted to see Kade after he proved what happened at Seacliff wasn't an isolated event to be blamed on demons. "Just Melissa. I've talked Bethany into letting me tell Sissa about her and Abe."

"They don't know?" Magdalene paled.

"Beth didn't want her to have to keep a secret from Freddy since he refused to allow Abe to call on her at their house. I think Melissa will be able to make him see reason when it comes to those two."

"Alex, what will it do to our relationship with Freddy and Melissa when they find out we've been helping Beth see a man her father refuses to accept as a suitor, allowing them to sleep under the same roof?"

"Frederick never forbid her from seeing Abe, just from entertaining him at their house. Besides, it's Bethany. The girl is as good as they come."

"Exactly, which is probably why Freddy didn't feel the need to spell out his guidelines. I hope it goes as well as you think."

***

After supper, Magdalene, Abraham, Bethany, Simon, Asher, and Amelia gathered in the morning room for dance instructions to benefit the islander. Not having grown up around experienced dancers—and lacking all sense of natural rhythm—Asher considered it his duty to ensure Abraham didn't look a fool while dancing with his half-sister in public.

Alexander leaned in the doorway to watch the fun until the doorbell rang.

"Darling Sissa." He kissed her cheek and waved to Frederick and Louisa before they backed out of the driveway.

"I have about an hour, dashing Poppy." She took his arm.

Kade bound down the stairs, stopping short at the bottom when he noticed Melissa.

Warm and friendly as ever, she smiled. "It's good to see you, Kade."

"Hello, Sissa. It's nice to see you as well." He quickly kissed her cheek and turned to Alexander. "I'm taking Mama's car. I'll be home later."

"If you happen to be at the same place as your sister, please keep an eye on Mr. Petty."

He guffawed. "I don't harass the elderly. If Tabby wants to hang out with a fossil, that's her deal."

They watched Kade until he disappeared through the kitchen.

"He's changed," Melissa whispered.

Alexander nodded and steered them to the morning room. "There's not much I can do for him that I haven't already tried, but I want you to see something before we go into my den. Don't say anything. Stand behind me and watch."

Melissa stood close, gazing over his shoulder. Just as he'd hoped, Bethany and Abraham were poised to dance. Asher circled them, pointing out Abraham's flaws. Once he was in the appropriate position for a tango, Asher motioned for Simon to start the music.

Five seconds later, Abraham tripped over Bethany's toes and she laughed.

"Stop giggling and allow him to right himself," Asher scolded. "He'll never learn if you get him laughing each time."

Bethany bit her lip as she gazed at her partner with complete adoration. Abraham's eyes went from her face to their feet in concentration. As time passed, a pleased smile found its way to the surface. He finished the tango with a flourish, dipping her back and leaving a quick kiss on her neck before he pulled her to his chest.

"I did it, Iris!"

"You were amazing!" Bethany snuggled against him as Abraham rested his head atop hers.

Alexander closed the door to his den and brought Melissa to the chaise—trying not to think what he'd done there with Magdalene a few hours before.

Melissa clutched his hand. "I knew she was happy lately, but I had no idea."

"She came to me after Thanksgiving and asked me to secure Abe an invitation to the New Year's ball. While the evening was ruined for everyone else, she managed to enjoy herself because she was with Abe. You know they fell asleep on the swing, right?" Melissa nodded and he continued. "Did you know she asked Freddy to allow Abe to return for Pancake Time?"

"No."

"She begged for Abe to be able to come back and he denied her. I know Freddy's worried about protecting her after what happened with Phoebe, but he's punishing Bethany through no fault of her own. He'll drive her away if he refuses to trust her."

Melissa's eyebrows furrowed. "So Abraham came to visit her this weekend?"

"He's been here every weekend she has since New Year's."

"Alex, that's not right! Maggie's mentioned him a lot lately, but I thought he was visiting with Kade."

"They're chaperoned, he's a gentleman, and Bethany is as good as they come. They don't deserve to be kept apart because Phoebe flew off the handle." He took her face in his hands. "Did you see her joy? The light in her eyes? When's the last time you saw that with our Beth?"

"Freddy will have a conniption."

"Then let him prove once more what a selfish brute he is if he's going to stand in the way of his daughter's happiness."

Worry creased Melissa's face. "I didn't say I agree with him, Alex. I agree with you, but the fact that you've kept this hidden—"

"I wasn't about to deny that sweet girl, not after all she's been through because of my sins. She suffered through her parents' divorce, possession, and kidnapping. Even if she has no memory of those things, I know what I did to her. But despite it all, she's the best girl around."

"I know she is." Melissa hugged him, her arms an instant relief from his tormented thoughts. "And she loves you, Alex. I'll talk to Freddy."

The doorbell rang and they stood together. When they made it to the hall, Amelia ran ahead and flung open the front door.

"Louisa, come see Abe and Beth dancing!"

Louisa followed the youngest Melling into the morning room, passing Melissa and Alexander in the wide hall.

Frederick turned the corner. "Did Amelia say Abraham was here?"

"Yes, Freddy." Melissa placed her hand on his arm. "Beth's been enjoying time with him."

"Not anymore." He went for the morning room with a limping gait.

Twenty-Eight

Bethany and Abraham were in the middle of the Charleston when Louisa bound into the room and took Simon's arm to dance. While Abraham was now adept at close partner dances, he was still a gangly monstrosity—in the cutest possible way—for fast ones. When the song came to an end, Bethany fell into his arms with laughter.

"Think I'm getting the hang of it?" His eyes were golden with merriment.

"Not by a long-shot, Abe." She kissed his cheek, fantasizing about kissing every freckle on his body. It would take hours.

"Could I get you a drink?"

"Yes, please. I'll come with you."

"No, Bethany Iris, you're coming with me."

Her heart went cold at the anger in his voice, but she turned to her father, holding fast to Abraham's warm hand. "I'm Poppy's guest for the weekend, Daddy. The same as always."

Magdalene ushered Amelia, Simon, Louisa, and Asher toward the door, but Bethany's half-brother stopped in the doorway when the others went out.

"Nothing good is coming from this arrangement. Your days of staying here are over."

"Don't keep my sister from me!" Asher's voice was hard and commanding—completely Melling. "Our mother wouldn't stand for that and you know it, Mr. Freddy."

Alexander stepped between his son and Frederick. "Phoenix Asher, please go with Maggie for now."

"He can't come in here and bully Beth!"

"I'm her father and know what's best." Frederick was red in the face and ignoring Melissa's attempts of placing a calming hand on his arm.

"We'll talk about it later, Phoenix Asher." Alexander crossed his arms.

With a final look at his sister, Asher exited.

"Freddy, let's talk rationally," Melissa offered. "I think you're upset over nothing, but help us understand."

"Nothing?" He raged. "I let Beth know I didn't approve of Abraham Walker months ago!"

"You did no such thing, Daddy. You only refused to allow me to invite him to our house, but you never said why or anything else on the matter."

"Why? Because you weren't raised to be shackled to a sailor educated in a one-room schoolhouse!"

"You need to stand down." Alexander stepped toward him. "What you're saying is insulting to my wife, Darla, and the whole Walker family."

"So be it. My daughter deserves better."

"I've had enough of this, Freddy!" Melissa got in his face. "The Walkers are our friends. We've had nothing but respect for Joe, Claire, and their children."

"Joe's just as crass as Alex and—"

"He's a man, Freddy! And honest, hardworking man who's built a respectable business that supports his family and employees dozens."

"Then why does his wife have to labor as—"

"Because she wants to, you prig! She has a profession she loves and helps people at the same time. Don't start in with your ideals about keeping the contrite wife home while you drag in the meat. There were years I worked while being a dutiful wife and mother because I wanted the fulfillment of doing something beyond my four walls. I had that with writing and Claire has that with midwifery, through no fault of a husband not providing. Your own business partner's wife does the same, in case you forgot."

Bethany couldn't stand the staring match that ensued. "Daddy, if you'd listen—"

"I needn't hear anything after seeing how deceitful you are in sneaking around my back."

"I didn't sneak. Poppy openly welcomed Abe here and people all over the city have seen us together. No one's lied. I've failed to share my joy with you because you were illogical the last time I spoke to you about Abe." Body on the verge of trembling, Bethany took comfort in Abraham's firm hand still holding hers.

"I'm disappointed in you, Beth."

Alexander pushed Frederick, actually causing him to reset his stance. "You're the world's biggest tyrant, Davenport! You're so stubborn, you can't see what's plain to everyone else. Bethany's the happiest she's ever been and Abe's a respectable young man. I'm proud to host him here and am glad to see them enjoy each other's company. Your unrighteous ideals have prevented you from seeing their relationship blossom these past months."

Frederick's hand went around Alexander's throat. While at one point in his life he would have lifted him off the ground in a show of strength, he merely grasped tighter. "Don't speak to me of relationships when your stepson took my daughter out of a masquerade to have his way with her!"

"Frederick Davenport, let go of him!" Melissa yelled. "And if you ever compare Bethany to Phoebe again, I'll slap you!"

Overcome by the arguing, Bethany went limp. Abraham eased her into the nearest armchair, making sure her head was supported by the backrest before kissing her forehead and taking her hand once more.

"Get your filthy hands off my daughter!"

Abraham straightened, not letting go. "Mr. Davenport, Bethany Iris doesn't need to witness her family arguing. I'm sure I'm not the type of man you envisioned for your daughter, but just because I don't wear a suit to work doesn't mean I'm not a decent fellow. I'm not perfect by any means, but we make each other perfectly happy."

Bethany brought his hand to her lips. "We do. I never thought life could be this joyful."

"I haven't told you because I didn't want to overwhelm you," Abraham said as he crouched beside her chair, "but I love you, Iris. No matter what other people say, nothing can change my heart. It's all for you. Every beat, every breath. I live my life for you from this moment on."

Arms about him, a tear slipped down her cheek. "I love you too, Abe."

Their tender kiss was broken when Frederick hooked an arm around Bethany's waist and carried her to the door. She felt him quiver with the exertion and marveled at her father's weakened state.

"Come on, Melissa," Frederick called over his shoulder.

"I'm not going anywhere with you when you're acting like this!"

He set Bethany on her feet and scowled at his wife.

Touching his hard face, Bethany stared into his brown eyes. "Don't you trust me?"

"I want to but—"

"Get out of my house, Frederick!" Alexander pointed toward the front door. "Any other young lady would be in hysterics right now, but Bethany's stoic even when her father makes an ass of himself. You don't deserve this girl's love when you can't see her true heart! You don't deserve your wife's devotion when you don't heed her opinions. Once again you've wrapped yourself into your own world of hurt and it's destroying everything good in your life!"

Frederick went heavily for the foyer, Bethany following several feet behind with Melissa's hand on her shoulder.

He motioned to the front room. "Come on, Louisa."

"She's staying with me." Melissa's voice was icy.

Frederick's glare of anger turned to pain as he looked back at his wife and daughters. He shook his head and limped into the night.

***

After crying for an hour in Abraham's arms, Bethany accepted a glass of lemonade from Alexander.

"I'm sorry I failed you, Bethany. I thought Melissa would be able to convince your father to see reason."

"It's not your fault, Poppy. And Daddy needed to know." She kissed Abraham's cheek. "I want everyone to know how I feel."

Melissa stood. "It's time for me to get Louisa home for the night."

"I'll drive you over and trounce the tyrant if needed." Alexander did his best boxing stance, which brought laughter from Magdalene and Melissa.

"I think you'd be safer suing him, dashing Poppy." Melissa held her arms out to Bethany and Abraham took her glass so she could embrace her stepmother. "I'm sure he's calmed down, but it might take a while for him to accept things fully."

Then Melissa turned to Abraham and took his free hand. "I couldn't be more pleased for you two."

"Thank you, Sissa."

Bethany's heart pounded to see his huge smile and settled against him once more.

Alexander took the two Davenports home while Magdalene chaperoned. When Bethany finished her drink, the lady of the house stood.

"I think it's time we get some sleep. Bethany has to be at work at eight." Magdalene went to herd the others upstairs, giving the couple a window of privacy.

Abraham wasted no time hugging her. "Iris, for me it was worth suffering through the argument to finally share how I feel and hear you say you love me too. I hope the good outweighs the bad for you as well."

"Your actions showed me that you loved me all these months, but it was glorious to witness you proclaim your feelings. I hope the need doesn't arise, but I'd choose you over my father if it came down to it."

His hot kisses replaced the lingering coolness of the lemonade with his tangy fire. Bethany clung to him as he continued his ministrations, allowing herself to be swept along with the mounting passion.

He walked her upstairs and whispered in her ear. "I'd do anything for you, Iris."

They parted with a sweet kiss. Bethany readied for bed with an air of hope despite the drama. She was soon asleep, only to be roused what felt like minutes later.

"Beth, I need to talk." Tabitha nudged her arm as she settled on the edge of the bed.

"What time is it?" She shifted to allow her friend the space to stretch out beside her.

Tabitha settled on the pillow, curling on her side facing Bethany as the scent of cigarettes settled over the bed. "Two-thirty. I'm glad you didn't come to the show tonight. It was terrible. Not the music, but what happened."

Instantly awake, Bethany blinked and took Tabitha's hand.

"Phoebe showed up with Hans and some of his rich art collecting friends. She was flirting with Brad while I could only glare at her from the stage, but I'm happy to say he didn't get wrapped in her scheme." She giggled. "I'm giving him enough for him to know which side his bread is buttered on."

"Tabby!"

"That's not the half of it. Kade showed up during our second set and he went right to Phoebe when she was dancing with one of Hans's friends, starting in on this naughty tango I haven't even seen Poppy attempt! Then Hans came over with his sketchbook, had Kade remove his jacket, and started posing them all sorts of ways so he could draw them. When he had Kade straddling Phoebe on a chair, the manager finally came over and forced them to stop. But they just packed up and took their exhibition elsewhere. I want to tattle on Phoebe, but if Poppy hears about it, Kade will lose the option of working with him when he finishes school. As much as I hate what he's doing, I'll not be responsible for that."

"Big brothers and sisters are the worst. Right up there with stubborn fathers."

"Be glad he doesn't know about you and Abe."

"He does now." Bethany sighed. "It was the best and worst day of my life. He and Sissa and Poppy were arguing but Abe stood in the middle of it and declared his love for me."

"Oh, Beth, that's wonderful!"

"I told him right back I loved him too. After we declared our love for each other and kissed for the world to see, Daddy carried me out."

"He didn't!"

"He did, but Sissa refused to go with him so he set me down. Sissa wouldn't even let him take Louisa home. Poppy brought them back later."

"You poor dears, but it sounds like you won out in the end."

"I don't know. Daddy is stubborn and said a lot of mean things about Abe and his family. But Abe and I are stronger than ever." Bethany fingered her lips. "His kisses were like nothing else once we were alone. Now that we know we love each other, there's no hesitation."

"I'm happy for you, but I'll let you get back to sleep."

"Goodnight, Tabby. I'll pray for Kade."

Twenty-Nine

Ready for a morning on the sales floor, Bethany donned a purple dress and took more pains with her hair than usual. She exited her room just before seven and met Abraham at the top of the stairs.

"My beautiful Iris." He turned her around to look her over before embracing her fully. Her lips met his with a spark of yearning. "Could I take you to the diner for breakfast and see you to work?"

"Only if you collect me afterward as well."

They descended the stairs holding hands. Alexander sat at the kitchen table with Amelia over bowls of oatmeal, each in their riding clothes.

Bethany hugged Amelia and kissed her stepfather's scruffy cheek. "We're taking breakfast at the diner and then Abe is seeing me to work."

"All right, Bethany. Did you want to go to the stables with us today, Abe?"

"No thank you. I'm going to stay in town this morning and bring Iris back at noon."

"I'll be sure you have a chaperone here." Alexander winked.

Bethany and Abraham took the trolley to Royal Street. The diner had a wait for tables, so they took breakfast at the counter where Abraham spent as much time chatting with a shop boy on his other side as with Bethany. She loved his easy-going personality and that he was friendly to everyone. Pleased to listen to his banter—and the fact that he introduced her as his girl—Bethany ate her waffles with a growing smile that only increased as they walked with an arm around each other to Mademoiselle Bisset's shop.

"Mr. Walker," her employer said as she unlocked the door for them, "it's always a good day when you stop in with that bright face of yours."

"It will be doubly so because he'll pick me up at noon," Bethany replied.

"So it shall," Mademoiselle Bisset said. "The alterations you finished for Miss Marley yesterday will be your priority, even if you're with someone else when she arrives."

"Yes, ma'am."

"No matter your skills with a needle, I do prefer to see you dressed for sales. Isn't it nicer to see her shapely legs than hiding them in those pants she prefers when sewing, Mr. Walker?"

He hooked his thumbs in his trouser pockets and grinned. "I'm not sure which is better, Mademoiselle Bisset, because the trousers draw attention to her other shapely assets."

She laughed and pinched Abraham's cheek. "Bethany my dear, if you don't keep him, I might have to. Now say goodbye. Women don't like to shop with a young man lurking about, no matter how charming he is."

Bethany walked Abraham to the door and he left her with a maple flavored kiss. "Love you, Iris. I'll be waiting for you out front."

The first hour and a half were slow, allowing Bethany time to reset the window display. Then, the Saturday shoppers arrived. Marie Marley, a twenty-six-year-old single woman, arrived during the bustling hour to try on her altered clothes. The lady's oldest sister, Grace Anne, had been friends with Lucy and her nephew was Robert

Woodslow, who Bethany could no longer stand after the Seacliff incidents. But Marie liked to play friendly with Bethany in an attempt to seek gossip tidbits.

"Don't you look fine today, Miss Davenport."

"Thank you, Miss Marley. I hope you'll find the changes I made to the clothes make them more enjoyable. We've saved the corner dressing room for you."

"You have such a fresh glow about you this morning. I doubt your friend Tabitha Campbell does. I suppose she's up until all hours since she joined that jazz ensemble. I'm surprised Mrs. Melling allows that with her daughter only being seventeen."

"Miss Maggie is proud of Tabby's talent. Now that's she's graduated, there's no need to keep her on short strings." Bethany pulled back the curtain to the changing room. "You'll find everything here. Let me know if you have questions or concerns. I'll be nearby."

Marie closed herself in the space, but kept talking at a louder volume so the whole store heard. "And what of you, Miss Davenport? I've seen you about several times in the past month with a young man I'm not familiar with, but his grin shows he's mighty pleased to be with you."

"I saw her with him this morning when we went for breakfast," another customer piped in. "He looks to be a cheeky rascal. I'm surprised Mr. Davenport allows his daughter to be with the likes of him."

Mademoiselle Bisset joined the fray. "Bethany's Abraham might have a naughty glint in his eyes, but he's a gentleman. I see him several times a month when he stops in town. He's as true-hearted as they come or I wouldn't let him near our girl."

"*Comes to town?* Don't tell me a Davenport is seeing a country boy!" Marie stepped out of the dressing room in a pale fringed evening gown.

"He's from Dauphin Island," Bethany explained. "His father owns a small fleet and Abraham is on track to become a captain. His mother is the island midwife who trained under Darla Adams's mother."

"Friends of the Darla Adams?"

"And the Davenports and Mellings," Mademoiselle Bisset added. "He's from a respectable family with good connections, ladies. And I think we can all agree a captain in uniform is nothing to slight. Why, Magdalene Melling's first husband was a captain with the Walkers."

A buzz went around the shop, for all the women respected Magdalene.

When the conversation continued without Bethany, Marie waved her over. "Do you think this gown makes me look like I'm trying too much at my age?"

Being shorter than average, Bethany had to hem the clothes several inches for her. "Miss Marley, you're still ever so sprite and have a lovely figure."

"But not young and pretty enough to catch the eye of Mr. Petty. I was excited when he moved to town and even shared a table with him at a charity auction last summer. I'm afraid to say he was all over Mrs. Melling. It's no wonder he took a liking to her daughter come New Year's. She's a sleek, modern version of her mother, though I do think Tabitha wears too much makeup."

"I'm sure you'll catch the eye of any number of men in this gown, Miss Marley. The length is just the right one to be flirty but retain your sophistication."

Miss Marley returned to the dressing room with a smile. Two outfits later, the bell on the front door rang. Mademoiselle Bisset, Bethany, and the customers turned to see who joined them.

"Why, Mr. Davenport," Mademoiselle Bisset said. "You're the very man we all wish to see! Your name even came up this hour in conversation."

He kissed her hand and leaned on his cane before looking at the smiling faces, falling to his daughter's last. "Hello, ladies. Beth."

"Are you here for something special for your lovely wife?" He shook his head at the question. "Well if you're here for Bethany, you'll have to get in line. She's assisting Miss Marley for the moment and her charming beau is expected to collect her at noon. All the ladies were aflutter about him, as you can imagine. I've never seen a young man as attentive of his girl as he is of Bethany. You must be pleased for the match, Mr. Davenport."

His forced smile faltered and he cleared his throat. "There is a matter I had hoped to discuss with you, Mademoiselle Bisset. In private."

Miss Marley stepped out of the dressing room in time to seek Frederick's opinion on a skirt ensemble, which he gave red-faced though friendly in the affirmative while his own suit hung loose on his once mighty body.

Dread grew within Bethany's chest as the minutes ticked by and her father didn't emerge from the back office. Miss Marley paid her balance and left with everything Bethany had seen to, but the conference continued. Customers came and went and the afternoon girl arrived. Still her father and Mademoiselle Bisset remained locked away.

As the clock struck noon, Bethany wrote her leaving time on her work card beneath the front counter and retrieved her purse.

"Aren't you staying to see your father?" the other worker asked.

"Abe's meeting me." She rushed out the door and into his waiting arms.

Taking his hand, Bethany wove their way through the crowded sidewalk. She went straight down the nearest block until they reached Government Street.

"Shall we catch the streetcar?" he asked.

"Don't stop."

She broke into a run, dashing across the wide street when there was a lull in traffic, not stopping until she fell onto a lounge chair on the back patio. There, she burst into sobs she'd held in the past hour.

Abraham dropped beside her, arms about her quivering frame. "Iris, what's the matter?"

"Daddy came to the shop over an hour ago and met in private with Mademoiselle Bisset. They were still in her office when I left. I know it's about me. He's going to do something to thwart our relationship. The only thread of hope is that she likes you. Maybe she'll talk sense into him, though I don't see how she can when Sissa can't."

"Are you going to allow your father to change your feelings for me?"

"Never, Abe."

"Then don't worry about it. I'm not going anywhere."

***

Washed and dressed for a Saturday night out, Bethany and Abraham sat with Amelia between them in the morning room before supper. They helped her with a crossword puzzle from a magazine she'd taken from her mother's stack. When the doorbell rang, Amelia left it on her seat and dashed for the hall. Bethany and Abraham each leaned over the puzzle until their heads touched. He took the pen to fill in another word. Someone came into the room, but they kept their concentration on the crossword.

Bethany snatched the pen and filled in more squares before passing it back. "There!"

"My clever girl." He kissed her cheek before going for another clue.

"Beth." Melissa's voice made her jump. Her stepmother stood across the room, her Kodak camera beside her forced smile. "I hope it's okay, but I took a few pictures. You two look so natural together. Could I get a few of you both looking at the camera now?"

Abraham moved the magazine and pen to the side table and shifted next to Bethany, arm about her shoulders without question. But Bethany's mind screamed her stepmother was there because of what her father had done that morning.

As though sensing her unrest, Abraham pecked her ear. "Remember, nothing can break us, Iris. And seeing your pretty face in a photograph will make me a happier man."

She couldn't help but smile.

"How about standing by the fireplace now?" Melissa asked.

"You'll be sure to share the photos, right?" Abraham led Bethany to the location.

"I'll order duplicates of them all, at the very least," Melissa promised.

Alexander came in and nipped a kiss on Melissa's cheek. "I'll want some as well, darling Sissa. Our Beth and her beau, forever captured in print."

While poised, Bethany saw the smoldering sadness beneath his charm. After Melissa took two pictures, she rushed to her stepparents. "What did Daddy do at Mademoiselle Bisset's?"

Alexander walked her to the sofa.

"What did he do, Poppy?"

He petted her hair and kissed her forehead. "Sissa will tell you, for she's dealing with it as much as you."

Melissa placed her camera on the coffee table and took an armchair. Turning to her stepmother, Bethany instinctively leaned against Abraham. He put an arm about her.

"Your father went to Mademoiselle Bisset to pull a favor from her she's talked about since you started working. He'd always told her he wouldn't think about sending you to Paris until you were eighteen, but he's changed his mind on the timing."

Bethany felt the color drain from her face.

Melissa took a deep breath before continuing. "They set it up that you'll leave by train on Friday for New York, and from there take a ship across to England before traveling to France. You'll be there through the end of summer, working and learning from Mademoiselle Bisset's friends in the fashion district of Paris."

"How could Daddy turn something wonderful into a punishment? Don't I have a say in my own life?"

"Oh, believe me, I spoke up for you when he came home and told me. He planned to travel with you and see you secured before returning, but I refused that notion. I haven't been to Paris since before the war, but I'm sure it's much the same in many ways. It wouldn't be safe for you to be there alone, even with trusted colleagues. You need a chaperone who understands your temperament and the possible dangers to young foreigners."

Abraham's arms tightened around Bethany. "Surely he doesn't think sending her around the world is safer than her being here with me?"

Melissa threw her hands into the air. "I don't know what's going on in his head, but I stomped out the utter devilishness of it and put him in his tyrannical place. He's not bringing you to leave you, Beth. He's not going at all. I'm pulling Louisa from school and taking both you girls. I telephoned a friend in New York and he's using his overseas connections to secure us a Paris apartment. I'll tutor Louisa while you work and several months abroad will be more than an education in itself. Your father can sit at home by himself and rot in his self-righteousness."

Alexander clapped. "It's about time you left him."

Bethany gasped at the thought of her father alone half the year—if Melissa decided to return. "But what will Daddy do?"

"Figure out his priorities, I should hope. Something's been eating away at him and he needs to get himself back on track."

Melissa sighed. "I don't plan on it being forever, but hopefully this will help him see what he's doing to you—to all of us."

Abraham, still clutching Bethany, looked to Melissa. "You're willing to leave your husband to prove Beth and I deserve to be together?"

"I do it to prove his bigotry is overshadowing common sense. The fact he was ready to drop his sixteen-year-old daughter in Paris for half a year proves he's not thinking rationally. Hopefully, he'll come out of the situation changed for the better."

"I don't want Daddy to hurt."

Alexander took Bethany's hand. "Sometimes through pain is the only way we can grow."

"You've always wanted to go to Paris, Beth," Melissa said in a softer voice. "It's just coming sooner than any of us realized. Set aside your frustration and focus on the good. You'll meet designers at House of Worth and even Coco Chanel. It's a tremendous opportunity."

"You'll do splendidly, Iris." Abraham kissed her cheek. "I'll put in more hours on the boats and work to get my captain's license even sooner, all while writing letters and gazing at what I'm sure will be fine photographs Sissa was kind enough to take. I won't forget you."

"Nor I you, Abe. Not ever."

Thirty

As much as Phoebe hated to admit it, Kade Campbell was a habit for her. Hans continued to grow his art circle in the Fairhope community, but his benefactors enjoyed weekends in Mobile with him and his muse. Phoebe would send word about where they were expected on a given Saturday, and Kade would show his handsome face for the chance to meet up with her. Hans turned a blind eye when she disappeared with him because he entertained others himself.

A Saturday night in mid-April, Kade walked into the dance hall with a swagger much like his stepfather. His attitude didn't go unappreciated by Phoebe. The fact that a man unknown to him had his arm around her while she sat at the table didn't seem to bother Kade in the least.

"Fancy running into you here. It's been about a month, hasn't it?" He kissed her slow on the mouth and Phoebe wanted to taste more of him.

"Whatever it was, it's been too long, Kade Campbell." She made introductions around the table, including to Jeremy Bridges, who had his arm about her waist.

"Are you stopping in to see your father while you're here?" Kade asked.

She rolled her eyes. "Why would I?"

"I thought you might with it being Easter tomorrow, seeing as how he's alone."

"Where are Sissa and my sisters?"

"They left him last month for Paris."

"And no one told me?" Phoebe pushed up from her seat and looked to Hans. "There's a bit of family dramatics and I need to see my father. Please excuse me."

Kade took her arm. "I'd be happy to drive you."

She looked to Hans.

"Find me by the time the ferry leaves Monday." Hans nodded toward Jeremy—who she was supposed to soften into purchasing a carving.

She gave Jeremy a playful smile. "I'm sorry to run out, but I'll return to the group before tomorrow evening. Save an Easter dance for me, Mr. Bridges."

Kissing her way around the table, Phoebe's last stop was Hans. "Sorry about this."

He glanced at Kade. "I bet you are, love."

Phoebe rushed from the club, Kade at her elbow. "Where are you parked?"

"Somewhere dark." He kissed her neck under the light of the full moon.

"If you gave me a story about Daddy to get me—"

"We both know I don't need to feed you a story to get you to come with me." He brought her down the side street to a parking spot off the road and opened the door to the backseat. "Ladies first."

"And we both know I'm no lady, Kade Campbell." She gave him a teasing smile before turning serious. "What about Daddy?"

"He'll still be alone whether in ten minutes or sixty."

The way he looked at her with hunger and appreciation made her cave to his blue-eyed demands. Even though they hadn't enjoyed a bed since their first time together, Kade was still her sweetest lover. She relaxed under his attentions and felt herself escape to the heavens as he satisfied their needs.

***

It had been almost a year since Phoebe was home. The last time, she had broken in to gather more of her clothing before escaping across the bay.

Kade pulled to a stop in front of the house. "I'll stick around, in case you change your mind."

"Thanks, Kade." She kissed him. "No matter what I've told you in the past, you're the best guy I know."

Though it was close to eleven, the parlor light was on behind the closed drapes. Phoebe rang the doorbell. When no one answered, she pounded against the window then waited with the screen door open.

More than a minute passed before the front door swung inward. Frederick Davenport leaned on his cane, eyes bloodshot, and smelling of whiskey.

"Daddy, what did Sissa do to you?" She fell against him, expecting his solid form but nearly knocked him over.

"Princess." He bowed his head over her and cried.

"Kade!" she screeched.

He was over in an instant, supporting Frederick so she could get free.

"Bring him to the sofa," she commanded. "I'll kill her for what she's done to you, Daddy!"

"I made her leave."

Phoebe settled beside her father, hugging his slim form. "You feel like you're wasting away. Aren't you going to the gym?"

He leaned back against the sofa, his gray hair a stark contrast to the hunter green of the fabric. "I haven't gone since last autumn. I haven't the strength to."

Chest tightening, Phoebe felt the lump rise in her throat until she couldn't breathe. "Don't say it, Daddy. Don't say it!"

She covered her ears and rocked. Eyes squeezed shut against her loving childhood home clashing with her current nightmare. Phoebe shuddered as Kade's hands lower hers.

"You're here because you care, Phoebe. Don't shut him out."

Clinging to her father, she sobbed against his chest. "Don't leave me again, Daddy."

"I was stubborn as always, not listening to the pain until it was too late. My body is riddled with cancer. The only thing left to do is dull the agony. I didn't want any of you around to watch my decline, so I planned to send Beth away knowing Sissa would never allow it and take her herself."

"Abe was your scapegoat." Kade's cold voice crackled with annoyance.

Frederick sighed in resignation. "I need to apologize to him."

"He's at the Adams's with his parents for Easter," Kade said.

Phoebe jumped off the sofa and gripped Kade's wrists. "Call Poppy and get Abe here! Both of them, now!"

Kade left the room and Phoebe paced before the hearth.

"Princess, please settle down."

"My body's on fire. I couldn't sit if you chained me to the chair!"

When Kade returned, Frederick motioned to Phoebe. "Please help calm her."

"It's better to let her go, Mr. Davenport. Either that or offer myself as a physical release, but now isn't the time or place for that."

Phoebe hissed out her breath as she watched the exchange. Her fears began to melt as her father appeared calm rather than aggravated.

"I need to apologize to you, Kade. I know you care for her and I might have made things difficult for you two. I'm sorry if anything I did pushed you apart."

"No!" Phoebe yelled. "Stay mad, Daddy! Stay mad at us and stay alive!"

The front door banged open, and Alexander rushed into the room. "My God, you look like hell, Freddy."

"He's dying! Why didn't any of you notice?" She was upon Alexander, beating him with her fists until Kade pulled her away in a bear hug. "He's been here alone and no one cares!"

"It's been my choice to be alone. I don't wish others to suffer with me."

Understanding lit Alexander's face with swift vengeance. "You damn fool! Did you learn nothing from Junior's death and the war? Your family needs you, even if you don't think you need them. They'll never forgive you if you keep them away, Freddy. They deserve to know, to be given the choice to see you through."

"I can't, Alex. It's as you said. Another wound to the old scars I already inflicted."

"Then I will, right now! A telegram is going to be sent to their apartment!"

Alexander stomped out of the house, his automobile squealing in protest as he cranked it around the front yard.

Frederick sank back onto the sofa. "I hate when he's right."

As her tension began to dissipate, Phoebe looked for ways to help her father. She propped a pillow under his arm and kissed his cheek. "Are you thirsty or hungry?"

"I haven't been hungry for weeks, Princess, but some tea would be nice."

She looked to Kade and he went for the kitchen. Phoebe paced behind the sofa, trying to hold herself together though the world was a haze beyond her own body.

Abraham Walker came in, red hair rumpled but he wore a pin-striped suit and a subdued expression. "You wished to see me, Mr. Davenport?"

"I want to apologize for using you as an excuse to send my family away." His hand went to his ribs as though cradling a sore spot. "As you can see, I'm not doing well. I didn't want my girls to see me suffer. I thought it best for them to be away, but Alex reminded me of my past mistakes in these matters."

Abraham perched on the coffee table in front of him. "What can I do for you, Mr. Davenport?"

"Tell Beth I understood my anger was unfounded when I woke on New Year's Day, but I was too ashamed to admit it. Tell her that I know you're a fine man though I used you as a way out. Be there for her and all her dreams, but protect her when needed. I know Melissa and Alex will be there, but she'll need more."

"I'll gladly do all that, Mr. Davenport, but I know she'll want to be here for you. Don't deny her closure."

He nodded. "Alex is seeing to that."

***

Wednesday afternoon, Phoebe stomped around the parlor. Anxiety over Hans's cold response to her telling him she wanted to stay with her father until her family returned continued to build after three days, as well as the silence from Paris. When Kade arrived after school, she came at him with her fists.

"Why haven't they telegrammed? They're punishing him by staying away!"

He took her strikes against his solid chest with a faint smile. When she slowed, he spoke. "Go get your riding clothes on."

"What a load of bricks you are to come here and order me around, Kade Campbell! I'm not leaving my father!"

"My mother is coming to sit with him so you can get some fresh air. I know Prince will be pleased to see you, and Poppy put in a special order of feed from Ingersoll's that's being delivered this afternoon."

She buried her head on his shoulder. "You're too sweet for words, and here I am beating you."

His arms snaked around her, lowering to grip her backside as they kissed. "I'll take good care of you, Phoebe."

Miss Sharon cleaned the downstairs and Phoebe asked her to listen out for Magdalene. Kade followed Phoebe into the guest room where her abandoned clothes from a year ago were stored, as well as it being her temporary home. Excited at the prospect of riding, she changed without hinting at seduction while Kade watched.

"I never tire of looking at you, Phoebe. If your father wasn't down the hall, I'd lay you on the bed and do everything we don't have the space for in an automobile."

She gave him a teasing smile as she buttoned her white top. "Find me sometime your mother isn't on her way over."

"You would? Here?"

"I don't know how long I'll stay on, especially with no word from Sissa. I can't be expected to go without." She saw a frown on the verge of showing. "But I'd welcome you anywhere, Kade. Don't you know that by now?"

"I've been hoping." He kissed her. "I'll wait for you downstairs."

"That's how it is, huh? Get yourself an eyeful and you're good for an hour or two."

"You know me better than that."

Magdalene was in the downstairs hall when Phoebe descended the stairs. "Come up, Miss Maggie. I've been a thorn in your side, but please know I appreciate you."

"You're being brave, Phoebe."

Willing herself not to cry, she bit the inside of her cheek and took Magdalene's hand to walk her to her father's bedroom. The woman immediately gasped and fled from the room in tears. Phoebe slipped downstairs and dialed Melling and Associates.

"I need to speak to Mr. Melling right away. It's a family emergency."

Less than a minute later, his voice came over the line.

"Poppy, please come as soon as you can."

"Did Maggie not arrive?"

"She's here and Daddy's asleep, but just looking at him gave her a shock."

"I'm sure she'll settle down before I arrive. Miss Sharon is there, isn't she?"

"Yes."

"Then you and Kade go on. He'll need to see to all the family's horses and the pony because the boys won't be going after school today. And Phoebe, try to enjoy your time."

"Thank you, Poppy. I love you."

"And I you, Knight Phoebe."

Thirty-One

Alexander took his final appointment not long after Phoebe's telephone call, and then readied to leave the office. With a fedora pulled over his eyes and a cigarette between his lips, he crossed the square toward Dauphin Street.

As though lying in wait, Kate Walters attached herself to his arm before he reached the corner. "Is it true about F.L.D.? Is he dying from a broken heart because his wife left him?"

"He doesn't suffer a broken heart, and Melissa didn't leave him. She accompanied Bethany to Paris for training." He lifted his chin to blow his smoke over his shoulder as they walked the next block. "But yes, I'm sorry to say, he's on his way out of this life. The family has been notified and asks for privacy, so don't get your gossip panties in a knot."

Her laugh was hollow. "It's tragic for those beautiful girls to lose both parents. I suppose you'll swoop in and be Daddy to them both. Not to mention care for the widow and her daughter as well." Kate winked.

Alexander released her hold and resumed walking without comment, snuffing his cigarette before entering the cathedral gates. After crossing himself, he lit a candle and moved to the pews to pray for Frederick, Melissa, and the Davenport girls, as he had each day since knowing his friend was dying.

When he arrived at Frederick's house, he was pleased to see the doctor's automobile. Magdalene rushed out the door, waving an envelope.

"This came to the house last hour. Simon ran it over." She handed him a telegram envelope and he tore it open.

RECEIVED NOTE TODAY STOP WE SPENT LONG EASTER HOLIDAY IN ITALY WITH CLAUDIO STOP WILL NOTIFY WHEN WE HAVE PASSAGE STOP HUG FREDDY AND TELL HIM WE ARE COMING HOME STOP

"Thank God!" He collapsed against his wife, the paper wrinkling in his hand. "They're on their way—or will be soon enough."

"What was the delay? Are they okay?"

"They spent Easter in Italy." He pressed his lips to hers. "I need to speak with the doctor."

"I'll wait down here."

Alexander took the stairs two at a time, skidding to a stop at Frederick's closed door. He rapped twice and tapped the telegram against the wall as he waited.

The doctor opened it a minute later. "Good afternoon, Mr. Melling."

"I have news for—"

"He's taking in what we've discussed—"

"Tell me, Alex," Frederick called from his bed. "Two weeks isn't so encouraging."

"Hang in, Davenport. Your girls are on their way!" Alexander thrust the paper at him—only realizing what confession it held a second later.

Frederick read the note and continued to stare at it. "Thank you, Doctor. I'll see you tomorrow."

"I'll leave a list of nurses with Mrs. Melling on my way out."

Frederick grunted in reply, sinking further into the pillows as he clutched the telegram to his chest.

"They're coming, Freddy. Hang on and allow them the chance to say goodbye."

"I'll look a fright to them, especially fresh from visiting Claudio."

"You pompous blowhard!"

Frederick managed a laugh. "Don't deny I'm withering away. I heard Maggie's tears but feigned sleep so I wouldn't embarrass her. Melissa fell in love with a boxing champion, not this waif of a man."

"She fell in love with you, Freddy—despite your stubborn pride."

"Tell Melissa I want her to keep living and loving. I know she'll care for the girls, even Phoebe in her own way. And you'll be here for them all."

Alexander nodded. "And Maggie and Darla and Henry and Naomi—"

"And Claudio." Frederick expelled a pained breath.

"Claudio chose the church."

"He settled for it because Melissa stayed with me. He'll come for her."

"What the hell would he do here if they don't call him as an exorcist?"

"He won't come as a priest, Alex. Not this time. And if he does come for her wearing the frock of your faith, he'll be nothing but a charlatan. If he's going to be true to Melissa and my girls, he needs to be honest about his choice to his superiors."

"He wouldn't do that. He's worked hard all these years training and—"

"You didn't notice them together the morning Lucy died. Claudio was committed, not to his faith, but to Melissa. He stood beside her, ready to forsake all and catch her if she turned from me. And she hesitated between us. I saw it in her eyes. She chose me, for better or worse, as pledged at our vows. Support them if it comes to it—and I believe it will, especially since she's been to him."

Seeking to defend his priestly friend, Alexander shook his head. "It's not like that, Freddy. The note said 'we'. The girls were with her."

"Hearts don't need sexual attention to be involved. She loves Claudio—she told me herself when I returned. Maybe I pushed her away after Junior died to prepare her for this, giving her a ready companion to succor her in her hour of need. I was neglectful to her again the months before she left because I didn't wish her to see how I'd weakened."

Alexander ran a hand through his hair and sighed in frustration. "Enough. Isn't it time for your supper?"

"I'm not hungry."

Calling on his last ounce of strength and bravado, Alexander squared his shoulders though he preferred to curl into a ball and weep. "You *will* eat, Frederick Lionel Davenport. Delicate Lucy clung to life to see you once more, and you'll do that for your girls as well."

***

A week later, Frederick's further decline was minor. Phoebe attributed it to the twenty-four hour nursing care, but Alexander thought it was due to his pep talk. Kade visited each afternoon, taking Phoebe to the stable every other day. Alexander stopped in after work, as well as Henry, who now ran everything at the accounting office. Magdalene, Darla, and Naomi paid short visits throughout the day, and Miss Sharon was employed from breakfast to suppertime to offer food to Frederick, as well as feed those watching over him and keep the house tidy.

The last Friday in April, a telephone call came through at Alexander's office.

"Melling."

"Alex, we're in New York. We'll be on the Limited tomorrow and home Monday."

"We need you, Sissa."

"He's still—"

"He's hanging on like the stubborn fool he is. He has much to tell you, but informed me of everything in case he's not strong enough to speak it all."

"Thank you for the telegrams. I'm sorry for the delay responding. We spent a glorious time in Italy, seeing more than we should have because now it's all a blur. Naples, Vatican City, Florence. We were even blessed by the Pope at Easter Mass. The girls were all begging to go back on the return train. They loved it, and Claudio was a spectacular guide."

"Did you keep the apartment? It might be good to get away while you adjust to changes. You could return to Paris and allow Beth to finish what she started."

"I let it go. I didn't think it best to pay rent on an empty place."

"Melissa, prepare yourself and the girls. You remember the change in Lucy her final weeks, it's even more pronounced in your champion."

"Your second telegram said cancer."

"His torso is eaten up with masses. They're starving his body as the pressure makes it difficult for him to eat. I hadn't seen him for a month, but for you and the girls it'll be twice that. Prepare the darlings—I can't say that enough. He's known since before

Christmas what was happening, but it was too late. He'd been having pains and fatigue for months. When he finally sought medical attention, he kept the news private and searched for a way to let you and the girls go to save you the pain. Don't worry. I berated him good for that."

"He's insufferable at times, but I love him."

"I know you do—as does he. Tell Bethany he's apologized to Abe for using him as the scapegoat to get you three out of town."

"He never meant to leave Beth in Paris?"

"He knew you would never allow it."

She sniffled. "And I thought he was raving out of his mind with hatred toward Abe."

"We all did, but they've made amends. Abe comes over a few times a week to check on him. Be sure Beth hears her father approves."

"I will, Alex. Thank you for everything. I suppose he was hiding at home. How did you find out?"

"Phoebe. Kade told her Freddy was alone when she was in town Easter weekend. She took one look at her father and had Kade to telephone me. She has stayed with him the whole time. It's amazing how she's holding together, but I think she'll be glad to free herself."

"I'm happy he had one daughter with him."

"We all are. I'll collect you on Monday, Melissa. Stay strong."

"Thank you, Alex."

He immediately telephoned home.

"Mellings' residence."

Is it just me or does her voice sound sultry? "Do you have any pressing engagements, sweetness?"

"Not today, Alex."

"Stay there, please. I need a hug. I'll be home soon to collect it. I love you."

He hung the receiver while Magdalene's soft laughter came through the line, but then picked it back up to dial the Davenports'.

"Miss Sharon, could I speak with Phoebe?"

"Certainly, Mr. Alex. The doctor's just come and gone."

A minute later Phoebe's breathy voice was on the line. "Poppy!"

"How's the patient?"

"He can no longer sit up by himself."

"Your sisters and Melissa are in New York. I'll collect them at the train station Monday afternoon."

"I'll tell him when he wakes." She hesitated. "Poppy, he's been talking about Sissa and all he's done to disappoint her through the years. I don't want to hear it. All I can think about is what Uncle Eddie told me, especially when Daddy said she didn't answer the telegram right away because she was with Claudio. I'm scared. My body gets tingly and I feel like I'm not really here. I don't want to be home when Sissa comes."

"Phoebe Camellia Davenport, you've been brave. I'm proud of you and your momma would be proud too. Leave whenever you feel like it. If you want to take the Sunday morning ferry, I'll stay with Freddy that day and Maggie will come after the kids go to school Monday so I can get to the train station. Just let me know and we'll cover things, Knight Phoebe."

"Thank you, Poppy."

"And be sure Kade takes you to the stables this afternoon."

"We just went yesterday."

"Tell him I insist. It will do you good. I'll stay until you return."

Alexander went for his automobile so he could rush into Magdalene's arms and find release for the mounting stress that threatened to break him in the coming days.

Thirty-Two

The train rumbled to a stop twelve hours behind schedule. Bethany, hand still gripping her locket as it had most of the journey, sat ridged in her seat as Melissa secured porters to help with their luggage.

Louisa pressed her face to the glass in the early morning darkness of Tuesday, wild auburn curls about her ears as she'd been allowed a coveted bob while they were in Paris. "Poppy's here!"

Bethany leaned over her sister's shoulder, but she didn't see Alexander. Her eyes fell to the tweed cap and the huge grin on a freckled face she'd been staring at in photographs in their weeks apart.

"Wait for Sissa," she told Louisa as she squeezed through the crowded passage to get to the nearest exit.

She flew off the steps, and ran headlong into Abraham's arms. Pressing her nose and lips to his neck, she breathed his salty scent and kissed his warm skin as she relished the sensation of his arms holding her.

"You feel wonderful, Abe." She squeezed him tighter. "I don't know if I could have made it without you any longer."

"You have fortitude, Iris, though I'm afraid I haven't made captain yet."

She laughed. "Nor am I a world class designer."

"That doesn't matter to me in the least, unless it's what you want."

Then they kissed, falling deeper into the other's arms.

Alexander nudged Abraham's shoulders. "Let me get a hug before you suck the life from her."

They broke their kiss with laughter.

Bethany turned to embrace her stepfather. "I love and missed you too, Poppy."

Alexander's hug was stronger than she remembered, but his kiss on her forehead was the same. He tucked her shoulder-length hair behind her ear and looked her in the eyes.

"Listen, Knight Bethany. It's going to be tough, but don't try to hide your sorrow. Abe is here for the week. He'll be sleeping at my house, but he's at your disposal all day. Don't hold in your emotions. Allow him to see you through the pain. I'll be here too, of course, but I'll have to help Sissa the most."

Bethany nodded and whispered her thanks.

Melissa and Louisa were greeted and the luggage piled into the back of the Mellings' second automobile. Bethany rode with Abraham and the luggage, following Alexander to the Davenports' house. They didn't speak, but they sat so they touched. When he parked in the oyster shell driveway, he took her in his arms.

"Your father loves you, Iris. Stay with him as long as you can. I'll be here for you."

Darla Adams met them on the stairs, hugging each Davenport in turn.

"Wake him, Melissa. He wanted to know as soon as you're here." Darla took Louisa's hand. "Give your mother a minute."

Bethany followed Melissa to the bedroom door. Seeing the arrivals, the nurse quietly left the room. Bethany's heart fell to her stomach at the sight of her father, pale and gaunt beneath the bedside lamp.

"Freddy," Melissa's voice trembled as she sank to the edge of the bed and took his hand. "Freddy, I'm home."

His head shifted toward her and his eyes opened. For a brief second, his old smile brightened his face before it was etched with pain.

He quickly took control of the display and raised her hand to his lips. "Happy Birthday, Beloved. These fifteen years you've worn my ring have been my greatest blessing. A gift I haven't been worthy of. I hope the good has outweighed the bad for you."

"We had a few rough spells, Handsome, but I've loved my life with you and our children."

As Melissa leaned over to kiss him, Bethany fled to her room, falling upon her bed in tears.

Alexander and Abraham carried in her trunk, setting it against the wall.

"Hold her, Abe," Alexander commanded. "Curl up beside her and let her cry. I'll get the rest of the suitcases."

"Iris, my love," he whispered as he lay behind her, tucking his body against her back. An arm went over her side as he kissed her ear. "I'm here for you."

She spooned with Abraham until the sun shone through the window and her tears dried. After washing her face, she returned to his arms.

Melissa came to the door. "Beth, your father wants to see you."

Abraham walked her to the other room, waiting in the hall.

"Little Princess." Frederick's smile was almost as big as the old days.

She leaned over to kiss his cheek, noting his glassy eyes. "I missed you, Daddy."

"I've told everyone how sorry I am, everyone but you. I didn't mean to harm, only to protect."

"I know, Daddy." But she didn't. His words were nothing more than deathbed confessions to help him and others feel better about the recent pain—different from what he admitted the previous summer about his behavior during the war. That time he didn't have to confess, this time he did.

"You're the most like me, Beth." He fingered the arch of her eyebrow. "You need someone equally strong to hold you accountable when you're too stubborn. Someone who loves you enough to put your relationship first in life. Sissa has been my match, and I think you've found that with Abraham Walker."

"I think so too," she whispered.

***

Wednesday after lunch, Bethany, Abraham, and Louisa took the streetcar downtown. They stopped in Mademoiselle Bisset's shop first, Bethany thanking her for the introductions she enjoyed while in Paris.

"They rave about you, Bethany! I keep getting letters from everyone you met in the district on how lovely and talented you are. Coco was ready to tuck you under her wing, both as a model and seamstress. They were all sad your stay was cut short, and send their blessings to your family during this time. You would be welcomed back whenever you wish to return, though I am happy to have you here."

"I'm glad to be home, but it was lovely. I'll let you know when I can resume work."

"I know you're needed with your father. I thought he looked worn that day he came to speak with me, but one does not say such a thing to a man like Frederick Davenport. Send him my love, Bethany. And his wife. I shall hate to see her clad in black when she needs earth tones to shine." She sniffed back a tear and embraced both Davenport sisters and then Abraham.

Their next stop was Davenport and Adams Allied Accountants. Ms. Neves—at the front desk as always—had tears in her eyes before the door closed behind them.

"Dear girls!" She rushed over with open arms. "Things aren't the same without your father in the office. He's called at least daily, but we haven't heard from him this week."

"He's not doing well," Louisa said. "But he told us to tell everyone hello for him."

"Then go spread the word, Miss Louisa, and show off your stylish Parisian haircut."

Louisa demurely made her way through the desks, speaking to each worker. Bethany paused long enough to introduce Abraham to the secretary. Then they went beyond the frosted glass door labeled FREDERICK L. DAVENPORT to the second office, and knocked beside the name HENRY H. ADAMS.

"Beth!" Henry pulled her into his arms and kissed her cheeks. He had always been more of an uncle to her than her Easton blood relations. His dark blue eyes shone as he looked her over. "Your time in Europe did a number on you. You'll be an old lady before we know it if you keep maturing."

She smiled and looked at Abraham. "So long as I don't pass Abe in years, it's all good."

Henry laughed before clapping Abraham on his back. "Are you doing all right, Abe?"

"Yes, sir."

"Mr. Henry!" Louisa jumped at him for a hug. "Mom doesn't want me to have friends over right now, but do you think I could visit Horatio sometime?"

"Stop by on your way home if you'd like. He's not scheduled to go to the stables today."

"Could I, Beth?"

Not wanting her little sister shut in the gloomy house, Bethany nodded. "We'll drop you there on our way home."

Once Louisa returned to Ms. Neves, Bethany looked at Henry. "Would it be okay if I go in Daddy's office?"

"Of course. We utilize it for meetings with a few of our clients, but it's empty right now."

Without taking Abraham's hand, she started toward the door. She fingered her father's name on the glass and breathed in the air when she turned the knob. Adding machine ink and aftershave—her father would live on there as long as his scent remained. She flipped on the light and turned to gaze at the space. The tops of the four-foot high bookshelves that lined the room held family pictures: baby photos from all four Davenport children, the girls through the years, and images of the Davenports, Mellings, and Campbells—most of them captured by Melissa.

She made her way through the memories and lowered herself to his desk chair. Looking at the tidy tabletop, Bethany studied at the wedding photo which sat on the right corner as long as she remembered. Frederick and Melissa stood in the gazebo. Bethany was in her father's arm and his other was around Melissa, who held Phoebe's hand. A new frame on the left side of the desk caught her attention.

"Abe!" her voice cracked.

He was at her side in an instant and she pointed to the photograph. It was the one Melissa took of them before telling Bethany she was being sent to Paris—Abraham's arm about Bethany's shoulders and his huge, easy grin.

"He hasn't been to the office for over a month. That means Daddy truly approved of us all along."

When Melissa went for her pre-supper walk Saturday afternoon, Bethany and Abe sat with Frederick. He was propped on several pillows to help his breathing, which had grown more labored, but his recent dose of pain medication made him talkative and artificially bright-eyed.

"Are you at peace with me, Beth?"

She took his hand in both of hers, surprised at the coldness. "Yes, Daddy."

"There's nothing more I need to explain or say to help ease your pain?"

Smiling, her own eyes glistened. "I always knew you loved me, no matter where you were." She touched her locket. "And you'll always be by my heart, just like Momma."

"Don't tell Sissa, but I think that's the best gift I ever gave."

Bethany smiled. "I think she'd argue her cameo was the best. She wore it always when we were gone."

"She didn't take the emeralds."

"It's not good to travel with things like that, Daddy. They draw too much attention."

"I told her she could sell them if she wanted. Even her engagement ring."

"She's wouldn't. Not unless it was a matter of life and death."

He gave a shallow laugh. "That's what she told me, or rather, if she was desperate to feed you girls, they'd be gone in an instant."

"Don't spend your remaining time worrying. She's sensible and she'll care for us. And there's Poppy and everyone else."

He shifted in a way the showed his discomfort. "Claudio."

"I don't know," she whispered.

"Why?" Frederick asked.

"She telephoned him from the train station before we left Paris. It sounded like they had an argument, and I haven't seen her write him since then."

"Did something happen on your visit to Italy?"

"Everything was lovely. We met the people in his parish, he had us blessed by the Pope, and introduced us to his family in Florence. It was only the telephone call that was amiss."

"What did she say?" His alertness was back and he squeezed her hand.

"She told him we were coming home because you were sick and then refused something he said. The station was noisy, but the last thing I heard was her telling him not to come."

"Little Princess, promise me something."

"Anything, Daddy."

"If Claudio comes, welcome him and help Melissa understand that it's okay." He took a heavy breath and closed his eyes. "Do you remember what I told you last summer when you questioned their relationship?"

Her skin broke out in gooseflesh. "Yes."

"Sissa might need you to remind her that I understood. I don't want her to be lonely." His brown eyes opened once more, looking to his daughter and then to Abraham. "I don't want anyone to be alone. Take care of my Beth."

Thirty-Three

On the afternoon of May fifteenth, Phoebe relaxed on the front porch of Jeremy Bridge's cottage overlooking the Fairhope pier. She took another drag from her cigarette and scowled when she spied Hans coming down the sidewalk.

When she had arrived back in Fairhope from her stay with her father two weeks previous, she found her things in a ragged box on his front stoop and a new girl installed in her room—the stranger's personal items all over the bookshelf her father had bought. Her pearls still hung from the side of the mirror over the dresser and her grandmother's scissors sat beside the wash basin. She snatched her items and barged into Hans's room that Sunday morning.

"What the hell is this, Hans?"

Sprawled on the bed, he shifted upright. "I didn't know when you'd be back and my work needed to continue."

"My father is dying!"

"Aren't we all?"

The back door opened. A flimsy brunette came in from the outhouse wearing Lucy's kimono.

"Get out of my mother's robe, you thieving bitch!" Phoebe slapped her across the face.

The new muse shimmied out of the silk, trying to cover herself with her hands once she passed it to Phoebe.

She laughed. "How is this chit inspiring, Hans? She hasn't proper posture, her breasts aren't symmetrical, and those are the knobbiest knees I've ever seen on a woman. But since you seem to be able to continue without me, let me take care of the rest of my things you forgot about!"

She stomped back into her old room, and picked up the spindled bookcase to smash it over the brass bedframe until it splintered into unusable pieces. Then, she used the Easton scissors to shred the upholstered chair bought by Frederick Davenport. But she didn't stop there. Phoebe tore open the kitchen cupboards, seeking dry goods she'd last purchased with her store credit. Gathering soup cans and an unopened bag of grits, she dumped them into the waiting box out front without another word.

It was too big to carry, so she dragged it toward town.

Two blocks later, Jeremy came across her on his morning drive and loaded the luggage and girl into his automobile, offering Phoebe a place to stay. Jeremy had been sensitive to her emotions and showered her with praises, including his opinion that the carvings of Phoebe were the pinnacle of Hans's career, and the new model he employed wouldn't amount to anything.

"He'll be back to nature carvings for tourists before he knows what hit him," was how Jeremy put it.

Two weeks of living with a maid and cook had her spoiled—not to mention Jeremy didn't mind sharing a bed with her all night, a comfort she had never before enjoyed. Phoebe was back to wearing her pretty clothes, which were laundered for her, and spending time in leisure rather than tedious domestic duties or sitting endlessly for scant praise.

Hans made it to the screen door of the porch and pulled two envelopes out of his pocket.

Phoebe stared without expression. "What do you want?"

"These telegrams came for you. The first arrived Friday evening when I was headed out. The second yesterday afternoon, but I was too hungover to do anything about it."

She unlatched the door and opened it enough to slip her hand out, knowing they held news of her father. He placed the envelopes in her hand and then grabbed her wrist. I'm on my third model, love. No one is as good as you."

"Let go of me!"

He tightened his hold. "Come back to me, Phoebe. I'll buy you a new bookshelf and chair."

"No!"

Hans twisted his grip, trying to drag her out. She screamed.

Jeremy ran from the house. "Let her go!"

Hans did, but sneered at the couple. "Don't think you own her, Mr. Bridges. She's a wild filly."

Jeremy's arm went about her waist as she clutched the telegrams to her chest. "If you come around again, I'll see you never sell another piece of art in this town."

Hans stomped off, and Jeremy guided her to the sofa where she tore open the envelopes and read the news with misty eyes. Phoebe laid her head on Jeremy's shoulder. He softly kissed her face.

"Daddy passed Friday afternoon. His funeral is at Trinity Tuesday morning. I want to go, but have nothing to wear." Which wasn't entirely true—she had dresses in Mobile that would do, but she didn't want two-year-old Sunday clothes.

"We can take the ferry tomorrow and shop for a few mourning dresses."

"That sounds perfect. How can I ever repay your kindness?"

"You know how, Phoebe." Jeremy brought her hand to his crotch, but his dark eyes were so seductive, it felt like pleasure rather than payment.

***

On Monday, Phoebe waltzed into Mademoiselle Bisset's shop with more cash in her purse than she had ever had at one time.

"Miss Phoebe!" The shopkeeper rushed to her. "My dear, we all feel your pain. Your father was the heart and soul of gentlemen in this town. At least half the ladies were in love with him at one point or another."

Thinking of her tirade at the New Year's Eve ball, Phoebe smiled. "I know, Mademoiselle, and I'm here for you to dress me for his funeral."

"It will have to be something off the rack. There's no time for alterations."

"I trust you." She smiled. "How's my sister?"

"She had a wonderful time in Paris, but is pleased to be back. Of course, having that charming beau has something to do with it, I'm sure. He's the dearest creature."

"Who?"

"Abraham Walker, of course. He'll be in twice a week just to say hello for half a minute before running back to the docks."

While she was shown every respectable black dress in the shop, Phoebe's brain mulled over the aggravating fact that in all her time at home, neither Kade nor her father mentioned Bethany and Abraham were a couple.

She walked out of the shop wearing a traditional drop-waist sheath Mademoiselle tried to tell her was too tight on her hips and a jaunty black hat with a partial lace veil. Her other purchases, and what she arrived in, were to be delivered to the hotel. Clipping her way down the sidewalk with an exaggerated sway, Phoebe had two offers to show her a good time so she'd forget her sorrow.

In the hotel room, Jeremy approved of her dress and then removed it so he could make love to her. The image of Abraham Walker's naughty grin as he felt up her thigh with his deliciously calloused fingers last summer was all she could think of while she panted and moaned for Jeremy's benefit.

Abe wants you, not Beth.

He only settled for her because you've been with Hans.

Kade was protecting both your feelings by not telling you.

Beth will never give a guy like that enough to keep him satisfied.

As typical after their time together, Jeremy fell asleep. Phoebe redressed and took the streetcar to the Mellings' home. No one answered the door. She went around the back, hoping to find a rear door unlocked. Instead, she found Abraham smoking on the patio.

"Abe Walker, you sly sailor." She stopped in front of his chair, hand on hip. "All those times you stopped by to see Daddy, I thought you were on errand from your family. But you were only trying to stay on his good side so you could get under Beth's skirt."

"You know nothing."

"I know her legs are locked at the knees, and a guy like you won't be able to hold out forever." She dropped into his lap. "I'll be my sister's stand in so you can get what you need."

Abraham stood so fast, Phoebe slid to the ground. Hazel eyes on fire, he stared with contempt. "You're still a conniving slut."

She forced herself to stand and appear unmoved by his words. "And you know you're unworthy of my sister!"

"You're the unworthy one, Phoebe. How will she feel to know her sister offered herself to me?"

"She might appreciate it if it keeps you from going elsewhere or exposes your true character to her delicate sensibilities."

"The only thing this conversation is proving is how loathsome you are." He dropped his cigarette in the ashtray, going for the kitchen door as the back gate opened.

"Phoebe!" Kade ran across the yard and took her in his arms, kissing her hard and deep like she enjoyed best. "No one knew if you'd make it home."

"I didn't get the telegrams until yesterday. I'm no longer with Hans."

"That's great to hear." His smile doubled before he caressed her backside. "We've got an hour or more before the family returns."

"I've always wanted in your bed, Kade Campbell."

"Then my bed you shall have, Phoebe Davenport." He held the door open for her.

"She offered herself to me a minute ago," Abraham said as they passed through the kitchen.

Kade paused, looking between the two.

Phoebe wiggled against Kade enticingly. "It was a pity offering. I know my sister's not giving him anything."

"She better not be."

"Don't tell me you're jealous, Kade Campbell."

"And what if I am, Phoebe? Would it make you give me more?"

Abraham slammed out the backdoor.

"I already gave you everything I've got. No other man can say he took my innocence."

The gleam in his blue eyes shot through her with yearning, and she hurried for the stairs. In his room, he removed her dress and laid it over his desk chair while he nudged her toward the bed. She kicked off her shoes, and then watched him release the garter straps and roll down her stockings with care. Once his own clothes were removed, he snuggled beside her on the soft bed.

"I can't wait to smell you on my pillow next time I go to sleep."

She attacked his lips, no longer able to control the passion he held over her. Their tongues tangled, and her hands explored him while he made her feel alive and forever cherished. The time and space was luxuriant compared to their recent romps. Content and feeling safe, they fell asleep in each other's arms.

It was nearly four when they slipped on their clothes. Kade kissed her once more and put a finger to his lips as he opened the hall door. Alexander leaned against the opposite wall, arms crossed, frown a mile deep.

"Both of you to my den. Father Quinn is waiting."

Phoebe raised her defiant chin. "We aren't members of the cathedral, or baptized Catholic for that matter."

"You're both half-Catholic and though those parents with that belief are gone from this life, you can bet they're disgusted with your lack of remorse for your sinful behaviors!" His frosty blue eyes bore into Phoebe's soul. "Haven't you learned from the past what these actions inflict upon those around you, not to mention yourselves?"

Phoebe reached for him. "Poppy, I'm—"

He stepped away. "Phoebe Camellia, I love you, but I can't allow you to invite evil within these walls. I'll be here to help both of you, but when you leave today you're not to come back unless I personally invite you. And Kade, I love you as my son, but you have until your autumn term to find new living arrangements. Now go to the den."

"If that wharf rat tattled on us when he fled—"

"I came back hours ago and heard the racket you two were making," Alexander said as he followed them down the stairs. "To safeguard my family, I immediately telephoned Magdalene to keep the children away and the parish so a priest would be at the ready to bless those of us unlucky to be within these unhallowed walls, and then to bless the house after the fornicators leave."

"Is that what I am now, a fornicator? Just because I've lain with two men today—"

Kade stopped in the hallway and grabbed her hand. "You said you were no longer with Hans."

"I gave him the icy mitt two weeks ago. I'm the houseguest of Jeremy Bridges at his cottage with a cook and maid on the bluff in Fairhope. He brought me across the bay, put us up in the Cawthon Hotel, purchased my mourning dresses, and then worked me until he exhausted himself. He may be rich, but he has no stamina. I still had plenty to give you, Kade."

Kade pushed her away. "Abe was right about you."

Hot pain slashed her chest from his contemptuous dismissal. Before she could rein her emotions, a tear slipped out.

Alexander whispered, "You need to make choices to bring you joy, not pain."

"I'm too far gone, Poppy."

"No one's beyond hope, Phoebe Camellia."

Thirty-Four

For the first time in his life, Alexander drove his automobile to Seacliff. Friday, July first, he brought Magdalene, Amelia, Tabitha, and Bethany while Melissa followed in her vehicle with Louisa, Simon, and Asher. For the grand total of two dollars and sixty cents, both vehicles drove more than ten miles across the five rivers at the delta of Mobile Bay on the Cochrane Bridge and causeway. The drive south from Spanish Fort through Daphne and on to Montrose was sweltering, but it was glorious to have the intimate companionship and travel on their timeline rather than deal with the public ferry.

When he pulled up the driveway, he glanced to Magdalene beside him. "That was fun!"

She laughed and kissed his cheek. "You're such a kid when it comes to new adventures."

"I'm incredibly simple in my likes and needs." He shut off the car and turned to her. "And right now I need a hug."

"Mama, Poppy, can Beth take me swimming?"

Alexander looked over his wife's shoulder at their daughter as she climbed out of the backseat. "If she wants to, Amelia Rose."

"I'd love to." Bethany took the girl's hand and they rushed to the porch.

Melissa unlocked the front door, and Simon and Asher hauled in the luggage—mostly for themselves and Amelia, who'd outgrown the play clothes and swimsuits they kept at the house. Tabitha opened the front room window and immediately began on the piano.

Alexander returned his attention to Magdalene, pulling her closer in the front seat. "May I bring you to your swing, Maggie?"

She blushed and nodded with that sweet smile she had whenever she thought of Douglas. He knew she felt closest to her first husband when sitting on the swing he built her. Leroy Watts had strict instructions to keep it in good condition. He also had extra plans to fulfill that week, and Alexander didn't doubt they'd been accomplished.

He escorted her into the old barn and held the ropes steady while she sat—admiring the curve of her hips in her lightweight traveling dress. After untying her braid and giving her shoulders a caress, Alexander pushed her forward to start her momentum.

"Is it just me, or does it smell like fresh hay in here?" she asked

Coming around in front of her, he smiled wickedly. "Must be all those erotic fantasies you have from your time with the stable boy."

"I'd punch you right now if I could reach you, Alexander Melling."

With a swivel to his hips he opened his shirt from the bottom up, showcasing his abdominal muscles. "Come on and hit me, Maggie. I can take it."

Whooping and hollering from the boys as they streaked toward the cliff filled the air. Then Melissa was in the doorway, wearing her swimsuit with a towel slung over her shoulder and a book tucked under her arm.

"I'm going down with them." She caught Alexander's display and did a double take. "I haven't seen you like that in a while, but you're—"

"The sexiest man you've ever met?" He winked.

She laughed, but it was short lived—typical for her solemn moods since Frederick passed. "I prefer my men tall and dark, but you're in fine shape, Alex." She looked to Magdalene on the swing. "You're extremely blessed, Maggie, just as he is. Enjoy each other while I have the kids. All except Tabby, but as long as you hear the piano, you know where she is."

"Speaking of music," Alexander said as he came at her with a grin. "I want to dance with you tonight, darling Sissa. Save a tango for me."

"Always, dashing Poppy." She kissed his cheek and lightly brushed his stomach with her fingers, causing his breath to hitch.

"Naughty Sissa." He grabbed her hips playfully as he kissed her cheek in return.

When she was gone, he returned his attentions to Magdalene. "She needs a man."

"Melissa Stone Davenport has always been independent," his wife reminded him. "She might want a man for companionship and lovemaking, but she doesn't need one to survive."

"We all need someone. That's what this life is about—love, the giving and sharing of it with body, mind, and soul." Alexander stood before the swing so she bumped to a stop against him. "Tell me you need me, Magdalene."

"I'd rather show you." Her arms went about his bare middle and she nibbled her way across his ribs.

With a groan of primal need, Alexander threaded his fingers through her loose hair as her lips continued to taste him. When her wanton eyes looked up, he grinned.

"Maggie, there's something I want to show you." He dashed for the ladder and steadily climbed, standing a couple feet from the edge of the loft before turning. After a brief hesitation from the dizzying sensation of looking down at her, Alexander raised his hands in triumph. "Your love helped me face my fears and become conqueror!"

When she went for the ladder, he hastily removed his shoes and pants. He stood in his underdrawers before a pile of clean hay topped with a velvet blanket when she reached the top.

"It's time for that romp in the hay I wanted last summer."

She unfastened the buttons at her chest. "Aren't we getting too old for this?"

"When we're too old to enjoy each other, we might as well be dead. And I'm nowhere near done loving you."

He managed to share pleasure with his wife for an hour before agreeing it was time to join the rest of the group. Magdalene went to their room to change into her swimsuit while Alexander prepared a batch of lemonade. When she came to the kitchen, he trailed a hand up her bare arm and pulled her in for a deep kiss.

Tabitha pushed through the swinging door. "Mama, *really*! You two should be well beyond the honeymoon phase. It's embarrassing!"

"I told your beautiful mother that when we fail to enjoy being together, life will be over. We're an example of what to seek in your own relationship. Don't bother with a man you don't wish to kiss all the day long."

"If I attached myself to a man the way you two go at it I'd be sent to a convent!"

Magdalene laughed. "I'd never send one of my daughters to a convent."

"Thank you, Mama. Though I wouldn't put it past Poppy."

He quirked a smile at her as he stirred the sugar into the water. *Amelia is so pretty, it might be safer for her to be in one. I don't look forward to the day boys start flocking to her—and they will! Dear God, don't make my beautiful daughter a punishment for all the women I mistreated in my youth!*

"I'll be sure Poppy doesn't ship you off," Magdalene said with a smile. "Did Bradford say if he's coming this weekend?"

"He'll be here Sunday afternoon. Please try to behave yourselves." Tabitha gave Alexander a cutting look before flouncing out of the room.

He glared at Magdalene. "You let her invite that cad here?"

"She's been seeing him half a year now. It's about time we invited him to a family gathering."

Alexander threw the ice cubes into in the pitcher with a little too much force and then gathered cups and a sack of peanuts, which he tossed into the picnic basket. After placing the roses for the sepulcher on top of the basket he frowned.

"Exactly like a spoiled boy." Magdalene pinched his cheek before kissing his lips. "I love you and I'm glad you worry about Tabby."

"Someone needs to stay immune to Mr. Petty's charms."

***

Before the sun began to lower over the bay, Asher and Simon piled the driftwood they'd collected for a bonfire so they could cook hotdogs for supper.

Alexander nodded his approval as he dried his torso. "It looks good, boys. Maggie, they have my permission to light it when they're done. I'm going to walk with Sissa."

Melissa pulled her beach jacket over her bathing suit. "You don't have to, Alex."

"I want to." He tossed his towel around his shoulders like a cape and hooked his arm through hers.

They headed north along the shoreline, leaving the sounds of the family behind them.

"How have you been, Melissa, really and truly?"

She leaned her head on his shoulder a moment. "I feel like I've lost my purpose. With Louisa out of school for the summer, I don't know what to do with her staring at me all day. I don't want to always farm her off to Magdalene or Darla, but I don't expect her to sit with me all the time. Beth's a dear when she's home, but I don't want either of them feeling like they need to entertain me to keep me from sadness."

"Have you tried writing?"

"What, 'A Widow's Guide to Survival'?"

Alexander chuckled. "At least you haven't lost your humor. How about you follow my advice from my widower days?"

"And remarry within months to defeat loneliness? I hardly have a harem to choose from."

"You have plenty of admires, Melissa."

"None of them are eligible."

"Is there one you fancy was available more than the others—you know, besides me?"

She ignored the joke. "I'll find my balance at some point."

"And I'll be your Turkey Trot partner in the meantime."

Melissa's smiled. "Freddy loved to dance. I remember his indignation when you taught Phoebe and Kade how to tango."

"God forgive me, I forgot about that. And now they're—oh Sissa, have I ruined the whole family?"

She stopped and fingered the scars on his chest. "You saved it, Alex."

He kissed her nose. "I wish I could save you now."

"Keep being my friend, dashing Poppy."

"Always." Alexander tugged her against his side as they continued on.

A figure walked toward them nearly half a mile in the distance, white shirt bright before the cliffs and baggage at his sides. As they grew closer, the man's dark hair and shape tugged at Alexander's memory, though the look of him in a pale shirt and trousers was completely new.

Melissa pulled away from Alexander and broke into a run. He followed in disbelief, remembering Frederick's words. *"...if he does come for her wearing the frock of your faith, he'll be nothing but a charlatan..."*

But Claudio was there as a layman. Melissa paused before him as though deciding the best course to take.

"*Eroina*, I know you told me not to come, but I could not stay away. I have been denying my feelings for fifteen years. We had a taste of what could be ten years ago, but it was not the correct time to see it fulfilled. I believe now is for us. If we do not cling to it, we will be lost to each other forever." He dropped his suitcases and raised his arms from his sides, eyes pleading. "I am released from my service to the church, though I still plan to honor God in all I do. Allow me your company as I transition to a new lifestyle and I will forever be your helpmeet."

Melissa dipped her head and wiped the back of a hand across her cheek.

Alexander squeezed her arm. "Someone to entertain you and be a dance partner," he whispered. "Frederick didn't want you to be alone. He told me to welcome Claudio when he came."

"He did?" she asked, eyes wide.

Alexander nodded. "He respected what you two shared and wanted me to thank Claudio for what he did for you during the war. Freddy knew you loved her, Claudio, and cared for her and Louisa like he hadn't been capable of since he lost Junior. He made me pledge to support your relationship. I promise you both now that I'll do all I can to see you through life together."

"Thank you, Alex." Melissa took him in a hug that knocked the breath out of him. Then she turned to Claudio. "I'd like to try."

Claudio's grin pulled every dimple and smile line into display. "As long as we are together, we cannot fail."

Then they were in each other's arms, mouths kissing in a hungry, haphazard way that made Alexander yearn for Magdalene. He wasn't sure which one initiated the move, but they lowered to the sand. Claudio cradled Melissa's neck with one arm as the other hand opened her jacket. Melissa caressed through his salt-and-pepper hair and he pulled her closer as their searching kisses continued.

Alexander cleared his throat and adjusted himself. "I guess I'll see you two back at the bonfire, though I think you have plenty of heat here."

They went on as though they didn't hear him. Alexander laughed, collected one of the suitcases, and returned to his family.

"Where's Mom?" Louisa asked as she dried her auburn hair.

"She stopped to collect something we found up the beach. She'll be here soon." He dropped Claudio's suitcase by a cypress tree and sat in the sand beside Magdalene, kissing her like he'd been gone all day.

"What happened?" she whispered.

"You'll see soon enough."

"Uncle Claudio!" Louisa ran for the approaching figures.

Magdalene's eyes widened.

"He's left the priesthood to claim her," Alexander whispered. "Freddy told me he would, but I didn't believe him. They sure put on a fine display."

Magdalene slugged his arm and stood. Claudio was already surrounded by the children, Asher with the other suitcase in hand and Louisa hugging his arm opposite her mother.

"The next family in our fold?" Magdalene asked Alexander.

"I hope so. He's always done well with us, but let it be known I'll never allow you to drink in his proximity. You were bad enough when he was a priest."

She leaned down to punch him but he jumped to his feet.

"If you're going to be naughty with someone, I want it to be with me."

"You've proven to be the most fun." She snaked a hand over his chest and tweaked a nipple.

"Hey!" Alexander jumped back, stumbling over a camp chair as he rubbed the sore spot.

Magdalene laughed and went for Claudio.

"Asher, Simon!" Alexander called the boys to him. "Collect Claudio's luggage and bring it to the room next to yours."

"Abe was going to take it tomorrow," Asher reminded him.

"Claudio might end up with Mr. Petty in the room come Sunday, but Abe could bunk with you. I doubt he'll care where he sleeps as long as he spends his days with Beth. And bring the hot dogs and fixings when you come back."

Alexander swung Amelia onto his back with a trail of giggles.

She kissed her father's cheek. "Are you surprised to see Uncle Claudio, Poppy?"

"Yes, Amelia Rose, pleasantly surprised. I'm happy to have him with us for the holiday and however long he wishes to stay."

"I haven't seen Sissa happy in a long time," his daughter said in a hushed tone.

"Her glow is the mark of a loving relationship."

"Like you and Mama, and Beth and Abe?"

"Exactly right, my precious." He squeezed her knee. "Don't settle for a boy unless he makes you shine as bright as all the stars in the sky."

Thirty-Five

Woken by a dream of her father, Bethany sat up in the Seacliff Manor room she shared with Tabitha.

"Tell her, Little Princess," Frederick had said. "You promised to welcome Claudio and remind Sissa I don't want her to be alone."

When Claudio had arrived that evening, Bethany hugged him and noted the pleased smile Melissa possessed. They stayed the center of attention the hours everyone spent around the bonfire, and Bethany didn't feel it right to speak such tender words in front of the whole group. Now, she knew she wouldn't be able to go back to sleep until she'd completed the duty her father reminded her of in the dream.

Slipping quietly from bed, Bethany peered into the room next door. With Abe and his parents arriving Saturday, Melissa kept her typical suite free for Joe and Claire to use and bunked with the girls. Louisa and Amelia slept peacefully in the double bed, but the single for Melissa was unslept in.

Bethany crept downstairs. All the lights were off except a pale glow from the game room. Bethany stopped in the doorway and smiled, thinking Claudio and Melissa looked like she and Abraham must have on New Year's Eve. Claudio's feet were stretched to the ottoman and Melissa was curled on her side, head resting on a pillow in his lap. His fingers were intertwined with Melissa's atop her hip.

She crossed the room lit by a single lamp and lowered herself to the opposite side of the ottoman from Claudio's legs.

"Sissa," she whispered before she lost her nerve.

Melissa sat upright, copper hair rumpled and her calico house dress askew. Bethany remembered the winter night when her father was at war, and she'd gone downstairs to find Melissa because Louisa had experienced a nightmare. Melissa was in disarray and smelled of Claudio. Understanding what she'd interrupted, Bethany blushed.

"What is it, Beth?"

"I need to give you a message, a message for both of you, but I didn't want to do it in front of everyone. Daddy came to my dream to remind me of my promise. I couldn't wait until morning."

Melissa took Bethany's cold hand in her warm one, a sad smile on her face. "It must be important."

Bethany looked to Claudio. "Daddy wanted me to welcome you, but everyone had you surrounded, and it didn't seem the right time. I'm sorry."

"I was welcomed by all, *Principessa*, but thank you for the special message." He opened his arms to her.

She breathed in his shirt, realizing he no longer smelled of incense. "I love you, Uncle Claudio. I always felt safe around you. Both you and Sissa."

"And I have always been comfortable with you and your family. I may have left my profession, but it feels as though I am finally home." He kissed her forehead.

She looked at Melissa. "And I was to tell you Daddy doesn't want you to be alone. He wanted you to keep loving someone. I think he meant Uncle Claudio because he told me both messages the same day."

Melissa hugged her and sniffed back tears.

"Will you be married?" Bethany asked.

Claudio smiled. "It is my hope, *Principessa.*"

"I'll look forward to it, Uncle Claudio, for all our sakes."

They went upstairs together, Claudio hugging Bethany and kissing Melissa outside their bedroom doors before going down the hall to his appointed room.

Later that morning, Bethany awoke after several hours of restful sleep. Dressed in her black striped swimsuit, she joined Melissa in the kitchen. The two smiled in greeting and worked preparing toast and coffee without words. Alexander stumbled in a few minutes later, shirtless and with his pajama pants riding low.

"Sorry, ladies." He tugged his pants up an inch and rubbed a hand across his scars. "I thought I'd be the only one up."

"It's after six-thirty," Melissa said with false indignation while Bethany placed a cup of coffee in his hand.

"Thanks, Bethany. I forget how you career-minded women take mornings seriously. Me? I prefer the nights." Alexander swiveled his pelvis, causing Melissa to laugh and Bethany's cheeks to warm.

Claudio entered. "Save that for Magdalene, Alexander. I am here to entertain Melissa and I doubt Bethany wishes to see displays like that from you."

"Thank you," Bethany whispered. "Coffee?"

"*Sí*, but I shall get it. I need more opportunities to familiarize myself in the kitchen once again."

Melissa kissed his cheek when he stopped beside her. "Why's that?"

"I wish to become a chef if there is an establishment in town that would have me."

"Wonderful choice!" Alexander slapped his back. "You always cooked the best meals when we were in Monroe."

"*Sí*, the parish was smaller and only provided a cook three days a week. I had the opportunity to explore the tastes of my homeland. All the other rectories I have been in had full-time cooks, and the priests were not allowed in the kitchen."

"I'm certain Melissa will let you in her kitchen anytime," Alexander said with a wink to her. "Be sure you partake of Claudio's baked ziti. It's an edible orgasm."

Melissa did her best to scowl, but the corners of her mouth turned up.

"But allow me to remind you lovely people to keep sin from happening within the walls of our homes."

Bethany inched toward the backdoor to escape the speech of such things.

"Knight Bethany." He pointed at her—freezing her progression. "That was a reminder for you as well. I know you and Abe love each other, but if he truly loves you, he'll be patient."

Her face felt like it was on fire, but she managed a "yes, Poppy" before dashing outside.

"Alex, how could you!" Melissa's voice escaped the house as Bethany ran for the mausoleum.

The cold air of the marble building gave her gooseflesh when she opened the door. Stepping over the roses Alexander left on the stoop the day before, Bethany ran a hand over her mother's glorious names. She felt her presence there, but her father was forever in his office, not Magnolia Cemetery where his body was laid to rest.

Returning her hand to the scrolling *Lucille*, she whispered, "Why do you never come to my dreams? Sissa is fine, but sometimes I need you. I hope you gave Daddy a big hug when he got to heaven."

Racing from her emotions, Bethany hurried to the shore and threw herself into the bay so her tears wouldn't be discernible. She swam to clear her head until a fishing boat brought her to a reminder of her aloneness, and she switched her direction for shore. When

Bethany reached the private pier, she pulled herself up on the end, tucked her knees to her chest, and rested her chin, allowing the morning sun to dry her.

The flapping of a sail as it lowered snapped through the air when the Walkers arrived. Bethany hopped to her feet and waved.

"Step back a bit, Beth," Joe hollered. "I don't want Abe to run you down when he jumps out to moor us."

Bethany moved back several paces. Abraham still aimed for her when he leapt onto the dock when the boat was five feet away. He gave her a quick kiss and then was on his knees, coiling the ropes to secure the sailboat to the cleats. Back on his feet, he offered a hand to help his mother step onto the pier.

Claire Walker went to Bethany with open arms. "Beth, it's been too long since I've seen you. You must visit us soon. I'll be sure to speak with Melissa about it." She released Bethany from the hug and looked her in the eyes with merry green ones that turned a shade darker with grief. "I'm sorry I couldn't make it to your father's funeral. There was a baby due, and the mother was in poor shape. I couldn't risk—"

"I know, Miss Claire. Abe explained it all. Daddy would have understood too."

Bringing her back into an embrace, Claire kissed her cheek. "Frederick Davenport was a fine man. We're all blessed to have known him." And in a lower voice she added, "And Abe is blessed to have you. You've done so much for my boy. I can never repay the debt."

"Enough with the touching reunion, Claire," Joe teased. "I need a hug from this pretty mite, and then I'm sure Abe wants to hold his girl and get more of that kiss he filched."

"Don't mind him, Beth."

"She has to know Abe got his way with ladies from me, though he took all his ma's charm and freckles." Joe flashed his crooked grin. "And that redheaded spitfire. Don't let him around you when he's mad, Beth. Lord bless you if he's ever a cantankerous cuss around ya."

Abraham whipped a cap out of his back pocket and shoved it low on his head to hide his blush.

Claire sighed. "Go give Alex your humor and spare the ladies your mouth, Joseph Walker."

He smiled at Bethany before taking his wife's arm and starting up the pier with her.

Abraham took Bethany by the hips and gently pulled her to him. "I missed you, Iris."

"Missed you too, Abe."

After a leisurely kiss, he led her onto the boat. "I can take it out if you think anyone would enjoy sailing."

"I'm sure they would. I know I'd like it."

Abraham opened the hatch and dropped into the hull without the use of the steps. Then he stood, head peeking out the top with his huge grin as he lifted his drawstring bag onto the deck. "Want to see the cabin? There's a snug table and two berths."

"Sure."

He heaved a big suitcase up and then offered his hand. The ladder was more of a steep staircase six steps deep. She forewent the handrail and stayed facing out, trusting Abraham's strength and guidance. Walking into his arms at the foot of the ladder, Bethany realized their utter privacy in the dim space. Emboldened by their seclusion, she wrapped a leg about him. His hand immediately went to her knee and trailed up until he reached the hem of her swimsuit on the back of her thigh. There he teased her bare skin as his kisses roamed from her mouth down to her neck and across her exposed skin below her collarbone.

Bethany's breathing came quicker. She clung to his shoulders and fought the instinct to press her intimate areas against him.

Momma, help me!

"Iris, you feel and taste amazing." He kissed her shoulders and back up to her lips as he lifted her to perch on one of the steps. She hooked her legs about his middle, ankles crossed behind him. Both Abraham's hands caressed from under her knees to her bathing suit hem, eyes half-lidded in ecstasy.

Kissing him back, Bethany tried to understand the sensations. "I've never felt like this before. Tell me what to do."

He grasped her backside and lifted her to him, bringing her across the cabin and stopping before a sleeper alcove.

"It's never felt like this for me either, Bethany Iris. You're wonderful, my perfect match."

Her legs locked about his waist and she felt the hardness of him beneath her. "What do I do, Abe?"

"Don't allow us to be alone this weekend, not like this. And you need to get topside before I take advantage and lose you forever." Voice husky, he held her waist as he lowered her to the floor of the swaying boat. "Get up those steps fast, Iris."

Halfway up, she held the handrail and turned to Abraham.

"You're stunning, Iris. Please wear a swimsuit everyday we're here."

"I'd be happy to, as long as you return the favor. It's been a while since I've seen those knees."

His laugh broke into a boyish grin. He handed up a covered basket and joined her in the sun. "Cornbread muffins. If you can carry that, I'll get the luggage."

"Of course, protector of my virtue." She felt the shine in her eyes as blood still raced to her core from their titillating exchange.

Hands full, he leaned over to kiss her cheek as they walked the pier. "Don't ever look at another guy like that."

"I don't think it's possible because I'm burning with love for you."

***

Sunday, after lunch, Bethany and Abraham took a blanket to the shady side of the stable and stretched out beside each other, holding hands. The adults were on the back porch talking. Alexander's and Joe's laughter rose above the others.

Amelia squealed as she ran across the yard and dove between Bethany and Abraham. "Simon's gonna get me!"

"I'll pay you a dollar to keep between them the rest of the day!" Alexander hollered.

Joe laughed. "That's a father of girls for you. The boy's Pa would shout 'better make it good and make her yours before she wises up!'"

Abraham shook his fist toward his father.

"All of you leave them be," Melissa responded.

Amelia looked at Bethany with her periwinkle eyes. "Do you want me to leave you?"

"You can stay if you'd like, Amelia. I'll protect you from Simon. What's Ash doing?"

"He went to the cliffs to draw. Poppy says that's where Aunt Eliza used to go. Did you know Aunt Eliza?" She linked her fingers through Bethany's, fully taking over Abraham's territory without realizing it.

Abraham rolled to his stomach and propped on his elbows to observe them.

"She died before any of our generation was born," Bethany answered.

"Poppy says she lives on in me and Asher—that we both have a part of her, just as we have parts of him and our mothers. Does that sound lovely or scary? I can't decide."

Bethany smiled at her earnest face. "I suppose it depends on how you feel about the people you're made up of."

"I love Poppy and Mama but all I know about Aunt Eliza Rose is that she was beautiful and talented."

"Then chose to have those nice things the parts of her you have."

"Does it work that way?"

Bethany shrugged, thoughts of her mother's madness dragging her smile into a frown. "I don't see why we can't try."

"Thank you, Beth." Amelia dashed to the house.

Bethany covered her face with her arms and tried to ignore Abraham's penetrating stare. Without seeing his green-gold eyes, she could pretend they were full of love instead of questions.

A finger ran along the inside of her arm eliciting chills. "Iris, my love, you only have the good parts of your mother."

Touched that he knew what worried her, a tear slipped out from her hiding spot. Tenderly, he raised her arm and set it across her stomach. He turned on his side and scooted closer until he rested against her shoulder and tucked an arm around her waist.

"You're the best parts of them all, Bethany Iris. A veritable rainbow of goodness."

Thirty-Six

Alexander tried to keep the smile from his lips as he listened to the jazz tune coming from the house as he oversaw Bethany and Abraham lying together from his seat on the porch. Those two were easy to tease—and Joe a willing participant—but he didn't want to say too much and cause hurt feelings. Taking a drag from his cigarette, his gaze switched to Magdalene who was curled in the papasan chair. She looked like a sleeping cat in a padded dish. He'd kept her up late with lovemaking Friday because she was shy when extra company was in the house and he wanted to enjoy their time before the Walkers arrived. But last night offered another excuse for them. The others had stayed at the bonfire when they brought Amelia inside and he and his wife enjoyed another exuberant session after their daughter's bedtime.

I'll let her sleep tonight—especially with Petty in the next room.

"What's on your mind, Melling?" Joe asked.

"Not in front of the ladies," he countered.

Joe smirked, but Melissa and Claudio laughed.

The piano quieted and Alexander cocked his ear toward the house. Tabitha didn't bring Bradford Petty to the back porch for over five minutes, but he had a hunch on how they'd spent their time. Besides rosy lips, pert peaks on her modest chest poked beneath Tabitha's navy swimsuit, advertising heavy petting at the very least.

"Brad's here. I think you know everyone except the Walkers and Uncle Claudio." Tabitha pointed to Joe and Claire. "These are Abe's parents, Captain Joe and Claire Walker of Dauphin Island. And Uncle Claudio De Fiore, as we call him, just returned from his self-imposed exile in Italy. Everyone, this is Bradford Petty. He works with the state department of transportation and is my biggest fan."

Hands were shaken and hellos made, but Magdalene slept on. Bradford looked her way several times, but didn't appear to leer though her hip gave a luscious silhouette and her mouth was incredibly inviting in its parted state.

Tabitha reclaimed Bradford's arm after his introductions were over. "Abe promised us a sail this afternoon."

"Be sure the youngsters are invited," Alexander told her.

"They went sailing yesterday, Poppy. I thought it would be just the four of us."

He gave her the Melling stare.

Tabitha huffed. "Go wait with Abe, Brad. I'll be back in a minute."

Bradford gave a nervous look at Alexander before exiting the porch. When he crossed the yard, Abraham stood and then helped Bethany from the blanket.

Tabitha slammed out the kitchen door. "Simon, Louisa, and Amelia are playing Parcheesi and they say Asher's on the cliff. Do I need to go find and personally invite him?"

"No, Tabby. Have fun, but remember I want everyone back by dark."

She ran for the others and Bethany came to the house.

"I need our picnic basket." She returned from the kitchen with it, slipping a cookie into Alexander's hand as she kissed his cheek. "Bye, Poppy."

"I feel I must have been good in some respect to be worthy of that one." He put out his smoke and took a sip of iced tea before taking a bite.

"She loves her poppy." Melissa smiled at him.

"And I love her to pieces."

Joe and Claire excused themselves for a nap during the heat of the day, and Melissa insisted on getting Magdalene to bed so she could stretch out properly. Alexander carried his wife upstairs and deposited her on top of the bedspread, closing the drapes halfway so the breeze still blew in and the ceiling fans did the rest to keep things manageable.

Leaving a kiss on her lips, she stirred enough to crack an eye.

"Sleep as long as you'd like, sweetness."

"Join me?"

"Not this time, but I'll hold you tonight, you can be sure."

Melissa sat at the desk in the library when Alexander passed through downstairs. She had brought a collection of Lucy's short stories to edit them for possible publication, though she hadn't gotten much work done with Claudio arriving. Alexander settled back on the porch, pleased to finally have one-on-one time with his best friend. They both lit up and stared at each other. The ex-priest continued to look strange to Alexander his in layman clothes.

"How was Mass at Church of the Assumption?" Alexander asked about Claudio's borrowing his automobile that morning.

"Fine. Many of the same people were there, and I was recognized."

"Did Melissa go with you?"

"She offered, but I wanted to go alone."

"She went to Trinity with Freddy twice a month, even brought the girls when he was overseas, but never was baptized. Do you want her to join you in our faith?"

"I wish for her to have a fulfilling life however she finds that."

"So you'll seek fulfillment in the bedroom before seeing to her spiritual needs?"

Claudio leaned forward, dark eyes intense. "When we are joined, I will not have you mock what we finally have. I went through hell with her when Frederick was gone to see her loved without taking advantage. Respect our journey and all she's been through."

"I do, Claudio. She and Freddy were perfect while it lasted, but you two will be just as wonderful."

***

Alexander paced the empty pier as the sun sank over the city across the bay. Magdalene wrapped her arms about his shoulders from behind.

"I told them to be back by dark," he muttered.

"It's not dark yet."

"They should be visible by now."

Magdalene moved in front of him, kissing across his jaw until she met his lips. He did nothing to return her desire.

She stepped back, hands on her hips over her blue sundress. "That was the worst kiss you've ever shared with me, Alexander. I demand a redo."

"Our daughters are out there with a young sailor and an old cad and you expect passion?"

"You're Alexander Randolph Melling. I expect passion no matter what." She turned and walked back to shore, going all the way to where the bonfire was being built and sat in Claudio's lap.

"Maggie!" Alexander shouted.

Magdalene gave an exaggerated wave and tucked against their friend.

"And she was so meek when she arrived here in '06," Joe remarked. "You've spoiled her, Melling."

He couldn't help but smile. "I suppose I have, but your boy better not be spoiling my daughter."

"I may joke, but I'd be the first to whup him if he ever does. We Walkers treat our girls right and marry up." Joe exhaled a puff of smoke and pointed toward Fairhope with the two fingers holding his cigarette. "There he is."

The sails lowered, slowing the progress.

"I only see two people aboard. If that insufferable fop has Tabby below deck I'll—"

Joe knocked his shoulder. "No use getting worked up until we see where they stand."

Bethany and Abraham followed the tide in the last hundred feet as he directed the tiller. Alexander hadn't been sailing since his summer in Newport, but he knew enough to appreciate Abraham's confident manner.

"Here, Iris, hold this steady," he called out. "That's it, just sit and relax, holding firm so I can throw the line."

Abraham went for the bow, taking the coiled rope in his hands. "Can ya catch it, Pa?"

"Got it!" Joe hollered back.

The younger Walker tossed the rope in a perfect arc to his father, who held tight as the boat came in the final bit, positioning himself near a cleat. Abraham jumped onto the end of the pier with the rear line in hand, mooring the back quicker than Alexander thought possible. He jumped back onboard and kissed Bethany as she stood from the tiller.

"You did swell, Iris." Abraham gave her sunhat a tug. "I'll get the basket."

He jumped down the open hatch and Alexander stepped aboard.

"Where are Tabitha and Petty?"

Bethany's eyes were wide as she looked back at him. "We tied up in Fairhope for half an hour to buy colas. Mr. Petty came across some men in the park he knew. I tried to get her to come back with us, but Tabby didn't want to pull him away from his friends. Abe insisted we return. He thought someone could go for them in the automobile so we wouldn't miss curfew."

Abraham climbed up, basket in hand. "Was that the right thing, Poppy?"

He couldn't fault the sincere look on the young man's face. "Yes, it's better for you to return and give us word so we aren't worrying about everyone. Thanks for bringing Beth home."

"She's my number one priority." His huge grin brightened the mood as he held Bethany's elbow for her to step onto the pier.

"Everything fine with the boat?" Joe asked.

"Great, Pa. No problems." Picnic basket hooked over an elbow, Abraham took Bethany's hand.

Alexander quickened his steps toward the bonfire. Fortunately, Magdalene was in her own chair rather than snuggling with Claudio. "Tabitha and Petty stayed in Fairhope. I'm going to drive over and find them."

"I'll come with you."

"You need to stay and be hostess."

"I don't want you going alone, Alex."

Claudio stood. "Shall I accompany you?"

"Yes, please," Magdalene said.

"Fine," Alexander grumbled. "Let's go while we have a bit of daylight left."

Magdalene kissed him "Don't embarrass yourself."

"If they've been up to no good, you can bet I'll let it be known with the righteous indignation of Douglas on my side!"

"*Calmati, amico.* Do not pass judgement until we see for ourselves."

Alexander ignored his remark and looked to his son. "You're in charge of the fire, Phoenix Asher, but if an adult gives you instructions, you had better heed them."

"Yes, Poppy."

"Simon, help keep an eye on Amelia for your mother."

"I will, Poppy."

Louisa looked to Alexander. "What about me?"

"Keep an eye on Bethany."

Joe and Abraham followed Alexander and Claudio up the path so they could collect the fish and corn to cook on the fire.

"Take it easy on them," Joe said as Alexander grabbed the keys from inside.

"How I react is up to those two."

"Do not allow others to dictate your response," Claudio said in his smooth way. "It is all up to you how you handle things, no matter what happens."

"I'm not in the mood to be preached at, Claudio."

Thirty-Seven

Phoebe finished applying her makeup and stepped back from the mirror to get the full effect of her ensemble. Red lips and blue-lidded eyes matched the short, red and blue sequined dress. A bit over-the-top to spend time in the park the evening before Independence Day, but she liked to make a statement. She trimmed a few strands that had grown longer than the rest of her curly bob and fluffed her hair even more.

Slipping on her new silver shoes, she exited the house in the twilight. Phoebe headed down the sidewalk for the make-shift party near the pier. The jazz band, laughter, and conversations created a cacophony of sounds. To lose herself in the moment, she started dancing as she reached the gathering—shimmying her assets to appreciative gentlemen as she kept an eye out for Jeremy. As the song came to a close, she spotted him across the way with a few familiar faces. He watched with rapt attention as Tabitha played her fingers along an invisible keyboard, as though she was showing off her skills. Bradford Petty and another young professional she'd met once appeared just as enthralled.

When the next song started up, Phoebe pranced her way into the middle of the group, causing Tabitha to lower her arms. She gave a flirty wink and air kisses to each man until she settled beside Jeremy with a real kiss on his cheek.

"Sorry it took me so long, Jeremy."

"Excuse us a moment." He put an arm around Phoebe's waist and steered her to a spot away from the crowd. With a loafer in the sand and the other at the edge of the path, he gripped her arm. "I might want you bold in the bedroom but I don't want you looking like a cheap hussy in front of my friends!"

Shocked at his roughness, Phoebe tried to recall when she'd ever done something to offend him before. They didn't go out much, but there wasn't a need as she was catered to by his help. Their times at the casino for dancing had always been pleasant, but she'd never flirted with anyone else.

"I'm sorry, Jeremy. Most guys are proud when their girl captures other men's attentions."

"I don't need you to draw attention in public, even if it's known that you stay with me. You're here to keep me satisfied while I'm in town, nothing more. Stop putting on airs or get back home."

His hand tightened and he yanked her up the path.

It took all her control to keep the quiver out of her voice. "I'd like a minute, please."

"You would do well to model your behavior after a classy young woman like Tabitha Campbell," he said before he stalked away.

A wave of heat washed her body at the name. She wanted nothing more than to claw his eyes out and shove them down his throat. Instead, Phoebe crossed her arms and tried to keep from scowling as tears evaporated behind her mask of emotions.

A swarthy man in a black fedora sidled toward her. "Hey, doll. Looking for a good time?"

"I don't need to go looking for it because I *am* a good time."

"Feisty, like all the best ones." He reached a hand to her. "How 'bout I take you dancing at the Bayside? I'll even buy you dinner, and then you can show me that good time you're so certain of."

"No, thank you. My guy's waiting for me." She might have swayed her hips a little more than usual as she walked away, but it helped her regain control of her riotous thoughts as she approached the group.

Phoebe didn't understand how Jeremy could hold Tabitha in high regard when she wore nothing more than a swimsuit and deck shoes. Certain she could find a replacement if he didn't cherish her, she plastered on her biggest smile.

"You should have your band booked to play Bayside Casino," Jeremy said to Tabitha as he motioned to the three-story building on the shoreline. "I'd love to hear you play again. I suppose I'll have to make another weekend trip to Mobile for that pleasure."

Tabitha smiled, dark eyes flashing. "That would be wonderful, Mr. Bridges."

Bradford Petty put his arm about her waist as a subtle reminder that he claimed her. His movement was one of a man familiar with the body he possessed. *Is perfect Tabby a wild cat with the men? I bet Poppy and Miss Maggie would be put out to know she's sharing more than kisses with him.*

"That would be fun," Phoebe added. "I haven't been to Mobile since my father's funeral."

"He was a great man, Miss Davenport. Your stepmothers are the most generous women I've ever met," Mr. Petty said. "You ladies have a remarkable family."

Jeremy looked between Phoebe, Tabitha, and Bradford with confusion. She realized that she'd never spoken to Jeremy about her family—other than her father's passing—but assumed he knew who her connections were.

With her winning smile, she pulled out her sugary voice. "Didn't you know, Jeremy? Tabitha and I are stepsisters of a sort. I'm sure her charm and good manners must be found in me as well, though possibly buried beneath my flamboyant ways."

"You're just as charming as Tabby, Miss Davenport," Bradford said. "You two are like day and night, both equally beautiful in your own ways."

His words earned him a sneer from Tabitha and a flirty giggle from Phoebe. "Hush now, Mr. Petty. Jeremy doesn't appreciate others complimenting me. I think he'd keep me locked away if he could. Would you hide me under a bushel if you had me?"

"Tabitha Campbell!" Alexander's voice boomed across the park, causing Phoebe to jerk.

Tabitha reddened, looking wide-eyed at the others. "Excuse me!" She dashed through the crowd.

"Pardon us," Bradford said. "I arrived with Tabby and should depart with her as well. Good to see you, Jeremy. And Arthur." He shook the men's hands and kissed the back of Phoebe's. "And it's always a pleasure to see you, Miss Davenport."

When he was gone, Jeremy took Phoebe by the upper arm once more, fingers digging in. "I think you should go on back to the cottage now. Fairhope has had enough of a display from you today. Behave yourself, and I might take you to the casino tomorrow night."

She grinned as she held back the tears once more. "Whatever you say, Jeremy."

Rather than taking the shortest way to the road, she went across the green to spy on Tabitha's talking to by Alexander. He fussed at her and glared at Bradford too intently to notice Phoebe hanging in the shadows, but the man beside him saw her. His olive face was as handsome as ever, though his hair was speckled with gray. He cut a noticeably fine figure in his half-unbuttoned sky blue shirt and khaki trousers. Phoebe felt she saw him for the first time— and she did, as a woman.

When she smiled, he came to her.

"*Principessa!*" With a hug, he kissed both cheeks and she warmed at his touch. "You are as beautiful as your mother, though you appear sad."

"It's nothing, Uncle Claudio." She fingered his open collar. "Did you finally get transferred back?"

"No, *Principessa*." His hands rested warmly on her shoulders. "I have left the priesthood, but I can still pray over you."

"Bless me, please."

She melted under the loving weight of his hands atop her head, heedless of the crowd around her as his Italian words filled her soul. Heartbeat returned to normal for the first time in ages, Phoebe smiled up at him when he finished.

"Thank you, Uncle Claudio." She kissed his hands as they lowered. "Have you come to visit Poppy?"

"Not to visit, to stay. But I have come more for Melissa than Alexander, though it is good to be with my friend once again."

"Sissa?"

"*Sí*. I have loved her all these years, and want to help her through her loss—help all of you. Losing both parents is not an easy thing. I know you have your extended family, but please rely on me as well."

She nodded, knowing her voice would betray her hatred toward Melissa for replacing her father so easily—especially with the man she was rumored to have had an affair with.

"May I escort you somewhere, *Principessa?*"

"No, thank you. I'm going home." *As close to a home as I have now.*

Alexander came for a hug. "Phoebe Camellia, you're dressed for a party!"

Smile fixed in place, she told him what she thought he'd wish to hear. "That's my life at present—one big festivity after another."

"Are you well?" The sincerity in his voice stabbed, the fire in his blue eyes burned.

She nodded and turned to continue home.

"Phoebe, we're at Seacliff until Tuesday if you need anything."

"Is Kade there?" she whispered.

"No, but he was invited to join us."

"Thank you, Poppy, but I won't ruin everyone's vacation by making an appearance."

The final block up the street was a blur through her teary vision. She went straight for the moonshine Jeremy kept in a parlor cabinet, chugging freely. In the bedroom, she wiggled out of the tight dress and pulled on her mother's kimono.

Ten minutes later, Jeremy found her draped across the bed.

"At least you're alone." Sarcasm dripped from his hard mouth like poison.

She sat up, tugging the silk closed. "What's that supposed to mean?"

"That was quite a spectacle you made with that man old enough to be your father."

"Who, Claudio?"

"A Latin lover is it? Will you be joining him at his villa, trading me up for a European?" He tossed his tie onto the chair in the corner.

"I'm not going anywhere with him. He's come to town for my stepmother, not me."

"Jealous, Phoebe? How does it feel to be on the losing end of someone's attention? Not much fun is it?"

"Leave me alone!" She jumped at him to push him away but he grabbed her wrists.

"You're in my house and do as I say. You're not to leave the remainder of this week to help you understand how strongly I feel about proper behavior when you're in public."

"Are you embarrassed by me, Jeremy? Is what I give you in bed not good enough to be known though you're quite pleased with me in private?"

"Ladies don't discuss such things."

"You've already told me I'm not your girl or a proper lady. I'm just your Southern concubine with apparently no shame or feelings." Fists clinched to keep her arms from lashing out, Phoebe felt the heat on her face as she yelled. "Maybe I'll take a walk through town tomorrow in nothing but my new shoes and let everyone know that you're only good for one thrust a day because that's all your little package can deliver!"

The back of his hand struck her clean across the jaw and light burst behind her eyes. Feeling like she was falling, her next awareness was of the bed beneath her and Jeremy on top.

"Have I been too gentle with you, Phoebe? Let me reassure you who is in control of this arrangement."

Thirty-Eight

As much as she loved both Melissa and Claudio, witnessing their wedding ceremony suffocated Bethany. The couple stood before old Father Quinn within the gazebo in Alexander's yard in the September heat. Everyone looked on from a single grouping of chairs that didn't differentiate between the bride's and groom's sides because the audience was intertwined in both their lives—Davenport, Melling, Campbell, Adams, and Walker. After they kissed to seal their vows, Bethany offered hugs to Melissa and Claudio before dashing upstairs.

Seconds after the first tears fell as she lay on her bed, Abraham knocked on the door. "Iris, please come out."

She curled tighter into herself, hugging her arms across her robin's egg blue dress she'd sewn for the occasion.

He knocked again. "Everyone's gonna be looking for you."

Silence.

Then the door opened and sandalwood filled the air. "Don't hide yourself like a stubborn Davenport, Knight Bethany. Allow those who love you to hold you through the pain."

"Poppy." She sat upright and reached for her stepfather, who pulled her into a hug. "Don't tell Sissa, but it hurt to watch."

"But you love Claudio."

She sniffed and wiped her nose with his offered handkerchief. "Seeing him and Sissa joined in marriage drove the truth to my heart. Daddy is never coming home."

"Little Princess, he's with you always." Alexander stroked her hair. After several minutes of allowing her to cry, he lifted her chin. "You'll have a lovely weekend on Dauphin Island with the Walkers, and when Sissa and Claudio return from New Orleans, you'll be in better spirits. Now, dry your tears and let Abe escort you to the party."

"Thank you, Poppy."

Alexander turned to leave, slapping Abraham on the back. "I'm counting on you to give her a fun weekend."

"I aim to do just that." Abraham's grin was that of the Cheshire Cat. When Alexander was gone, he wrapped Bethany in a hug and kissed her ear. "Wash your pretty face, then I'll see you downstairs for refreshments. I'll tell Pa we can head out early."

"Don't interrupt your parents because I'm feeling sad. Your mother hardly gets to town, and I know she enjoys time with Darla."

"Then I'll have to kiss the sadness out of you."

His lips roamed from her mouth to neck and his strong hands held her waist, pressing them together. Bethany fell under the spell of Abraham's attentions and willed the sensations to overpower her thoughts. Arms about his neck, she deepened the next kiss.

"You're gonna get busted!" Louisa said from the open door. "Mom's asking where you went. Should I tell her you're necking with Abe in your bedroom?"

"Poppy was just in here. We've only been alone a minute. I'll be down soon."

Bethany washed her face before returning, and managed to enjoy the party.

Sadness swept her once more as Melissa and Claudio made their rounds to say goodbye before the hired car picked them up to bring them to the train station.

"*Principessa*," Claudio whispered as he hugged Bethany, "thank you for welcoming me to your family. I look forward to settling in upon our return."

"Take good care of Sissa."

His eyes crinkled at the corners with his dimpled smile. "I promise you I will. We shall see you and Louisa here for supper next Friday."

Alexander put an arm around her shoulders as everyone waved the couple off. "You will be blessed with his wisdom in your home, Bethany."

While Abraham helped Bethany collect the luggage from her room, Louisa unpacked her own suitcase as she was staying with the Mellings while her mother was out of town.

Bethany hugged her half-sister. "I'll see you Monday, Louisa."

"I'll try to keep your room clean, and you better behave." She gave Abraham a stare much like their father would have.

"I'll give her a proper island welcome." Abraham winked.

Bethany hadn't been to Dauphin Island in almost a decade. What once seemed like rustic fun was now a world of difference to the daily comforts she enjoyed when they arrived at the Walkers' home that evening.

After a late supper, she was glad to be out of the primitive interior and on the front porch swing with Abraham. There she could focus on nature and the night sounds as opposed to plain walls, oil lamps, and lack of indoor plumbing. Abraham used the darkness to his benefit, nibbling her neck and sneaking his hand under the hem of her dress to caress her bare knee.

Joe Walker's shadow spilled through the screen onto the planking of the porch. Bethany brushed Abraham's hand from her leg.

"Your ma and I are going to bed. I trust you'll behave yourself, Abe. You're not to step a foot into Beth's room, night or day."

Abraham straightened. "Yes, sir."

"Put out the final lamps when you come in."

"I will, Pa."

"Thank you for inviting me, Captain," Bethany said.

"I hope you enjoy yourself, Beth."

The floorboards creaked as Joe retreated. Abraham quickly returned to his previous administrations. Breath warm on her cheek, his calloused hand crept up her leg. "You're so soft, Iris."

Tangled in touches and tastings, the chains supporting the swing squeaked with their movements. Bethany nearly jumped when someone in the yard called out.

"Who ya got up there, Walker?"

Abraham stood and peered into the darkness. "Tom?"

Another laugh. "Yeah, and who's with ya? She sounds like a good time."

Abraham led Bethany through the yard. When they reached the flowerbed at the edge of the sandy lot, a flame leapt within a lantern. The young man raised it, lighting his weathered face. He smiled and his dark eyes widened.

"Don't tell me this is your city girl." He whistled as his gaze traveled down her blue dress, all the way to her anklet. "How'd you ever manage to snag a classy gal like this, Walker?"

Abraham shrugged and ruffled a hand through his tousled hair. "Must be lucky, I guess."

"I'll say. No wonder you've given up the local talent." He turned to Bethany. "Abe's been a real bore since he went to Mobile for Thanksgiving last fall. I've been dying to see who tamed him."

Abraham's grin shone in the eerie light. "I told ya she was worth it."

Bethany blushed, but before she could protest, Tom spoke again.

"There's a bonfire tomorrow night at the dunes. A real kicker. Be sure to bring your city gal to show her how we live it up. Maybe she'll even learn a few tricks to take home."

Abraham laughed and shoved him. "Go on with ya."

Tom raised a brow and grinned. "Have fun tonight, Walker. And you, Miss Mobile."

The lantern swung in his hand as Tom retreated into the night with a jaunty whistle. Left in the yard with only the light of the waning moon, Abraham claimed Bethany with a hard kiss. Beneath the layer of pleasure was a thrumming unease. Abraham's first friend to meet her saw her as a plaything to be fondled on a dark porch and taught tricks.

"He's a good guy, but a bit of a cad when it comes to girls."

Kade had warned her last summer, but all Bethany saw was the charming smile amid his boyishly freckled face—a breath of fresh air in the city that had shunned her mother and gossiped of her extended family. Abraham gave no hints to his past transgressions though he once told her he was experienced. Something about being with a few girls and not shying away from action is what he had admitted. But when he looked at her so earnestly, she couldn't believe he'd ever looked on another girl like that. There was no past, only the two of them and his devoted heart.

His agile fingers went for the buttons on her dress but Bethany drew away. "I'd like to go to sleep now."

"Iris." He kissed her cheeks and then her lips. "We finally have privacy. What's wrong?"

She sighed, hoping it sounded more like exhaustion than nerves as she tucked her head under his chin. "It's been a long day and I'm tired."

Hands roaming her back, Abraham kissed her again. "Then by all means, get your sleep. I want to be up early for the beach, and then we're going to the bonfire tomorrow night."

***

Exiting the outhouse, Bethany tried to straighten her bathing suit—a difficult task in the confined space. At the water pump, she rinsed her face and ran her hands through her hair to dry them.

"Come on, Iris." Basket and blanket hooked over one arm, Abraham linked his other through hers and headed for the road with all the exuberance of a boy on his birthday.

The sun was barely above the horizon, but people already walked the streets with purpose. Abraham's bare feet led the way and she kept pace with his long strides. She wore only her navy and white bathing suit and deck shoes, and he a white shirt and pair of old pants cut above the knees. Abraham greeted those who called to him with his huge smile and a hearty hello.

Once they reached the forest on the south side of town, Abraham dropped what he carried and embraced her. His lips were warm and sweet like the coffee he drank before leaving the house, caresses on her bare arms a thrill that quickened her heart.

"That's how I'd like to greet you every morning. These will be our best days. Sissa isn't here to see you blush when we kiss too long, and Poppy's knowing gaze won't fall upon you for two more days. Forget society regulations, sharp-eyed stepparents, and kid sister. It's just you and me on the island. Anything could happen."

"But your parents are watching."

"They watch from afar, trusting you, trusting me. Do you trust me, Iris?"

In the dappled light of the pine canopy the gold flecks in his eyes sparked dangerously, but she couldn't help leaning in for another taste as she nodded.

Once they were through the pine trees and on the beach, Abraham spread the blanket and set the basket on top to keep it from blowing away. Bethany slipped off her shoes and he pulled his shirt over his head. Abraham's lean torso was pale and dusted with freckles. She'd only ever seen him in one of Kade's old bathing trunks with an attached shirt. Fingers reaching, Bethany trailed her touch across his chest as she followed the haphazard freckles she found so endearing.

He sucked in a breath. "Please touch me all day."

A tingling in her core caused her to flee from the sensations. "You'll have to catch me!"

She ran into the surf, scattering a flock of seagulls. Abraham's splashing rained droplets on her back as he closed the distance. Bethany tried to rely on her swimming capabilities to outdistance him, but he grabbed her ankle displaying his shells and pulled her close.

Nestling behind her, Abraham kissed her neck as his arms snaked about her waist. "May I touch you?"

Bethany took a few steps into deeper water. The hard planes of his torso stayed flush with her back. With the lapping water and his breath in her ear, she'd never felt more alive.

"Tell me, Iris. I need to hear you say it so I know it's what you want."

She shifted against him before realizing she was rubbing against his pelvis. With a whimper, she felt her morals shift. "Touch me, Abe, but don't remove anything."

"I'll continue to honor you, Bethany Iris Davenport." He kissed her shoulders and gently urged her further from shore.

She was chest deep in the warm water watching a pod of dolphins when Abraham's hands shifted from her waist up her ribs. A few feet in front of them, a mullet jumped. Bethany flinched. He laughed and kissed her neck.

"He ain't gonna hurt you. I won't let anything touch you except me." Both hands rose to cup her breasts. "You're perfect, Iris."

They spent a breathless hour exploring each other in the shallows. Respecting her wishes, no clothing was removed, but by the time they lowered to the blanket, Abraham was well acquainted with the body under her clinging suit.

Curling beside him, Bethany rested her head on his shoulder and fingered across the sparse auburn hair on his chest. "You make me feel glorious. I hope I do as much for you."

"You're all I need in this life, Iris."

***

Back at the Walkers' house, Bethany insisted on time to brush her hair and pull on a sundress to take dinner with Clara Jane. Printed with orange hibiscus flowers, Bethany had sewn the dress especially for the weekend, basing it on tropical vacation wear she'd seen in fashion magazines.

Like many of the town's men, Clara Jane's husband was on a boat for the day, but they enjoyed a boisterous midday meal with Abraham's oldest sister and her three children. The two boys climbed all over their uncle and did their best to frighten Bethany. Abraham's assurance that the island was snake-free kept her from yelping when she caught sight of scaly things in the boys' hands. Fortunately, it was only anoles.

When they left his sister's house, Abraham took Bethany to the docks. His grin was bigger than ever as he paraded her before the returning fishermen. By the time they reached the village center, she wished she'd worn one of her old Seacliff Manor outfits rather than the new summer frock. While Abraham chatted to an elderly man outside the market, several young women stood across the way and whispered, nodding in her direction. A particularly bitter looking one shifted a baby from one hip to the other, trying to still the child's distressed whines.

Holding Abraham's hand, Bethany gave him several firm squeezes. He nodded to the man. "Excuse us, Mr. Collier. I need to get my girl out of the sun, but it was great speaking with you."

He tipped his hat. "Likewise, Abe. And it was a pleasure to meet you, Miss Davenport."

Before she could warn him, Abraham led her directly toward the chattering females. He gave them his charming grin.

"Good afternoon, ladies."

"It's great to see you on the island for your time off, Abe," a drugstore blonde said. "We thought you'd forgotten your old friends."

He laughed. "That's not likely, Kelly."

"Is this your city girl Tom was bragging about?" Another asked, sneering at Bethany as she waited for an answer.

"The one and only, Miss Bethany Iris Davenport." To Bethany's embarrassment, he lifted their joined hands and spun her around. "One kiss from her and I knew I'd found my perfect match."

The brunette with the baby made a sound of disgust and shouldered past Bethany, pausing long enough to whisper "I had him first," before stomping across the dirt road.

The others closed circle around Bethany like sharks.

"Are you sorry you had to kiss so many of us before you found a keeper?" Seeing Abraham's puckish smile, Kelly dug deeper. "I hope you at least enjoyed all the practice. I'm sure several of us can attest to helping you perfect your techniques, but who taught such a sweet society doll to kiss well enough to capture an experienced sailor like you?"

Abraham's smile fell into a scowl and his arm went protectively around Bethany's waist. "Iris doesn't need to hear such things."

"Does she claim to be a good girl?" the blonde mocked much like Phoebe with a hand on her hip. "If she's so upright and moral, why is she still with you when everyone knows you never gave a girl a second chance if she didn't give a little something the first time? Tom did say you were having a go with her on your porch last night."

It took all Bethany's self-control to keep her chin up as the venomous words assaulted her image of Abraham.

He stepped in front of Bethany and towered over the blonde. "Go to hell, Kelly."

"Is that what you said to Charity when you broke her heart mere days after taking her innocence?"

"That was three years ago, so shut your mouth." The hardness of his voice was unlike anything Bethany had ever heard from him.

"But you always wanted my mouth open, Abe Walker, or have you forgotten?" Kelly smirked.

"You bitch." Abraham looked at her with complete disdain. "And you wonder why I had to find a girl off the island."

Taking Bethany's hand, he led her away. Once they were in his parents' yard, he turned her to him.

"Don't listen to them, Iris. They're nothing to me." He kissed her and swiped the tear that cascaded her cheek. "I ain't touched any other girl since I kissed you on your birthday, but I told you New Year's I wasn't a saint before choosing you."

"They all looked at me like I wasn't worthy of you. Like I—"

"God, no, Beth."

Hearing him speak her name sobered her, and then he took her face in his palms.

"It's me who isn't worthy and they know it. They're jealous of your beauty and style. And if they got to know you, they'd be in awe of your gentle soul."

Bethany sniffed back tears and tucked against his chest. "I know you haven't hidden anything from me, but to see the faces of the ones you—"

"I admit I played my cards of being the son of the man with the biggest fleet on the island to tumble with the girls. They all seek for what comforts and stability they can when looking for a husband, and a Walker is about as good as you can get around here these days. Emmett had his choice of every unmarried lady from fifteen to thirty when he was ready to settle down. I started testing the waters early without wanting to be chained to any one girl. Several were willing to do whatever I wished in an attempt to prove their worth, but I wasn't serious about any of them."

"That blonde…"

"Kelly," he spat the name. "Don't get worked up over her. She fusses about Charity—the one with the baby—but she was more than happy to indulge me after I supposedly broke her best friend's heart. What does that make her? Something not fit to say in front of you."

She wanted to flee before Abraham could wound, though the past ten months showed him completely faithful to their budding relationship. Everything he had said and done proved his changed life, his dedicated love. If he was still that guy looking for release with a willing girl, he could have taken her on the beach that morning with little protest after their provocative explorations.

"Forget them all, Iris." Abraham held her tighter. "It's you I want forevermore."

***

"Do we have to go?" Bethany asked as they walked through the twilight.

"For a little while. I haven't been to one of the bonfires all year. My old chums are strangers now that I spend all my free time with you. But that's no hardship. You're much nicer to look at." Abraham flashed his broad smile and kicked at the sand. "There'll be some moonshine, but you don't have to drink."

"Can we leave before things get rowdy?"

His bold laughter drowned the noise of the surf. "What do you think's gonna happen?"

"I heard a few stories from Miss Darla about what her brothers would do on Saturday nights."

"That was years ago. Our generation is more sophisticated."

They rounded a dune and sparks sprung to the indigo sky beyond the next mound of sea oats.

Abraham still wore the same cutoff pants he had on that morning, scratchy with dried salt water as he rubbed his knee along hers. "It won't be as bad as you think, but stay close."

"Walker, ya stranger!" a guy shouted when they neared the fire. "Now we can live it up like we did last summer when Kade was home!"

Tom shook Abraham's hand. "I'm glad you came. And it's great to get a better look at your girl."

Abraham's arm went around Bethany, tugging her closer. "Don't look too long or you'll have a black eye."

Several men joined them, rugged clothes faded and ripped. A few were without shirts, showcasing their bronzed bodies from hours in the sun and muscle-hardened from their labors. Kelly and another young woman Bethany recognized from the exchange that afternoon came closer. Feeling overdressed in her vibrant tropical print against the faded tones kept Bethany from relaxing, though Abraham's arm around her usually melted all insecurities.

Another couple arrived, each with an earthenware jug. A shout went up and the jugs were passed. Swallows were followed by whoops and animal sounds as the alcohol seared life into those partaking.

When a jug reached Abraham, he guzzled from it and let out a rebel yell louder than anything previous. He reached beyond Bethany to pass it to Tom.

"What, the society princess doesn't drink moonshine?" Kelly glared. "Our stuff ain't good enough for you, Mardi Gras Queen?"

"I'll drink her share." Abraham pulled it back for another drink.

Bethany touched his hand as he lowered it, an expectant look in her eye.

"Take it slow, Iris."

Wary of everyone watching, she used both hands to lift the jug to her lips. The smell was enough to singe her nostrils as the liquid fire choked her. To control the coughing fit threatening to overpower her, she swallowed saliva to coat her throat as her eyes watered. Tom took the jug and Abraham smashed his lips to hers, his tongue sweeping the lingering burn from her mouth.

A wave of acceptance washed over her as Abraham broke their kiss with his huge grin. "You don't have to prove anything, but I'm glad you tried it."

"I preferred the wine on New Year's."

He nipped her cheek. "You have refined taste, Iris. I can't get over the fact you like me."

She leaned against him and whispered, "I love you, Abraham Jeffery Walker. And your kisses are sugary sweet, even with the flame of alcohol."

The moonshine continued to make its leisurely rounds. After several more passes, the jagged circle of people settled around the bonfire. Bethany drank once more and felt heaviness in her head she'd never experienced. As though sensing her unsteadiness, Abraham stood behind her and lowered them to the sand until she sat nestled between his legs. Closing her eyes, she tried to imagine they were on the beach at Seacliff, except for the fact that Abraham wouldn't be periodically nibbling her neck or trailing his hands about her middle.

Abraham continued to joke with his friends. The words and laughter rumbled his chest beneath her back, creating a hum of life that soothed Bethany.

"That moonshine's done turned her into a drowsy kitten, Walker," a rough voice said. "Sit her in my lap if you want a taste of one of your old flavors while she sleeps."

"Don't even think about it, Grayson." Abraham stroked Bethany's hair and she drifted further from the bonfire in her mind. "I'll take another swig if there's any left."

The next thing Bethany heard were rowdy shouts. She lifted her head from Abraham's shirt that kept her face from being in the sand. An amorous couple lay a dozen feet away, paying no mind to the commotion as they all but made love with their clothes on.

Standing, Bethany wobbled. The others were splashing in the water, the guys all shirtless and the handful of females with their skirts tucked in their waistbands or their pants rolled above their knees. Abraham was the object of Kelly's attention in what appeared to be a water battle. While the other men would make a grab at the girls splashing them, stealing a kiss or a touch, Abraham seemed content to sling handfuls of water at the blonde.

Slipping off her deck shoes, Bethany went for the water. It felt like she walked on cotton candy, but she didn't let the sinking feeling stop her.

"Walker, your girl's up!"

She felt the water inch over her toes and reached for the hem of her dress.

"Abe's got himself an exhibitionist!"

"Woah! She's gonna skinny dip with the pack of us!"

"Bethany Iris, stop!"

She pulled the hibiscus dress over her head and let it fall behind her. Groans of disappointment over her swimsuit beneath followed. Abraham splashed over and tossed her dress onto the dry sand so the tide wouldn't pull it out to sea.

"Where ya going, Iris?"

"To swim. I need to clear my head."

Abraham's arms clamped around her middle. "It's too dangerous."

"You can play out here with your old girlfriends but I can't take a swim?"

"It's the Gulf, not the bay, Iris." He kissed her cheek but she flinched away. "It's dark, you aren't used to the currents, and there could be sharks. Not to mention you're a bit drunk."

Kelly laughed, her soaked shirt straining against her heaving chest. "Are you jealous your man has a playful side you don't know how to fulfill?"

Fists clenched, Bethany wanted to strike. "I give him everything he needs!"

The words spewed from her mouth before she realized the source—the horrific memory. She stumbled forward, throwing herself into the water as soon as she was waist-deep. The action awoke her coordination and her solid strokes pulled her from the group.

"Iris!"

The tears came along with the images as she swam. Cowering in the entrance of St. Mary's School with Asher and Louisa while her mother shouted those very words at Sister Prudence as she beat her.

I'm like Momma!

Something brushed her foot and then her leg. Flipping over, Bethany found herself in Abraham's embrace. Treading water, he hugged her as best he could while they stayed afloat.

"Don't ever do that to me again!"

"What?" She trembled as she took in the utter darkness of their surroundings.

"Leave me. The Gulf isn't safe at night. We need to go back."

Looking to the beach, Bethany saw the bonfire half a mile in the distance. The others stood along the shore like ants.

"It's so far." Something splashed a few feet away and Bethany clung to him.

"It was only a fish that time, but start swimming. I'll be right beside you."

"But—"

"Now, Beth! We need to get somewhere safe."

She stopped every few strokes to look around and hold Abraham's hand, making the trip even longer. Once they were able to stand, her lips quivered as the tears overpowered her.

"I didn't touch her, Iris." Abraham spoke into her ear as he held her. "You don't need to be defensive, though I'm glad to know you'll bite back if you feel threatened."

"Momma," was the only word she could get out between catching her breath from the swim and her falling tears.

"You ain't done nothing like your mama. You've got hooch in your veins and that rotten hellcat pulled on a bit of your pluck. Your Daddy was a fighter and you were brave in speaking the truth and swimming into the dark." He roughly kissed her cheeks but still she fought for control. "You hear me? What you said was the goddamned truth, Bethany Iris! You give me everything I'll ever need."

"But we haven't even—"

His hard mouth claimed her before he pressed his forehead to hers. "It doesn't matter that we haven't shared it all because one kiss with you overshadows any paltry experience with another girl. They can all go to hell for all I care."

"Your pa was right, Abraham Jeffery Walker." Her legs wrapped about his waist. "You are a cantankerous cuss."

The harsh set of his jaw softened into his dazzling smile. "And I'm all yours."

Thirty-Nine

Alexander looked up from his paperwork when someone in work pants with white sleeves rolled to the elbows stopped in his opened doorway.

"Do you have a moment, Mr. Melling?" Abraham Walker stood with cap in hand; chin down though he met his eyes.

"God help you if—"

"Iris is good. I just came from dropping her at the house. Miss Maggie and all the others were happy to see her."

His face relaxed a tad and he waved him in. "Then why do you come to my office and *Mr. Melling* me when I've been Poppy to you for months?"

Abraham hesitantly crossed the room and took the seat opposite. "Because I want to make sure you keep an eye on Iris while Sissa is gone. Please be a listening ear if she needs to complain about what happened over the weekend."

"If you took advantage—"

"Never, Poppy." But his smile gave way to the truth. Abraham *had* enjoyed intimacies with Bethany, though they were welcomed by her. "I treat my flower with respect."

Knowing his stepdaughter was comfortable with her beau—
and that he in turn was man enough to come forward with
concerns—helped Alexander remain calm. He took his cigarette case
from a pocket and handed it and a lighter to the young man. "What
has you worried, Abe?"

"I'm no saint, Poppy."

His laugh tightened his belly with its force. "You and me
both, but that's nothing new."

Abraham shrugged and sucked on the cigarette a moment.
"The island's a small place. We ran into a few of my old girls, I guess
you'd call 'em, though I never claimed one long enough for a
relationship. They weren't kind to Iris—or me for that matter, but
that's not the issue."

The remembrance of Lucy's face upon seeing Consuela
dropped like a boulder. "The poor darling. It was traumatic for her,
wasn't it?"

Abraham nodded. "But she was brave. There was a bonfire
Saturday night and we all had several nips from the jug."

He gripped the edge of his desk. "You better be glad
Davenport isn't alive or he'd—"

"I know, Poppy. And I told her before we got there she
didn't need to drink, but those bitches were calling her names and
she took the moonshine to prove herself."

"Was she all right? Did she get sick?"

Abraham grinned. "She took it like an old sailor and blinked
back the tears. A glorious sight, though she fell asleep half an hour
later."

"Frederick always held his drink well, unlike me." Unable to
stop a chuckle, Alexander immediately cleared his throat to mask the
amusement. "So you confess you got my daughter drunk and broke
her heart a little, huh?"

"Yes, sir."

"You probably felt her up several times between all the drama too."

He blanched beneath his freckles. "I…we—we love each other. She sets the limits and I respect her. I promise I won't force anything or take from her what honor should be held for her husband."

"That leaves plenty of room for mischief." Alexander smirked, eyebrows raised.

"I'm no saint, Poppy," he repeated, "but Iris is cherished."

Alexander inclined his head and stared at the young man a minute before speaking. "It means a lot that you come to discuss these things with me. Both of you, as it was Bethany who approached me at the beginning of your relationship to secure the New Year's invitation."

"Thank you for being a father to her, especially since Mr. Davenport passed. Iris loves and respects you."

"She's been a joy to me since the day she was born. Just remember you now have Claudio watching her as well."

Abraham nodded. "Knowing she's well cared for makes our separations easier."

"Thanks for stopping in, Abe. Come anytime." Alexander offered his hand. "And thank you for treasuring Bethany Iris as you do. You're a better man than I ever was."

At supper, Alexander gazed across the table at his stepdaughter. Bethany sported a tan from her weekend on Dauphin Island, but nothing appeared amiss with her. After eating, Asher, Simon, and Louisa retreated to the back porch and Tabitha to the piano.

Amelia came for a hug. "Will you play checkers with me, Poppy?"

"In a few minutes, my precious girl." He kissed her. "Go ahead and set the board."

Amelia skipped out of the room and Magdalene shifted in the chair beside him as though to stand. He laid a hand on her knee to still her as he turned to Bethany.

"Did you have a good weekend, Knight Bethany?"

"I did, thank you." Her smile had a hint of darkness in it. "And I'm feeling better about Sissa and Uncle Claudio."

"They could do with our love and support. So could you." Her eyes widened and he continued. "Abe stopped by my office this afternoon. He's concerned you experienced a few upsets and wanted to be sure I would help you in any capacity you might require."

A spark of alarm reached her eyes and her arched eyebrows rose. "When I went to the island as a child, I only saw the wilderness and fun. This time, I saw the drastic differences in our lifestyles. Everyone's clothes and skin are rough and hardened. Miss Maggie, how did you save your delicate hands and complexion?"

A dreamy smile appeared on her lips. "Douglas kept me well supplied with skin creams from the city and lovely sunhats."

Alexander couldn't help kissing Magdalene as he threaded his fingers into hers. "Yet another thing to thank your mighty Scot for."

She blushed and looked to Bethany. "You must have stood out like a lighthouse amid the locals."

"I brought all the wrong clothes and was the only one in a proper bathing suit." She looked to her hands, breath halting as she fought back her emotions. "The girls hate me and Abe's friends think I'm some trophy he's training for fun. He kept reassuring me, especially about those girls he…. Oh, Poppy, why does it hurt to know the choices he made before he loved me?"

"No one's perfect, darling. You've seen and heard about the mistakes of others, but I'm afraid the more you love someone that the deeper the pain strikes when they disappoint you." He was by her side in an instant, arm about her as the well of emotions rose in his throat. "Abe loves you and has matured into a fine man."

"What if I'm not enough?" Her voice wavered with unshed tears. "What if I don't continue to please him as things progress?"

"You have your mother's tender heart, Bethany." Several hot tears slipped from his eyes as he gazed through the blurriness at the jewel before him. "Lucy worried the very same thing with me in the beginning. I can assure you that you're more than enough for Abe. Your purity and beauty, both inside and out, are what he craves. After experiencing true love like you two share—what I shared with your mother—there's no going back. Never doubt your worth or the power of love."

Bethany clung to him until he felt her breathing calm. Her lips found his cheek before she pulled away. "I wish Momma was here to talk to, but I love you, Poppy."

"I love you like my own, though there's no denying your father in you."

"Thank you for being understanding and patient." Bethany hugged him once more.

After she left, Alexander met Magdalene at the end of the table for a healing embrace.

"You're a great father, Alexander Melling. The fact that your stepdaughter called you patient is proof of that."

He laughed and kissed below her ear where her fragrance gave him a head rush. "I'm only as good as the wife beside me."

***

To make sure he was the first to welcome the De Fiores, Alexander paced the foyer Friday evening.

Abraham arrived and brought his weekend bag to Kade's old bedroom as the oldest Campbell had moved into an apartment near the university the previous month. Then, the young man settled on the loveseat in the front room with Bethany. Alexander looked upon the couple with a pleased smile, knowing they pulled through last weekend's upsets better than he and Lucy had after the Mystics of Dardenne masquerade.

Alexander flung the door open before the chimes finished ringing and took both Melissa and Claudio in a giant hug as he kissed each of their cheeks. "My dearest friends! Please tell me the marriage is consummated and all is glorious."

"You should never ask that of a lady, Alex." Melissa forced a frown before a grin filled her face. "But all is glorious, as you say."

"*Sí*, and you shall see the next time we dance that our tango has been perfected." Claudio swayed against Melissa.

"Dancing after supper it is!" Alexander ushered them in and called out to the others. "The newlyweds are here!"

Bethany came first, hugging Melissa and then looking upon her stepmother's husband.

"*Bentornato, Papá*," she said with perfect inflection as she looked at him shyly. "May I call you *Papá* now, Uncle Claudio?"

"*Sí, Principessa*. It would be an honor." Claudio held her to his chest, smiling over her shoulder at Alexander and Melissa.

"I believe I should take offense," Alexander said. "Melissa was deemed 'Sissa' after being in town a few days, Claudio is given a nickname the first week he is in the family, yet I had to wait nearly two years before earning the title of Poppy."

Bethany kissed his cheek. "You know we love you."

"Mom!" Louisa rushed down the hall like a little girl though she was nearly as tall as the adults at fourteen. "Did you have a marvelous time?"

"Yes, but it's good to be back."

Louisa turned to Claudio. "Are you really coming home with us tonight, Uncle Claudio?"

"*Sí.* We have already dropped our luggage at the house and it appears Alexander delivered my other things while I was gone."

"There are a few items I wanted to ask about," Alexander said. "Come with me. We'll just be a minute, everyone."

Alexander led the way to his den.

As soon as the door was shut, Claudio laughed. "You want details, no?"

"Yes!" Alexander grabbed his shoulders. "How was it? Are you both fulfilled?"

Claudio stepped back and lit a cigarette. "We met a few of my New Orleans friends for several meals and social hours, and we satisfied each other many times a day, even in the sweltering heat. Creole food and love making go well together."

Alexander's face ached from his huge smile. "And is Melissa as naughty as she seems?"

The ex-priest arched an eyebrow. "As we are married, no confessions are needed."

A sharp rap on the door followed by it immediately opening. Melissa walked in with an accusing eye on Alexander. "Please announce supper, Alex. I really don't think you need more time questioning my husband about our honeymoon."

He raised his hands in a show of surrender. "I must know my friends are content."

Melissa took Claudio in an amorous embrace to which he responded by running his hands down the back of her green dress until he provocatively grasped her rear. In a fine show of passion, they kissed and caressed for the better part of a minute. Straightening, she ran her tongue over her lips as though capturing every last taste of her husband.

"Are you mollified, Alex?"

With a primal growl, he leapt at the couple to hug them once more. "May you keep this beautiful passion always, De Fiores!"

Forty

Bethany stepped out of Mademoiselle Bisset's shop and tugged the purple scarf around her neck against the northerly wind. She rushed to catch the next streetcar going west. Exiting at Catherine Street, she refastened the buttons on her coat to prepare for the final leg of her journey home.

A jaunty figure in a gray pea coat waited on the porch. Bethany's smile felt as big as the grin Abraham sported that February afternoon.

"Captain Abraham Jeffery Walker, what a pleasant surprise!" She used the title he'd earned that winter each time she saw him.

Abraham laughed as he always did, pulling her into a hug.

"You think I was going to let you leave the country without a special visit?" His kiss stirred her entire body to life as he traveled from her lips to her jaw and up to her ear. "I'm going to miss you, Bethany Iris."

"I'll miss you too, but we'll both keep busy. It's only seven weeks."

"I've seen you at least twice a week for months on end. You've become quite the habit."

"You can keep on seeing me with all those photographs we've amassed thanks to Sissa. Weekends together, the New Year's ball, Christmas, my seventeenth birthday—"

"That one's my favorite. Fashionable Bethany Iris Davenport in a silly party hat. Those designers in Paris can say what they want about you, but I know my girl likes to wear rumpled trousers when she's home and will go all week at Seacliff wearing nothing more than a fresh swimsuit every day."

He tugged the scarf loose so he could get at her neck. She pressed closer, wishing they weren't so layered with clothing as she ran her hands through his windblown hair.

"Perhaps it is best to bring this display out of the cold."

Blushing, Bethany looked to Claudio as he climbed the front steps carrying a grocery sack. His coat was topped with the wool scarf she'd made him when he worked as an exorcist in Naples. "*Mi dispiace, Papá.*"

"*Molto bene, Principessa.* You will do well when we are in Italy." He kissed her cheeks, then Abraham's. "You are saying a final, *final* farewell this time, no?"

"*Sí, Papá.*"

They followed Claudio inside and removed their outerwear.

"We are to have a late supper if you would like to stay." Claudio told Abraham. "That would give you almost two hours to keep saying goodbye."

"Thank you."

"Do you need any help in the kitchen?" Bethany asked.

"No, you two enjoy your time together, and I will prepare an Italian feast. Can you not smell the sauce? It has been simmering all day. Bethany, would you see to the music for me?"

"I'd be happy to."

Claudio kept the kitchen door open so he could listen to recordings of his cousin while he cooked. Bethany started one playing in the dining room and led Abraham to the parlor where she shut the drapes against the darkening sky. In an attempt to memorize the feel of him, her hands roamed over his shirt as they kissed. He in turn caressed her curves.

"Everywhere you go," he whispered as he held her hips, "think of me. The next time you go overseas, I'll be the one to take you. No more parents or chaperones—it'll be you and me. Decide on all the lovely places you want us to share."

"I'd like that." She snuggled against him.

The trip Bethany and her family were leaving on the following day would bring them by train to Florida, then by ship to Italy for two weeks to visit Claudio's family before traveling to France for the remainder of their time. It was a work trip for the newlyweds—Melissa to research and write a retrospective on Paris a decade after the armistice for the local newspaper, and Claudio to receive intensive instruction under French chefs for three weeks. It would also allow Bethany another stint in the fashion district with Mademoiselle Bisset's contacts. Louisa was coming as her mother's assistant and Bethany's companion so the half-sisters could keep each other busy while the De Fiores enjoyed a bit of privacy while traveling.

Bethany and Abraham were deep in another kiss when the back door opened.

"We're back!" Melissa called. "And it smells wonderful!"

The couple untangled themselves as Louisa's light steps clipped up the stairs.

"How do I look?" Bethany whispered.

"Flushed with passion. Your lips are even more kissable when we've been at it."

She went to poke him in the stomach but he took her around the waist, swinging her about until he nestled into her neck from behind.

"You're breathless from kissing and your heaving chest beckons me. One of these days I'll explore all of you."

Thinking of the times he'd touched her over her clothing, she guided his hands up her ribs. Abraham turned her in his arms and pressed a hard kiss to her lips.

"Not now." His breath danced across her face.

"Claudio informed me we have a supper guest," Melissa said as she entered the parlor. "I can't say I'm surprised to see you, Abe."

"An extra week without seeing Iris proved too much. I switched my days with another captain to come. I have to be at the dock at five in the morning for a run up the river, so tonight will be it." He kissed Bethany's cheek but kept an arm about her. "I do have good news, though. Something to keep me busy while you're gone." His smile was infectious.

Bethany grinned. "What is it?"

"Pa's promised me my own boat this summer. He said if I can gather regular routes in the north bay, delta, or up the rivers I can be stationed in Mobile rather than the island. You can bet I'll be scouting all the leads I can in the next few months to set-up cargo, ferrying, and whatever else I can figure out to work from town."

"That would be wonderful!"

"I hope to be well established here before your birthday." He held Bethany's face, tracing her cheek with his thumb.

Words weren't necessary because he'd already promised to give her a ring when she turned eighteen. "I hope you are too," she whispered.

"I wish you the best, Abe. Be sure you tell Alex, Henry, and Maxwell so they can spread the word. I'm always surprised at their connections. Some of the men they're acquainted with probably know people along those routes." Melissa patted his shoulder and smiled at Bethany. "I need to supervise Louisa's final packing. We had to run downtown to purchase new shoes and a few other things she's outgrown in the past month."

Once they were alone again, they settled on the sofa together. Abraham enfolded Bethany in his arms. "Tell me about your day."

They chatted about work, kissed, and laughed until supper was ready. Bethany still had a hollow spot in her heart at not seeing her father at the table, but Claudio was excellent company. And his meals! Miss Sharon didn't have a chance with him around, but the evenings he worked at the restaurant they enjoyed her cooking. Claudio had quickly made a name for himself in town and hoped his training in France would open more possibilities. He led the prayer and eagerly passed the platters and bowls. Penne pasta with shrimp marinara sauce, salad with his special vinaigrette dressing, garlic toast, and green beans. He watched like a boy awaiting birthday presents as they ate their first bites until it was declared perfection. Then he kissed Melissa before starting on his own.

"To everything there is a season, and a time to every purpose under the heaven" the words from The Bible came to her as she linked her hand with Abraham's under the table. *Just as Momma had her season with Daddy, and then Poppy, now it is Sissa's season with Claudio and Poppy's with Miss Maggie. I only pray I have more time with Abe than they were given with their first loves.*

Bethany volunteered herself and Abe to do the dishes. Claudio readily accepted. Upon seeing the state of the kitchen, Bethany decided to never again offer cleaning after he cooked.

"I think he used every pot in the cabinet," she told Abraham as he carried in a stack of dishes from the dining room. "I need to remind him there are no paid washers in the house on Miss Sharon's off days."

"It means we'll be together longer and that sounds great to me."

On their last trip to the dining room, Claudio came in to start the gramophone. The quick Latin beat was one for a tango. Bethany didn't need to look into the parlor to know he and Melissa danced in their sensual way.

Once the load of dishes was deposited on the counter, Abraham positioned Bethany for a dance of their own. His focus was too intense for it to be a natural stance for him, but it endeared him all the more that he applied such effort.

"Abe," her voice whispered with longing, "I want you to touch me tonight."

"Iris—"

"I want you to feel my heart beating beneath my skin and remember me."

"I'll remember you always. Your sweet lips, your angelic eyes, the feel of you as we dance." Both hands went to her hips and he held her against him as his movements mimicked the rhythm Alexander had often displayed with her mother.

She backed toward the door, releasing the iron they used to prop it open by sliding it aside with her foot until the door swung closed. Then her hands were at the buttons on her chest.

"You don't need to—"

"I want to, Abe. I may not be experienced, but I know what feels good. I think I've understood when you find pleasure in our connections as well." She smiled and pressed against him as he gave a sharp intake of breath. With the top four buttons unfastened, she laid open the left side, exposing her black silk brassiere.

Without hesitation, his head lowered to her creamy skin and left a kiss on the swell of her chest that sent desire racing to her core. "You're beautiful. I'll love and cherish you forever."

"Do you know how to leave passion marks? Poppy always marked Momma's breast with one to show who possessed her heart. I want you to mark me yours, Captain Walker. I want to carry you with me everywhere I go."

"It'll fade eventually."

"My love won't. And when I return, you can keep a fresh mark on me because you own my heart."

His eyes darkened with the exception of the golden flecks. "It might hurt a bit, especially as you aren't used to contact there."

"I'm ready for more."

His finger traced the top of the brassiere, nudging the silk lower. Bethany wanted to watch, but the cupping motion with his strong hand set her eyes looking heavenward as his lips laid claim to her virgin skin. The urge to hold him to her breast until he conquered the whole prize doubled when Abraham's other arm encircled her body. He took her backside in a firm grasp, communicating to her all he would do when the time to explore everything was upon them. The momentary disappointment that it couldn't be now was chased away by the sensation his mouth produced. When the sucking pinch stopped, his tongue laved the tender flesh before he moved to the valley and left another kiss there.

Abraham raised his head to meet her gaze. "Thank you for sharing yourself with me. For trusting me."

With a smile, she nipped a kiss as she closed two of her buttons. "My redheaded cantankerous cuss."

His laughter was beautiful and bold—everything she wanted. He finished fastening her buttons and hugged her as he tasted her neck.

"Abe, if we don't start on the dishes soon Sissa might grow suspicious."

The door swung inward. "What of the wary stepfather? Do I need to send Louisa down to chaperone?"

Bethany rested her head on Abraham's shoulder. "No, *Papá.*"

"Then keep the door open." Claudio gave them a knowing look before fixing the iron on his way to change the music.

"He's understanding but firm," Bethany remarked as she tied on an apron. "I can't help but think Daddy would have stormed about if he'd caught us embracing in a closed room."

"I'm glad you get along with Claudio."

She nodded and started the sink filling with sudsy water. "I've always loved him, but I still miss my father. My mother, too."

"I know you do and don't be afraid to let it show. I'll be here to help you through the pain, just as I promised Mr. Freddy."

"That's all I'll ask of you, Abe. Share my pain and joy, my upsets and thrills."

"With all my heart, Bethany Iris."

Forty-One

Alexander returned to his air conditioned office on the sweltering afternoon of August seventeenth after having walked to and from George's Candy Shop to buy Amelia a box of fudge for her birthday. His daughter turned nine that day, and the extended family and friends were all invited to a supper party. A category one hurricane was making its way up the Florida Gulf Coast, sure to dump plenty of rain and ruin the weekend for riding or Seacliff Manor. But Amelia wouldn't care what they did so long as they were together.

He stood before the air conditioning vent to dry the sweat from his white shirt when a knock sounded. Turning so he faced the door, he called "Come in!"

Melissa held a box before her. "I didn't want to wait until supper and take away anything from Amelia's special day."

"The advance copies?"

She nodded. "I thought we should both inscribe them."

"Why should I—"

"Alex, you were her muse. Those poems were all for you except the handful about her children, but you even bleed into most of those."

He took the box from her. "Yet there wasn't room for my limericks. How's that?"

"The world isn't ready for your poetry, Alex of the Marble Palace."

"Too sultry?" He worked his hips in his favorite rhythm.

"Much too sultry, dashing Poppy."

Tears pricked Alexander's eyes when he opened the lid. He fingered the embossed image of Lucy on the lavender hardcover, her stubborn chin, gorgeous eyes, and hair streaming around her face in waves. Her likeness had been copied from Eliza's sketch of Lucy drawn at their tea with her that first month of courtship. Gold letters scrolled above the image.

Selected Poems and Short Stories of Olive Kent

Edited by Melissa Davenport De Fiore

"It's beautiful, Melissa." He hugged her. "I'm sorry to see you lose 'Stone' from your writing name, but I know Freddy would be pleased you kept his."

"I hope so. Be sure to look at the dedication page."

Alexander turned beyond the title page and paused at the bold declaration.

For Alexander Randolph Melling,

who inspired his queen more than we will ever understand,
and Camellia, Iris, and Ash,
proof that love continues to grow from one generation to the next.

"It's perfect, Melissa. And using the middle names allows Camellia to also speak of the one she lost without adding a fourth name. Thank you." He gently flipped through the book to see the layout before hugging it to his chest. "Even all these years later, seeing this makes me want to run home and make love to her."

"'Like a good gent'?"

Their laughter filled the room before they settled across from each other, writing special notes first to one another before tackling the others: Phoebe, Bethany, Asher, Magdalene, Claudio, Naomi, Darla, Claire, Maxwell, and finally Mr. Fearn—the chairman for the new public library that was opening the next month several blocks down Government Street from the mansion. It was Mr. Fearn's idea to have a new Olive Kent title in conjunction with the opening. Noble Publishing was all too happy to assist with the collection because they'd been making as much money off Lucy's novels as ever by releasing twentieth anniversary editions for her titles over the last few years.

"Freddy would have loved to read this," Melissa remarked as she repacked the final book. "Several of the stories were completed when we brought the girls out west our first summer together and Lucy was home alone."

"Do you think it's time to tell the girls about their share of the royalties? Phoebe is twenty-one next week and Bethany nearly eighteen. That money could mean a lot to her with any travel or business plans she might have for the coming year."

"You're probably right."

"I'll check with Kade about where to find Phoebe. May I give you a ride home?"

"Thank you, but I drove. Claudio took the streetcar to work this morning. I'm picking him up from the restaurant on the way back."

"I still get a kick out of the two of you being married." He laughed. "Don't take this the wrong way but—"

"Now I'm scared."

He rubbed his discolored jaw and grinned. "I think of him being seduced and tormented by Eliza and all those years he denied his natural man afterward. I can't help but believe you're his reward for good behavior. You're the grand prize upon release from priestly prison."

"I'm not sure how I could take *that* the wrong way." She kissed his cheek. "I'll see you at the house later."

"There's one more thing." Alexander fingered her copper hair. "Have you noticed a change in Bethany and Abe this summer?"

"They've been more intense since we returned from Europe, like they've advanced to a new level of intimacy." Melissa blushed becomingly. "You don't think they're—"

"No, but they have to be exploring some things. Abe's no innocent but he's been a gentleman all this time—nearly two years since he gave Bethany that anklet. They're both working hard and saving for some future goal I've yet to hear specifics about."

"Before we left in February, Abe told Bethany he wanted to be established in the city before her birthday." Melissa fingered the emerald ring Freddy had given her for her thirtieth that she now wore on her right hand. "I think he means to propose and I doubt they'll want to wait long."

"I don't blame them."

"She's young, Alex."

"Bethany's been through much and learned from others— both their mistakes and triumphs. All this has matured her beyond her years. Even you've helped with that through your travel adventures. Don't compare her to you at that age or even her mother. Lucy was sheltered and your upbringing in New York was much different. She's been working and is on track to do anything she wants through her professional connections."

"But what if she throws it all away for Abe?"

"How can you say something like that after what Claudio walked away from for you?" Anger boiled so quick, Alexander was shaking by the time he finished the sentence. "True love is worth any sacrifice and you of all people should understand that. You left New York for Freddy, for God's sake!"

"I didn't mean—"

"But you did. Abe is no less worthy of commitment than anyone else. If Bethany never sews another dress except for her family and is happily married to Abraham Walker, I'd be pleased as punch for her—for both of them! If they keep their true love at such a tender age, so much the better. It'd spare them the hell her mother and I went through." He tried to calm his voice when he saw the fear in Melissa's eyes. "But she wouldn't give it up. And Abe wouldn't let her. Look at what Freddy and Lucy had when they were married. He supported her writing. Her timing might have slowed with motherhood, but she kept going with his blessing. And you with your articles, essay collections, and newspaper column. Marriage doesn't have to stop Bethany."

"You're right, Alex. Beth's goals aren't the same as mine were at her age. I was working on my education in order to get out of my parents' lifestyle. Beth is already on solid ground and working her way up. I don't want her to deny love but—"

"You dated Freddy two months before marriage. Can you imagine having those feelings for two years and *not* making love to your champion?"

She shook her head.

"That's what Bethany and Abe are dealing with. The poor guy is gonna pop his load the minute they say 'I do.'"

"Alex!" She covered her face with her hands. "Don't talk about them like that!"

"Beth might be our baby girl, but they're still human. Adult humans with yearnings and emotions, same as us."

"Not the same as you, so help me—"

His laughter was bawdy. "I'll speak with her."

"No!"

"I'll do it privately. I *can* be discreet and sympathetic. You should know that from all the times you've come to me for advice. I'll handle Beth with compassion."

"I hope so, for all our sakes."

***

Alexander watched Amelia perform a Beethoven piece on the piano after supper and present time—her first concert recital since she began lessons that summer. Her sky blue gown was perfect with the long brunette plait that hung down her back. *So much like her mother!* When Amelia jumped to her feet afterward, his gaze was the first she sought. He clapped the loudest then opened his arms.

"You did wonderfully, Amelia Rose." He hugged her.

She went to Tabitha next, who stood near the door with Bradford as they were headed out for one of her concerts that night.

"My little *protégé*, you did well! I told you there was no reason to be nervous." She kissed her forehead. "I'll see you tomorrow, birthday girl."

Alexander watched Amelia as she thanked each person in the room—De Fiores, Davenports, Campbells, Adamses, and Asher before going to Magdalene.

"I'm proud of the young lady you're becoming, Amelia. All your hard work showed effortlessly. I look forward to hearing more."

"I saved the best for last, Mama, because I knew you'd say the sweetest thing." She snuggled against her breast. "Poppy calls you 'sweetness' for a reason."

Magdalene caught his eye over their daughter's head. "I'm helpless against you and your charming children, Alexander Melling."

"I'd say I prefer you that way, but that's not true. I like you spicy, Magdalene."

The love in Magdalene's warm brown eyes made him wish to thrust into her to let her know what she did to him. *So much passion and heat after all these years! I would have loved to populate the world with our beautiful children. A daughter or son for every time we made love would be an awesome sight.*

As though reading his thoughts, Darla cleared her throat. "It's time for us to get home."

The Adams family said their goodbyes, and Claudio looked at his watch and stood. "Thank you for sharing your special day with us, Amelia. Melissa and I need to bring your brothers and Louisa to the cinema now, but we will see you soon."

"Thank you, Uncle Claudio and Aunt Sissa. I love the ribbons and horse book."

Louisa went to Bethany. "Why don't you come with us since Abe didn't make it?"

"No, thank you. I'd like to play a game or two with the birthday girl and then have a quiet night reading." She had kept Lucy's book with her since Melissa presented it earlier in the evening, the lavender cover bold against her white summer dress.

The others left, leaving only Amelia and Bethany with Alexander and Magdalene. Before he could collect Bethany for the talk, the doorbell rang.

Kade stood on the veranda when Alexander answered the door. "You needn't ring here, Kade."

"I wanted to pay an official birthday call on my half-sister and see if I could take her out for ice cream."

"You were invited to supper and she's already had cake."

Kade folded his arms across his chest. "I studied late after working at the stables and lost track of time."

"Studying?" Alexander raised his eyebrows.

"Yes."

Alexander accepted the excuse he didn't believe, moving aside so his stepson could enter. "You missed her piano recital, but I'm sure she'd give an encore performance if you ask. She's in the morning room with Bethany."

"I'd like to join them, if that's okay."

"Of course." Alexander took his arm before he could leave. "Are you in touch with Phoebe?"

"Yes."

"I sent her an invitation for supper and also one from me, Claudio, and Melissa asking to take her out next week for her birthday, but we haven't heard anything. I have a few other things to discuss with her as well. I'm not sure we have her current address."

"You don't."

"She's not still with what's his name, the man after Jeremy?"

Kade shook his head.

"You won't tell me?"

"That's up to Phoebe, but I'll let her know you're trying to get in contact with her."

Not wanting her to set upon Magdalene, he clarified the ways to get in touch. "Tell her to call or come to the office or to Sissa's. Are you looking out for her?"

"I'm trying, but when she's in a mood there's nothing to be done." Kade squeezed his eyes shut a moment. "I wish I could get her to listen to me, to come with me, but I know better than to force her when she's unstable."

"How bad is she, Kade? Do I need to come in with medi—"

"It would break her. Most of the time she's clinging to sanity by a thread, but if she thinks she's being forced into something, she'll snap."

"I owe it to her parents to try to help. Promise you'll come to me if things get too much."

"I'll do my best, Poppy, but I can't promise anything. On her worst days she refuses my company. Let me see my little sister for now."

Alexander followed him down the hall, noticing the way Kade carried himself—like a man with the weight of the world on his shoulders—but his voice was chipper when he reached the morning room.

"Happy Birthday, Amelia! How would you like to go for ice cream?"

"Kade!" She ran to him and he tossed her up like she was still a tiny girl. "I miss seeing you at the stables when we go early in the morning. But, yes, I'd love ice cream! I already had cake and fudge today, but I shared those. The ice cream will be all for me!"

"Go get your shoes, birthday girl." Kade looked to Bethany and held his arms out to her. "How are you doing, Tiger?"

Her smile was one of grace without a hint of the school girl infatuation she used to hold for him. "I'm wonderful, Kade."

He spun her around, appreciating her in a way Alexander was sure would earn him a strike to the face from Abraham. "You're gorgeous, Tiger. I haven't seen you in white since your graduation. Don't tell me you're still hanging around with Abe when the world is yours for the taking."

She tilted her head. "Hasn't he kept you updated?"

"I'm sorry to say we've drifted apart this past year, but I hear he's a busy captain these days. No time for a measly college boy, especially when he's got a woman like you to see to."

"We'd love to get together with you sometime."

Amelia tugged on Kade's arm.

"Want to come with us, Tiger?"

"No, thank you. You two have fun."

After Kade and Amelia left, Bethany smoothed her dress and gathered her book.

Alexander held out his arm before she could leave the room. "I need to speak with you, Knight Bethany. Sit with me a minute?"

She held the book to her chest and settled on the sofa with him.

"You know you can talk to me about anything, right?"

"Yes, Poppy."

"I may tease you, especially when others are around, but that says more about me than my feelings for you. People expect me to be filled with innuendos, but I know your personality is different, even if your passions are the same."

"My *passions*?" Fear quivered her voice.

"Passion is normal, healthy. Your mother and father were two of the most passionate people I ever knew. They loved hard and gave their whole hearts to those lucky enough to capture them. You were raised by them and have been surrounded by people like me, unashamed to express desires. I know you and Abe love each other. It's natural for you, after all this time, to want to elevate your relationship. After a few months, a kiss isn't enough. A few months more and caresses on the arm only make you want to touch more."

She nodded and—though blushing—maintained eye contact.

"I know he's not pressuring you into doing more. That's not what I'm getting at. I'm trying to help you understand that it's natural for you both to *want more* of an outlet of expression for your feelings. When I was first engaged, your Grandpa Easton was thrilled to hear Lucy and I wanted only a few weeks engagement because he understood how passions, even between two committed people, can grow out of control and lead to heartache. It doesn't happen badly for everyone, but it did for us. Your mother and I let our passions rule our better judgement and I lost the love of my life for more than five years because of it."

He took the book from Bethany, holding it so Lucy's image faced her. "Yes, you are your mother's daughter, but you're not your mother. You are gloriously different, but you're human and have desires and needs. Abe is a hundred times a better man than I was at his age."

After letting that admission out, Alexander took a deep breath before asking the next question.

"Do you have an understanding for a future together?"

Bethany nodded. "He wants to propose on my eighteenth birthday so no one can say I'm too young, but I know there are girls on the island that are married as young as fourteen."

"That's not typical for your social circle, Beth. Abe doesn't wish to bring unnecessary criticism to you, which is admirable. But at the same time, it could be damaging if you're waiting in an attempt to be proper when it has the potential to lead to sinful behaviors. I'd much rather give you my blessing for marriage than console broken hearts."

"You would allow—"

"Oh heavens, yes! You're both mature people. You've been working years now and he's an established captain. I'm telling you rather than him because I didn't know the plans nor wish to assume things. And I don't know if Abe will ask my permission since your father is no longer with us."

"He's with us." She held her locket to her chest.

"I haven't looked inside in ages. May I?"

Bethany unclasped it so Alexander could hold it at his leisure. Frederick and Lucy were displayed upon opening.

"I keep it like that now since they're both in Heaven and you and Sissa are still here."

"I like that idea, and Sissa is a fine figure to be stuck staring at if I'm to be in a locket."

Smiling, she hooked it back on. "Will you talk to Abe when he comes?"

"You may be sure of it. I want my Bethany happy." *Even if Melissa gets upset my talk didn't go the way she was planning it to.* "And I have news that could help you two. Before your mother died, she prepared a detailed will. In it were directions for her royalties. Not only is part for the upkeep of Seacliff Manor, but all these years the remainder has been divided between you, Phoebe, Asher, and me. There's a sizable nest egg waiting for each of you. Sissa's been overseeing your account. See her for the details. I hope it will help you settle comfortably or finance any business opportunities that may arise."

"Thank you, Poppy!" Her hug was a soothing balm to his troubled soul.

"I promise to see you and Abe joined properly." *Despite what Melissa might say to the contrary.*

Forty-Two

Phoebe lay in her latest bedroom and stared at the white plaster ceiling, imagining Alexander in the room during his exploits. Two decades later, the Mellings—father and son—were still legends within the district, but for different reasons. The head Madame of the house had known both and admitted to being victim to George Melling several times in her youth, but with a gaze of remorse she informed Phoebe she'd never been lucky enough to land the younger Melling.

"He was devoted to his special girls and rarely deviated from them unless he was completely plastered. Then, he might have grabbed whoever was closest, but he'd make it up to his girls later," she'd said.

Sighing, Phoebe spoke her pain aloud. "Would you have taken me, Alexander? I'm no worse than your Prudie, who Momma drove to kill herself. Is that my only way out of this hell?"

It was too late to think what might have been had she accepted Kade's offer of marriage after they were together at Seacliff Manor two years ago. Instead, she'd welcomed Hans, Robert, and an audience into her shame. *But the demons made me do that!* Hans and his crude lifestyle weren't a good fit, but Jeremy was—until the violence began. When he returned to Chicago, he'd passed Phoebe to a friend who was equally rich but filled with fetishes that degraded her further. Her planned escape with an older yacht owner was worse than all the others combined, making her move to Mobile's red light district look like a respite.

But always she contacted Kade and told him where she was. He'd begged her to come to him after each relationship ended, but it was too late. *Even if he loved me once upon a time, I don't think I could tolerate his tender touch knowing I could have had it exclusively. At least here I'm in control of my own room, but how long would the privacy last? Will there be a line when word gets out that the daughter of the great romance novelist and war hero is taking clients?*

For now, the only knocks on the door were from the Madame when a man arrived and all the other girls were occupied or a regular was looking for someone fresh to cure his boredom. And Kade. Kade brought her money and gifts that supplemented her spotty income, but they hadn't been intimate since her time with Jeremy. Jeremy had caught them together and beaten her afterward. She'd kept covered in front of Kade to hide the bruises that were constant since that day. Now, the final purplish marks were merely yellow. Those visual reminders of her past would be gone, but the pain would remain.

Mid Sunday morning was the quietest time of all in the district, but a knock rapped on her door. Wearing her mother's silk kimono tied over lace underclothes, Phoebe crossed the room.

"Good morning." Kade smiled and offered a brown paper sack. "The Danishes at the diner looked so good, I picked a few up for you."

"What do you want, Kade? You were just here Friday evening."

"I have a message." He kissed her cheek and set the bag on her dresser. "Poppy and Sissa have been trying to get in touch with you. They'd like to see you for your birthday tomorrow. Uncle Claudio would love to see you as well."

"Did you tell them where I am?"

"I only told Poppy I'd pass the message. He's concerned about you, Phoebe. He wants to help."

"I'm seeking to support myself rather than rely on others." She sounded defiant though she knew she wouldn't be able to eat most days if it wasn't for Kade's generosity.

"I know, Phoebe, but I'm not offering handouts. I want to share a life with you."

She shook her head. "You're just saying it out of habit."

He didn't deny it, but he lifted her chin and kissed her lips. "Meet with them. They haven't seen you in so long."

"I have no desire to see Sissa with Claudio. She remarried even quicker than Poppy did after Momma died."

"Uncle Claudio came halfway around the world for her and had no home otherwise."

"I won't see her!"

"Then I'll tell Poppy that he and Uncle Claudio can meet you. Would you want to go downtown or to Sissa's house?"

"My *father's* house! And it was Momma's and Grandpa Easton's before that."

"Would you take a meal together?"

"I'll eat dinner with them at noon. Will you accompany me?"

"I'll drive you over, but I think it would be better if you were alone. There might be private matters to discuss. Family things."

She shrugged, her robe slipping open with the motion.

"I'll telephone and let you know if that's good for them before I leave."

"Kade, you need to stop coming here. Someone is bound to see you and when word—"

"I know why I'm here, and you know why I'm here. That's all that matters." He pulled her kimono closed. "If you're that concerned with my reputation, come home with me. I've got a little apartment with plenty of room in the closet for your dresses and space to add a shelf for your mother's books."

She scowled to hide her sorrow. "Go away, Kade Campbell."

***

At a quarter to twelve the following day, Kade pulled to a stop behind the house to collect Phoebe. He was smart enough to stay silent on the drive and Phoebe rewarded him with a kiss before she got out.

"I'll be back at two," he told her.

"Thanks." She smoothed her skirt and made sure all the buttons were fastened on her blouse before going for the porch—the home of her childhood battles of Melling Militia verses Kingdom Davenport.

Claudio opened the door and kissed her cheeks. "*Principessa!* How glad I am to see you."

He was as striking as ever in a plain shirt, unbuttoned in the European way to display his masculine chest and sleeves rolled past his elbows. His navy trousers were well-cut, displaying the definition of his lower half, which Phoebe couldn't help but look at as she followed him into the parlor.

No matter her faults, Sissa has fine taste in men.

Alexander stood to greet her. Phoebe snuggled against him, feeling safe for a fraction of an instant.

"I've missed you, Poppy."

He smiled and touched the tip of her nose. "And I've missed you, Knight Phoebe."

"I have chilled pasta and green salads for our luncheon this hot day," Claudio said as they sat on the sofa, Phoebe in the middle.

"We can eat whenever it is convenient and there is carrot cake for our birthday girl."

"You remembered?" Phoebe couldn't keep the surprise from her voice.

"*Sí.* My times with this family were the highlights of my days. I am blessed to be here permanently."

"And we are happy to have you and host Phoebe on her twenty-first birthday." Alexander gave her his dashing smile and lifted a wrapped book from the coffee table. "This is for your collection. Happy Birthday, from Momma, Sissa, and me. It doesn't release until September, so keep it safe."

The lavender and gold cover was exquisite, the image completely capturing her mother's essence. Melissa's name was the only flaw, but Phoebe knew she was in charge of the literary side of her mother's estate.

"It's beautiful! Momma would have loved it. Are all her poems included?"

"Not all, but many. Most of the short stories were written when you were about five. A few of the characters might even remind you of yourself and Bethany, especially the story of the two princesses."

She turned the first few pages, skimming over the handwritten notes and falling to the dedication page. *At least Sissa got something right.*

"Would you like to eat now?" Claudio asked.

Alexander laughed. "The man is eager for you to try his food. I believe he works for compliments instead of the Lord these days."

Phoebe's mood brightened at their lightheartedness. She smiled further after noticing the photograph of her father displayed on the mantel by his boxing trophies.

They ate under the electric fan around the Easton's old wicker dining set. The nostalgic space made it difficult for Phoebe to swallow the wonderful food.

"It's all terrific, Uncle Claudio, but I want to be sure to save room for cake. Would it be all right if I take some of the extras home with me?"

"*Sí*, you may have whatever you like."

"How many people will eat with you?" Alexander's question, though asked respectfully, was pointed.

"I've given up trying to live within other's boundaries. I'm in charge of myself, Poppy."

"I'm glad to hear that. Is there anything you need as you get established?"

"My room was furnished, though Kade helped me purchase new linens."

"You're in town?"

She nodded and accepted the plate Claudio presented with a large slice of cake.

"Would you like to come to family supper sometime?" Alexander looked expectant, almost pleased.

"I don't think it would work out, but send word through Kade if you'd like." She took a bite of the chilled carrot cake and nearly melted to the floor. "It's divine, the best I've ever tasted!"

Claudio's dimpled grin was huge. "Come to family suppers to partake of this regularly."

Phoebe smiled without meaning to. "It's tempting."

"Surely you'll want to wish your sister and her beau well," Alexander urged. "We expect a formal announcement within the week."

"She's still with Abe?"

"They're an unlikely couple at first glance, but perfect for each other."

"Abe's told me off on several occasions, though I deserved it. But I don't think I could look at him with his arms about my sister." Eyes huge with worry, she took Alexander's hand. "Is Beth still sweet and innocent, Poppy? He hasn't spoiled her?"

"She's as fine as ever, Phoebe. Abe's been a gentleman."

Her tight shoulders deflated. "Good."

"I have some other news that might cheer you and help you on your way to independence. A percentage of Lucy's royalties have been gathering interest in your own account." He pulled a bank booklet from his pocket and slid it across the table to her. "I reminded Sissa that it was time it was turned over to you."

"Because I'm twenty-one now?"

"There was no age stipulation on it for any of you. I suggested it was time to turn them over to you girls with Beth approaching marriage and you—"

"I'm an afterthought! Only when perfect Beth needs a boost will anyone remember me!" Phoebe opened the booklet, skimmed through the regular deposit amounts in the hundreds from the last several years alone. Turning to the final registry page, she choked at seeing the total. Gathering her voice, she slammed the book on the table. "Why the hell did no one tell me?"

"Your mother and I always discussed that it would be presented to each child when the time was right."

"Right according to who, Sissa? She's been a thorn in my side ever since she arrived in town with that cursed brooch! She stole my father, tried to take my mother's place, created more children that shattered Daddy when one died, and made him run away from us to war!"

"That's not true, Phoebe." Alexander reached for her hand.

She jumped away, pointing at the account papers. "Do you have any idea what that would have meant to me two years ago? What heartache it could have saved me, let alone dear Kade?"

"Tell me, Phoebe. I need to understand." His voice was soft, pleading.

"I've relied on men to keep me since I ran away from the Moores' house. I've been tossed out and passed around and even tried to run away, but I was nothing more than a live-in whore to four different men who shared me with their guests. I took Kade on the side just to feel a connection to someone who loved me rather than used me for sex. When Jeremy found me with him, he began beating me regularly to remind me of my place as *his* plaything."

Alexander paled.

"After that, I stopped seeing Kade because I couldn't hide the bruises Jeremy and the others inflicted. But I always told him where I was. A few weeks ago, I went to where I thought I could be in control of myself. I'm learning it's just as much relying on men as before though I have a room to call my own."

Tears streaked Alexander's scarred countenance.

Your mother's reputation was lost because of him, her first marriage ruined. It's his fault you've been reduced to a whore. His sins brought you to his playhouse!

She sneered and rammed the next words to strike his heart.

"I'm in possession of Sister Prudence's old room. The house Madame has only brought a handful of men to me in the past weeks, but I'm sure word will get out soon. After all, who wouldn't want a piece of the notorious Lucille Amelia Easton Davenport Melling's daughter? I did cause stirs at several masquerades last year with my see-through gown, so they'll all know what I have to offer. Will I be well sought-after, Poppy? Would I have been what Consuela was to you back then or more like your dear Prudie?"

"Forgive me for failing you, Phoebe."

"Why don't you bring me home this afternoon? Madame lamented you never bedded her. I'm sure if you give her a good romp she'll only send the best clients to my door. *That* would be incredibly helpful."

"*Principessa*," Claudio prattled on in Italian, words that made Phoebe's head swim and her soul shake.

"No!" She clutched her ears. "Don't pull me out of the darkness! It's my home! The only place I know I'll be safe!"

Alexander reached for her, but she shoved him away, stumbling out the screen door and through the yard.

"Phoebe!"

Dodging traffic, she flew across Dauphin Street and made her way northeast until she stumbled up the back stairs. In her room, she locked the door and stripped off her clothing.

He's trapped you in this life of sin. You tried to love him, but he rejected you. There's only one way out. Go to your parents. They're the only ones who love you.

Wrapped in her mother's kimono, she approached the dressing table. Grandma Easton's scissors were fisted, silver and sharp. Phoebe's skin gave way with each of the dozen slashing motions.

The room spun with the sight of red and the coppery tang. Falling back on her bed, she closed her eyes.

At last, the pain dripped from her tired body.

Pounding.

"Phoebe Camellia, open the door!"

"Mr. Melling, you can't behave in such a way. The others will become upset and—"

"Give me a key or we're breaking it down!"

Bodies slamming, but this time it wasn't her head hitting a bedframe.

Walls rattling.

Wood splintering.

"My God, my little Camellia!" Warm arms about her cold body. Lips on her face.

Too late.

"We need an ambulance, *signora*!"

Prayers.

Rocking.

Binding her wrists.

Too late.

Too late.

Forty-Three

On the morning of September fifteenth, Bethany sat on her bed with knees tucked to her chest under her cotton nightgown. She stared at the last Davenport family photograph, gaze focused on the shine of Phoebe's pale hair and the dress she had sewed for her sister that Christmas.

Melissa and Claudio both came to her open door several times during the past hour, Louisa once. But no one spoke. No one wanted to push her to come out. It might tip her over the edge. She could lose her grip—go crazy like her mother and sister. Her beautiful life would cease to continue.

No autumn wedding.

No lovemaking with Abraham.

No personal design label.

No offspring to continue the curse of the Easton madness.

Not even the smell of pancakes and bacon could rouse her from the emotional stupor she'd been in since Phoebe took her own life.

Everyone else seemed to be moving along—especially on that important day—but Bethany held the weight of her possible future on her soul, unable to see hope like the others could.

A new figure walked into the room. He appeared as defeated as she felt in his wrinkled clothes that he might have worn all night during an attempt to outrun his demons.

"Tiger, why did Poppy have to find me and ask me to talk sense into you? You're not one to mope, but you look terrible."

A half-smile found her lips. "Hello to you too, Kade."

He climbed onto the bed, placing his arm about her so she rested her head on his shoulder. "It hurts like hell, doesn't it?"

"Yes."

"But you know what I realized this week? She's out of pain and no one can ever hurt her again." He stroked Bethany's hair. "I knew she was bad off, but I didn't know how much until Poppy told me afterward."

"I don't see how she fell into all that. She was strong, willful. She could have made a name for herself with horses, performing, modeling, anything!"

"But Phoebe was sick. She should have been in an asylum, Tiger, but no one wanted to cage her wild beauty. She's free now, with your parents and Junior."

She nodded, wiping her tears.

"I bet they're all watching us, our guardian angels. I think I can hear them. Listen." Kade cupped his hand around an ear. "Yep! Mr. Freddy is calling out your stubborn streak in refusing a private audience with Abe for almost a month."

She stared at his blue eyes, dark lashed and intense as always.

"I've been in contact with Abe these past weeks. He was always my best friend, but I allowed my feelings for Phoebe to consume most of my energies, leaving little for school and work and nothing for friends and family. Your father tried to warn me she wasn't fit for a relationship, but I thought I could love her out of madness. It didn't work." He kissed Bethany's forehead. "But Abe, the poor soul, is dying to give you a certain ring he's been carrying around. He wants to see your names printed in the society column, watch you walk down an aisle to him, and then do all sorts of naughty things with you that will no longer be wicked because you'll be married."

"Kade!" She pushed him away with an attempted laugh that choked on the lump in her throat. "I can't marry him now. I might go mad too. I can't put him through that."

"You're the sanest person I know, Tiger, but if you don't marry Abe *he'll* go mad. He's been loving you all these years and putting aside his physical needs to see that you're treated with respect. Don't crush my friend's spirit. Marry him and let him finally have his way with you."

Cheeks heated, she pushed him once more. "And to think, I once fancied I was in love with you!"

"You did?" His bright eyes and smile carried a hint of mischievousness.

"I did for years, and you shattered my heart that New Year's Eve you kissed me only to apologize. My first kiss. I thought I did something wrong because you felt bad for doing it."

Kade laughed. "Do you hear that, Abe? I was Tiger's first kiss!"

"Abe?" Heart pounding, Bethany looked to the hall.

Abraham stepped into the doorway, his teasing grin subdued to a gentle smile. "I wouldn't send this cad into my girl's room alone. And now that I know he hurt you, I want to clobber him."

"Please do, but not here. Both of you need to leave." She covered her thin blue nightgown with the sheet.

"Kade," Abraham said with a take-charge air, "tell them Iris will be down in ten minutes for breakfast. And shut the door on your way out."

"Sure thing." He left with a smirk that further colored Bethany's face.

Abraham dropped to a knee beside her bed. "Miss Davenport, I understand your pain from the loss of your sister and I've allowed you this month to grieve. But as I promised your father, I'll not leave you alone. I've come today to—"

"Captain Walker, I'm in my nightdress!" She clutched the blanket to her chest.

"And it's a fine sight I hope to enjoy every morning the rest of my life in the very near future." His cheeky grin was back full force. Taking her left hand in his, he retrieved a gold and diamond ring from his pocket. "Bethany Iris Davenport, you're the love of a lifetime. Will you marry this cantankerous cuss and make me happy the remainder of my days?"

He slid the ring onto her finger and she moved to the edge of the bed to kiss him. "Yes, Abraham Jeffery Walker."

"The way I figure, we owe each other three and a half weeks of loving." His hands trailed up her bare arms to the shoulders of her nightgown. He eased her backward as he lowered to the mattress on his knees. "Please allow your future husband to express a bit of the love he has for his bride."

With Bethany's smile, Abraham's kiss started gentle, but he quickly claimed her mouth with plundering tongue. Just as desperate for his taste and touch, she tugged his shirt loose and ran her hands across his stomach. Core tingling with sensations, Bethany kissed her way down his jaw, nipping and licking at his sharp Adam's apple and the pulse throbbing beneath his freckled skin.

"Iris,"—his breath hitched with the word—"may I touch you?"

In response, she arched into him, enjoying the feel of his lean body pressed to hers. He sat back, eyes studying her until he brought his hands simultaneously to her hips. His fingertips pressed to feel the give of her slight curves.

"Perfection." He leaned forward to feather a kiss on her cheek. "When it's time, I'll see to your comfort, Iris. Always."

Then his hot hands moved up her nightgown, palms open as he felt across her belly. He paused a moment beneath her breasts, golden fire burning in his hazel eyes.

"I'm yours," Bethany whispered in hopes of him ending the ache for his touch.

She gasped though he was soothing with his circular caresses. Her pulse quickened with Abraham's attentions and the fabric ceased to be a barrier and became a means of delivering more stimulation. The hunger in his eyes burned stronger than anything Bethany had ever seen.

"I think you're overdue for a marking, Iris." He inched her neckline down and wasted no time suckling a passion mark. When he was done, he brought her to her feet and pressed against her. "Do you feel how perfectly formed we are for each other?"

"Yes, and I understand how wonderful it will be. Only with you, my captain."

A kiss—deep and fulfilling—followed.

"You're going to have to dress real quick to make that ten minute mark."

Bethany rushed to her closet and pulled out her hibiscus sundress, tossing it to the bed.

"Face the other way," she said as she retrieved a full slip from her highboy.

She pulled off her nightgown and brought the undergarment over her head. When she turned back, she met Abraham's reflected gaze in her dressing table mirror.

"I did what you said, Iris. Next time, tell me to close my eyes because that was pure torture to see your bare back and the shape of your buttocks in those little undies you wear. I've never seen the like."

She joined him with a smile. "All my lingerie is French."

"Maybe I could help you design American lingerie perfect for playful Southern newlyweds." He thumbed over her chest and flashed a grin.

Laughing, she hugged Abraham. "I'd like that, even if it's just for you and me. I bet you'd look fine in a pair of silk shorts."

He waggled his straight brows at her. "Anything to help you, Iris."

As soon as she pulled on her dress, Abraham opened the bedroom door.

Claudio stood in the hall with his arms crossed. Bethany half-expected to see him brandish a crucifix at them. The thought made her smile.

"*Papá*, don't tell Sissa I showed you first, but look!"

She held out her left hand and Claudio's serious face broke into his dimpled grin. "*Sono felice per te, Principessa.*" He kissed her cheeks and then Abraham's. "I am happy for you both, Abraham."

Bethany went ahead of them but heard Claudio's words. "Do not spend any more time in a closed room with her if you wish to live."

She descended the stairs with a smile. "Sissa! Louisa!"

She ran to Melissa, kissing her before showing the ring. Then Louisa took Bethany's hand and squealed.

Louisa hugged Abraham when he entered the kitchen. With the room full of family and best wishes, Kade came over for a kiss.

"Congratulations, Tiger. If Abe doesn't treat you right, I'll be the first to beat him."

"We shall have to take turns," Claudio said. "You, me, Alexander, Henry, Asher, and probably Joe as well."

Abraham laughed. "Pa would throw me overboard. But I'll never hurt my flower. Now stand back. My bride needs breakfast."

"Join her if you want," Melissa said as she brought the platters of pancakes and bacon over. "There's plenty."

Claudio brought the coffee. "When shall the wedding be?" he asked.

"I always thought Naomi's October wedding was beautiful," Bethany replied.

"Then October it will be!" Abraham gave her a syrupy kiss on the lips.

"You're still seventeen, Beth."

"She has an old soul, *Eroina*. One month early will not harm anyone, but it could make a gulf of a difference going the other way." Claudio looked to Bethany. "Would you like to be married in Trinity?"

Knowing Abraham was raised Catholic and attended Mass with Alexander when he was in town, she didn't want to commit to an answer without discussing it with him. "I don't have my heart set on the where so much as with whom."

"I'd be happy to be wed in your church if they'd have me, Iris."

"I'm sure the dean would be willing," Melissa said. "He loved Freddy and the congregation has known you since you were born."

Abraham squeezed Bethany's hand. "Don't worry about it now. The family has a big day ahead of them."

Both households were to be at the opening ceremony for the new public library that evening. In Phoebe's memory, the families purchased a thousand copies of Lucy's new anthology to be given away to the first patrons. Alexander and Magdalene, who often donated to the library fund, were among the honored guests as well.

When they were done eating, Bethany leaned against Abraham's sturdy shoulder. "I want to tell Poppy about our engagement."

"He's at the stables, but should be home soon." Kade took the last strip of bacon and nodded to his friend. "I'll drive you two over."

"And stay until Alexander returns," Claudio added.

"Tabby is home."

"But is the night owl expected to be alert at this time of the morning?" Claudio countered.

Kade smirked and thumbed toward Bethany. "This one's trouble, huh? Fine, I'll chaperone the love birds."

Melissa pressed her lips together and remained silent. Bethany collected her shoes and hurried to the foyer where Abraham and Kade waited. She climbed in the middle of the front seat and took Abraham's hand as Kade pulled onto Catherine Street.

"I don't think Sissa is happy for me."

"She thinks you're too young. Being a career woman herself, she'd choose that path for you," Abraham said. "Not that I'm going to keep you from your work. You know that, don't you?"

"Of course, especially after what you offered to help me with this morning." She laughed as her cheeks warmed.

"What?" Kade looked at her sideways.

Abraham kissed Bethany and looked to his friend. "Be sure you study patent laws. We might need your help if this passionate brain of hers thinks up something completely amazing."

Forty-Four

Alexander, Magdalene, and Amelia returned from the stables late morning and found Bethany, Kade, and Abraham on the back patio. The couple was snug together on one of the loungers, and Kade sprawled on the love seat. Smoke wafted up from the guys' cigarettes and was blown about by the ceiling fans, reminding Alexander of the toxic vapors from the burning lilies in Seacliff Cottage. With a slight shudder, Alexander shook off the memory.

"Poppy, look!" Bethany met him at the edge of the patio and held out her hand, showcasing a classic solitaire.

"Darling, how wonderful!" He hugged Bethany and kissed her cheeks.

"Alex, you're filthy!" Magdalene, in her own sweat-stained riding clothes, fussed. "Let her go."

"I was one of the first people to hold her and I'll hug her all the more before she up and leaves us for a wharf rat."

Bethany laughed. "Poppy, will you walk me down the aisle?"

He claimed her in a hug once more. "Yes, my knight. It would be an honor and a blessing."

"You've always been a father to me."

He didn't hide the moisture that shone in his eyes when he moved back a step. "I don't think you understand how proud and happy I am for you."

She frowned and looked at her shoes. "I don't think Sissa is either of those things."

"Don't mind her, Knight Bethany." Alexander took her Easton chin in his hand and looked in her Davenport eyes. "You found true love and you're old enough to conquer the world. Sissa has trouble understanding your situation because her own life was so different, but she'll not stand in your way. And even if she did, I wouldn't let her. I'd toss her in the bay and tell her to swim back to New York. You're going to make it, Bethany Iris, and I promise to do all I can to help see that it happens."

She kissed his cheek. "Thank you, Poppy."

Magdalene and Amelia congratulated Bethany while Alexander shook Abraham's hand. "You've won the best prize in the state."

"I know it." Abraham's grin said it all. "Thank you for your support."

"I better go shower before Maggie fusses again, but know I love you both as my own."

***

That evening, Alexander stood in a gray suit in the new library at the table celebrating his first love's literary legacy. Melissa was at his side in a sophisticated green dress. They took turns handing out the final complementary copies of *Selected Poems and Short Stories of Olive Kent.* Magdalene was off with Amelia and Claudio in the children's area and Asher roamed about with Simon and Louisa, though he had worked a bit at the table and looked pleased to hear the kind words about his mother's books. Bethany was there as well, milling about with Abraham and Maxwell.

When the next lull in visitors allowed room for conversation, Alexander brought up the most pressing subject. "Doesn't Bethany look happy today?"

"She does," Melissa said.

"It's even nicer to see after these painful weeks, though you don't appear pleased."

Melissa sighed. "She's a child, Alex."

"There's no better way to grow and mature than with the one you love by your side. Bethany deserves the opportunity to make her choices despite the mistakes of her family."

She turned away from him to greet the mayor and his wife. "I know you're a fan, Mrs. Schwarz. Please accept this copy in behalf of the family."

"Thank you, Mrs. Dav—De Fiore. Such an exotic name you have now." Mrs. Schwarz offered her hand to Alexander. "And Mr. Melling, it's always good to see you at events with your lovely wife. I spoke with Magdalene and your daughter not long ago. That girl is as pretty as a picture."

"Thank you. I enjoy both of them and all the others in the family, Melissa included. She did a wonderful job organizing the book. There are several poems about me that are a bit steamy, so keep a fan nearby when you read." He winked.

Mrs. Schwarz's cheeks grew rosy as she smiled. "You're a naughty man, Mr. Melling."

Melissa stared at Alexander after the couple left. "Did you really just say that to the mayor's wife?"

"Please don't tell Maggie."

Melissa's laughter brought the attention of several guests. Alexander took the opportunity to hold up the book. "Claim your free copy of the new Olive Kent collection. There's something for every reader, from child to feisty adults!"

"You cad!" Melissa whispered as he distributed three copies.

"But you love me, just as you'll come to appreciate Bethany's relationship with Abe."

"I apprec—"

"You can't count blessings when you're riddled with worry." He looked into her brown eyes with a determined stare. "They'll be married next month, and for the love of God, please be the supportive, loving mother our girl needs at this time in her life."

"I will, dashing Poppy." Her broad smile showed a lightening of her cares. "I have the sneaking suspicion you may be right about them."

***

Friday, October twelfth, Alexander woke on his forty-sixth birthday to his wife snuggled against his scarred chest. He kissed Magdalene's forehead and caressed her shoulder until she arched against him with a mumble of semi-alertness.

"Good morning, Magdalene."

"Happy birthday." She kissed the marks on his torso as her hand roamed lower.

"I need a taste of you this morning."

"Only a taste, my lion? I want it all."

He grasped her hips. "Then all you shall have."

Afterward, Alexander showered and pulled on pajama pants before going in search of Magdalene. He found her making omelets with Amelia.

"Happy birthday, Poppy!" His daughter ran for a hug. "I'm glad Beth is getting married today. It makes your birthday extra special."

"So it does, Amelia. I look forward to seeing my girls in the wedding party and my boys as best man and groomsmen."

Asher and Simon joined them to eat, and after breakfast, they all readied for the midday wedding.

Tabitha had stayed the night with Bethany so she could help her as maid of honor. Kade—the best man—was to collect Magdalene, the boys, and Amelia and bring them to Trinity Episcopal Church.

Suited for the special event, Alexander drove away in his automobile for a lone mission. His first stop was the florist, where he purchased two dozen red and white roses in a crystal vase. Then, he went in George's Candy Shop for a sampler of chocolates which he brought to State Street.

When Abraham and Bethany began looking for a home to call their own, she found her father's first house on the market. With it being close to the river, the couple considered it providence that it waited for them. Thanks to her mother's royalties, Bethany had the means to purchase it outright—much to Melissa's distress, though the stepmother kept quiet about it.

As Alexander had hoped, Abraham had already left for the church. Alexander unlocked the front door of Frederick Davenport's old home with the spare key he had borrowed. Walking into the house brought him back to the nights he had lived with Frederick while he tried to stay sober before marrying Lucy. The solid, functional home had been a great fit for Frederick and was a perfect match for the newlyweds.

Thanks in part to Maxwell and the Easton and Sons warehouse, the home was already partially furnished. A sofa, rocking chair, coffee table, and bookshelf were in the front room. Alexander settled the vase and box of chocolates in the middle of the empty table and continued his self-guided tour. The study was set as Bethany's workspace with her sewing machines. Fabric bolts and notions filled the built-in shelves rather than books. The dining room was empty, but there was a simple four-person table in the kitchen.

Upstairs—he couldn't resist peeking—the master bedroom was arranged with Bethany's touch. A beautiful blend of greens and cream against the oak Craftsman furniture were pleasing to the eye in their artistic simplicity. He went to the guest room where Abraham stayed the last two weeks—waiting to use the master suite with his wife as Alexander planned to do when he was in the duplex all those years ago.

But Abe made it to his wedding day without deflowering his love.

Closing his eyes, Alexander recalled the Thanksgiving Bethany Iris Davenport entered the world and the look on Lucy's face as she held her daughter to her breast to nurture her in that room.

"I've done my best to care for your children, my queen," he whispered. "Thank you for allowing me back into your life and sharing your final years with me."

With tears in his eyes, he locked the house and drove the few blocks to Trinity. He found Claudio pacing the front steps.

"*Amico*, what should I do? I am used to preparing for the wedding sacrament before a service."

"It's past time we gave our girl the pre-marriage talk." Arm about his friend's shoulders, Alexander steered them to the bride's room. He paused, listening to the buzz of happy chatter beyond the closed door. With a sharp knock, his voice boomed. "The fathers would like a word with the bride!"

Melissa opened the door with an annoyed expression. "We still need to set her veil."

"I'd rather see her face. Give us five minutes."

Melissa motioned Magdalene, Claire, Tabitha, Louisa, and Amelia outside.

Darla took Charlene by the hand and scowled. "Don't you dare upset Beth with any of your harebrained stories." She stopped in front of him and kissed his cheek. "But happy birthday."

He gave her a teasing smile. "I always knew you cared, Darla."

With the door shut, Alexander looked across the room for the first time. Bethany stood with hands clasped before her white lace sheath. Her father's locket and Abraham's anklet and ring were the only jewelry she wore. The scallops at her shoulders and knees trimmed the gown perfectly and her angelic smile shone like the face of heaven.

He kissed her cheek. "Your parents are smiling down on you right now, Bethany Iris."

"Not all of them." She kissed him in return and then Claudio's cheeks. "I'm blessed to have mothers and fathers still on earth with me."

"*Principessa*, you do us all a great justice with your words."

She held a hand from each of them. "What is it you wished to talk to me about?"

"Well," Alexander cleared his throat, "when a man loves a woman, he—"

"Poppy!" Bethany laughed. "I've known all about that for ages."

He smiled at her joy. "We wanted to tell you how much we love you and that we're happy for you and Abe. If you ever need anything, even just to voice concerns, come to one of us or Melissa or Maggie. We are always here to help."

"I know you are, Poppy. Thank you. And you, *Papá*. I love you both."

Alexander and Claudio made their way to the groom's room next. The space was filled with laughter and smoking. Joe, Emmet, and Kade led the jokes while Asher and Simon were red-faced over their yellow neckties because of the subject matter. Abraham looked ready to faint with anxiety—or because his harvest orange bowtie was too tight.

"Come on, Son." Alexander put an arm about him. "You need some fresh air."

Once they were outside with Claudio, Alexander went for the shade of an oak on the opposite side of the church.

"We just came from seeing Bethany," he told Abraham. "You will fall in love with her all over when you see her, and then again when you bring her home. Seek for ways to fall in love with her every day. That's what keeps a marriage fresh, and if I have anything to say about it, you two will be together for decades upon decades."

Abraham nodded.

Alexander tightened a hold on the groom's shoulder. "I'll tactfully remind you if I think it's needed. And please remember if you ever hurt our girl, you'll be in a world of pain."

"*Sí*. She is a jewel to be treasured always. Be gentle with her."

Alexander's grip squeezed Abraham's shoulder. "She only knows the touches you've shared and it had better been a *long* time since you've—"

"Yes, Poppy. Since before I first kissed Iris."

He patted his freckled cheek. "Good. Keep yourself in control the first bit. You'll go fast, but your body will adjust to the lovemaking with her. Don't be afraid to explore once things are comf—"

"Perhaps," Claudio said, "it is best for him to figure it out and ask questions if needed."

Alexander laughed and slapped Abraham on the back. "You get the idea."

"We need the groom!" Kade shouted from the door.

"Thank you, Poppy. Claudio." He gave a nervous smile and went for the door.

"I do not think you scared him, but you came close." Claudio elbowed Alexander in the ribs. "You are calmer than you used to be, but still too much for most people."

"Alex!" Magdalene came around from the front of the church. "It's time!"

"As long as I'm never too much for that woman, my life will be blessed."

Magdalene hooked an arm through each man's and they entered the building. Claudio joined Melissa and led her into the chapel to take their seats on the front row.

"You'll do fine, Alex." Magdalene kissed his cheek and straightened his sky blue bowtie that matched Kade's tie. "Do you still have extra handkerchiefs in your pocket?"

"Yes, sweetness."

When he joined the bride's group, he kissed Amelia—the youngest bridesmaid—and then Tabitha and Louisa. When the music began, Charlene Adams led the way as flower girl. Amelia followed in her yellow dress, then Louisa in a matching one. Tabitha's gown was sky blue and the result of the wedding procession was the sensation of golden mums against a harvest sky because Bethany planned the wedding colors to showcase the season and complement each member of the wedding party.

Bethany's arm trembled slightly, the orange chrysanthemums quivering in her hands, as they walked the aisle.

"It's all right, Knight Bethany," he whispered. "This is your finest victory to date for Kingdom Davenport."

When they reached the front, he couldn't help but smile over Abraham's large eyes and straight face. Alexander stood before Bethany at an angle he knew would allow Abraham to see her fully when he raised the blusher of her veil.

"Iris," her name escaped the groom with a breath of longing.

Alexander quickly kissed Bethany's cheek and turned to give her hand to Abraham—who sported the biggest grin ever.

Taking a moment to look at the congregation before he sat, Alexander realized that everyone who loved Bethany was there, including Naomi's family in the back corner. If he had noticed them earlier, he would have moved them to the front, but he knew Naomi wouldn't want a fuss made.

Taking his seat, he immediately linked hands with Magdalene on one side and Melissa on the other. A few minutes later, he had to lose their touches to fish handkerchiefs out of his pocket, handing one to his wife. Seeing Claudio give one of his own to Melissa, Alexander kept the other for himself.

When it was time for Abraham to kiss his bride, they went at it so long the dean had to clear his throat three times to get their attention. A rumble of laughter rolled through the chapel.

With the wedding party still in place, Melissa stood to get pictures.

Seeing all his children before the pulpit renewed Alexander's zest for life—the life he'd ruined and rebuilt over the decades through pleasure, pain, faith, and love.

Epilogue

Twenty-five years after the time Alexander and Lucy began their relationship that wreaked havoc upon their lives, another gathering took place within the Government Street mansion. On Christmas Eve 1929, the extended family and friends of Alexander Melling convened at his house as he and Magdalene hosted a party—despite the challenges facing the nation after the stock market crash two months previous. Alexander had lost capital on much of his parents' investments, but their local accounts were in decent order for the time being.

Claudio and Melissa De Fiore were in good cheer. Melissa had a newspaper column about scenic destinations along the Gulf Coast and Claudio a position as head chef in a local restaurant. Beyond work, the couple led a satisfying personal life full of passion that even Alexander coveted—and he often remarked over when swapping stories with his best friend.

Louisa Davenport was coming out at the New Year's Eve ball the following week. At sixteen, the auburn haired beauty was eager to claim public dances with Asher, Simon, and Horatio. She fancied they were all in love with her because the boys had begun to squabble over their time together. Unsure which one she preferred, she enjoyed them all. Asher Melling stole kisses in the camellia garden— if he wasn't too busy painting in the studio above the garage. Simon Campbell preferred to try his luck while dancing with roaming touches. But Horatio Adams, who she saw the least, liked to hold her hand whenever he was nearby. His indigo eyes were mysterious, his features masculine without being rough. If he asked her, Louisa would save her first dance at the ball for him.

Amelia Rose Melling kept busy with Virginia and Charlene Adams, both at school and at the stables. They all rode well under their fathers' instructions, but Amelia was the best of all and had the awards to prove it. At present, the three girls played a round of cards while comparing their new dresses.

Henry Adams had the most cause for alarm those days, trying to keep Davenport and Adams Allied Accountants afloat with an uncertain financial future looming. Many of his clients suffered great losses and though the company was hurting, he managed to keep all his employees through the holidays. But the dawn of 1930 could alter those circumstances.

The Rollins family stopped in to greet the assembled guests on their way to their own Christmas gathering. Naomi gave everyone a hug and fussed over the children while Paul kept silent on the sidelines. Samuel, named after the hero in *Winter of My Heart*, was eleven. The youngest Melling liked to watch his dark hands when they played together.

"Sam," Amelia called to him. "Sit in on a round with us."

"I don't have time, Miss Amelia. We're going to Mattie's house, but I'll sit with you a moment." Samuel settled on the floor beside her with a shy smile because he loved to see the spark of joy in her bewitching blue eyes.

Then the final guests arrived, only two more because Tabitha was in New Orleans with her band for a special engagement and Kade was celebrating with his girlfriend, Jessica Godwin—Maxwell Easton's niece.

Abraham and Bethany Walker entered the room, faces bursting with more joy than their normal good cheer. "Merry Christmas, everyone!"

Bethany dazzled in a red silk gown of her own creation, her husband in a matching bowtie with his navy suit.

An arm lovingly about her waist, Abraham spoke loud enough to hush the room. "We have an announcement. According to the checkup Bethany Iris had this week, we'll be pleased to welcome the newest member of the family in July."

All the ladies exclaimed with surprise except Darla. She was happy for the announcement because she had wanted to rush to Melissa with the news after Bethany's appointment.

Alexander reached the Walkers first, slapping Abraham on his back. "I was beginning to think you didn't have it in you."

"Poppy!" Bethany's face held a mix of mortification and humor. Then she dropped her voice so only her husband and stepfather could hear. "We were using a planning method Darla taught me to prevent things until this fall. The first month we dropped the protocol proved successful, so all of Abe—and me—are in working order. I plan to give you many grandchildren."

Abraham gave his cheekiest smile. "And you can be sure we'll enjoy every attempt."

"That's the spirit!" Alexander kissed them both and set them free to collect congratulations from the others.

"I know you have great support with your family and Miss Darla, but I'd like to help when your time comes," Naomi told Bethany. "I loved those days with your momma when you were all born. I'd be pleased to lend a hand."

"Thank you, Miss Naomi. I'd enjoy your company and experience."

Naomi and her family bid everyone goodbye. Then the food trays Claudio and Miss Charlotte prepared were brought to the dining room for people to help themselves.

Melissa caught her stepdaughter in a hug. "I'm happy for you, Beth. Freddy loved the idea of big families and admired your grandparents and the passel of grandchildren at the Easton dinners. I'll do my best to show the love your parents would have to your children, and I know Claudio, Alexander, and Maggie will as well."

Bethany hugged her in return. "I know you will, Sissa. I've always loved you like a mother. Just as with Poppy, my memories are full of the two of you, as well as *Papá* and Miss Maggie, as far back as I can remember. I love our big, jumbled family."

Abraham joined them, his hand caressing Bethany's middle. "It's time to feed the baby. I don't want you to grow faint before Mass."

Melissa took hold of his arm. "Keep loving and caring for her, Abe. And let me know if either of you need anything."

"Thank you, Sissa. We've already discussed that if the child is a boy he'll be named Frederick."

Melissa's throat tingled with rising tears. "He was happy for you and Beth. Even in his pain, seeing you together gave him the greatest pleasure."

"And don't worry about my career, Sissa," Bethany said. "I've been getting plenty of commission pieces and have my sewing room at the house. I'll be able to work from home if I no longer wish to work through Mademoiselle Bisset's shop. She's already told me she knows I'll get too big for her one day."

Melissa's finger traced the arch of Bethany's brow. "I just want you to be happy, Beth."

"I am." She tucked against Abraham's lanky frame. "I'm joyfully blessed."

After everyone finished eating, the group gathered in the front room to exchange a few modest gifts and sing carols.

Bethany had once stolen the limelight with her hand-sewn presents, but that night Asher surprised the family. Bringing a wrapped frame in from the hall, he presented it to Melissa.

"Asher, you didn't need—"

"It's for your household." He ran a hand through his blond hair and smiled at Louisa. "I hope you all enjoy it. Poppy bought the frames, though he didn't know what the money was for."

Melissa opened the paper, exposing a lovely rosewood frame encompassing a portrait in oil paints of Frederick Lionel Davenport—broad shouldered and smiling in a business suit.

"Daddy!" Louisa fell on her knees before the painting. "Asher, it's terrific!"

"You captured him perfectly, Asher," Melissa said. "It's a wonderful legacy."

"I have a slightly different one for you and Abe, Beth." Asher returned, impish grin bright.

Everyone in the room watched expectantly as Bethany opened hers. With a laugh she hugged the oak frame.

"Ash, you're simply marvelous!" She turned the painting to the others.

Frederick posed in the boxing ring during his victory lap with young Bethany on his shoulders. The portrait of the photograph that once graced the front page showed the rippled muscles of his body and the pride on his face that Asher managed to convey was more for his daughter than the win. Bethany passed it to Abraham so she could hug her half-brother.

"You get two," Asher whispered. "Think that you're holding one for Phoebe if needed."

He hurried to the hall to collect another parcel. That one depicted Lucy nestling a blonde baby to her breast, eyes cast down at her bundle, lips smiling.

"They're breathtaking, Ash. Thank you."

Next he brought his stepmother her gift, a striking depiction of Lieutenant-Commander Douglas Campbell in dress uniform, blue eyes sharp and an eyebrow arched. Simon took his mother's hand and stared at his father's likeness.

"A seasoned professional couldn't have depicted the portraits better. Thank you, Asher," Magdalene said. "I wish Tabby and Kade were here to see it."

Alexander's heart raced when his son left the room to collect another gift. He knew what it would be and the thought of it thrilled him. With hands that slightly trembled, he peeled the paper to reveal a handsome mahogany frame four feet tall—twice as long as all the others. The backdrop was the camellia maze, pale blossoms speckling the bushes behind a full-length Lucy in the white and silver gown she'd worn to the Mellings' Christmas party in 1904. Hair loose and golden against the dark foliage of the garden, lips rosy on her ivory complexion.

"Phoenix—" Alexander choked on a sob amid the silent reverence in the room.

Bethany came to her brother's side and took his hand. "She looks like an angel."

"She called me her angel," Alexander's voice was raw, "but it was she who was the light in my darkness all those years. I nearly destroyed her, but she saved me."

Magdalene embraced Alexander, comforting the ache in his soul. "You saved each other."

Alexander kissed her cheek and turned to Asher with glistening eyes. "You captured her essence, Phoenix Asher. You highlighted her body and soul with your brush. No one could have done this but you—her beloved son."

When emotions calmed, Amelia settled on the piano bench. She accompanied her parents singing "The First Noel" in a duet that was all the more poignant in the room inhabited with pictures from the past as they looked to the future with their greatest possession—family.

THE END

Author's Note

Thank you to all the readers who've traveled this journey with the Melling, Easton, Davenport, and Campbell families—plus all those characters' friends and enemies. When I set out to write one Gothic horror novel, I had no idea it would evolve into a family saga with eight novels, one novella, and nearly a dozen short stories. (That's not including The Malevolent Trilogy, which is now available, and any other related projects that may arise in the future.)

To say The Possession Chronicles took over my life is an understatement. In the two years it took to actively draft the main books—and several more years to edit them all—the likes of Alexander, Claudio, Eliza, and more were near constant companions in my head while driving, weeding flower beds, washing dishes, and grocery shopping. (Don't bring Alex into the produce section! There are more than enough innuendos and dirty jokes to be told there.) With the publication of the final novel in the main Possession Chronicles cycle, I feel like I can breathe a bit easier, even through the tears.

Many thanks to Alisha Vincent with Bienvenue Press for taking a chance on this Southern Gothic family saga when books of this style weren't topping the best-seller charts. It's been an adventure, and every new reader is celebrated. The BP family also introduced me to Ashley Byland with Redbird Designs, who helped set the tone of the series with her cover designs through all nine books on the first edition run. And to Sara Miller, who offered keen insights into edits for this manuscript.

Appreciation, as always, goes to my family and critique/beta circle. John, Mom, Dad, Angela, and my children, plus Candice, Sandi, Joyce, Lee Ann, and Jennifer have heard me lament over characters, answered odd questions, and looked at way more visuals than they ever wanted to see over the years—including all the McAvoys. Thanks for coming along for the ride and redirecting me when needed. Here's to the next literary discoveries!

About the Author

While experiencing the typical adventures of growing up, Carrie Dalby called several places in California home, but she's lived on the Alabama Gulf Coast since 1996. Serving two terms as president of Mobile Writers' Guild and five years as the Mobile area Local Liaison for the Society of Children's Book Writers and Illustrators are two of the writing-related volunteer positions she's held. When Carrie isn't reading, writing, browsing bookstores/libraries, or homeschooling her children, she can often be found knitting or attending concerts.

Carrie writes for both teens and adults. *Fortitude* is listed as a Best History Book for Kids by Grateful American Foundation. She has also published *Corroded*, a contemporary teen novel about friendship and autism, several short stories that can be found in different anthologies, as well as a multitude of Southern Gothic novels for adults.

For more information, visit Carrie Dalby's website:

carriedalby.com

www.ingramcontent.com/pod-product-compliance
Lightning Source LLC
Chambersburg PA
CBHW030357200726
48286CB00015B/1476

9 781957 892368